CW00833158

Praise for *Esme*

"*Esme* is a beautiful story of sacrificial love, the renewal of our most intimate dreams for ourselves, and that profound, heartfelt journey toward the mirroring of our souls that we all deeply long for in another."

J. Reuben Appelman, Author of
The Kill Jar and *While Idaho Slept*

Book Clubs will love *Esme* as members of The Overbooked Ladies Literary Society in Gig Harbor, Washington attest to:

"*Esme* is an unputdownable book. It's a story about life's choices and their consequences. It's about struggles and redemption, joy and sorrow, strength and sacrifice, prejudice, mental illness, motherhood and magic. It will take hold of you from the beginning to the very end."

Lori Hammond

"Just finished *Esme* and I could not put it down. For me it was probably the best book club book this year, even including my own book choice."

Sharon Smith

"*Esme* was a thoroughly enjoyable read. The different sections were like separate stories, but they all came together perfectly. The book touched on so many subjects and definitely kept my interest until the very end."

Mary Beth Hines

"I enjoyed *Esme* on many levels … Thank you for sharing your wonderful book with us! It was a joy to read."

Lori Williams

ESME

SHONI DAVIS

ISBN: Paperback 979-8-9890099-0-9
ISBN: Hardback 979-8-9890099-2-3
ISBN: E-book 979-8-9890099-1-6

Library of Congress Control Number: 2023915833

Esme is a work of fiction. Names, characters, incidents and places, either are the product of the author's imagination or are used fictitiously. Any resemblance to actual persons, living or dead, events, or locales is entirely coincidental.

The quote, "A person often meets his destiny on the road he took to avoid it."(Jean de La Fontaine, 1621 - 1695) is Public Domain.

First printing edition December 2023

Interior formatting, book design and cover illustration by Formatted Books

Published by SK Davis
sdavis3305@msn.com

For Vera Morrow, my first-grade teacher. For over a century, you were everything a teacher ought to be. Even years later, you remembered your students' names. You taught simple and enduring lessons: kindness, gratitude, encouragement, unconditional love, and always comb your hair for birthday parties. I know wherever you are, you're serving tea out of dainty China cups with a cat in your lap.

A person often meets his destiny on the road he took to avoid it.

(Jean de La Fontaine)

PROLOGUE

WHEN SAM PARKER WAS A JUNIOR IN HIGH SCHOOL, A FORTUNE TELLER came to his campus as part of the annual school fair. The fortune teller, a Romani woman, read palms for fifty cents. She sat at a table in the quad where students gathered in small groups to hang out and socialize. Other than a bohemian-style cloth draped over the table, her set-up had no fanfare—no crystal ball, no deck of cards, nothing to suggest she was a psychic.

Standing with a group of fellow students, Sam kept glancing at her. He thought she'd make a good character for one of his stories. He was always looking for characters for the novel he planned to write. He watched as the fortune teller inhaled a long drag off her cigarette and then lazily exhaled, tilting her head upwards to allow a slow stream of smoke to billow overhead. Nicotine yellowed her fingers; her hands were gnarled and arthritic. Age and bad habits had wrinkled her face, making her skin look sallow. Sam couldn't guess her age. He figured she probably looked older than she was. Despite it all, Sam noticed a twinkle in her eyes and a teasing grin that bad habits and hard living hadn't diminished.

He was embarrassed when she looked over and noticed him watching her. He started to look away, but she motioned him over with her hand holding her cigarette. He hesitated momentarily, then slipped away from his friends and walked to the table where she sat.

"You got any money, kid?" she asked. Sam handed her two quarters which she pocketed. "Sit down," she directed him, nodding to a folding chair on his side of the table. Sam did as she instructed.

"Let me see your right hand, kid." The fortune teller took Sam's hand, her cigarette dangling from her lips, and turned it over, palm up, to examine it. "What's your name, kid?"

Sam introduced himself. "I'm Sam. Sam Parker."

"Ah, look here," she muttered, intent on Sam's palm. "You've been around for a long time, Sam." She said it matter-of-factly.

"What do you mean?" Sam asked.

"You've had previous lives." She looked into his face and grinned.

"Previous lives? You're joking, right?"

"No joke, kid, you've had many before this." She said it with certainty.

"How can you tell?"

"I can see it in the lines on your palm. Look, you can see it here," the cigarette was still hanging from the fortune teller's lips, the ash about to drop. She ran her finger down a distinct crease on Sam's palm that ran on a diagonal. "Your karmic prophesy's very clear. You've been here before, Sam Parker, no doubt about it." She continued her examination like she was unraveling a mystery.

"Ahh, here's something interesting." She found something else that caught her attention. She pointed to the horizontal line running from the side of Sam's palm underneath his little finger. "You have a soulmate you travel with in every life—a girl." She raised her eyes, looked at Sam, her smile mischievous. Sam noticed she was missing a couple of teeth. The fortune teller removed the cigarette from her lips and flipped the ash onto the ground. She returned the cigarette to her lips and took a deep drag, exhaling another cloud of smoke above their heads.

"Who is she?" Sam couldn't tell if she was messing with his head.

"I can't get the specifics. She's someone who travels with you in each life."

Sam was enthralled. The idea that he'd lived past lives and had a soulmate he was bound to in each life was far out. Sam wanted to know more. "Where is she now?" he asked.

"I don't know that, either," the fortune teller admitted. "I can't tell." She leaned back in her chair and studied Sam's face.

"When will I meet her?"

"You'll find her when the time's right. She helps steer your destiny." The fortune teller returned her attention to Sam's palm. "This line here," she directed Sam to the long line running from his wrist to his third finger, "your destiny line, it's very revealing. Fate will play a big part in your life, Sam; it'll be waiting for you around every corner."

The fortune teller stubbed out her cigarette, indicating that her prophesying with Sam was complete. He reluctantly stood. He didn't want to leave, he was full of questions, but the fortune teller had pushed back her chair as though to stand. It was clear she had no intentions of saying more. Sam started to walk away, hesitantly, toward his group of friends. When he'd taken a few steps, she called after him. "Hey kid …" He stopped and turned around, trying to anticipate what she'd say. She was still sitting at the table, watching him. "Your destiny, Sam," she said, as if in forewarning, "involves sacrifice. You'll be forced to choose."

PART I

SAM

1

THERE ARE MANY WAYS TO DESCRIBE SAM PARKER. BRIEFLY, ONE could say he was a "nice guy." But even nice guys have hard knocks, and Sam had his share throughout his journey. Some might say more than he deserved. Others might say what happened during Sam's journey was meant to happen. It all depends on how one looks at it.

Sam was born in 1971 and grew up in the Pacific Northwest in Oak Harbor, Washington, a family-friendly community of twelve thousand residents named for the Garry oak trees that line its main streets. The town is situated on pretty-as-a-picture Whidbey Island. His parents were Jack and Sid. Jack knew the minute he walked up the driveway of Sid's house to deliver the mail when he was just twenty-one that she was the girl for him.

Sid was in the garage standing at her easel, painting, when Jack walked up the drive. She wore jean shorts and a ripped t-shirt covered in paint, her long sandy-brown hair knotted at the back of her head. A streak of blue from her paintbrush smudged her right cheek. She was the typical girl-next-door, with freckles sprinkled across her nose and her cheeks slightly blushed. She'd looked up as Jack approached, took in his reddish-blonde mullet and short beard, his body in good physical shape from walking his mail route five days a week, and smiled. Jack was smitten immediately and still felt the same way years later.

Sam was their only child. They made a conscientious decision when they married to have no more than one child. Sid believed in limiting the number of children brought into the world. She was an environmentalist, a hold-over from her high-school hippie days when she and her friends marched with their banners flying to protest any issue that threatened Mother Earth.

By the time she was twenty, Sid had foregone her patchouli perfume and love beads and traded in her tie dyes for jeans and paint-splattered t-shirts. She gave up marching for one cause after another and spent her free time painting. She captured the beauty of the Pacific Northwest on canvas: the pristine waters of Puget Sound, the snowcapped mountains, the meandering sloughs, and marshy wetlands, home to waterfowl and wildlife. Her art became her voice to the world. She hoped her paintings would inspire others to preserve nature's beauty, care for the planet, and respect Earth's limited resources.

Jack's worries were less global. He worried more about the high cost of living, retirement savings, and supporting his family. He started working for the post office when he was nineteen, right after he was found ineligible for military service. He'd registered for the draft right out of high school like all boys his age were required to do when the Vietnam War was in full swing, but a history of childhood asthma disqualified him.

He saw working for the post office as a golden opportunity. He knew he wasn't college material. He wanted a job that would put enough money in his pocket so he could move out of his parent's home and live independently. He wanted a job that he could move up in, settle into. That the post office offered retirement, health insurance, paid vacation, and sick leave seemed too good to be true to Jack. Plus, in his mind, the federal government paid well.

All in all, Jack appreciated the stableness of a government job. "Call me a bureaucrat," he'd sometimes joke, "there's nothing wrong with that. I get weekends and evenings off, three weeks annual paid vacation, sick leave; what more could I ask for?" He worked through every position the post office offered over the years until his gradual ascent to postmaster.

Sid and Jack married within a year of him walking up her sidewalk to deliver the mail. They wasted no time in planning their future. On weekdays while Jack was working his post office job, Sid marketed her artwork to galleries as far south as San Francisco. Within a few short years, her paintings began selling in art galleries up and down the west coast. The money she earned from the sale of her art supplemented Jack's income, and by the time Sam came along, they were able to purchase a modest home in Oak Harbor that had a backyard with a swing set for Sam, a garden where they could hone their skills at growing vegetables, and a large shed that they turned into a painting studio for Sid.

They named Sam after Sid's Grandpa, who taught her how to paint when she was a young girl, when she and her younger sister and their parents would visit him and their grandmother during the summers at their cabin on Diamond Lake in northeastern Washington. Sid remembered her Grandpa Sam's snowy white hair and the smell of whiskey that often lingered on his breath after he took a nip, which he frequently did. Losing him suddenly when she was eighteen was Sid's first real trauma that life forced upon her.

As with every endeavor they undertook, Sid and Jack approached parenting as a team. They balanced each other out. Jack was a hands-on dad chaperoning school field trips, coaching minor league baseball in the summer, tag football in the fall, and soccer in the spring. During the summers, he joined other Dads in organizing weekend campouts on the beach. He surprised Sam and his best friend with Mariner tickets in the spring and Sea Hawks tickets in the fall.

Sid's painting career allowed her to be a stay-at-home mom. She loved the daily routine of managing the house and never saw it as a burden. What some might call chores, Sid saw as self-expression.

She got up early every morning, took the dog on a long walk, and then got busy with that day's goals, canning fruits from the trees in their yard, harvesting her vegetables, baking bread, or making food for the family dog that kept his coat shiny. She applied fresh paint on dingy walls, recovered furniture, and, as Sam got older, taxied him and his friends to the movies, the mall, or the basketball court in the back of the high school.

While Jack tended to overlook minor infractions, rules meant to break, like coming home late or skipping class with his buddies now and then, Sid always held Sam accountable and taught him that his actions, even small ones, have an impact. The lessons that Sid taught Sam carried with him into adulthood, made him, in part, the man he'd become. They were subtle but profound—finish what you start, apologize when you're wrong, always hold the door open for others, and root for the underdog. She taught Sam by example to step up in life, take a stand, always be willing to listen to what others say, and don't be afraid to stick up for what you believe in. "Don't complain," she taught Sam when he was a boy, "unless it's something worth complaining about. Then don't stop complaining until things change."

2

JACK INSTILLED IN SAM HIS LIFELONG LOVE FOR FISHING. THIS PAS-
time would define Sam and, years later, would lead to the inevitable
circumstances that would change the course of his destiny.

Jack started taking Sam fishing when he was too young to reel
in even the smallest fish if he was lucky enough to hook one, just
as Jack's dad had done with him when he was a boy. Jack and Sam
would head out to Cranberry Lake in Deception Pass State Park
early on Saturday mornings with Jack's aluminum fishing boat in
tow. He'd teach Sam the basics of trolling, how fast and deep to drag
bait, and what lures work best for which types of fish: bluegill, trout,
or smallmouth bass. Other times, they'd find a spot on the shore of a
river or stream where Jack taught Sam the art of fly fishing—how to
cast the weighted lure out onto the water with enough momentum
to carry the bait to the exact location they aimed for.

One of Sam's proudest achievements was reeling in his first
big fish. A fifteen-pounder! He was fourteen years old, and he and
his dad were fishing for coho salmon on Puget Sound. Sam would
never forget the thrill of suddenly feeling the tip of his rod bend and
realizing a big fish had taken his bait and his dad excitedly talking

him through how to keep the fish on the hook by quickly reeling in his line until he felt it tighten.

Sam recalled the power of the fish plunging downward into deep water, fighting to free itself, every muscle in his young arms burning from pulling his rod up while reeling the fish toward the surface, keeping the tension of the line just so until he was able to gradually bring the fish close enough to the boat to net it, while his dad stood by, cheering his efforts. Afterward, Jack poured Sam a cup of black coffee from his thermos. "You can't pull in a fish like that without a cup of black coffee," he told Sam. It was a coming-of-age moment for Sam, a memory he would always cherish.

Sam came to know the Pacific Northwest through the lens his parents provided, a lens of wonderment; a wonder that would shape his ideals and provide the backdrop for the stories he would someday write. Even as a child, Sam loved the distinctiveness of the Pacific Northwest, the ferry boats dotting back and forth across Puget Sound from the San Juan Islands or the Olympic Peninsula to the mainland, the bewitchery of Mount Rainier, the way the mountain could completely conceal herself when the clouds were low and then suddenly reveal herself in all her glory for miles around. "Oh look, she's out today!" was a familiar proclamation he grew up hearing the locals exclaim.

When he was a young boy, he accompanied his parents on drives through the picturesque Skagit Valley farmlands north of Seattle, where his mom, equipped with paints and an easel, would search for landscapes she would capture on canvas. While Sid looked for the perfect scenic backdrop, his dad drove the back country roads, where refurbished farmhouses dotted the landscape and cultivated vegetable gardens protected by scarecrows nestled alongside old barns. In the distance, Puget Sound glistened below the snowcapped peaks of the Olympic Mountains.

In winter, they'd drive out near the tiny town of Edison, where sloughs fingered their way through the marshy wetlands inland from Puget Sound, where Sid captured on canvas eagles that gathered to feed on the carcasses of salmon that spawned in the nearby Skagit River. Once when Sam was only seven or eight years old, on their way back to the ferry from a long drive, they'd counted thirteen eagles roosting in a barren red alder tree standing starkly in a field near the roadside. Close by, another eagle was sitting atop a fence post feasting on the small rodent it had swooped up in an adjacent meadow. It reminded Sam of an Easter egg hunt—everywhere he looked, he could spot eagles resting on pieces of driftwood along the boggy shores of a slough, flying low over the verdant fields or roosting in evergreen shrubs that clustered along the soggy marshlands, so many of the beautiful creatures that he lost count. At his young age, it seemed to Sam that they'd wandered into a mystical, magical fantasy land.

Fields of brilliant tulips carpeted the Skagit Valley landscape each spring. The first time Sam's parents drove him to see the tulip fields near La Connor, the quaint seaport town located on the Swinomish Slough that flows into Puget Sound, when they were still a distance away on the country road leading out to the farms, Sam mistakenly thought he was looking at the low tops of enormous circus tents, spread out in all directions, colorful and delightful. They were tulips, Sam suddenly realized in awe. As far as the eye could see, field after field of blooms painted the farmlands like a whimsical circus scene. He carried that image in his head into adulthood. It never lost its fairy-tale flair when the sight would cross Sam's mind.

But it was the snow geese that most enthralled Sam. They would crowd into Skagit Valley, thousands of them in early spring, on their migration south from Wrangel Island off the coast of Russia, where they'd gone to breed. They'd settle in the marshy tidelands, estuaries, and bays to evade being hunted by eagles. One of the most remarkable moments in Sam's young life happened one morning when he and his folks had taken an early ferry ride from Whidbey

Island so Sid could capture the flight of the snow geese as they foraged, landing and taking off from field to field.

That morning, they'd come upon a pure white grassland, which tricked Sam's mind into believing it had snowed. "How can it snow in just one field?" he'd asked his parents. His dad pulled the car over so Sid could set up her tripod and camera while Sam and Jack walked to the edge of the field to get a better view.

"Stand very quietly, Sam," his dad instructed. As they stood watching, the ground slowly began to move. Thousands of pure white snow geese began to take flight in the distance at the far end of the field. In synchronous order, like a choreographed dance, row after row of the beautiful birds lifted off the ground like a vast wave, becoming a white cloud filling the sky. It was the sound of their mighty wings lifting them into the air that Sam remembered most, like the rumble of a jet plane flying low overhead.

Of all the places Sam grew to love, his favorite was the Hoh Rain Forest on the Olympic Peninsula, with its hundred-foot-tall trees draped in shrouds of moss and its perpetual dampness. Even as a small child, Sam dreamed that someday he would live in a cabin on a river in the forest where he could be close to nature, immersed in the places he grew up loving.

Sam wanted to be a writer ever since he could remember. By the time he learned to talk, his active imagination was full of wonder and fascination. He wrote his first story in the fourth grade—about a hunter in the Olympic Mountains who continually got outsmarted by a pack of wolves he was tracking. After that, he wrote one story after another. He created imaginative worlds on paper when he should have been paying attention to his spelling lesson, social studies project, and the salt dough volcano that erupted in science class. He'd get swept away into a fantasy world and forget the goings-on around him.

Sid kindled Sam's love for storytelling. When Sam was a young boy, Sid told him stories when driving in the car, taking walks along the beach, and at night when she tucked him into bed. She was easily awed by the natural wonders of nature. She believed in magic and mysticism. She looked for miracles wherever she went and usually found them. She loved sharing her discoveries with Sam. "Isn't it a wonder, Sam," she would ponder, "that a honey bee can wiggle his abdomen up and down in a dance movement that tells the other bees exactly how far and in what direction a watering hole is from the hive?" Or, "Isn't it mind-blowing, Sam, that when we look up at the stars, we're looking back in time and seeing them thousands or even millions of years ago?"

By the time Sam was in high school, his writing had developed depth and curiosity. He was writing about universal topics everyone could relate to, mainly triumphs and losses and the enduring nature of the human spirit. He created characters that were unusual in attractive and appealing ways, with quirky, peculiar, eccentric traits. His words made his characters jump off the page: "Thoughts tumbled around her head like laundry in the dryer," and "He sounded like a bad-tempered bulldog when he barked orders."

Sam's high school literature teacher, Mrs. Morrow, recognized his talent, full of empathy and uncanny awareness, and took him under her wing. She assisted him in applying for college scholarships for future writers. She pushed him so that he would be competitive on college applications. At her urging, Sam became the school newspaper editor his senior year. He wrote a column in each edition; whether somber or humorous, he prided himself on always provocative editorials.

With each story Sam wrote, his writing got better and better, bringing him closer to the writer he would one day become. But it would be many years before Sam found his true passion, a love that would form the basis for his stories and bring him to full fruition as a writer.

3

SAM'S BEST FRIEND GROWING UP WAS BOBBY GILLESPIE. SAM MET
Bobby on their soccer team in junior high, and the two became
inseparable ever since. They did what most kids do in small towns,
hung out at the mall and their favorite fast-food restaurant, went to
the movies and the arcade, skateboarded up and down the streets of
Oak Harbor, and shot hoops with their buddies in the back of the
high school.

Sam and Bobby's favorite playground was Deception Pass State
Park, just minutes from Oak Harbor. With its shadowy lagoons
and rugged cliffs, old-growth forest, meandering hiking trails, and
gravelly shorelines, the park became a utopia where the boys would
meet up with school friends to explore and play games of tag, Red
Rover and Ghosts in the Graveyard. Digging for cockles and butter
clams along Ala Spit beach south of the Deception Pass bridge and
swimming and fishing in Cranberry Lake or the icy waters of Puget
Sound became memories Sam and Bobby carried with them always.

They played varsity football in high school, Sam a wide receiver,
Bobby a running back. They went through girlfriends and breakups
together. They buoyed each other up when something was getting
one of them down—a crush that was getting too serious, a class

kicking butt, or a lousy football practice. They told each other everything and shared secrets about their insecurities that they wouldn't trust with any of their other friends.

Bobby was a tease; he could turn on the charm, and girls couldn't resist. They loved his long brown curls, pulled back in a ponytail. They loved that he was intelligent and funny. Sam, while not quite the jokester that Bobby was, was an even bigger hit with the girls. He was more introspective and cool, with an easy laugh that girls couldn't resist. His smile and the way he'd look someone right in the eye when he spoke felt like a spotlight, warm and inviting. Girls flirted with him. They'd slug his arm and find excuses to engage him in conversation.

Dressed in slim-fit jeans, hoodies and lace-up Vans, good for skateboarding, Sam and Bobby caught eyes walking down the halls of their high school on their way to class or football practice. They'd be greeted with high-fives from other guys. Girls who saw them approaching would nudge each other, exclaim secretively, "Here comes Sam," or "Don't look now, but Bobby's coming." Sam and Bobby would be greeted with smiles, dreamy looks, and flirtatious remarks.

With Sam, it was his outdoorsy looks that girls loved, his reddish-blonde hair that always looked tousled and slept on, his naturally tanned complexion, and his blue-green eyes. The fact that Sam was known for his writing made him seem even more dreamy to girls. "Have you written any new stories, Sam?" they teased as they passed him in the hall.

To their disappointment, Sam had a girlfriend. Her name was Claire, and she ran on the track team and took advanced placement courses to help her get into pre-med when she entered college. Girls both envied and respected her for being the one to land Sam Parker. Claire loved walking down the halls at school, holding his hand. She tried to make it look like no big deal, but inside, she was beaming. Sam and Claire dated on and off during their sophomore and junior years, and then in the summer between their junior and senior year, became "an official item," as her friends labeled it. She was Sam's girlfriend through their senior year until they both went off in different directions for college. Claire remembered Sam into her old age as her first love, the one she let get away.

The day in May of 1989, when he opened the envelope from the University of Washington's Admissions Department to learn he'd been accepted into the English Department's creative writing program, was one of the best days of Sam's life. His dedication and hard work paid off. His dream of becoming a writer was within reach.

That fall, Sam shared a room on campus with Bobby, who'd earned a spot in the Architectural Design Program. Architecture appealed to Bobby. It satisfied his creative thirst while challenging his analytical skills.

Everything went well for Sam during his first couple of years at college. He and Bobby enjoyed campus life and lived together in student housing in a room containing two single beds, a couple of desks, a small refrigerator, and a microwave Sam's parents brought on one of their visits. Finally, in their junior year, they moved to the upper floors and got an apartment-style dorm with a private bathroom. This felt like a luxury after sharing a community bathroom with other students for the first two years.

Sam and Bobby played pranks on each other and on unsuspecting classmates, went out for beers, and shared girl problems with each other. They bucked each other up if a girl turned one of them down for a date. They came up with great come-on lines they believed would impress girls but never had the nerve to use.

They promised themselves not to get distracted, not to get serious with anyone, to keep things casual, an occasional date, but no commitment. Bobby was happy playing the field, dating a girl once or twice, and then moving on, but Sam preferred something more stable. He dated a girl named Susan, whom he met in his sophomore year. She was athletic and played on the girls' volleyball team. She had short brown hair and a natural, healthy complexion. Sam wasn't in love with her, he didn't see them planning their future together, but he liked her. They had fun together and enjoyed hanging out. Like Sam, Susan was an aspiring writer. She grew up in San Diego and came to the University of Washington for the creative writing program. They spent hours in coffee houses discussing books and writers.

After hanging out platonically for a couple of months, they slept together. It seemed like the next natural step. Sam was an inexperienced lover. He'd only had sex on one previous occasion, with Claire, in high school. Just before they left for college, Claire brought Sam to her house one evening when she knew her parents were out. She wanted her and Sam to have sex in her childhood bed. She decided it was the perfect way of saying goodbye to her childhood and stepping into adulthood. While the experience was sweet, neither knew what to do except follow their instincts. It was clumsy and awkward, but whenever Sam thought about it, even years later, he remembered Claire affectionately.

Susan was more experienced than Sam when it came to sex. She'd slept with a handful of guys the summer after high school and during her first two years of college. Sam and Susan's relationship wasn't passionate, but they had fun together; their sex life felt playful. Susan wasn't self-conscious or embarrassed, nor did she hold back during sex. She told Sam what she liked, what felt good. She coached him and helped him refine his moves.

He was grateful, letting her teach him. They never talked about a future, just took each day as it came, and enjoyed their time together. They didn't put expectations on each other. They studied together and understood when one had to spend a Saturday night in the library or a Sunday afternoon studying for an exam. When one was busy, the other would go out with friends, grab a beer, or go home early to catch up on homework.

Sam's trouble occurred toward the end of his junior year. The problem started when Bobby developed a crush on a first-year sorority girl he met in the dining hall one evening when he ran over to pick up a pizza for dinner. They struck up a conversation and exchanged phone numbers. A few days later, she called Bobby to invite him to meet her at a frat party on campus that Friday night.

Fraternities didn't interest Sam or Bobby. In fact, frat parties represented everything they avoided: excessive drinking, partying, and hazing. There was always heavy imbibing, and it wasn't uncommon for drugs to be passed around, drink-spiking to occur, and for students to pass out in a drunken stupor. Even date rape wasn't unheard of.

Sam and Bobby avoided wild parties, preferring to hang out at one of the many coffee houses or pubs around campus. But this invitation, Bobby convinced Sam, was too good to pass up. "We'll just go for a while. In fact," he told Sam, "you don't have to stick around."

The party, it was rumored, was going to be wild. Susan couldn't go because she was preparing for a literature exam on Monday and had to study. Sam agreed to go with Bobby only until Bobby found his girl interest, then Sam planned to leave. He told Susan he'd stop by around ten o'clock when she was finished studying.

What seemed like a good plan Bobby would later regret. He always blamed himself for dragging Sam to the party that night—a fateful night that could neither be forgotten nor undone.

PART II

JOANNA

4

MOST UNIVERSITY OF WASHINGTON SORORITIES HAD STRICT PROTO-
cols for socializing at fraternities. If caught attending a frat party, sorority girls risked significant penalties, even expulsion. There were always sorority girls, however, willing to take the risk. Frat parties were a great place to meet up with friends, pick up guys, drink, and get high. There was always plenty of free liquor, beer, and weed.

Joanna Melrose was one of the sorority sisters who took the gamble that night. She was a senior business major, set to graduate that May, top in her class. Joanna knew to avoid frat parties—they led to trouble. But tonight, she felt like going out, doing something sneaky. Attending a frat party would be a novel experience that her dad would likely shame her for even considering. She wanted to go just once to say she'd been.

A frat party, she rationalized, couldn't be that much different from the drinking parties she used to go to with her friends back in high school. She remembered the parties when someone's parents would be out of town. She'd smuggle liquor from her parent's house, and she and her friends would get drunk. She and her girlfriends would compete to see who would succeed in hustling the cutest boy at the party and making out with him, maybe even going all the way.

In college, though, Joanna rarely fraternized with her sorority sisters. She knew they talked about her behind her back and thought she was a snob and moody. They called her the "Ice Queen." She didn't much care what they thought of her. Aside from one or two of them, she found them all immature and silly. She came from Mercer Island, with its wealth and privilege. She'd grown up to believe that anyone less advantaged was below her standards, which it seemed were most of the girls in her sorority.

Now when she felt like partying, Joanna preferred to go it alone. She'd sometimes take a cab into downtown Seattle and go to a nightclub where no one knew her, where she wouldn't be recognized, and she'd drink, dance and pick up guys. She never let on to her sorority sisters this other side of herself, where she went, or what she did.

A frat party on campus, however, was riskier. Joanna figured it was better to show up with a group of girls rather than arrive alone. She made an exception and decided to tag along with a few of her more tolerable sorority sisters. Once they got to the party, Joanna planned to ditch them. She didn't want to be stuck with a group of prissy do-gooders. She wanted to dance, get drunk, get hustled, maybe even have sex with someone. She felt like breaking the rules; what did she care? Graduation was only a few weeks away. After that, she could follow her own rules, not somebody else's.

Joanna had her plans for after graduation. She intended to live and work in Europe. Her dream was to eventually manage an exclusive hotel in Paris. She recently interviewed for an internship that would train her for entry-level administrative positions with Hilton Hotels. It was a one-year commitment, and she'd be assigned to various Hilton Hotels nationwide. She did well in the interviews. She believed she had a good chance of being accepted.

Joanna fell in love with Paris during her first trip to Europe with her parents when she was twelve. She loved the city's history, the Seine, and how the river threaded through the many arrondissements, stitching them together to form the city proper. She loved everything Parisian: the musical, romantic diction of the French language, the museums, the cathedrals and cemeteries, the fashions and trends.

In her head, she already lived in Paris. She constantly day-dreamed about what her life would be like. She dreamed of living in a French flat, visiting museums, and throwing dinner parties for international friends—designers, and artists. She fantasized about taking a lover and having a standard poodle she'd walk on the boulevards on weekends. She'd make her own money. She'd travel, purchase expensive art and dine in exquisite French restaurants. She believed living in Paris would make all of her problems magically disappear.

Fate brought Joanna and Sam together at the frat party that Friday night. As soon as Sam and Bobby arrived, Bobby disappeared. He went off to search for the girl he came to meet. The party was packed with wall-to-wall people. Most everyone was drunk or working on getting there. Music was blaring from loudspeakers. Sam was left to finagle his way through the crowded living room. People were laughing and hip-bumping to the music. Some girls, obviously drunk, with eye makeup smeared and hair loose around their faces, danced provocatively, arms in the air, swaying their hips while boys reached out to touch and grab. There was spilled alcohol and vomit on the floor. Girls who weren't yet drunk stood around in groups to ward off unwelcomed touching and groping by frat boys. Couples were making out, some headed upstairs to find a private spot, a deserted bedroom, while others, less concerned for privacy, groped each other in crowded spaces.

Sam knew right away he was in the wrong place. This type of gathering wasn't for him. He wandered into the kitchen, which seemed like the least crowded place to hang out, to wait and see if Bobby hooked up with his girl before leaving. It was then that he noticed Joanna. She was standing alone by the back door. She had long, silver-blonde hair and distinct green eyes. She looked Norwegian. She was gorgeous, strikingly so. Her looks spoke of money. There was a hint of arrogance about her that Sam picked up on. She gave off an expression of superiority. In this setting, she looked out of place.

A frat boy, drunk and glassy-eyed, was trying to get friendly with her. He swayed back and forth when he talked, sloshing his beer out of his cup and onto his and her shoes. Joanna tried to move out around him, but failing to read her cues, he wouldn't move out of her way. Sam figured she'd appreciate somebody sober intervening. He approached her. "Crazy party, huh?" The frat boy didn't object to Sam's intrusion; he gave up and moved on.

"I was about to leave, but a couple of my sorority sisters asked me to wait and said they'd be right back," Joanna answered with irritation. "I'm about to leave without them. It's disgusting here."

"Me too," Sam offered. "I'm waiting for my buddy who came to meet up with a girl. As soon as he finds her, I'm out of here."

A bit of small talk led to more. Someone passed around a fifth of tequila, and partygoers drank straight from the bottle. Sam and Joanna began taking swallows when it was passed to them. Each swallow of the fruity-tasting liquor made the next one easier to go down, and before they knew it, they were drunk after a second bottle was passed around. Their drunken banter led to innocent flirting. Sam was aware of Joanna touching his arm, leaning in close when she spoke. Bobby was nowhere to be seen. Sam figured he either found the girl he came to hook up with or someone else equally as enticing.

When Sam and Joanna went off looking for a bathroom, they found an empty bedroom. A few drunken kisses got out of hand, and before they knew it, they were having sex on some frat boy's un-made bed. The act, short-lived as it was, sobered them both up. Sam felt embarrassed when it was over. Their conversation was awkward as they quickly redressed. Joanna didn't wait for Sam; she made an excuse for a quick getaway.

When Sam got back downstairs, Joanna was nowhere to be seen. He needed fresh air and walked outside. Going to Susan's now seemed wrong. Instead, he headed back to his dorm. He'd call Susan tomorrow and tell her he got drunk and went straight home. Lying didn't feel right, nor did telling her the truth.

He wished it had never happened. He'd have liked to apologize to Joanna. She deserved better than he'd given her, but he let it go. He pushed it out of his mind. Over the next few weeks, he thought of his encounter with Joanna less and less until the entire event was nothing more than a passing memory, a college experience, something to reminisce about in his old age. But as fate would have it, that was not the end of it. Six weeks later, Joanna, who never missed a birth control pill or her period, discovered she was pregnant.

5

WHEN JOANNA'S PREGNANCY TEST TURNED OUT TO BE POSITIVE, SHE refused to believe it. She thought the pee stick was incorrect. It had to be. How could she be pregnant when she took the pill every day and never missed? But her period hadn't come when it was supposed to, and her cycle was always regular. She could narrow it down to the exact day she would start.

She thought about calling her mother, but she was pretty sure her mother would be anything but understanding. Her parents would see this as a betrayal. It'd be worse than her sister, Francine, running away to Florida with her boyfriend. Her father might want to punish her. He might withdraw the financial support he promised to provide while she completed her internship and established herself in Paris.

Joanna didn't have anyone in her sorority she could confide in, nor did she trust any of her high school girlfriends; they'd devour a story like this. They thrived on gossip and drama, and this would be too juicy not to run with. Joanna knew, she'd been one of them.

She walked around for several days in a state of disbelief. She hoped her period might miraculously arrive if she didn't think about it. "A watched pot never boils," her mother, Gladys, liked to say. When the nausea came, Joanna was forced to pay attention. Morning sickness.

"Oh, God," she moaned. She was sitting in her finance class when it first hit her. She had to get up and run out of the classroom to the women's bathroom, where she barely made it in time to lose her breakfast in the toilet.

Joanna thought about abortion and even called a clinic near campus. She was told by the friendly receptionist she could have the procedure done within a week; all she had to do was come in for an introductory appointment. It seemed too easy. She could go in, have the procedure, and her life would go on as planned. One week and this could all be behind her. No one would have to know. Except God would know. According to the Catholic priest who presided over her mother's parish, God knew everything she did. "He's always watching," the priest told her once. It gave Joanna the sense that a peeping Tom was always prowling around, peeking in her windows.

Joanna was raised Catholic. Her mother came from a long line of Catholics. While not overly religious, her mother tended to fall back on the teachings of the Church to guide her decisions. Gladys passed that notion on to Joanna and her sister, Francine. "When in doubt," her mother taught them, "say a Hail Mary."

When Joanna and Francine were growing up, Gladys made it a point to attend Mass with the girls every Sunday. Joanna and Francine went through catechism and took their first communion when they turned eight. After that, it was an expectation that the girls would go to confession once a month.

Joanna always had to think of what offenses to confess to the priest. She tried to keep her admissions of wrongdoing to a minimum to avoid lengthy atonements. While she might admit she chewed gum in school, which was against the rules, and skipped class to go shopping with a girlfriend now and then, she'd avoid declaring bigger sins; stealing liquor from her parent's liquor cabinet, or letting Larry Butte, a neighborhood boy, put his finger inside her once when they were making out outside the high school dance.

Joanna tried to think of how she'd handle confession if she had an abortion. It's a big one to gloss over, the absurdity almost making her laugh. Abortion was probably the equivalent of three or four normal-sized sins. Lying about it on top of everything added a couple more infractions. The Hail Marys were more than Joanna dared to think about.

"Abortion?!" She could hear her mother now. "Oh my God, Joanna, you can't have an abortion. We'd be excommunicated. What would people say if they found out?" Her mother sat on several committees for her Catholic parish. How could she look other women in the eye when her daughter committed the biggest of all sins? It wasn't so much that her mother was against abortion; Joanna doubted if she ever gave it much philosophical thought. It was more about what others would say behind their backs. It was always that way with Joanna's mother.

Joanna thought about contacting Sam. She didn't because she didn't know his last name or how to reach him. They'd shared very little about each other that night except the basics. She did remember that he told her he came from Oak Harbor and that his father worked for the post office. She vaguely remembered him talking about wanting to be a writer. What good was that? That told her nothing about how to locate him.

Joanna wanted to avoid involving Sam, even if she knew how to contact him. While part of her thought he should at least be informed—he shouldn't get off scot-free—Joanna knew Sam wasn't her type, wasn't the kind of guy she'd ever give a second thought to. Telling him she was pregnant felt personal and intimate. Sam wasn't the type of guy she wanted to share that information with.

Had she gotten pregnant by someone in her Mercer Island group of friends or by the son of a friend of her parents, it might be different. It wouldn't feel so personal. Instead, the situation would be defined by her parents simply as a "predicament." Her parents and the boy's parents would get together and decide how best to proceed. Inevitably, in situations like this, the pregnant girl would disappear from the scene for a while, reappear a few months later, and pick up where she left off. Joanna couldn't see her father sitting with Sam's blue-collar dad to brainstorm this problem. She and Sam were from different worlds. Joanna had no desire to blend the two. She had no idea what Sam would want her to do and didn't care to know.

Joanna lay on her bed. She felt alone. She realized she had no one to call. No one really cared about what happened to her. She could phone her sister, but she knew what she'd hear, "You let Mom and Dad lead you around by the nose. They don't have your best interest at heart; they never have. How do you know this Sam may not be a good guy? He might at least support you through all this. You should call him; give him a chance."

Joanna put her head back on the pillow. She felt tears coming and buried her face in her pillow and cried until her eyes were swollen, and her complexion, which was usually fair and milky, turned an angry red. Her stomach tossed. She got up, went into the bathroom, and vomited into the toilet. She lay on her bathroom floor, letting the cold tiles cool her body. She was overcome by anguish. Everything in her life was falling apart, especially the future she'd planned since she was twelve.

She pulled herself up from the floor, tossed cold water onto her face, and blew her nose. She walked back to her bed and sat on the edge. She felt like the world had slid out from underneath her. Everything she'd been excited about just a few weeks ago—graduating, doing an internship for Hilton Hotels, getting her career started, moving to Europe—had been replaced with feelings of gloom and regret.

She suddenly wanted her dad to be involved. He was good at making problems go away. Whenever his own good standing was on the line, he'd find a way to make the situation disappear. Being pregnant by someone none of them knew anything about would be unacceptable. Her dad wouldn't tolerate it. He'd find a way to fix it. She'd go home as soon as graduation was over. She'd tell her dad. It would become his problem to solve, not hers.

Joanna felt a little better. Just having a plan helped. She knew her dad would scream and yell when he first found out, and her mother would scuttle around, sweeping up the destruction left behind from his anger. She'd gone through it before; she could endure her dad's rage. Sooner or later, her parents would settle down, as they always did. They'd figure out what to do and get it taken care of. She decided that's what she'd do—graduate and head home.

6

RIP, JOANNA'S FATHER, WAS A SUCCESSFUL PERSONAL INJURY AT-
torney in Seattle. He was the primary shareholder and equity partner
of the law firm that belonged to his father and his father's father
before that. He was of average height, bulky, and out of shape—he
never went to the gym; he considered golf his workout. He had balding hair and a face that rarely smiled. He enjoyed sitting on the patio
at his private golf club after playing eighteen holes and bragging to
other club members about how much money he made that year, the
seaworthiness of his sailboat, his ever-shrinking handicap on the golf
course, the cabinet of Cuban cigars he recently ordered.

Rip was a no-nonsense kind of guy. He raised his daughters with
a hands-off approach, leaving the day-to-day parenting to Gladys or
the daytime nanny at the house Monday through Friday. The expectation was that both of his daughters would become independent
and successful. He pushed Joanna and Francine to take up sports in
school and to excel in their grades. It wasn't that Rip believed women
were as capable as men. He wanted his daughters to become financially independent, so they could support themselves if, by chance,
matrimony didn't work out for them.

Rip didn't have the temperament for the drama that girls can generate. His daughters learned that the house must run smoothly and quietly when Dad got home. No drama. Spectacles weren't Rip's concern—a boyfriend break-up, a girlfriend squabble, a bad haircut, or someone showing up at the prom in the same dress. Giggling or crying outbursts made him uncomfortable. Squealing and excitement that slumber parties or birthday celebrations evoked were intolerable to Rip. All of it gave him a headache.

This wasn't to say that Rip didn't love his daughters. He did but in his own way. He liked bragging about their accomplishments to his law colleagues and friends. Joanna won doubles in the high school tennis state championship. Francine took second place in the school debate team's competition. Both girls were riding in the equestrian competition on Mercer Island.

The family took annual trips overseas, and by the time Joanna entered high school, they'd traveled throughout Europe and parts of Asia. Rip felt it was important that his daughters experience different cultures and learn the customs of countries other than America. It wasn't because Rip subscribed to a multicultural philosophy. He had only a few friends who weren't white and affluent, but he believed that success meant one was *familiar* with the world and aware of social issues that plagued the globe. The inequalities among social classes were rarely thought about by Rip other than to believe that poverty was one's own fault. He thought of people who lived in poverty as being generally lazy, who would rather live on welfare than get out and find a good-paying job.

Gladys met Rip in college at the University of Idaho when she was twenty. The year was 1961. She was a political science major and went one afternoon with a few of her classmates to hear a local politician speak on campus about the homeless crisis that the politician claimed would only worsen. "If we allow homelessness to take root, we'll no longer know our beautiful state as it is now," he warned. The politician offered little in the way of solutions, nor did he address the root causes of homelessness. Gladys felt gloomy when the talk ended, wondering what the future would look like when she was older.

She lingered around outside after the event with a group of her classmates. As she stood talking to a couple of girls from her sorority, she saw a not-so-handsome but impressive young man eyeing her. She held his gaze for a moment and then looked away in embarrassment. She knew he continued to watch her, but she was too shy to look his way again. A while later, he caught up with her on the path when she was walking back to her sorority. "Geez, you're making this hard," he teased. This time she allowed herself to look at him. She smiled. She was unsure why Rip picked her out of the crowd that day. Gladys wasn't beautiful but tall, slim, intelligent, and self-assured in everything except flirting. That was the start of her and Rip.

They began dating and continued as a couple until they graduated. Rip, Gladys soon learned, came from old money. He grew up with entitlements and was accustomed to getting whatever he wanted. Gladys admired Rip's ambition and his family's ability to make things happen, like for instance, Rip was given a permanent deferment from the draft right out of high school because a US Senator from Washington owed his grandfather a favor.

Gladys, at first, was impressed with the power and money Rip grew up with, even though she often felt overshadowed by his self-imposed grandiosity. She typically felt she had to hold back around Rip and keep her thoughts and opinions to herself. He had a habit of finishing her sentences, and the two rarely embarked on deep conversations about politics, news stories, or current events—topics integral to her political science studies. When Gladys broached these subjects, Rip jumped in, negating much of what she had to say, offering up a different version of the same story, one he declared was more accurate.

In truth, Rip believed the male species naturally had a better grasp on intellectual topics than women. "Men are more analytical," he'd contend. "Why do you think Gladys, engineers, mathematicians, scientists, and the like are nearly all men?"

While it angered Gladys, she didn't make much of a fuss about it. "Pick the mountain you want to die on," her mother would say. Within the first year of their relationship, she learned to take Rip's perspective on most subjects to avoid an argument.

While Rip could be arrogant and insensitive, he knew the dating rules. He always brought Gladys flowers when he came to pick her up, and he never forgot Valentine's Day or failed to plan an exciting gala for New Year's Eve. Gladys deceived herself into believing that these actions were proof enough that Rip loved her. She overlooked his arrogance because he never missed an opportunity to show her that he cared. The truth was that Rip really did care for Gladys. She was the perfect match for him: an all-around good sport, easygoing, didn't try to take over and always made him look good. He couldn't have done better if he tried.

That Gladys sometimes lost her identity with Rip didn't deter her from going headlong into the relationship. They began sleeping together after only a month of dating. Sex with Rip seemed aggressive compared to the few other boys she'd slept with. It wasn't that he hurt her, but he got so caught up in his own physical pleasure he forgot to tune into Gladys.

He tended to sweat when he had sex and would make grunting noises that Gladys didn't find sexy. They reminded her of the noises farm animals make. At first, she'd tried to enjoy the experience and let herself go, to climax simultaneously with Rip, but she could never catch his rhythm. Finally, she learned the best way to get through sex with Rip was to bear down, brace herself, and hope it wouldn't take too long. Rip never seemed to notice. If it was good for him, he figured it was good for her.

Thankfully for Gladys, she wasn't interested in having a passionate love life. Sex, she learned, was something that guys needed, but she could take it or leave it. It was more like something she did to satisfy him, to keep him clear, running at peak performance. Gladys wanted to marry Rip for the other benefits she knew it would bring. Her mother taught her what to look for in a potential husband, and Rip met most, if not all, of the criteria. He would be successful, he was ambitious, they'd live well, they'd travel, they'd run in affluent social circles, and he was a guy's guy and not interested in flirting with her girlfriends.

She looked forward to being the wife of a successful attorney, as she knew he would become. Gladys didn't care if she had her own career. Instead, she'd do what the wives of successful men do: volunteer, sit on boards, and become involved in the arts and human services to bridge cultures and strengthen community values—all the things she'd been taught by her parents were worthy outlets for women.

In 1963, when Rip and Gladys were both twenty-two, they married. Gladys graduated with a degree in political science, and Rip earned his law degree and passed the bar. He was assured a position in his father's personal injury law firm in downtown Seattle. The newlyweds found an affordable apartment on nearby Capitol Hill. They fell comfortably into the day-to-day routine of being a married couple. Gladys knew she'd need to work until Rip started making good money. She worked at the box office in one of Seattle's downtown theaters.

Gladys was a hard worker and could be counted on to do a good job. Within a few months, she was promoted to House Manager. She loved ensuring that each performance ran smoothly. She liked thinking on her feet and solving problems to ensure each performance was a success.

In a few short years, Rip earned enough money as a personal injury attorney to allow Gladys to quit the theater job. She didn't give resigning a second thought. The theater's Managing Director encouraged Gladys to stay on and grow a promising career with the theater. She could move up the ladder to better and more challenging positions. Gladys thanked him but declined. She felt her place was to support Rip in his career. After all, she believed if Rip wasn't successful, neither would she be.

With help from Rip's parents, he and Gladys purchased their first home in Queen Anne, a neighborhood in downtown Seattle with a mix of stylish shops, cafes, and tree-lined residential streets that tout nineteenth-century houses. Gladys got busy becoming the wife of an up-and-coming attorney, serving on several community boards, and joining a lady's group at the yacht club whose mission was to conduct clothing and food drives for those in need. She began to host dinner parties for Rip's colleagues in her newly decorated dining room and backyard barbeques for neighbors and friends. She learned to shop at exclusive dress shops when items went on clearance, took a painting class, and joined a museum-touring group to hone her art appreciation skills. Gladys took to her role as Rip's wife with enthusiasm. She saw her position as a silent partner in Rip's climb up the corporate ladder. She provided the backdrop that every successful man needs.

Both Francine and Joanna were born during the time Gladys and Rip lived in Queen Anne. Gladys didn't take well to being pregnant. She was nauseous and so tired in the early months of both pregnancies that it was challenging to keep up with her activities. As the months wore on, nausea and exhaustion were replaced with Gladys's body ballooning into something twice its previous size and shape, making it hard for her to walk long distances or to be on her feet for long periods. Rip was of little help, convincing himself that if he downplayed the situation, Gladys would adapt faster. When he reminded her to pick up his shirts from the dry cleaners or drop off his suit jackets for alteration, or swing by the liquor store to pick up his favorite liqueur, Gladys would sigh heavily and roll her eyes, obviously perturbed.

When Gladys became particularly out of sorts, she'd seek the council of her local Catholic priest, where she attended mass on Sundays. The young priest would listen to Gladys's complaints with an empathetic look and then set about convincing her that men are not always the best caregivers and that she shouldn't take Rip's inattention too seriously. After all, the priest pointed out, Rip worked hard to provide Gladys and their growing family with security and opportunity. Look at all he did for her, the priest reminded Gladys. "Try not to be hard on him," he'd murmur.

When Francine and Joanna were in middle school, Rip stretched his pocketbook enough to purchase a home on Mercer Island, one of the wealthiest neighborhoods in the Seattle metropolitan area. The island, located in the south end of Lake Washington, lay between Seattle to its west and Bellevue to its east. It was known for its private beaches, pristine parks, and hiking trails. Mercer Island's town center was a vibrant array of trendy local restaurants, fitness clubs, chic home décor shops, exclusive boutiques, and bookstores.

Although a strain on their budget, Rip and Gladys purchased a dated waterfront home with views of Mount Rainier to the south and the downtown Seattle skyline to the west. Even covered in wallpaper from the fifties, shag carpet left over from the sixties, a kitchen with outdated walnut cabinets, and bathrooms that sported blue toilets, Gladys loved the house. It was her trophy for all the sacrifices, as she had come to think of them that her marriage and Rip demanded of her.

She wasn't unhappy but had begun to tire of Rip's know-it-all attitude and braggart ways. As his success grew, he often, after consuming several alcoholic beverages, boasted about his accomplishments—his money, his career achievements, his possessions—to folks they ran into at the theater, a silent auction, or some other community function. Gladys grew weary of it. She made a point of looking disinterested when Rip started in about himself. Sometimes she'd start a conversation with someone standing by her side to drown him out.

As the years passed, Gladys began to speak up more when Rip talked over her or negated something she'd say. She and Rip sometimes quarreled about a decision he failed to include her in. Her alcohol consumption increased in the evenings. She sometimes criticized Rip in public when she disagreed with something he said. In short, the honeymoon was over. Gladys and Rip no longer considered the state of their marriage, if it was everything they hoped it would be, or if they were happy. That they were slipping apart was never discussed. They failed to recognize that they had stumbled into a comfortable state of discord.

Joanna and Francine became accustomed to the relationship Gladys and Rip shared. The girls disconnected from their parents early on. They had their own full plates, trying to live up to the expectations heaped upon them by their parents, their schools, their social circles, and their affluence.

When Francine was twenty-one, she dropped out of college, ran off, and married her scuba diving instructor, Joe Grossman, a man three years her senior. They ran to Florida, making it harder for Rip to come after her. They took up residence in a small beach shack in Vero Beach, a tiny seaside town on the Atlantic Ocean across the Indian River Lagoon. Joe did several jobs that brought in a small income; besides teaching scuba diving, he worked on fishing boats and as a tour guide, sometimes bartending and waiting tables.

Francine started cleaning other people's houses and, within a short time, acquired enough weekly cleaning jobs to keep her busy five days a week. Her clients loved the quality of her work and began to drop her name to friends, family, and colleagues. Francine's business grew. She eventually had to hire two helpers to keep up with the demand. Francine found she loved the work. She liked being good at her job and having her clients appreciate her efforts. Francine and Joe were satisfied with what they had in Vero Beach. They resided in year-round sunshine, lived on the beach, worked at what they enjoyed, even if it wouldn't make them rich, and lived how they wanted, not according to someone else's expectations.

Francine's elopement threw the Melrose family into turmoil. Rip was furious that Francine would disregard everything he and Gladys had given her. That she chose poverty, living in some shack, and working as a maid over the future Rip had planned for her, was beyond his imagination. Gladys was equally outraged. How could Francine have chosen Joe Grossman for her husband when "he didn't have a pot to piss in?" What, she worried, would others think?

Gladys and Rip met Joe once when they came home and found him sitting on the porch with Francine at their house. They had no idea at the time their daughter, that very evening, was planning her escape with Joe as her co-navigator. The only good thing that came out of the whole mess was that Rip and Gladys finally found something to bond over.

The one who felt the most impact from Francine's departure was Joanna. With Francine gone, the heat was on Joanna to be the saving grace for her family. She envied Francine for her newfound independence and what appeared to be happiness. Francine made it look so easy. When Francine spoke to Joanna on the phone a few weeks after arriving in Florida, she encouraged Joanna to break away from the pressures her parents heaped on her. "It's easy," Francine jibed. "You don't have to accept their beliefs." But Joanna wasn't Francine. Francine always balked at her parents' rules and expectations. Joanna was more compliant. While she often felt overpowered by her parents, especially her dad, she'd resort to letting them make her decisions.

7

JOANNA WENT HOME IN JUNE AFTER GRADUATION. SHE SPENT THE first week at home lounging around, went to her favorite hairstylist, had a manicure, went to lunch with a couple of friends from high school, and sunbathed by the pool, but waiting for the right moment to reveal her pregnancy to her parents caused anxiety. The longer she put it off, the harder it became.

"What happened to the internship with Hilton Hotels you applied for?" her parents wanted to know.

Finally, one afternoon when Joanna accompanied her mom to a fashionable boutique specializing in upscale designer clothing, one of her mom's favorites, she figured this was the time. Now or never. "Mom, have you noticed anything different about me since I got home?"

Gladys inspected Joanna up and down. "What's different?" she asked.

"I'm pregnant," Joanna said flatly, knowing her mother wouldn't scream in front of others.

"What?" Gladys, admiring a Valentino evening gown with a price tag of ten thousand dollars, stopped and stared at Joanna. "If this is your idea of a joke, it's not funny."

Joanna kept her voice low and steady. "I'm pregnant. I'm almost three months along."

Gladys stood holding the Valentino gown, staring at Joanna. Joanna stared back. Finally, Gladys replaced the dress on the rack and started walking out of the store. "Follow me."

When Gladys told Rip that Joanna was pregnant, he raged and paced back and forth in front of their bed at night, demanding to know what Gladys intended to do about it. He couldn't deal with it and refused to speak to Joanna for days. His alcohol consumption increased dramatically; he stayed late at the office.

Gladys shook her head in disgust every time Joanna walked into the room. "Look at the trouble you've caused, Joanna. How could you be so careless? We raised you better than this. Your father's beside himself. How could you do this to us after all we've given you?"

Joanna didn't talk about Sam to her parents other than what Rip demanded she tell him; he was a struggling student, wanted to be a writer, grew up in Oak Harbor, and his dad worked for the post office. That was all she could tell them because that's all she knew. Rip wanted to check his background, but Joanna didn't know his last name.

Rip wanted to keep Sam from being involved. "It's a good thing this kid, Sam, doesn't know Joanna's pregnant," he told Gladys. "That's the way I want it. For all we know, he'd see this as an opportunity to marry into money. He probably thinks all he has to do is knock up some rich girl at a frat party and then claim ownership of her inheritance. He can think again." Rip knew the legalities of these types of situations. Sam hadn't officially been declared the biological father. There was no DNA test. Without a legal declaration of parentage, Sam had no rights. That's how Rip intended to keep it. Joanna could deny that Sam was the father if push came to shove.

Rip and Gladys agreed that no one beyond themselves would find out about Joanna's pregnancy. How would they possibly explain to others if it got out that their daughter had gone to a frat party, got drunk, had sex with a total stranger on dirty sheets in some frat boy's bedroom, and ended up pregnant? It caused Gladys anguish, fearing others might learn the truth. This could be her fall from grace.

It was bad enough that Francine ran away with her scuba diving instructor, but at least they had the good sense to go to Florida, and she hadn't been pregnant. Amazingly, Francine and Joe were still together and going strong, to Gladys's knowledge. Gladys learned to keep it short and vague when someone asked about Francine. "Oh, she and her husband live in Florida. Francine has her own business and is doing well." She didn't mention that Francine ran a house cleaning business. All the women who Gladys socialized with had housekeepers. To think her daughter was one of them was too much to bear.

The situation was even more challenging for Rip. Just weeks ago, he'd bragged to a group of his men friends at the Yacht Club that Joanna was top in her class and ready to graduate. "She'll graduate shortly and has applied for an internship position with Hilton Hotels. It's almost certain she'll get accepted. Of course, if she doesn't, her ol' man can intervene. I know someone on the Board of Directors. I could sway them." Rip's friends laughed. They knew how that worked.

Now Rip found himself avoiding the Yacht Club, his golf club, and work lunches and instead stopped off for a drink, or several, at an out-of-the-way bar on the way home in the evenings. He feigned work issues, used the excuse that he was working on a significant legal case, and couldn't get away for a few weeks. How could he explain Joanna's situation? The whole mess gave him an ulcer.

Rip considered marrying Joanna off to someone from their circle of friends or acquaintances. Joanna had a lot to bring to the table. She'd be a good catch. A middle-aged gentleman, who Rip had known through various business dealings over the years, had just gone through a divorce. Although overweight and balding, he was a reasonable prospect, wealthy, and a stockbroker. He'd probably jump at the chance to marry Joanna; she was beautiful and from a wealthy family. And yes, pregnant, but that could be negotiated. There were always nannies and private schools. But Rip worried that Joanna might balk at the idea of marriage. She always said that she didn't want to get married. She planned to stay single and live overseas. He couldn't exactly force her into marriage.

There was one other possible way to avoid a lifetime of problems—adoption. Joanna could agree to give the baby up for adoption. She'd always claimed that she didn't want children and had no desire to become a mother. If she agreed to adoption, Rip could put her in an apartment some distance from Mercer Island for the remainder of her pregnancy, less than six months. They could conceal the situation for that long if they played their cards right.

Rip thought through the details carefully. They could explain to their friends Joanna had gone to Europe for a few months. She wanted to travel around and decide where she might settle. Then, when it was over, Joanna could reappear on the scene as though she'd never been gone. This could work as long as no one learned the truth. As long as this boy, Sam, didn't cause problems. Just thinking about Sam caused Rip to feel agitated. He convinced himself Joanna would never willingly get into such a compromising situation as she did with Sam. Whoever this boy was obviously got her hammered, then led her upstairs and took advantage of her. He might decide to cash in on his good fortune if he found out she was pregnant.

Rip and Gladys approached Joana with the possibilities of marriage or adoption, one or the other. These were the best ways to minimize the damage. They'd help her, they told her, but she must agree to their terms. She must never let the boy who got her pregnant learn of the situation. "We don't want this kid involved in any of this," Rip told Joanna. "Think hard and fast before you decide to contact him. I'll withdraw every penny of your inheritance, Joanna, I promise. I'll not allow some young punk, without a dime to his name, to come along and claim ownership of anything we have. You'll be on your own if you get him involved."

Joanna agreed to adoption. She certainly wasn't going to marry some old divorcee her parents pawned her off on. Plus, she never wanted to have children. Adoption was the way to go. Someone else could raise the baby better than she could. She'd be doing something good, making another woman happy, someone who wanted a child but couldn't get pregnant or stay pregnant. She'd think of it as a sacrifice she could make for the good of her fellow man—or woman. She'd give some disheartened childless couple their dream come true. Then she could go back to her life. Her atonement would be complete.

Gladys remembered the name of an OBGYN who a friend of a friend's daughter went to for her delivery and was able to get Joanna an appointment. The doctor knew of a couple in their thirties who wanted to adopt. They'd tried for several years and couldn't carry a pregnancy to term. They might be good candidates to adopt Joanna's baby. Rip instructed the doctor to get the ball rolling. They had under six months to work things out and get everything into a foolproof legal package. Of course, they would want to meet this couple and check their backgrounds, financial status, and living situation.

They located a two-bedroom apartment for Joanna in Wallingford, a neighborhood on the north shore of Lake Union in Seattle. It overlooked Gas Works Park and had a peek-a-boo view of the Seattle skyline from the living room window that one had to look out over the parking lot to see. "How am I supposed to live in this dump for six months?" Joanna asked. The building was inhabited by a mix of college students, struggling young couples trying to make ends meet, and an occasional young family with small children. Joanna missed her old room, sitting on the patio of her parents' mansion, sipping iced tea the housekeeper served her, and going sailing on Lake Washington.

Rip and Gladys told everyone, including the household help, that they were taking Joanna on an extended European trip. "We plan to travel around and check out places where Joanna may want to settle," they told their friends. In reality, as soon as they got Joanna situated a comfortable distance away from everyone they knew, Rip and Gladys flew to Europe, just the two of them. They wanted to get away from the whole ugly mess. Joanna had put them through so much. They deserved a reprieve.

Joanna had nothing but time on her hands in her new hideout. She had no social outlet and no support network. Her few friends from high school weren't supposed to know Joanna was hiding in some dingy apartment waiting to deliver a stranger's baby. She was alone with nothing to do. One day melded into the next. Resentment toward the baby consumed her. She felt like a host to a hungry, demanding parasite. Oh, for it to be over and done with.

At her next OB appointment, the doctor mentioned that the couple who were interested in adopting Joanna's baby would like to set up a meeting. "It will be your chance to interview them," the doctor told Joanna. "So you can decide if they're the right parents for your baby. So that you can feel good about who will raise your baby. You can ask them any questions you'd like."

Joanna agreed to meet them in a little coffee house around the corner from her apartment. She didn't know what to expect. She felt nervous. What was she supposed to ask them? Her doctor told her to ask questions about their philosophy on discipline, their aspirations for the child, and where they planned to live. Joanna was more nervous about what they might ask her, for instance, who the father was. What was she supposed to tell them?

They met one morning when Joanna was in her sixth month. Joanna thought they were a nice enough couple, Rose and Phil, although mediocre. They were nothing to get excited about. He was a physical therapist, and she was a dental hygienist. They'd been married for twelve years. They'd tried over and over to get pregnant and carry a baby to term, but Rose had one miscarriage after another. Finally, they decided on adoption.

During the meeting, they tried to be everything they thought Joanna would want them to be. They assured her they were a happily married couple. They went to church regularly. They didn't care if it was a boy or a girl; they'd love either. They'd give the baby a wonderful home, they promised. Joanna was more than welcome to stop by and visit their home if she'd like. Joanna could contact their employers, interview friends, or do whatever she wanted to feel good about her decision. They'd save for the child's college education. They'd ensure the child had everything needed to grow up healthy, happy, and loved.

Joanna found it all overwhelming. She told her doctor that she was good with the adoption. Her father could get everything in order when he returned from Europe. She'd sign the final papers after the baby was born. The doctor could inform Rose and Phil that they could plan on adopting her baby when the time came, which, for Joanna, wasn't soon enough.

8

JOANNA STROLLED THROUGH THE UNIVERSITY OF WASHINGTON grounds one morning in her seventh month of pregnancy. She missed her college days and the beautiful campus with its stately buildings and park-like settings. Hoping to watch the rowing team do their practice sprints in Union Bay on Lake Washington, she made her way to the Conibear Shellhouse, where the boat crews gathered. Grabbing a coffee, she found a bench on the shore of the lake with a good view of the rowers. By now, her pregnancy was apparent and impossible to hide. She knew it was risky to be on campus; some of her sorority sisters were still in school and might notice her. Her father demanded that Joanna stay out of sight of anyone who might recognize her. "We don't need a kink in our plan, Joanna," he repeatedly told her. "This won't be forever. Then you can go back to your life."

It was the first part of November, and winter was anxious to push autumn aside, but autumn wasn't giving up easily. While the day was chilly, the sun was out and felt warm on Joanna's face. She closed her eyes and soaked it in. She sat watching the rowers glide along the smooth, calm waters of the lake. The sidewalk was frequented by students hurrying to class, people out for a stroll wanting to soak up the last of the season's sunshine, and runners and joggers. She noticed someone jog past, and vaguely, out of the corner of her eye, she saw him stop a few feet ahead of her and turn around. She thought nothing of it until she heard him call her name. She looked up and saw Sam staring at her several feet down the sidewalk.

"Joanna, is that you?"

Joanna immediately recognized him and panicked. "Oh my god, what should I do?" she thought. Her first instinct was to get up and walk in the opposite direction, but by then, Sam was walking back toward her. Joanna pulled her jacket around her middle, hoping to hide any sign of her enlarged belly.

"Joanna," Sam was now standing in front of her, "I thought that was you when I ran past. How are you?" Sam wondered, by her reaction, if she even remembered him. "It's nice to see you. I was sorry we never got the chance to talk after that frat party. I wanted to tell you I was sorry I let things get out of hand that night."

Joanna stared at him with a blank look on her face. She had the feeling of being caught shoplifting. Her heart was pounding inside her jacket. She tried to come off as casual but couldn't pull it off, instead coming across as stifled and rigid. "There's nothing to apologize for. It's in the past." She remained silent, hoping it would dissuade him from saying more, that he would turn around and continue his jog.

"How have you been? Did you graduate?"

"I'm fine, and yes, I graduated. I'm not really in the mood for small talk, Sam. If you don't mind?"

"Sure …, no problem. I'm glad I ran into you, Joanna." He hesitated briefly and then jogged off.

"Thank God he's gone," Joanna wasted no time getting up and walking in the opposite direction, away from him, but she heard him call after her. "Shit," she mumbled under her breath. "Play like you don't hear him, keep walking."

"Hey, Joanna, wait up a sec."

Joanna walked faster. Sam jogged back in her direction.

"Joanna, wait up a sec." Sam caught up with her. "I was wondering if you got on with Hilton Hotels. I remembered you telling me you applied for an internship with them."

Joanna froze, not knowing what to do. She stood with her back to him for what seemed like an eternity. It was like getting caught breaking into somebody's house. "No, I didn't get the internship," she answered with her back still to Sam. While she stood there, a skateboarder whizzed past her, forcing her to step out of his way. When she did, her profile was visible to Sam.

"Oh, Joanna, you're gonna have a baby! Congratulations! … Wow! When's the happy event?"

"First part of January …" Joanna was practically inaudible, staring at the ground. "Please, Sam, just go," she thought.

"If I remember correctly, you never wanted to have kids or get married," Sam laughed. "Someone must have changed your mind," he teased.

"Not really. I have to go, Sam." Joanna started to walk away.

Sam watched her go. Two and two at first didn't add up, but clarity flickered in his brain and remained on. Joanna was due at the beginning of January. Sam did the math. That would be nine months after he and Joanna had gotten together at the frat party. A sense of dread clutched him. He started running after her. "Joanna, wait up," he hollered. "Joanna, please, wait up."

"Fuck," Joanna thought. She heard him running up behind her. Anger took over. She spun around. "What do you want, Sam? I told you I'm not in the mood for small talk. Please leave me alone. Take a hint; I don't want to talk to you."

"Joanna, I may be way off base here, but I'm doing the math in my head and …" Sam didn't know how to finish what he started to say. He knew if he were wrong, she'd think him an idiot, but he had to say it anyway. "Are you pregnant with my kid?"

Joanna stared at him without saying a word. Her mouth was dry as the moment lingered. Finally, she said, "No."

"Joanna, I'm not trying to butt into your business, but I think we should meet and talk. Can I have your phone number? I'll call you."

"No, I don't want you to have my number."

"Then, please, Joanna, call me so we can talk. My phone number's really easy to remember, 321-6006." Sam spoke the numbers slowly so she'd have time to process them. "Just a simple cup of coffee is all I'm suggesting."

When Sam ran into Joanna, he was twenty-two years old and in his senior year of college. His studies were going well. He'd gotten a short story published in a journal that looked for fresh new writers. His grades were good. He'd even been able to do an internship with the editorial staff at a Seattle-based publishing company as part of one of his classes. His future looked bright.

He dreamed about graduating in less than a year and beginning his writing career. He'd rent a tiny studio apartment on Capitol Hill in downtown Seattle. He'd live a Hemingway-type existence on a shoestring budget and spend his free time in coffee houses and comfortable bookstores like Elliot Bay or Twice Sold Tales, imagining stories and putting them down on paper. He'd bartend two or three nights a week to pay the bills. He'd hang out with other writers and discuss books, Faulkner, the classics, and the latest best sellers. Now, without warning, his world did a complete three-sixty.

Sam didn't return to his dorm as he typically did after a morning jog. Instead, he walked around campus thinking. He found himself wandering aimlessly along the Lake Washington shoreline, past the rowing house and over the greens scattered with students enjoying the intermittent sunshine that peeked out from behind a layer of grey rain clouds that had begun to roll in from the west. Running into Joanna had been surreal. He'd been caught off guard. It felt to Sam like suddenly finding out that the path he'd been traveling to get to his future was really nothing more than a circle leading nowhere.

He did the math again in his head. If Joanna were due at the beginning of January, that would put her precisely nine months from the night of the frat party, the night they met. Sam knew, almost without a doubt, that the baby was his. That's why Joanna was acting so odd. She didn't want him to know. He stopped, bent over, and put his head in his hands. "She's over seven months pregnant, and I'm just now finding out," he thought.

Thoughts swirled through his head. How could he have gotten a girl pregnant who was on the pill? He remembered learning in his biology class that one percent of women who take the pill daily get pregnant. Joanna had assured Sam that night that she was on the pill. "I never miss," he distinctly remembered her saying. A one-time chance encounter, five minutes together at most …

Ninety-nine times out of one hundred, the pill would have done its job, protected her from becoming pregnant. Still, somehow Joanna had drawn an unlucky card from life's game of chance. He hadn't worn a condom that night and hadn't given it any further thought after learning she was on the pill. Now he was kicking himself.

"Always have a condom in your pocket," the college counselor who'd spoken during first-year orientation three years ago had warned. The counselor talked about safe sex, consensual sex, and the consequences of getting drunk and having sex. Why hadn't Sam paid closer attention?

He straightened up and looked to the sky. The world up there was spinning, and Sam couldn't tell if he was being whirled upward into space or rocketed downward from somewhere far above. He couldn't even remember the direction back to his dorm for a moment. *Why had he let Joanna walk away?*

Joanna drove the short distance back to her apartment. She closed the door behind her and leaned against it. Her father would be furious if he found out she'd run into Sam. Even worse was that Sam had figured out the baby was his.

What, she wondered, *had just happened?*

For two days, Joanna thought of nothing else. She felt like a fugitive who had just been found out by the authorities. What if Sam doesn't let it go? According to her father, he didn't have any rights. There was no evidence linking him as the father. But what if he wanted to pursue it? What kind of trouble could he cause? He might demand a DNA test. She had to prevent him from trying to butt in. She had to let him know he was off the hook. She didn't want anything from him other than for him to stay out of things. She'd call him, she decided. She vaguely remembered his phone number, 213, 321? She remembered the last four digits had two zeros and two sixes. She jotted down different combinations. She'd keep trying until she got the correct one. She'd get a handle on things before they got out of control.

It took several attempts to get the correct number, but finally, on the fifth try, Sam picked up.

"Hello?"

"Is this Sam?"

Sam knew who it was; he could tell by her voice. "Joanna, I'm so glad you called."

"I'm calling to let you know how important it is that you stay out of all of this. I'm not asking you for anything; I don't want anything from you. I'm asking you to stay out of my life, Sam. You could make things very difficult for me. Seriously." Joanna hoped she was coming across clearly.

"What do you mean, Joanna? Who's making this hard for you? If that's my baby, I have a right to know what's going on. I need to know, Joanna; I *want* to know."

Joanna snapped. Damn, this guy. "Sam, I'm dead serious; stay out of this. Butt out. The baby's being adopted. There's a couple already lined up. My father's handling the adoption. He says legally, you don't have any rights. There's no DNA test to show that you're the father. I can do what I want without your input. If you try to interfere, I'll deny you're the father. My parents don't want me near you. Stay out of my life, Sam." She hung up the phone.

9

WHEN SAM TOLD BOBBY THAT JOANNA WAS PREGNANT, BOBBY TRIED
to be helpful. "Dude, think about your future. I'm unsure what I'd
do in your shoes, but Joanna and her parents have things figured
out. I get this is a big deal, but maybe you should leave it alone." Sam
wished he could think like Bobby. He wanted to put the whole thing
out of his mind and move on, leave it alone, as Bobby put it. But that
was impossible. This situation was life-changing. He would never
forget this, never be able *not* to think about it, at least sometimes.

The dread of telling Susan about Joanna caused him to lay awake
at night, fretting. He rehearsed scenarios in his mind as to how to
approach the subject. He thought about what to say. "Susan, the
other day when I was out jogging, I ran into a girl I got together
with one night when you were studying and found out she's seven
months pregnant with my baby." How in the world could he tell her
that story without hurting her? He could confess he was drunk the
night it happened, but that sounded like an excuse.

He wanted to get it out in the open but avoided it. Even though
they agreed their relationship was casual, they slept together, hung
out, studied, and shared meals. They'd gotten close to each other. He
didn't want to upset whatever it was they had going on. He couldn't

imagine how Susan would take it, finding out that a girl he hardly knew was about to have his baby. He didn't know if she'd consider his being with another girl cheating since they never professed to be anything more than friends.

Finally, one Sunday afternoon after they went for a jog, Sam told her. She didn't take it well. Sam figured she'd be surprised, maybe even angry, but he thought she'd be supportive, understanding. He didn't expect her to dump him flat out without discussion. They were at a coffee house on campus when he told her. Susan was quiet while she listened to him tell his story, but she wouldn't look at him. She didn't want to know the details or talk about it. She made an excuse to return to her dorm and hurried away, leaving Sam feeling terrible.

They had a short conversation over the phone a couple of days later, and she told him she was "disappointed." She avoided him after that. Sam tried calling her every couple of days. "Can we meet and talk, Susan?" She told him she was busy. When they saw each other in class, she was evasive, distant. She didn't sit next to him anymore, and they didn't meet in the library to study. Sam missed her more than he expected. He saw her on campus a couple of weeks later with another guy. They were laughing and talking as they walked down the sidewalk together. Susan was listening attentively to what the guy was telling her and didn't notice Sam walking toward her across the lawn.

Sam could never figure out whether Susan's "disappointment" was a result of him having sex with another girl behind her back or if it stemmed from her feeling sorry for Joanna, for Sam not doing his part to prevent the whole fiasco, for not carrying a damned condom in his pocket as the college counselor had warned of so long ago.

Sam finally talked to his dad. They were in the backyard when Sam told him. Sam had gone home to Oak Harbor for the weekend. He knew he had to have this talk with his dad face-to-face. After hearing about his son's situation, Jack thought, "What the hell? What a careless thing to let happen. Making a baby is life-changing." He didn't say it aloud. He didn't want to make Sam feel worse than he already did. He didn't want to say something that would mar his son forever. Sam would undoubtedly remember this talk with his dad for the rest of his life. Jack knew this was a teachable moment but wasn't sure what to teach. He removed his glasses and rubbed his eyes with both hands, which he did when trying to figure out something. It would cause a momentary blurriness in his vision, and when it cleared, he'd feel refocused and back on track.

Jack remembered his own youth. He'd been luckier than Sam; that was the only difference. He didn't know much about his son's sex life, but getting drunk and having sex without a condom at a frat party with a girl he'd never met before was hard to chew on all at once. It didn't sound like Sam. He realized he'd never had a talk with Sam about safe sex. Why not? He was kicking himself now.

"Look, Dad, I know it was a stupid thing to do. It was careless." Sam hated disappointing his dad. His dad had always shown such pride in him. "What was I thinking?"

"You sometimes *don't* think in those situations, Sam," was all Jack could say.

10

SAM'S MOM, SID, BELIEVED IN FATE, THAT EVERYTHING HAPPENS FOR
a reason. "Look for the lesson," she encouraged Sam growing up.
"There's a lesson in everything that happens." Some of those lessons
had been hard, like when Sam entered a poetry contest during his
sophomore year of high school sponsored by the Oak Harbor public library. The volunteer librarian in charge of sorting through the
entries had purposely withheld Sam's poem because she disagreed
with what he had to say about bigotry. While the volunteer had been
relieved of her duties because of the ordeal, the contest was over
before Sam's poem got approved.

"Where's the lesson?" Sam demanded. "It was completely unfair."

"I'd think awareness," Sid offered. "You'll remember this your
whole life. It'll make you more aware of the prejudices that exist in
the world, something writers need to know. It'll make you a better
writer," she soothed, touching his cheek as she brushed past him
with an armful of laundry.

Maybe it was the romantic in him, the writer, but like his mom,
Sam grew to believe things turn out how they should. "If not," he'd
argue with himself, "what's the purpose of all this? What meaning

does life hold if we aren't here to reach our calling, complete some preordained mission, enhance our souls?"

On the other hand, Bobby believed in free will, that people can make their own choices, create their own destiny, and if things don't work out, they can choose something else. Our life, Bobby believed, is what we make of it. "We only get one go-around," Bobby would say, "so make it a good one."

It wasn't that Sam didn't believe in choice. He did, but he thought that everything does happen for a reason and that his choices have consequences that shape his future and teach him what he's here to learn. That's why Sam was sure it was fate that put him and Joanna in the same spot at the same time while out on his jog. He'd have never known she was pregnant had he not encountered her. Now he had a choice, to stand back and let Joanna follow through with the adoption plan or fight it and try to intervene.

Either choice included a lesson. It reminded Sam of the fortune teller who read his palm back when he was in high school. She'd warned him that he'd have to make sacrifices, that he'd have to choose. He thought he was beginning to understand what she meant. But how can you tell if you're making the correct choice? He was confused and had no idea what to do. Sid helped put things into perspective for Sam. "Look inside yourself, Sam. Listen to your gut. If you listen to your heart, your decision will be based on emotion—whatever you're feeling right now, guilt, anger, fear—your head, on the other hand, will rationalize and make excuses. Your gut won't lie to you. Follow your gut; that's where you'll find your answer."

He felt one way one minute and another way the next. His thoughts were up and down. Finally, he forced himself not to dwell on it for several days. When it came into his mind, he got busy doing something that required concentration, like homework or writing. His mom taught him when he was younger that if he quit thinking about something that was bothering him, a decision he had to make, the correct response would naturally surface. "Thinking about it's like stirring the pot," she told Sam. "It keeps everything moving around inside your head. Let it go and quiet down; what you're looking for will float to the top."

A few days later, he woke up and knew what to do. He'd hire an attorney and find out what his rights were. He wouldn't accept being kept in the dark. For all he knew, Joanna and her parents would try to prevent him from knowing when the baby was born or even knowing the sex of the baby. Bobby encouraged him to leave things alone. "The less you're involved, the easier," he warned. Sam couldn't let it go.

"Can you help me find a family law attorney?" he asked his parents. Sam's father got the name of an attorney who worked in Bothell, a bedroom community north of Seattle. Jack and Sid agreed to help Sam with attorney costs. Jack accompanied Sam to the appointment. The attorney's name was Marty Bigelow. He was a large man in his mid-forties. Most of his girth was flab, not muscle. He had a robust voice and kind eyes. He kept a small office with just one receptionist. The office was unpretentious, and the furniture needed to be updated. He wasn't in it for the money, obviously. He listened to Sam's story. "Boy, kid, you got yourself into a jam."

"Can you help me?" Sam asked.

"First of all, do you have the girl's or her attorney's contact information? We have to be able to reach her before we can make anything happen."

"All I know," Sam was embarrassed to admit, "is her name is Joanna Melrose. I get the feeling she comes from money. But I don't know for sure. She mentioned that her dad was the one handling the adoption. She acted like her dad knew everything about the legal ins and outs of all this. I took it he might be an attorney."

"The first thing we have to do is locate her. We'll need to hire an investigator to help us. First, we'll try to locate her father and determine if he's her legal representative. Worst case scenario, we'll have to find out where Joanna lives and serve her with papers."

Bigelow paused briefly, then added, "There's another thing you need to know before we proceed. Once you voluntarily claim to be the biological father, you're in it for the long haul. Even if you discover you're not the biological father, you could still be held financially responsible until the kid turns eighteen by voluntarily claiming your paternity. You sure you want to do this?"

"Tell me what I have to do?" Sam already knew he was responsible for the child.

Sam got a phone call from Marty Bigelow less than a week later. "Good news, Sam, we located Joanna's dad. His name's Rip Melrose; he's a big-shot personal injury attorney in Seattle and lives on Mercer Island, a waterfront home. The bad news for us is he's loaded."

It felt like some espionage takedown to Sam. "What do we do now?" he wanted to know.

"I'll file all the necessary paperwork, a declaration of parentage. It's a paternal responsibility agreement; it legally establishes you as the presumed father. You'll need to come in and sign the paperwork. I'll order a DNA test to be drawn from the baby's cord blood after it's born. Adoption can only occur with your authorization once the paperwork is finalized. You'll have the same rights to the baby as Joanna. Then we notify Mr. Melrose and wait for all hell to break loose.

"Another thing, Sam, it'd be good to get a part-time job to show you're being responsible. Don't make any major changes in your life; don't move in with your girlfriend or anything like that. Stay in school, show you're working toward your future."

Sam got a job as a bartender at a pub close to campus, a popular hang-out with college students. He worked four evenings a week, from five until closing, and dealt with loud, drunk, and sometimes rude customers. Servers became angry at him if a drink order got messed up. He typically returned to his dorm around twelve thirty in the morning. He had early classes he'd occasionally miss. His grades dropped a notch, and the submission deadline for a short story he was hoping to get published got overlooked.

Marty Bigelow came through for Sam. He went to court, filed the necessary paperwork, and ordered a DNA test for when the baby was born. As Joanna's authorized representative, Rip learned that Sam was legally recognized as the baby's father, and Marty Bigelow demanded that the birth certificate identify him as such. If Rip tried to interfere, Bigelow was ready to go to court.

Rip thought he had everything taken care of, under control. Finding out Sam had finagled his way into the situation was infuriating to Rip. "Well, if this doesn't fuck things up, I don't know what does!" Rip roared at Gladys. "How could you raise such an idiot daughter?"

"What does this mean?" Gladys wanted to know.

"It means," Rip spoke to Gladys like she was a child who wasn't capable of understanding, "that *Sam*"—he said Sam's name with disdain—"has legal rights as the baby's father. He can stall the adoption, even stop it if he chooses. It means, Gladys, that this baby, and this Sam, whoever the hell he is, may be in our lives forever. And according to what this Bigelow fellow tells me, Sam's done everything right. He'd shine in front of a judge. How, in God's name, did we ever get into such a mess?"

Joanna couldn't believe what was happening. She couldn't believe Sam hired an attorney, that he got an investigator to locate her father. "*What does he want? Why is he interfering?*" She tossed and turned at night. She cried. She fretted. Her parents were no help. They were too angry to be nurturing. They acted like somehow this was worse on them than it was on Joanna.

11

ONE NIGHT CLOSE TO JOANNA'S DUE DATE, TOWARD THE END OF SAM'S
bartending shift, he had a visitor. It was late, just after midnight.
Most of the patrons were leaving the pub, heading back to their
dorms or apartments, counting on their fingers how many hours of
sleep they still might squeeze in if they went directly home, knowing that tomorrow morning would come too soon. Sam noticed a
middle-aged man walk in and sit down at the bar. The man didn't
match the profile of the typical customer. He wasn't a student and
didn't look like the average professor on campus. He looked more
like a businessman, influential, at least he appeared to think so.

The man took a seat at the bar, adjusted his tie. He moved his
shoulders back and forth and rolled his neck muscles to loosen them
up, much like a boxer entering the ring. He tugged at the cuffs of his
shirt from inside his suit jacket with his thumb and forefinger. He
was around fifty, not in good physical shape, and balding. Sam half
greeted him as he continued stacking dirty glasses in the dishwasher.
"Sorry, sir, but we're closed. I can't serve you after midnight."

"Are you Sam?" The man sat with his arms on the bar, hands
folded.

"Yep, you've got the right guy." Sam had gotten used to customers calling him by name. He found that customers, especially regulars, liked to be on a first-name basis with the person pouring their drinks. It was a bonding ritual.

"My name's Rip Melrose. I think you know my daughter or at least you're familiar with her."

Sam picked up on a snide tone in the man' voice as he turned to look at Rip. He dried his hands on his apron. "You're Joanna's dad?"

"Yeah. I thought it was important we had a little man-to-man talk. Wouldn't you agree?" Before Sam could respond, Rip went on condescendingly. "I've been wondering, Sam, why a *boy* your age is willing to claim financial responsibility for a child you don't even know for sure is yours from a girl who's a total stranger to you."

Sam sounded agitated. "Age has nothing to do with it; it's my kid."

"Okay, Sam, I'll get to the point; we have a couple lined up to adopt the baby when it's born. Pulling the carpet out from underneath them is late in the game. I can't believe for a minute that a young kid your age, a struggling student, is interested in assuming financial responsibility for a baby conceived when you were too drunk to know better and with a girl you'd never met until that night. So, why don't you tell me, Sam, what *do* you want? Money?"

Sam needed to be sure he heard correctly. "Money?"

"Would ten thousand dollars squelch your interest in this affair? I can make that happen."

"Is that a bribe?" The words came out almost excitedly. Sam felt like a character in one of his imaginary novels. He felt inclined to set Rip straight. "Look, Mr. Melrose, I just learned about all this, or I would've been involved sooner. I *want* to be involved. It's my kid. I want to know who the people are who plan to adopt it when it's born. I want to meet them." Sam stood across the counter and looked Rip directly in the eye.

"Think about my offer, Sam. You'll never get one like it again."

"I hope not," Sam responded.

Rip got up from his bar stool. He turned to face Sam once again. "What should I tell the couple who thinks they're adopting the baby?" Rip said it almost like a dare.

"The truth." Sam looked at Rip like it was a no-brainer.

Rip and Gladys had their reasons for not liking Sam. They didn't need to know him to form their opinions. They wanted someone or something to blame for their daughter's calamity, and Sam was the easiest target. He had, after all, gotten their daughter pregnant. But for Rip, it was even more profound. Rip measured one's worthiness by their financial standing, and Sam didn't make a remarkable impression with his middle-class background and struggling student status. To make matters worse, Rip couldn't intimidate Sam.

Rip felt certain Sam would jump at an offer of ten thousand dollars to stay out of the way. That money would go a long way for a kid like Sam. Rip hadn't counted on Sam accusing him of bribery. He could deny it if he had to, but what if someone in the pub had overheard him? It would look bad if Sam's attorney knew what Rip had done. Sam was turning out to be an even bigger pain than Rip anticipated.

Gladys had her own reasons for not liking Sam. He didn't meet her eligibility criteria. Try as she might to adhere to her Christian values, accept others, and look for character, Sam came up short. Most of the boys Joanna's age, whose parents were in the same social circle as Gladys and Rip, were finishing college with degrees in law, medicine, and engineering. Many were following in their fathers' footsteps. Gladys wanted sons-in-law she could parade around and show off. She pictured her grown daughters and their partners accompanying her and Rip to the theater or the symphony. She wanted her friends to look at them and remark on what a beautiful couple they made, and wasn't Gladys proud of how well her daughters had turned out? Instead, both her daughters got mixed up with boys who, she hesitated to find the right word, were "unimpressive." Sam was the definition of unimpressive. She'd forever need to sugarcoat him when she spoke of him to others, just like when Francine's Joe came up in conversation.

The day after meeting Sam at the pub, Rip called Joanna and blamed her for being careless in revealing their plan to Sam, especially after making it clear that keeping it a secret was of utmost importance. Rip admonished her for blabbering the entire plan to Sam, which included their strategy of keeping him from knowing about her pregnancy. He insisted that if Joanna had kept her mouth shut, the adoption would have been smooth sailing. He lectured her that if they could have gotten the adoption papers signed before Sam found out, there would have been little he could do, as undoing a finalized adoption was tough. Rubbing it in Joanna's face, Rip chided her for her mistake.

"I visited Sam's place of work last night to try to talk sense into him," Rip told Joanna sarcastically. "He was less than cooperative, Joanna. He's gonna cause problems, mark my words. His name will be on the birth certificate. He can call the shots. All this trouble, Joanna, because you couldn't do what I asked. Unbelievable."

When she hung up, Joanna lay down on her bed. She didn't know for how long she lay there. She didn't get up to eat, use the bathroom, or shower. A sense of doom lay heavy on her. She couldn't move from the weight of it. Somewhere along the way, she'd lost her power. Everything she'd planned for her life fell apart. She felt like a pawn; something pushed around a gameboard racking up consequence after consequence. She hated men. She hated her father; she hated Sam. She hated her mother for not being strong enough to stand by her, to stand up to Rip. She hated the baby growing inside of her. She hated herself.

She wished she could go to sleep and never wake up. The thought of ending her life went through her mind. No pills were in the apartment, not even a razor blade; her mom had ensured that. She couldn't even figure out how to kill herself. Even death wasn't an option. Living was her only choice. She was so exhausted she didn't have the energy to do what life required. She fell asleep. She woke the next day to the sound of her phone ringing. She had no idea what time it was.

"Joanna, it's Sam." Dead air was on the other end of the line, so he continued. "Your father paid me a visit at the pub where I bartend the other night. He's something else, Joanna. We need to figure things out without him involved, just you and me. This is our problem to solve, not his."

The silence on the other end of the line continued. "Joanna, are you there?"

"Sam, what do you want?"

"We need to talk. We need to hear each other out." Silence. He continued, "Look, Joanna, we don't need to be enemies. We're having a kid very soon, whether we like it or not. I don't know about you, but I need to be sure I do what's best for the baby, so I can live with myself."

When she replied, her voice sounded weary, tired. "You have no idea how hard you've made this for me, Sam. There's a couple who wants the baby very badly. It's all arranged."

"I need to meet them, Joanna. I want to know who they are. This is huge. This will change our lives. It's not your father's problem to sweep under the rug." There was silence on the other end of the line. Then the line went dead.

Sam dreamed he was running after someone he couldn't see because they were too far ahead. He kept yelling for the person to slow down, but whoever it was ran faster and faster. Sam woke up in a sweat, confused, trying to figure out what the dream meant.

He'd once watched a show on TV that interviewed parents who'd given up their babies for adoption. Sometimes, one or both biological parents interviewed opted to see and hold the baby before signing the baby over to the new parents. Sam remembered how some of those parents described feeling "messed up" for the rest of their lives. They couldn't get the memory of that tiny baby out of their minds. Others opted to sign the baby over sight unseen. Some parents talked about how never holding the baby left a considerable void. They believed they would have dealt with their loss better if they had rocked the baby and said goodbye. Sam wondered which option he'd choose. He already knew that adoption would be hard for him. He knew he'd think about the child for the rest of his life, every birthday, Christmas, Halloween.

12

IT WAS A COLD AND DAMP MORNING IN JANUARY WHEN JOANNA started having labor pains. She was making a cup of tea in the kitchen when her water broke. Joanna immediately called her doctor, but the nurse informed her that the doctor was performing a c-section and was unavailable. The nurse advised Joanna to wait until her contractions were three to five minutes apart before going to the hospital.

Joanna tried to call her mother and left a message on her phone when she didn't answer. For a couple of hours, the pain was bearable. "Is this as bad as it gets?" Joanna hoped. Then things picked up. When she knew it was time to go to the hospital, she could still not reach her mother. Joanna couldn't drive herself; her pains were too intense. She felt desperate. She didn't know anything about labor. What if she waited too long and the baby started coming? As a last resort, Joanna phoned Sam. He didn't answer. She hung up without leaving him a message and called a cab.

Her contractions were coming hard and regular when she arrived at the hospital. She was put in a labor room by herself. The nurses were in and out, checking on her. She thrashed out at them and pleaded for a spinal. When her doctor arrived at the hospital, her labor was too advanced for an epidural. "Can we call anyone for you, Joanna?" the nurses questioned. "The baby's father? Your mother?"

Joanna held her breath during each pain. There'd been no Lamaze classes. She went into labor unprepared. The baby's heart rate fluctuated. Her doctor came in to check on her and instructed her to turn on her side and breathe through each contraction. She resisted. She yelled at the nurses. They attempted to hold an oxygen mask to her face during each contraction. She batted it away. Her cervix refused to dilate completely, and her labor continued into the afternoon. She was sweaty. Her hair stuck to her face. Her lips were dry. The nurses fed her ice chips which she vomited back up.

The labor pains were relentless. They'd start slow and gradually build in intensity until Joanna felt like she was in the grip of a vise that kept tightening and tightening around her middle. She'd grab the bed rail, the nurse's hand, anything. Her body tensed with each contraction, and her muscles stiffened—her jaw, lower back, neck, and shoulders. She moaned. The nurses explained that by fighting each pain, she was prolonging labor. If she could work through each contraction, breathe and try to relax, things would move along faster. "I can't," she whimpered.

She closed her eyes. She felt the next contraction coming on. She was exhausted. She felt limp. How would she get through another contraction? And another? She felt like a long-distance runner who was too tired to take one more step yet still had miles to go. Just then, she felt a hand take hers. It felt warm, strong, and comforting somehow. She squeezed it when the contraction began to tighten. "Breathe, Joanna, take a deep breath, then let it out slowly. Concentrate on exhaling very slowly." It was a male voice, calm, reassuring. She listened and did as he instructed. She made it through, and the pain subsided. She waited until her body relaxed before she opened her eyes. There was Sam at her side, holding her hand. He smiled at her. "The nurse says it won't be much longer."

"How'd you find me?" Joanna asked.

"I saw on my phone that you called but didn't leave a message. I took a guess."

At a little after five in the evening, Joanna delivered a six-and-a-half-pound healthy baby boy. He had brownish-blond hair, lots of it, and deep blue eyes. The nurse placed him in Joanna's arms. Joanna felt awkward, unsure of how to hold a baby. He looked swollen to her, his face puffy and red. "What's wrong with him?" she demanded. She peeked inside the blanket and looked him over. Dread swept over her. "Sam, take the baby." She was surprised to see how easily it came to Sam. He took his new son in his arms, cradled and talked to him, and kissed him on the forehead.

"Joanna, look at him," he exclaimed softly. Joanna watched Sam with the baby. "He's beautiful," Sam said, awestruck. Joanna didn't say a word.

Sam's name appeared on the birth certificate as the baby's father. The hospital staff drew a sample of DNA blood from Sam and the baby's cord blood. Sam didn't need to wait for the results; he knew the baby was his. He could tell. His parents said they saw the similarities when they came by the nursery later to look at the baby through the window. "We can't tell you what to do," his parents told him. "Whatever you do, we'll support you."

Joanna signed the adoption papers. She was ready to let the baby go. Rose, Phil, Rip, Gladys, and Joanna were all waiting for Sam. The decision seemed monumental to him. By far the most significant decision he'd ever make. Should he sign the baby over to Rose and Phil? He met them. They seemed like genuine people. Rose had nearly pleaded with him, and Phil had tried talking to him man-to-man about the responsibilities of raising a child. Sam was so young,

Phil emphasized. Sam was sure Phil and Rose would give the baby a loving home. But it wasn't just *a* baby; it was his son.

When he was thirteen, Sam remembered begging his parents for a puppy for which a neighbor down the street was trying to find a home. The puppy was named Minor, a black Lab, around six or seven months old. Sam pleaded and promised he'd be responsible for the dog's care. Finally, his parents gave in. For the first few months, Sam fed Minor, took him on walks, trained him to retrieve a ball, and taught him "sit" and "off."

Gradually, Sam became more and more lax about how much time he spent with Minor. Soccer and football practices were time-consuming, schoolwork was demanding, and girls took his attention. Minor was often left alone in the backyard for most of the day. Sam often felt guilty, but the situation didn't improve.

Eventually, Sam and his parents contacted a family looking for a young Lab. The family fell in love with Minor the minute they saw him. The dog ended up in a loving home. Still, Sam never got over feeling guilty for failing him and letting another family do what he promised. Sam remembered saying goodbye to Minor when he and his mom dropped him off at his new home. Sam's heart ached for weeks. It still invoked feelings of guilt and regret when he thought about it.

Sam telephoned Marty Bigelow from the hospital lobby. "Marty, this is Sam. I've made my decision. You can notify Rip that I want custody of the baby. I can't give him up."

"Have you thought through this, Sam? How you'll finish school, work, and pay for an apartment? There's so much to this decision. I'll phone Rip and give him the news if you're sure."

"I'm ready, Marty. Call Rip. And Marty, thanks for everything you've done. You've been a great help." Sam hung up. His heart ached for Rose and Phil. He wondered what their future would hold. He hated to be the cause of their anguish. He thought of the empty nursery in their home, ready for a baby that wouldn't be coming. What would Joanna do now? Would Rip and Gladys be willing to forgive her for disrupting their lives? Sam didn't care if he ever saw Rip and Gladys again, but he felt sorry for Joanna. She had so many expectations to live up to.

Despite it all, Sam was eager to face his future. His life had turned on a dime. He headed back toward the nursery. He didn't know what his life had in store for him or what obstacles or surprises fate would impose, but he was in charge of how he responded. Somehow, that made Sam feel better, more in control. He had no idea what tomorrow would bring, but he was a father now. He'd figure it out

13

WHEN JOANNA AND HER PARENTS DISCOVERED THAT SAM REFUSED TO sign the adoption papers and that he was taking custody of the baby, Rip flew into a rage, shouting at Gladys because she was nearby and available. Gladys was more concerned with how to break the news to her friends. The grim reality of the situation settled over Joanna. One fateful encounter, one night, and her whole life turned upside down. She'd taken precautions. She'd been on the pill to make sure she never got pregnant. She never wanted children. The thought of taking care of another human being was overwhelming, almost laughable. She could hardly take care of herself. Sometimes, just getting through a day seemed like an impossible task. She tried to imagine doing so with a child in her care. Impossible!

She laid back in her hospital bed, rested her head on the pillow, and let her mind drift back to her high school days. That's when things began to go wrong. That's when her mood swings began. At first, she thought it was hormonal, PMS. Feelings she and her friends experienced and bragged about. "God, I'm a bitch today; I'm PMSing," they'd boast. But Joanna's moodiness felt more extreme to her. Her moods were fluid. She'd swing from euphoria to hopelessness in a matter of days.

It started in her junior year. A feeling of apprehension settled over her that she couldn't shake. It felt to her like something terrible had happened the day before, or was going to happen that day, a feeling of constant butterflies in her stomach. Once, her anxiety got so bad that while sitting in her English lit class, she suddenly felt like she couldn't breathe or get air into her lungs. It felt like everyone in the class was watching her and snickering. She got up and ran out of the classroom. Her teacher, who came looking for her, found her in the girl's bathroom in a stall, curled up on the floor in a fetal position.

Then, without warning, Joanna's anxiety slipped into something worse: hopelessness and doom. It seemed to come out of nowhere. She became obsessed with her health and convinced herself she had some dreadful disease, leukemia, or another form of cancer. She fretted that she only had weeks to live. When checking out her body in the mirror, she saw herself as emaciated, hollow, and skeletal. She started avoiding her friends. She hated herself, the way she looked, the way she felt. She took her self-loathing out on her family. She was defiant and belligerent. She couldn't understand why her parents didn't notice she was dying and do something to help her. She hated them for it. She hated her sister, whose life went along pleasantly unmarred.

The first time it happened, the feelings of doom and gloom lasted for almost three weeks. After that, it began to reoccur every couple of months. Each episode seemed to get worse than the one before. Her despair felt so heavy that she concluded that being dead would be the best thing for everyone: her parents, her sister, her friends, herself. Thoughts of death consumed her. The pull to end her life both frightened and energized her. Planning her death gave her a sense of self-control; it put her back in charge of her life. She spent hours figuring out how she'd take her life—maybe by overdose or with a gun from her grandfather's gun cabinet or a bedsheet she could hang herself with. She thought through each scenario—how she'd get the gun from her grandfather's cabinet, where she'd loop the bed sheet in her parent's house. She studied how to tie knots securely enough to hold her weight.

She researched pain pills and found that mixing narcotics with valium and alcohol could lead to overdose and death. She began stealing valium from her mom's medicine cabinet and stashing them in her bedroom. Narcotics were proving to be a bit more challenging to come by. She thought of ways she might injure herself or break an arm or leg in order to be prescribed pain pills. She planned and schemed; she'd plotted. Acknowledging that she *could* take her life, lifted her mood slightly—not much, but enough to save her.

And then, after a few weeks of feeling depressed, Joanna would begin to feel like her old self again—"normal," she called it. Her energy level would slowly return, and her mood would lift. She'd fall back into the rhythm of her life; she'd go shopping, hang out with her friends, and her appetite improved. But then her mood would shift once again. Feelings of hopelessness and despair would return. Thoughts of wanting to kill herself would fill her mind. It terrified Joanna; she didn't feel safe in her own body. She didn't know what to do or who to tell. How do you tell someone you spend all day thinking of ways to kill yourself? What if they thought she was crazy? *Was* she crazy?

Joanna feared the next downer, the obsession of wanting to die. She didn't know how to stop it from happening. Her anxiety worsened. She began to withdraw, to stay in her room more and more. She lived on sweets that she'd stash away. She gained weight. She hated herself for being weak.

And then, without warning, she felt better than she'd felt in months. Her energy came back in a surge. She felt giddy and revitalized. It was the same feeling she felt when she and her friends would sometimes do a line of cocaine when they were out partying on weekends. She danced around the house, played music loudly, got up early, and jogged on the beach before school. She felt invincible, omnificent. She flirted with boys, laughed too loud at something someone might say, was animated and talkative around her friends.

In her revved-up state, she felt hypersexual, like a dog in heat, or how a stallion must feel when he gets a whiff of a broodmare. She brought her boyfriend home and had sex with him in her room while her parents were downstairs. Her boyfriend loved her in this state. He had no idea what had come over her, and he didn't care. He didn't question a good thing.

The high she was on continued to escalate for several days. She smuggled liquor out of her house for her and her friends. They got drunk and showed up at a party of some college boys Joanna and her friends met a few days earlier while cruising the downtown streets of Mercer Island. The party was crazy; there was lots of drinking, the air was thick with the smell of pot, and a group of kids was sitting around the coffee table, taking turns snorting lines of cocaine through a rolled up dollar bill.

Joanna's girlfriends weren't into it; they told her they were leaving. She told them to go without her. She hooked up with one of the college boys she'd met while cruising around. He followed her into the bathroom, and she had sex with him on the bathroom floor, her mini skirt hiked up around her waist, while her head bumped into the wall with each drunken thrust from the boy. Later he drove her home and dropped her in front of her house. She never heard from him again.

Stimulating herself sexually, she discovered, somehow calmed her thoughts and provided an outlet for her anxiety. Sitting at the chemistry lab worktable one afternoon, she put her hand up her skirt and inside her panties and rubbed herself under the table. It was exciting, sitting there, right in front of other students and her teacher, getting herself off.

But after a couple of weeks, it became too much. Joanna's thoughts became erratic and raced around inside her head. Her vivid, busy dreams left her feeling unrested and tired in the morning. The over-confidence she started out feeling turned into confusion, and she couldn't concentrate on one thought before being bombarded with another and another. She didn't know how to slow things down. It was like her throttle was wide open and stuck. She went without eating. She stayed up two nights in a row organizing and reorganizing the clothes in her closet and dresser drawers, writing in her journal, and rearranging her bedroom furniture. It took a couple more weeks for her brain to slow down.

After that, the highs were as likely to come on as the lows. Joanna never knew which way her moods would swing. Her schoolwork began to suffer. When she felt high, a typical essay assignment could become a lengthy discord on something unrelated to the subject matter. She'd write in long, run-on sentences, and her train of thought would become a word salad, everything chopped up and tossed together. Finally, in her senior year, her history teacher, after trying to make sense of something Joanna had written, referred her to the school counselor, who contacted Gladys and suggested she take Joanna to their family doctor.

Gladys didn't believe the situation was an emergency, so she waited a few days before calling the physician. She was sure Joanna's behavior was nothing more than typical adolescent moodiness. So it wasn't surprising that things got out of hand before Gladys got around to scheduling the doctor appointment.

Joanna got into an argument with one of her closest friends one day at school during lunch break when her friend said something to her that sounded to Joanna like ridicule or belittlement. Other girls standing close by had laughed. Maybe they were laughing at something else, but Joanna thought they were laughing at her. Her paranoia made it tough to know what was real from what was in her head. She walked away, angry. Later that day, she thought she overheard her friend talking about her to another classmate. Joanna's pent-up agitation turned to uncontrollable rage. She approached her friend and classmate, standing at their lockers in the hall. "You rotten bitch," she screamed at her friend, causing other students who were close by to stop what they were doing and gather around to see what the commotion was about. In her rage, Joanna swung her shoulder bag through the air, purposely hitting her friend in the head and knocking her to the ground. Joanna got expelled for two days, but she didn't care. It was worth it at the time. After that, her group of close friends began to ignore her, exclude her, went out of their way to avoid her.

The family doctor diagnosed Joanna as having bipolar disorder. "It's a chemical imbalance in your brain," the doctor explained. "In your case, Joanna, your mood swings occur fast and frequently. It's called rapid cycling. That's why, several times a year, you experience severe ups and downs in mood swings, each episode sometimes lasting for weeks. You'll need to take the medication I prescribe daily, Joanna. Consistently. That's the best way to keep your emotions in balance."

Joanna remembered attending a family meeting the doctor had scheduled. He'd phoned Gladys to recommend the whole family come in so he could educate them about the disorder. "We need a coordinated effort on this one, Gladys," he said, sounding upbeat. During the family conference, Joanna listened, not saying a word. All that registered was that she was mentally ill, a nut case, crazy. What would her friends think if they found out? She'd be a laughingstock, a target. She'd be ostracized.

Gladys and Rip shied away from the term "mental illness." It sounded worse than having the plague. Rip refused to accept that Joanna's disorder was serious. "We aren't going to molly-coddle Joanna about any of this," Rip demanded of Gladys. "We'll treat her like normal. If we aren't worried about it, neither should she be." It was all crap, in Rip's opinion. Everybody has mood swings. "Isn't there some kind of therapy that will cure it?" he demanded of the doctor.

"Of course," the doctor had tried to sound reassuring. "There's therapy, medications. It's important to maintain a healthy lifestyle. Bringing it out in the open is the best way to handle it, keeping it transparent. Talk about it as a family; make it acceptable," the doctor encouraged. "If you try to hide it or cover it up, Joanna may feel ashamed. That will only make things worse for her."

"Without proper management," the doctor explained, "bipolar disorder can be hard to live with. Those afflicted with the disorder often harbor suicidal ideations. There's a higher-than-average suicide rate among bipolar patients. They may go without eating or sleeping for several days, risking their physical health. They tend to be very impulsive when in a manic state. They may become sexually promiscuous. Joanna's a teenager; she's already struggling to find herself. Bipolar disorder, on top of everyday adolescent challenges, is a lot for a kid her age to handle. She'll need your support. There's no reason why she can't have a normal lifestyle, but it will require careful management. I want to recommend some books for you to read."

Only Francine, nineteen at the time, took anything the doctor told them seriously. In Rip's mind, he heard the doctor say Joanna was disabled, which meant, in Rip's opinion, that she was damaged. All Gladys was sure of was that she would be the subject of gossip among their social group if it got out. "Isn't it just awful about Joanna?" the women from her parish auxiliary would mutter behind Gladys's back. "Do you think it's safe for Joanna to associate with our kids?"

Gladys and Rip meant to read the books the doctor recommended on how to parent a teenager with manic depression, support her, and help manage her disorder, but they never got around to it. Finally, Gladys returned the books to the library with the promise that she'd renew them soon. She never did. Only Francine picked up the books and read through them. When Francine tried to discuss it, Joanna snapped at her to shut up. "I won't talk about it, Francine, so save your breath." In Joanna's mind, if she refused to think about it, then everything would be fine.

Joanna hated the medications the doctor prescribed for her. They had side effects that made her feel awful. She felt queasy and lost her appetite; she felt sedated and sometimes confused. Occasionally her hands would visibly shake. Her doctor periodically weaned her from one medication and started her on another to minimize the side effects. It became a constant juggling act.

Sooner or later, Joanna would tire of the whole thing and go off the medications without telling anyone. She wouldn't wean herself off slowly as her doctor did; she'd stop abruptly, all at once. Within a week or two, maybe more, she'd again feel her mood change, up or down, never knowing which direction it would go.

As time passed, Joanna withdrew from her friends and social life. By the time she got into college, into the sorority her dad had pulled strings to get her accepted into, she had withdrawn from most social contacts. When in a manic state, she'd convince herself that she was superior to those around her, more intelligent, more knowing. She looked down on her sorority sisters and classmates, snubbed her nose, and refused to join in, treating them like they weren't worthy of her time or attention. Just as quickly, however, her perceptions could change with her mood. Joanna's bluster would wane and she'd feel inferior to her fellow students, like they could all tell what was wrong with her just by looking.

14

JOANNA COULDN'T BELIEVE SAM TOOK CUSTODY OF THE BABY; IT would tie him and the baby to her forever. At some point, Joanna worried Sam would have to explain to the child who his mother was and why she refused to get involved. Joanna already felt guilt nibbling away at her. She would never be able to make a clean break. Her eyes filled with tears as regret swept over her. She despised Sam for approaching her that night at the frat party. She wished she could go back, undo it. She would have walked away when she saw him coming, walked out the door, and left the party. Now she would have to go through the rest of her life knowing that a guy she'd be embarrassed to introduce to her friends, who she wanted nothing to do with, was raising her child. How was she supposed to deal with this? What was she supposed to tell people?

Joanna was jostled from her thoughts by the nurse. The baby was having trouble suckling from a bottle. The nurse was concerned. "Your baby's blood sugar won't stabilize. I'd like you to try breast-feeding to see if he latches on. We don't want his glucose to continue to drop. We'll have to start an IV if his glucose doesn't come up soon, which means admitting him to the newborn intensive care unit."

"I'm not breastfeeding," Joanna told Sam. "I'd feel like a dairy cow."

Joanna gave in. She felt pressured by the hospital staff. Her doctor explained how good breast milk was for a new baby and how it was protection against allergies and viruses. "You'll be giving your baby a big advantage." How could she say no? What would they think of her? They'd think she was a bad person. She *was* a bad person—she didn't want anything to do with her child.

To Joanna's surprise, the baby latched on immediately. He suckled from her breast, rooting and pulling at her nipple. It hurt. Something came over Joanna when she felt the first tug on her breast. She felt a connection she'd never felt before. This baby had grown inside her for nine months and now fed off her body. It dawned on her that the whole time she'd been miserable, while her parents were chastising her, punishing her for letting them down, this baby had been busy growing into a tiny human being. Nothing had stopped him; he'd carried on despite them all.

As he rooted at her nipple, grunting and tugging, his face buried in her breast, he imprinted onto her. She knew then that, like it or not, this child would be a part of her life forever. There was no way out. The weight of it all was overbearing. All the planning she'd done for the past nine months was for not. Rose and Phil were going home empty-handed. Her father's plan had fallen through. There would be no reintegration back into her old life. Her parents were grandparents to an illegitimate child, the baby's father being someone they'd never accept. The child would always be a reminder to her parents of how Joanna had failed them. To fall asleep and never wake up sounded inviting. Joanna withdrew further into herself.

Sam worried about how he'd care for a new baby during his final two-quarters of school. Living in his dorm with a baby was against the rules, and he didn't make enough money bartending part-time to support himself, much less another person. He could pay rent on a studio apartment with his salary, but that didn't leave enough to hire a sitter to care for the baby while he was away at school or work. His folks offered to help care for the baby. Still, they lived almost eighty miles from the university, which involved taking a ferry.

Sam thought about moving back to Oak Harbor, living in his old room at home until he could figure things out. But it wasn't feasible. The trek to and from the university was two hours, depending on the ferry schedule. Some of Sam's classes started early in the morning. The ferry schedule would prevent him from making it to those classes on time. On nights when Sam bartended, he got off work after twelve thirty a.m. The last ferry back to Clinton left Mukilteo at eleven forty-five p.m. That would leave him stranded on the mainland on the nights he worked. Where would he sleep? It all seemed impossible.

The solution was one that neither he nor Joanna had considered. Sam could move into Joanna's apartment with the baby until he finished school, just a few months away. The hospital social worker, whom Joanna's doctor had referred, suggested it. She thought the idea was a good one. It would give Sam and Joanna time to figure things out and decide Joanna's role in the baby's life.

"You know, Joanna," the social worker said, "even if you choose to sign over your parental rights to Sam and not be a part of your baby's life, you'll think about him, wonder about him. It's only natural. This way, you and Sam can start on good terms and decide how much involvement you'll have. It'll work out so much better for all of you if you can be friends, approach this as adults, and devise a plan that works for all three of you so that you feel good about your decision."

Sam attempted to talk to Joanna about the possibility. "Look, Joanna, we just had a baby together. Neither of us asked for it, it's not what we planned on, but we're equally responsible. We don't have to be enemies. I intend to take full responsibility for the baby's care. I know you're not ready to take on motherhood, I get that, but who's to say you can't know him, be a part of his life? He's here now; he's not going away. What do you want me to tell him about you, his mother, when he gets older? Why can't we be friends and work through this together?"

Joanna didn't want to be friends with Sam. Allowing him and the baby to move into her apartment seemed like a terrible idea to her. If Sam wanted the baby, so be it, but she didn't want to be involved. She'd always been clear about that. Plus, what would her dad say? He'd cut her loose and end her financial support, including paying for her apartment. He'd ridicule her for not sticking to their plan to get the baby out of their lives so they could all move on.

Joanna understood that if she allowed the baby into her life and spent time with him, she'd inevitably become attached to him. Her guilt would eat away at her, and she'd feel obligated to get involved. She didn't want to get hooked. She wanted to live in Europe, get her life going there, and be free of all this.

And then there was the issue of Sam—he was the last person she wanted living with her. How awkward it would be, having a stranger living in her apartment, caring for her baby whom she had planned to give up for adoption. The whole situation seemed unreal. How did it get to this?

She thought about moving back home, but knew it wasn't an option. Her dad was too furious. He blamed Joanna for the whole debacle, for spilling the beans to Sam and allowing him to get involved. Gladys was too self-absorbed, worrying about what to tell anyone who might find out that their daughter just had a baby with some kid from the other side of the tracks who planned to raise it on his own! How would they explain it to their friends? What would people think?

In the end, Joanna gave in. She felt ramrodded, coerced with no voice or power. She wondered if she'd ever had any power to begin with. Her dreams of living in Europe died—she wouldn't live in Paris and manage a hotel. It was all a pipe dream; it had never been real. Her only reality was her highs and lows and that now she had a child. Whether she was involved in his life or not didn't matter one way or another. She'd feel guilty either way.

She felt her mood slip. She was afraid to be alone; she knew her feelings of gloom could morph into something worse—thoughts of suicide. It terrified her. She feared she'd hurt herself if left alone, maybe kill herself. The bottomless pit that was pulling her down was unbearable. It was a dark and murky place. It felt to her like being on a small raft, alone with no oars, on a lake of thick, ominous black oil with no land in sight. If she fell in, it would fill her lungs and consume her. It felt safer to have someone, *anyone*, around. She gave in, told Sam he and the baby could move in.

When Rip found out that Joanna agreed to let Sam move into her apartment with the baby, he was livid. "That boy has wormed his way into our lives!" he thundered at Gladys. "This kid, Sam, thinks he'll live off Joanna. He knows an easy ride when he sees one. I'm cutting her off, Gladys. I won't pay her way with that freeloader living there."

When Gladys suggested that Sam seemed genuinely commit- ted to the baby, Rip waved away the idea. "Tell me one kid we know, Gladys, who would give up everything to become a parent at twenty-two? Joanna's never getting out of this now. She's let that baby into her life and won't be able to turn her back. We're screwed, Gladys."

"Rip," Gladys said, trying to talk some sense into him, "you can't just cut her off. Joanna's depressed, I can tell. When she gets this way, it can take weeks for her to recover. She shouldn't be alone when she's depressed. She gets all sorts of crazy ideas in her head. She might try something stupid. At least with Sam there, he can keep an eye on her. We won't have to worry about her. We can give it a little time for things to settle down. Let Joanna get back on her feet." She took a deep breath and added, "Whether we like it or not, Rip, Sam's our grandson's father. Sooner or later, we'll have to work out a way to deal with this. People are bound to find out. Maybe embracing it would be the way to go. Act like we're all on board."

Rip had been shuffling through a stack of mail on the counter and looked up. "Don't refer to that child as my grandson, Gladys.

If Sam Parker thinks for one minute that I'm going to accept his offspring into our family, that I'm going to share what we have with that child, he has another thing coming. Especially when I know that he practically forced himself on Joanna at that frat party. He probably saw her and got dollar signs in his eyes. She got manipulated into drinking and led upstairs. He either strongly persuaded her to lay down for him or downright forced himself on her. Joanna got tricked into having that baby. And now, just as I predicted, Sam has weaseled his way into living with her. Unbelievable!"

Sam imagined he and Joanna living like roommates—not permanent, just something temporary until they both could figure things out. Sam and the baby would take the extra bedroom. Sam's parents purchased everything needed to care for a newborn: a crib, dresser, rocking chair, changing table, a mobile to hang over the crib, tiny baby clothes, diapers, and baby blankets. Sam would sleep in the baby's room on a cot he and his dad used to take on camping trips. Sam would be the one to get up in the night and care for the baby. He kept reminding himself, "It's just temporary until I get my feet on the ground, just until I graduate."

To Joanna, having Sam and the baby there felt like an intrusion. She reacted belligerently. She took her resentment and disappointment out on Sam. She refused to take part in caring for the baby. "I planned to give the baby up for adoption," she reminded Sam. "Don't try pushing him on me. I swear I'll be extremely difficult to live with if you do." Sam named the baby Jamie. Joanna refused to get involved in the naming. "Call him what you want," she told Sam."

15

HAVING SAM AND THE BABY THERE DID NOT ACHIEVE WHAT JOANNA hoped for, avoiding becoming depressed. She withdrew further into herself each day, staying in her bedroom except to use the bathroom. She'd go all day without eating until Sam brought her a meal. He'd sit on the edge of her bed, trying to get her to take a few bites. She wouldn't look at him; she'd stare straight ahead as though Sam were invisible. She barely responded when he tried to talk to her. She refused to get dressed, bathe and slept on and off all day.

The first time Sam tried to get Joanna to engage with Jamie, she rolled over and turned her back on both of them. Once, she screamed at Sam to get out of her room. Sam realized Joanna's behavior went beyond being spoiled; she was in a dark place. He didn't know how to approach or pull her from where she had sunk. He feared she would slip further into her abyss if she didn't eat or leave her room.

Joanna became practically catatonic, reminding Sam of a caged dog who had surrendered to hopelessness. The only signs of life Sam could detect were occasional tears that slid down Joanna's cheeks as she lay curled up in a ball on her bed. He telephoned Gladys, hoping she'd would know what to do and could help out. She told Sam that

Joanna occasionally got "down in the dumps" and gave Sam the number to Joanna's doctor.

"Joanna's more than down in the dumps," he wanted to tell Gladys but instead contacted Joanna's doctor. She was diagnosed with postpartum depression.

"Women with postpartum depression often reject motherhood for fear they'll do something wrong, hurt the baby somehow," the doctor explained. "They sometimes want nothing to do with the baby."

During her pregnancy, the doctor had kept Joanna on a very low dose of antidepressants. The doctor put her back on a higher amount, but it would take several weeks, he explained, for the medication to take effect. The doctor emphasized the importance of not leaving Joanna alone, especially with the baby, and warned Sam to watch for signs of suicidal ideations. It became Sam's obligation to look after her as well as Jamie. He coaxed Joanna to eat. He tried to engage her in light conversation. He listened for anything that might indicate she felt suicidal. He worried she might hurt herself, although she could hardly move, and hurting herself took energy. He encouraged her to shower. Finally, after several days, he got her to walk to the bathroom and would have helped her get undressed, but she told him to get out.

On top of caring for Joanna, Sam had a newborn to care for. With Joanna refusing to breastfeed, her milk quickly dried up, and Sam switched Jamie to formula. Jamie had trouble suckling from a bottle and became colicky; he spit up half of what he ate at each feeding. Jamie's fussiness increased. Sam was in near panic, worried Jamie wasn't getting enough nutrition to survive. He walked the floors day and night, trying to comfort Jamie. Sam, exhausted from lack of sleep and constant worry, ran on fumes and stress.

Each day was like the one before. Sam feared he couldn't handle everything heaped on him. To say he was overwhelmed was an understatement. He functioned like a zombie in a state of exhaustion. He got through each day by putting one foot in front of the other.

He tried not to think more than a few minutes ahead, focusing only on what was right in front of him, the next most important priority. He had no previous experience with postpartum depression, or thoughts of suicide. He had no previous experience caring for a newborn. Keeping Jamie alive and Joanna from hurting herself had become his full-time responsibility. Just a few weeks prior, his biggest worry had been passing his next exam. He felt like an old man in a kid's body.

Gradually, things improved if only slightly. After several weeks of colic, Jamie became more satisfied and less fussy. It took almost five weeks for Joanna's antidepressants to take effect, but slowly, she began to come around, to feel her depression lift. During the day, she'd sit in the living room and stare out the window. Sam brought her meals and tried to engage her in light conversation. She took to sitting in the rocker that Sam's parents brought over. One day Sam handed her Jamie and asked her if she'd rock him for just a few minutes while he tended to the laundry. She found that rocking Jamie soothed her anxiety. The rocking and Jamie's rhythmic breathing relaxed and lulled her. As soon as Jamie became fussy, Joanna handed him back to Sam.

After that she'd rock Jamie while he slept. She made no effort, however, to get involved in caring for him. If he cried, needed his diaper changed, a bath, or to be comforted, she left it to Sam to get done. She'd retreat to her bedroom, shut the door, and crawl into bed. It was Sam who got up in the middle of the night, walked the floors when Jamie cried, prepared bottles of formula, fed Jamie on demand, changed diapers, comforted, rocked, and soothed.

Joanna felt detached from the reality of the situation. She felt like a spectator, watching what went on around her from the sidelines. In her mind, Sam was a roommate who happened to have a baby. Sam's parents made the trip several days a week to watch the baby while Sam was in school or working. Joanna would disappear into her bedroom when they were there. She made no effort to interact with them and had no desire to form a relationship, even when Sid and Jack tried to engage her.

As Joanna's depression lifted, she was left feeling sluggish and disinterested. Most days, she still wouldn't get dressed. She slept during the day and couldn't motivate herself to go out for a walk or a jog. She made unhealthy food choices and craved carbs. She lived in the past. She'd close her eyes and picture bygone days when her friends would pull into her parents' circular driveway on Mercer Island and honk; she'd come running down the stairs in her bikini, yelling at whoever was in the house, "Be back later, we're going swimming at Lisa's!" Then, reality would hit. Those days were long gone. Joanna couldn't run down the stairs, out the door, and into her little world ever again. She was a grown-up now, stuck in a dumpy apartment with a guy she had nothing in common with and a baby she never wanted. Her future seemed glum.

Sometimes feelings of guilt would spread over her. She knew that, according to nature, she should feel maternal toward Jamie, but she didn't. The hormones she read about that bond a mother to her child hadn't kicked in for her.

And then there was Sam's mediocrity to endure. It was glaring to Joanna; it was all she could see when she looked at him. She resented him for his failure to be what she wanted. She punished him with hostility for being a nice guy. She was on edge around him, short and curt, detached. She knew she was spoiled and entitled, but regardless, that was the world she'd grown up in. She hadn't asked for her entitlements, just as Sam hadn't asked to be ordinary.

A couple of months after Jamie was born, Joanna went to confession and told the priest everything—how she hated her pregnancy, had considered abortion, had planned to put Jamie up for adoption, felt no interest in her child, and resented the father of her baby for his commonness. She did her Hail Marys, prayed for forgiveness, and went to mass for a few Sundays, hoping God would notice her more easily if she were in his presence. He didn't. She couldn't shake her guilt. She tried counseling but found it too tedious and painful. It was too difficult to look at her shortcomings, so she quit her counselor, didn't show up for her next appointment, and didn't call to cancel.

One day, when Jamie was a few months old, Sam put him in his stroller and talked Joanna into walking the short distance from their Wallingford apartment to Gas Works Park on the north shore of Lake Union. It was a popular place for young families to gather, fly kites, picnic on the grass. It's where Sam and Bobby used to hang out on weekends when they roomed together on campus. It was where they'd come to play frisbee or throw a football. Now Sam was taking his infant son on a walk on the same paths that he and Bobby used to skateboard on not so long ago.

Most days, Joanna didn't have the energy to shower or comb her hair, much less go on a walk, but on this day, Sam talked her into coming along. The doctor told him that getting Joanna out of the apartment would do her good. Sam pointed out that the sun was shining, a rarity for February in Seattle.

Joanna felt flabby and out of shape. She and Sam sat down on a bench facing the lake so they could watch the commercial boats as they came and went. As Joanna sat enjoying the sun on her face someone called her name. She looked up to see a small group of her high school friends from Mercer Island approaching. Joanna froze. They gathered around her, staring at her and Sam who was holding Jamie. They were all talking at once, hurling questions at her like, "Joanna, is that you?... You look different ... You've gained weight ... Is that your baby? ... You mean, all this time, we thought you were living some glamorous life in Europe?... Oh, you poor thing ...." Joanna felt the door to her old life slam shut. She'd been found out and could never pick up where she left off. By tomorrow, everyone from her past would know she'd disappeared to have a baby.

Joanna prayed the ground would open up and swallow her. It was the final humiliation. She sat motionless, hardly responding to her former friends' barrage of questions, not looking at any of them. She didn't introduce Sam. Finally, she stood and walked away without saying goodbye or telling Sam where she was going. She headed for home. She lay on her bed for the remainder of the day. Periodically, Sam would check in on her. Once, he asked her if she was okay. "Leave me alone, Sam," was all she could get out.

16

THERE WERE ALWAYS THINGS AROUND THEIR APARTMENT THAT NEEDED doing. Groceries needed buying, dishes stacked in the sink needed washing, laundry piled up on the floor needed to be washed, and clean clothes that rarely got folded and put away ended up back with the dirty laundry again. Joanna failed to notice when something needed to be done, or she'd tell Sam she felt too overwhelmed. Sam felt like he was drowning.

There were no breaks or timeouts for Sam. He didn't get to crash on his bed and nap through most of a Saturday afternoon when he didn't feel like doing anything else like he did when he roomed with Bobby. Sleeping in on weekends was a mere memory. He didn't get to go for a beer when he felt like neglecting his responsibilities for a few hours or go out for a jog when he needed to clear his head.

He thought about his life before Jamie, before Joanna. It hadn't been that long ago that he was hanging out in his dorm, watching *Beverly Hills 90210* or *Cheers*. Sam thought about times when he and Bobby would meet up with friends to shoot hoops at Denny Field on campus in the late afternoons before making their way to the college cafeteria for dinner. Sometimes, he thought of Susan and wondered how she was doing. Did she plan to go back to California after graduation? He missed their easy-going relationship. He thought about calling her, but he didn't.

Sam continued to bartend in the evenings. On nights when his folks couldn't make the trip to care for Jamie, Sam obtained the help of a neighbor, Chris Wyler, a widow somewhere in her sixties who lived in the apartment next door. Chris had raised four children of her own and had nine grandchildren. She was lonely after her husband died, and helping out filled a void for her. Sam trusted her, thought she was a baby expert. Plus, she had a calming effect on Joanna.

Sam's grades in his final quarter of school suffered. He cut classes, missed assignment due dates, and skipped an opportunity to compete in a short story writing contest. He was on the cusp of flunking a couple of his classes. His academic advisor met with him to let him know he was at risk of failing, and the program director placed him on academic probation. He'd need to make up several major assignments immediately to graduate. His professors were willing to create a study plan for him. They encouraged him to hang on. "Don't give up; you're almost there," they prodded him.

Sam had too much riding on his shoulders. It all felt impossible. He wanted to give up and drop out of school. Graduating seemed insignificant now. The support from his parents, his college professors, Bobby, and Mrs. Morrow, his high school literature teacher, who occasionally checked in to see how his writing was coming along, buoyed him. Somehow, he pulled off his final quarter. He wrote essays on his breaks at work and papers in the middle of the night while he bounced Jamie in his baby backpack. He finished a story that was his final project in his Short Story Composition class while his parents took Jamie for a weekend. In the end, he scraped by enough to graduate. He wasn't proud of his final performance; it didn't reflect what he'd worked so hard to achieve.

Sam's academic record, which once could have helped him get hired into a writing job, now reflected only a B minus grade average. He took a chance anyway and applied for a few writing jobs. The publishing company he interned with his junior year was no longer interested in him. They instead hired a couple of star students from his class. He applied for a job with a non-profit agency that wrote reviews of art events around town. He didn't get called for an interview. He held on to his bartending position. It paid the bills—barely.

Shortly after Sam graduated, when Jamie was nearing five months old, Rip invited Joanna to meet him for lunch. Rip chose a classy sushi place in downtown Seattle that he knew Joanna would enjoy. He was already seated when Joanna arrived at the restaurant. Being a man who liked to get straight to the point, Rip didn't waste any time explaining his reason for wanting to see her. "Your lease on the apartment is up at the end of the month. I don't see any reason to renew it. You can move home, and now that you're getting your strength back, you can look for a job. If you're still interested, I can get you into the internship with Hilton Hotels. I know a couple of guys on their board. Or you can go to Europe for a while, I'd support that. You've always said that's where you want to live. You can get something going over there. Regardless, you can be done with all of this …" Rip hesitated while he searched for the right word, "inconvenience. You can legally terminate your parental rights; the baby will be with his father. It will work out for everyone. I can prepare the necessary paperwork for you to sign."

Joanna couldn't believe what she was hearing. This whole fiasco was finally going to be over. Joanna could look ahead and almost see her future within reach. She informed Sam that she was moving back home—as planned, she reminded him. Sam and Jamie would need to find somewhere else to live before the lease lapsed. Her father, she told Sam, would draw up papers to give Sam full custody of Jamie. She would sign them.

Sam felt the vise tighten. Where would he and Jamie live? He and Jamie could move back to Oak Harbor and live with his parents until he got on his feet. Would that ever happen? For every step he took forward, he got knocked backward three steps. His life was different from what he expected it to look like as a college graduate. He had less than one month to figure things out. If he moved back home, he'd have to quit his bartending job in Seattle and look for a new job in Oak Harbor.

Sam couldn't help but think that Rip waited until the last minute to break the news to Joanna to make things difficult for him. Sam could see why Rip didn't like him, but he couldn't believe Rip's lack of concern for Jamie. And how would it affect Jamie when Joanna just walked out of his life? Jamie was attached to her; he wouldn't understand if she disappeared. He was too young for explanations.

Sam brought it up. "Joanna, are you planning on making a clean sweep of things with Jamie? You know, do you plan to cut all ties with him? If you sign paperwork to legally terminate your parental rights, you're agreeing to permanently remove yourself from Jamie's life. Is that what you want? You need to be sure. You can't erratically pop in and out of his life. It could mess him up. If you plan to remain in his life, we need to get things legally worked out—you know, establish regular times he can count on seeing you."

Joanna felt a tug on her conscience. She'd become fond of Jamie; the very thing she'd tried to avoid had happened despite her efforts to keep her distance. She couldn't walk away permanently. For reasons not clear, Jamie responded to her. When she came into the room, he'd light up and smile at her, his gums showing, drool sliding down his chin, making her feel like an imposter. "Don't get attached to me," she'd silently plead. "I'll only let you down."

Joanna told Rip she wasn't sure she wanted to terminate her parental rights. She asked if he could set up visiting rights so she could see Jamie every week or at least every other week after she moved home. She was in Rip's office when she made the request. "Joanna, if you establish visiting rights, you will have to pay child support. Sam will have every right to demand it of you. And furthermore, where would you have these visits? You need a location, a physical setting."

"What about our house?" Joanna knew there was no reason why that wouldn't work. There was plenty of room. Her mom could help with the baby. They could set up a nursery for Jamie. She saw it as a way to bond with Gladys. It might make them closer, mother and daughter. "One weekend a month," she offered. They could start slowly.

Rip pushed his chair back from his desk with too much force and practically lunged out of it so he could face Joanna. "Joanna, you aren't getting this, so let me try to clarify," his exasperation came through loud and clear. "You're not bringing the baby to our house. If you recall, the plan was for you to put the baby up for adoption and sever all ties so we could all get back to our lives. If it had worked out, it would've been a clean break, we would've been off the hook for any financial responsibility for the baby, and he would have been in a good home."

Rip continued, "The fact that Sam ended up being the one to take possession of the baby is unfortunate because it means that for the rest of our lives, that kid will be in our face, one way or another. Sam can demand all sorts of financial responsibility from me. I've had to change my will to protect our assets. I've had to move accounts around and get clever with where I put my money to keep Sam from trying to home in on what's ours. The more you're involved with the baby, the more Sam can demand from you, from *me*. That's not what any of us want. You can resume your old life if you agree to sign an order to terminate your parental rights. It will relieve you, relieve *us*, of any financial responsibility for the baby. You can start working toward a job in Europe. You can have the life you've always wanted."

So, that was it. Rip's generous offer to let Joanna move back home was about ensuring his wealth and getting Joanna as far away from Sam and the baby as possible. Joanna felt her old weariness come on. "So, what exactly are you saying, Dad, that if I take your offer, I sever all ties permanently with Jamie? Is that what you need me to do to make you feel more secure?"

"That's the offer, Joanna. Take it or leave it. If you want to be involved with the baby, and Sam for that matter, then you'll be responsible for yourself. If you want to settle for some mediocre, middle-class kid with nothing going for him, go ahead. You deserve each other if that's the case."

Joanna stood to leave. Something came alive in her that she hadn't felt for a while. Anger. "Dad, just out of curiosity, where does your grandson fit into all this? Is he as disposable to you as I am?"

17

JOANNA'S NEWFOUND ANGER BROUGHT WITH IT A SURGE OF RENEWED energy. She felt alive for the first time in months. Her old desire to be independent once again took hold. She'd show her dad. She'd flaunt Sam and Jamie right under his nose. She'd show up with Sam at places where she knew her folks would be, the theater, the symphony, and their favorite restaurants. She'd force Rip to tell his friends that his daughter had an illegitimate baby with some kid with no credentials and not a penny to his name.

Joanna informed Sam that she wouldn't be moving home after all, that she couldn't walk out of Jamie's life altogether, and that she'd decided not to sign away her parental rights. Her father, she let Sam know, had cut her off financially. "Look, Sam, I don't have any money, nor do I have a job. I can't pay rent, buy groceries, or anything. We both need each other right now. You need help with Jamie, and I need a place to live. We could continue to live together until we get on our feet. We can renew the lease on this apartment. I'll start looking for a job. We'd be like roommates, co-parenting roommates."

Sam called Marty Bigelow. "Marty, Joanna's decided not to sever her parental rights; she wants to live together as roommates and co-parent. Are there any downfalls, anything her dad could do to screw me over? He can't stand me, as you know."

"From what I know of Rip, there are several things he could do. Perhaps most importantly, if you aren't married, Joanna could take you to court and demand full custody of Jamie. If Rip wants to make you sweat, he could agree to support her and Jamie financially, put them up in an apartment, and give her an allowance to live on. Joanna could argue to the judge that she's more financially secure, that she doesn't have to work and can be home with Jamie all day, that she can provide for him better than you."

Marty Bigelow continued, "Rip's attorneys could lay into you, show in court that you're barely making it financially. You'd have to show the judge you have a place to live and accommodations for Jamie when you go to work. Even if the judge didn't grant Joanna full custody, she'd get partial custody and maybe even a larger slice of the pie than you'd get. The bottom line is you'd only be able to have Jamie half the time. He'd be with Joanna the other half. The truth is that the courts favor mothers in custody cases. She'd have to do something awful for a judge to deny her."

"Another thing," Marty added almost as an afterthought, "Joanna can take you to court whenever she wants to demand child support or ask for an increase in child support or to demand that she gets Jamie on holidays or birthdays. If Joanna decides to move into her own place, she can demand that Jamie attend school close to where she lives, making it inconvenient for you. Joanna could demand to claim Jamie as her dependent on taxes. The one he lives with the most gets to claim him. That's another thing you'd have to figure out. I've seen it become a never-ending nightmare with couples. In and out of court. Dealing with huge legal fees. It depends on how one partner feels about the other. If you don't get along, one or the other can make it a miserable situation."

"What do I do, Marty? She has me at a disadvantage."

"You know, Sam, from a business perspective, marriage is advantageous. It would solve most of the problems. It'd be cheaper; expenses could be shared. Custody wouldn't be an issue. Marriage offers more stability for you and Jamie and protects you, and Joanna for that matter, from child support warfare."

"I don't love her."

"Well, Sam, people get married for all sorts of reasons."

Sam thought about marriage to Joanna. She was beautiful but not the type of girl he was attracted to. Outdoorsy, intellectual girls who liked to throw a football, go for runs, discuss good books, and dine in hole-in-the-wall restaurants were who appealed to Sam. He couldn't imagine Joanna doing any of those things.

He thought about what he wanted in a wife. She'd be quick to laugh and good-natured; she and Sam would be partners, friends, and lovers. He had no idea what being married to Joanna would be like. If her behavior toward him up to that point was any indication, marriage to her would have its problems. He thought about the relationship his parents had. They'd sometimes eat from the same fork, lick off the same ice cream cone, and share a meal when dining out. He tried to imagine sharing that level of intimacy with Joanna.

Sam remembered the fortune teller who read his palm when he was in high school. She told him somewhere out there was his soulmate, the girl who held his heart, the woman who guided his destiny. "You've been with her through many lives." The memory of the fortune teller had faded over the years, but Sam never shook the notion that somewhere in the world was the person he belonged to. He wasn't sure about having past lives, but he liked believing that the girl destined to be with him was looking for him like he was looking for her. He fantasized that someday, when he'd least expect it, he'd look up, and there she'd be.

Sam had told his mother about the fortune teller's prophesy. She didn't think it was frivolous or foolish. "You'll meet the right girl,

Sam. When you see her, you'll know. You'll feel like you've known her for a thousand years." He'd been willing to wait. If he married Joanna, his chances of finding his special someone disappeared.

"We could get married, Joanna," Sam suggested. "It's best for Jamie. Plus, it makes financial sense. I know it's not ideal. We could try to make it work."

Joanna didn't want to marry Sam but was backed into a corner and needed a survival strategy. She wasn't in love with Sam. She hardly knew him. There was a massive gap between what they had grown up with. With privilege and money, she was used to having someone around to pick up after her, fix her meals, and clean her room. She grew up going to the theater with her parents, dining in expensive restaurants, and getting a new car every few years. Sam was middle class. His parents were unrefined. His mom's pride and joy was her vegetable garden, and his dad's idea of a great vacation was camping out. But marrying Sam would be a slap in her dad's face. What a great way to get back at him. That part appealed to her. Joanna would marry Sam to show her dad.

Joanna realized there'd be other advantages to marrying Sam. Having Sam around made it easier for her with Jamie. He was so much better with Jamie than she was. She didn't want to walk away from Jamie. She wouldn't be able to live with herself if she did. What would Jamie think of her if she abandoned him? What would others think of her when they eventually found out? They'd think she was an awful person. What kind of mother walks out on her child? The guilt would be unbearable.

When Joanna informed her parents that she and Sam were getting married, Rip yelled and hollered at Gladys. "What the hell is that crazy daughter of yours thinking? She's throwing her entire future away. They'll have nothing. Mark my words, Gladys, they'll be crawling to us in no time, begging for a handout."

Rip drew up a prenuptial contract protecting Joanna's assets from Sam. It would legally protect Joanna's bank accounts, investments, purchases, and anything of value that was in Joanna's name from Sam claiming ownership if they split up. "If Sam gets into financial trouble, the prenuptial will protect your assets. He won't be able to use them to pay off his debt," Rip told Joanna. He convinced her to sign it.

Sam had Marty Bigelow look at the prenuptial contract before he agreed to sign. "It contains typical language for this type of contract. It stipulates that the marriage can be terminated at any time. Income, savings, investments, and material assets that legitimately belong to one or the other of you can't be claimed by the opposite spouse or used to pay off the other spouse's debt."

This wasn't the way Sam imagined his marriage would be.

There was no wedding celebration. Sam and Joanna married on a Thursday afternoon in late June at the Seattle County Clerk's office. Bobby stood up for Sam, and a lady who worked for the county clerk stood up for Joanna. Sam's parents were in attendance, but Joanna hadn't mentioned it to her parents. She didn't want them there.

Sam officially moved into Joanna's apartment. He put his clothes on one side of her bedroom closet, his toothbrush in the bathroom, set up his computer on the secondhand desk in the living room, and placed his favorite books on the bookshelf. He traded in his cot and sleeping bag for the left side of Joanna's bed. It felt awkward to share the bedroom, and the bed, juggling the use of one bathroom. It was uncomfortable. They found themselves avoiding each other. There was nothing romantic between them. They slept on separate sides of the bed, their backs to each other.

18

JOANNA'S MOOD STABILIZED. SHE WAS NEITHER UP NOR DOWN. SHE got busy job hunting. Without Rip's help, she couldn't afford to hire a headhunter; they cost a fortune. She'd have to find a job the hard way, sending out applications, going on interviews, and waiting for a second interview which may or may not come. She sent out resume after resume. She applied for anything that remotely resembled the type of job she dreamed about having, a management position in a hospitality setting.

She felt exasperated. She had yet to receive one call to schedule an interview. She called a couple of hotel corporations to inquire about her application. The hotel spokesperson told her she didn't qualify. "What qualifications don't I have?" Joanna asked.

"Experience," came the response. "You don't have any experience. You're competing with applicants with twenty-five years of experience."

She telephoned Hilton Hotels to inquire about the internship she had to withdraw from last year and hoped to reapply for this year. Could she do the entire training in one or two hotels in the Seattle area? She had a baby, she explained. "Sorry, we don't adjust the schedule. You must be available to go where we send you," the hotel employee on the other end of the line told Joanna in a couldn't-care-less voice.

All through college, Joanna believed she'd go to school, walk out into the world, and get a good-paying job doing what she liked. Instead, she was getting door after door slammed in her face. She wished her dad could intervene. He knew people. He could get things done. He could help secure her a job, a good job. God, she wanted to phone him. She knew Sam would find out. He'd find it inexcusable and would never even consider letting someone go to the board of directors of some big corporation and bribe a board member to hire him as a payoff for some past favor.

They were living on Sam's bartending salary. Bills piled up. Sometimes, Sam had to decide what bills to pay that month and which ones to let slide into the next month. It was a constant juggling act, trying to make ends meet. Diapers alone cost a fortune. Joanna went without manicures, hair appointments, new clothes, the little luxuries she'd enjoyed her whole life. She didn't like going without. She didn't do it gracefully.

Every dime Sam earned was accounted for and went toward necessities, diapers, baby food, groceries, the power bill, rent, and car insurance. There was nothing left over at the end of each paycheck for anything frivolous, like dining out or going to the movies.

The apartment was dismal; the carpet was old and worn, the bathroom was outdated, the kitchen counters were stained from years of use by one renter after another, and the tiny balcony looked out onto the parking lot below. Somedays, Joanna thought she'd lose her mind. She'd sometimes sneak out when Sam was home to watch Jamie and drive to her favorite mall or boutique neighborhood, where she'd wander around window shopping, remembering days gone by.

When Joanna was still living at home, she'd never been on a budget or told "no" to anything she wanted. She'd had a credit card since high school. New boots, a new outfit, a haircut, a manicure, a facial, got charged. She occasionally treated her friends to lunch and never gave it a second thought to rack up miles on the new car her parents bought her. Auto repairs or gas for her vehicle was someone else's worry, not hers. She never saw the bills. Someone else took care of all that.

Joanna and her sister, Francine, were essentially commodities her parents could brag about when they did something worthwhile or criticize when they let one or the other of their parents down. Joanna learned to imitate her parents' behavior. She learned to judge others and became entitled. She couldn't be bothered by people she considered beneath her. Labels and brands became more important to her than quality relationships. She wouldn't be caught dead in high school hanging out with someone who didn't dress according to the latest trends, who didn't drive to school every day in a BMW or Audi.

She learned to lie to her parents, to sneak out and be places she wasn't supposed to be. Her mom looked the other way. Gladys didn't want to be bothered as long as she didn't have to get involved in a mess or have to handle something Joanna got caught up in, like the time Joanna and her friends got pulled over by the police on their way to a school football game with an open bottle of alcohol in the car. Gladys was furious. What would she and Rip's friends think?

Sam took on extra hours at his bartending job. He felt like he was on a treadmill, running as fast as he could and getting nowhere. His life felt like a bad joke. It did no good to complain. There was no going back. He had a child. He knew he needed something more than bartending. He had to make a living, one they could survive on. In his mind, he still thought he could get a writing job somewhere. He hadn't done any serious writing since he'd graduated. To be good, he needed time to write, daily slots of two or three hours set aside. He didn't have that. The couple of times he did find to write, he got so groggy from lack of sleep that he found himself dozing in front of his computer screen.

He scoured the newspaper every day, looking for openings for beginner writers. He sent applications to marketing agencies, small companies that needed newsletters or blogs written, and a publishing company that needed editorial assistants and copy editors. Every job opening he looked at wanted candidates with top-notch credentials or at least three to four years of experience. He was going to have to find something else in another field. The reality of that hurt—all those years of wanting to write so badly only to find out that he wasn't good enough and didn't have what it took. Jobs went to other, more qualified applicants.

Joanna's mood took a turn. She became angry, agitated, and difficult to get along with. She complained constantly. She needled Sam when he couldn't get a writing job. "I knew this would happen. How many students from your writing program do you think are working in their field, Sam? I guarantee you very few. You'd better find a real career or be poor your whole life."

The one person who could make Sam forget his worries was Jamie. Sam loved to sit on the balcony of their apartment in one of the secondhand patio chairs that his parents brought over, with Jamie on his chest. He'd bring out one of his favorite books, *A Tale of Two Cities,* or some other classical treasure he loved and read to Jamie. He loved how Jamie relaxed into him; his breathing would get rhythmic and heavy, and he'd squirm now and then to settle in. Sam loved the way Jamie smelled. When Jamie smiled at him, it felt to Sam like he was witnessing something miraculous.

19

ONE YEAR INTO THE MARRIAGE AND JOANNA HAD HAD ENOUGH. SHE couldn't tolerate her life as it was any longer. She'd die having to endure one more day like they'd been living. Marrying Sam had been a big mistake; it was hell.

She should have listened to her dad. She'd promised never to ask him for anything again, but she didn't know how hard things would get. He could rescue her from this nightmare. She was suffering for nothing; help was just around the corner. On a whim, she forgot how angry she was at him. She'd go to him and ask for help. She'd beg if need be.

One afternoon, when Sam's parents were over helping with Jamie, Joanna slipped out, claiming she needed to run an errand. She drove to her father's law office in downtown Seattle, sat across from him at his desk, and implored him to help them. "Just for a few months, Dad, until I can get a job. We're never going to make it on Sam's salary. We can't even afford to pay our bills every month. I've applied for job after job. I've gotten nowhere. I need a headhunter to help me get my foot in the door. I know I've screwed up my life and let you and Mom down, but if you could help us until I get a job, I know I can turn things around. Please, Dad, just for a few months."

Rip heaved a sigh of frustration, even though inside, he was gloating, knowing he'd been right. "This is what I warned you about. I told your mother when you married Sam, you'd be back, asking me for help. As long as you're married to Sam, you'll struggle and be poor. You could have avoided all this if you'd done what I offered."

"Dad, I have a child to think about. Please."

"Fuck," the word came out louder than he expected. "Okay, Joanna, here's what I'll do. Go out and buy some clothes. Put them on my account. Get a headhunter, and charge it to me. Start lining up interviews." Rip knew the sooner Joanna got a job and started making good money, the sooner she could leave Sam. They'd all be happier without him.

"Joanna, I'll help you and the baby out until you get on your feet, on one condition. I want to talk with Sam, man to man, and I want to do it with you there. If he thinks he's getting a free ride out of me, he has another thing coming. I want you and Sam to meet your mother and me this weekend for dinner. It's time Sam and I had a little meeting of the minds."

"Dad, please. Is that necessary?"

"It's my condition, Joanna. If Sam's going to live off my good graces, he can sit across the table from me and face me like a man."

Joanna felt a sense of dread. Sam would be furious. He thought Rip was an ass. But she wasn't willing to pass up her father's offer. If Rip was inclined to help them, then Sam should be grateful. It would be a relief, having their hard times behind them. They just had to get through dinner with her parents. If Sam had to endure Rip's ranting for a couple of hours, then so be it. In the long run, it'd be worth it.

Before Sam left for his bartending job, Joanna told him about her meeting with her dad. She confessed to asking her dad for financial support. "He wants us to meet him and Mom for dinner this Saturday evening. We have to take their help, Sam. We can't go on like this anymore. We're struggling. I don't like to struggle, Sam."

Sam listened. He felt his jaw tighten. "Everyone struggles in the beginning, Joanna. I have every intention of getting my feet on the ground. In case you haven't noticed, I've been preoccupied these last few months since Jamie was born. We'll make it, Joanna. You'll get a job, and I'll get a better job. Things will look up."

"This has been harder than I thought it would be. There's nothing wrong with asking for help while we get on our feet. It's not like my dad can't afford it. He's very rich, Sam."

Sam turned to walk down the hall to the bedroom. He needed to get ready for work. "What should I tell my dad about meeting for dinner Saturday? This is the first time he's invited us anywhere since before Jamie was born. I want to go, Sam. I want a relationship with my parents. Please go with me. They'll expect you to come."

"Tell him we'll meet 'em." Sam shut the bedroom door.

They met Rip and Gladys at Ruth's Chris Steak House in downtown Seattle. It was a high-end restaurant, far out of reach of Sam's budget. Joanna acted nervous. She fidgeted in her chair, laughed at her dad's jokes, and talked too much and too loudly. Rip and Gladys ordered double martinis. The three of them were obviously tense; even their small talk sounded restrained. Sam had very little to say. Rather he sipped on a glass of ice water while he listened to Joanna and her parents make superficial conversation. When they'd finished eating, over coffee, Rip finally got down to business, ensuring Sam knew which of them was top dog. Sam listened; he was quiet.

"Joanna's mother and I aren't going to sit by and watch our daughter go without," Rip used his most condescending voice. "I'm sure you understand how we feel. I can't tell you what to do with your future, Sam, but I can care for my daughter and grandson. So here are my conditions …"

Before he could get his words out, Sam interrupted. "Rip, I appreciate your offer, but Joanna and I won't take one cent of your money, now or ever. I'll support my family; I don't need or want your help. Thanks for the offer, though."

Rip, staring at Sam in astonishment, opened his mouth to say something, but Sam continued before he could get a word out. "Joanna's perfectly capable of getting a good job. She has a business degree from the University of Washington, she'll be fine. As for me, I don't need your help. I'll never let my son go without anything he needs to live well. I don't need you to provide for him."

Gladys looked at Rip as though to say, "What now?" She'd never heard anyone defy her husband, much less someone twenty-three years old, and wasn't sure how Rip would take it. It was intriguing somehow. "Go, Sam!" went through her mind, but she remembered he was the problem. She kept quiet.

Joanna looked confused, "Sam, what are you doing? My dad's trying to help us."

"We don't need your dad's help, Joanna. We're both capable of caring for ourselves and our son." Sam stood. "Come on, we need to get home. I have to be at work by nine o'clock. I'll drop you off on my way." He pulled Joanna's chair out so she could stand. He reached into his pocket and pulled out a one-hundred-dollar bill. That would have bought a week's supply of groceries or paid the monthly utility bills. Instead, he laid it on the table. "That should cover Joanna's and my dinner." Sam headed for the lobby. Joanna had no choice but to follow.

Sam and Joanna were quiet on the way home—Sam because he had nothing to say, and Joanna because something told her not to open her mouth. Later that night, while Sam was bartending, Joanna sat on the couch going over what had taken place at dinner. Jamie was at Sam's parents for the night. She wanted to enjoy this one night of peace and quiet. She laid back on the couch and tried to relax, but she couldn't turn off her thoughts.

She got up, walked into the kitchen, and poured herself a glass of wine. She stared out the window into the darkness. She thought of her life, where she'd ended up. She tried to imagine herself living in Europe. That was such a faraway dream. She couldn't bring the details into focus like she used to. Instead, she found herself thinking of Sam. Somewhere not too far away, he was pouring drinks for par-tygoers. There were girls all around him. They'd be drinking, getting drunk. They'd hang around his workstation, sit on their bar stools and try to draw him in. They'd flirt with him; he'd smile, laugh at their jokes, pour more drinks.

Joanna knew how other girls looked at him when they were out together, at the grocery store, walking through the park. She'd never considered Sam her type, but she'd grown to recognize his appeal. He had an outdoorsy look, a downhill skier look. He'd look just as natural as a ranch hand as he would tossing a football in the park. Maybe it was his reddish-blond hair that always looked windblown or his habit of running his fingers through it to push it off his fore-head. Perhaps it was his slightly tanned complexion or how his facial hair grew out all stubbly after one day of not shaving. His body was transitioning from boy to man, that in-between stage when he wasn't completely done maturing but had an appeal that women of all ages appreciated. What made him sexiest to women, Joanna knew, was his unawareness of his appeal. He didn't use it or work it. Rather, he wore it like a comfortable pair of jeans.

Joanna knew Sam would come home when his shift was over. He'd get up tomorrow and attend to whatever needed to be done; he'd pick up Jamie, run errands, and prepare for his evening shift. Joanna went into the bedroom and got into bed. She stretched her arm across Sam's pillow and was still awake when he came home a couple of hours later and crawled into bed beside her. Feigning sleep, she rolled towards him—nude. She wrapped her leg over his, and pressed closer, feeling him respond. She felt his hands on her body. She allowed him to roll over onto her. They made love. She wasn't sure what made her want him that night. There was something about how he'd stood up to her dad, his strength, his resolve. It felt like her dad couldn't bully her with Sam around. With Sam around, she felt protected from her own demons.

20

ON SAM'S DAYS OFF, HE'D PUT JAMIE IN A BACKPACK CARRIER OR A jogging stroller, and they'd head for different places around the city where they could explore. They'd walk around Green Lake, Gas Works Park, and the University of Washington campus. Sam was a magnet for girls when he had Jamie with him. They'd think it was sweet and ask, "Oh, is that your baby?"

"Yeah," Sam would answer.

"Oh my gosh, he's adorable. What's *your* name?" they'd ask Sam. He and Bobby'd laugh about it when they'd meet for coffee.

"Dude," Bobby would exclaim, "can I borrow Jamie now and then? I could use a little kickstart in my love life."

One day in early January, when Jamie was just over a year old, Bobby called and asked Sam to stop by his office—he wanted to talk to Sam about something. He was waiting when Sam arrived with Jamie in tow. Bobby still had his curly brown hair that he wore in a man bun and was dressed in khakis, a tie, and a faded Levi's shirt. He worked for an architectural firm that specialized in high-end commercial buildings located in Seattle's trendy Bell Town neighborhood. Bobby had been there a few months and loved it. He'd interned with the firm during his senior year of college. They liked him and had guaranteed him a position when he graduated.

Sam and Bobby ordered specialty coffees at a nearby coffeehouse while Jamie made a mess of a blueberry muffin. "Hey man, listen, my dad wanted me to talk to you about something." Bobby's dad was an Oak Harbor tax attorney Sam had known since childhood. He occasionally taught a course on tax law in the School of Law at the University of Washington. He was well-connected with the law professors within the department.

"Once a year, "Bobby told Sam, "the law school awards a needs-based scholarship to one applicant who might never get into law school because of the financial burden. My dad thinks you should consider applying for it. He thinks you'd make a good attorney. He'd put in a good word for you and present your application at the next Admissions Committee meeting."

"If you remember, Bobby, my grades sucked at the end of my writing program. My college transcripts aren't very impressive. Plus, I've never taken any classes that would make me competitive in law school. You know, political science, law classes."

"According to my dad, it doesn't matter. Until the last quarter, your grades were great; you got a short story published and interned with a publishing company. Plus, you have a lot of real-life experience; that counts for something. My dad thinks you'd make a great candidate."

"Bobby, I love ya, man, but I can't take a handout. I don't qualify for law school. I'm not even sure I'd like it. It's so far removed from writing."

"Dude, think of it this way: a law degree is a good backup plan. You could make a good living and still be able to write in your spare time."

"Spare time," Sam moaned, "What's that? I haven't had any of that for a long time."

"Jamie'll get older; he won't demand as much of your time in a few years. You'll find time to write. But in the meantime, you could make a good living as an attorney."

Sam was silent for a moment. "Your dad would do that for me?" It seemed like a lot to Sam.

"Yeah, it was his idea. He thinks you'd be good, thinks you'd do fine with the courses. Don't think of it as a handout, bro. Dad sees your potential. It wouldn't be like Rip, who buys his way through life. You'd have to earn this one. Dad can help you get your foot in the door. You'll still need to go through the interview process."

"Law school." Sam rolled it around on his tongue. "What do I have to do?"

"Dad will call you. Maybe you should wear Jamie on your back when you go in for the interview. That might help you cinch the deal." They all laughed, Jamie included. He clapped his hands, pounding on a chunk of blueberry muffin on the tray of his stroller.

Bobby's father secured an interview for Sam at the law school. The rest was up to Sam. He decided to be himself, not try to impress the Admission Committee members superficially. His situation was what it was. His grades had suffered in his writing program due to circumstances beyond his control. He told them the truth; he was the primary caregiver for his infant son, as his wife, the baby's mother, had been diagnosed with post-partum depression and couldn't care for the baby. Sam took over the care of his son and his wife. Plus, he'd taken a job at night to make ends meet. His school work had suffered.

The Admission Committee liked Sam's genuineness, not to mention the letter the owner of the pub where Sam worked had written in support of Sam, saying that out of all the employees he'd ever hired, Sam was the most "reliable, honest, and levelheaded" of any he could remember. Sam got into law school. He started in March, the spring quarter.

He received a needs-based scholarship. His tuition was minimal compared to what it would be without financial assistance. Sam took out student loans to pay for the rest and worried about paying them off. He couldn't allow himself to think of the debt that was piling up around him. He felt buried under it.

Law school added another layer of stress to Sam's life. He changed his bartending hours—he now worked Friday through Monday nights and did a double shift on Saturdays and Sundays. The law courses were challenging. He studied his notes while he pushed Jamie around the neighborhood in his stroller. Instead of the classics, he read to Jamie from his law books. He rode the public bus to and from work to study en route and save on gas and parking. He found much of the material dry compared to creative writing. Regardless, he applied himself. He got good grades, and his professors liked him, thought he showed promise as an attorney.

21

DURING SAM'S FIRST YEAR OF LAW SCHOOL, JOANNA WORKED IN A flower shop in downtown Seattle's South Lake Union neighborhood. The job had been a last resort. She happened upon it one day while strolling around South Lake Union, waiting for her car to get an oil change. On her way back to the car, she saw the Help Wanted sign in the flower shop window. It was a busy shop. It supplied flower arrangements for elaborate events throughout the Seattle metropolitan area. She inquired about the position on a fluke and walked out with the job. She could start the following Monday.

Life for Joanna and Sam fell into a routine. Joanna's added income improved their financial situation, if only slightly. They were at least finally able to make ends meet every month. Joanna initially found it difficult to adjust to the demands of holding down a job and keeping up with things at home. Her exercise consisted of walking Jamie around Green Lake in his stroller a few evenings a week. She learned how to cook simple boxed dinners on a budget, work the vacuum, and clean the inside of the toilet bowl.

Despite all the adjustments she had to undergo, Joanna felt settled in. She began to accept her life with Sam and Jamie. Her mood remained stable, neither up nor down, "normal." She and Sam took

Jamie on walks on their same days off or to the playground at the park, where he loved to swing. They stayed up late on Sam's nights off and watched movies on TV. Even their sex life improved to a degree. Joanna overlooked her disdain for Sam's shortcomings. She found, with a glass or two of wine, that she enjoyed occasional sex with him.

Gradually though, Joanna's contentment was replaced with boredom and restlessness. She felt her mood begin to change. She didn't want it to happen, she wanted things to stay the way they were, but it was like the earth was shifting underneath her feet, and she couldn't stop it. She became increasingly agitated. She began to complain again. She withdrew and left Sam to pick up the slack around the apartment. She isolated herself from Sam and Jamie and refused to interact or participate in family routines or activities. She was short with Jamie, easily angered by anything he did that rubbed against her nerves. She was dismissive of him, even when he brought her a picture he had colored just for her.

Joanna felt her mood slip lower. Getting up in the mornings, getting ready for work, feeding Jamie breakfast, or being productive felt nearly impossible. Everything she did was an effort. It was like trying to swim against high tide. Sam noticed the change in her mood and saw signs of the same behavior she exhibited after Jamie was born when the doctor diagnosed her with postpartum depression. He tried to talk to her about it, but she refused.

There were days when she missed work, wouldn't eat, and went without bathing or combing her hair. She'd try to interact with Jamie, sit on the floor and play with him, read to him, but she felt bored, disinterested. Being with him didn't bring her joy; it made her irritable. In a short time, she dipped so low that she felt like there was nothing to live for. The desire to die once again crept into her thoughts. She'd lie on the bed in the dark, drinking wine. One or two glasses calmed her anxiety and took the edge off.

Then, after several weeks, her energy gradually lifted. Rather than leveling off, returning to her "normal," her mood continued to rise. All feelings of doom and gloom were gone, vanished, and replaced with a sense of excitement. She liked it when this happened. It was refreshing to feel good after feeling so bad. It was a feeling like spring fever. She experimented with new ways to style her hair, and her make-up became excessive with blue eyeshadow and red lipstick. She could feel a buzz inside her head. She became hyperaware of her senses, of her body. Sexual thoughts flooded her brain. She felt like doing something devious behind Sam's back, like going to a bar and picking up a guy.

Joanna would sneak into the bathroom at work, lock the stall door, put her hand inside her panties, and stimulate herself until she climaxed. She became hypersexual at home. She'd strip down naked and climb into the shower with Sam when he was getting ready for work or walk around the apartment scantily dressed when she knew Sam was studying.

She went without sleeping and eating. She got up to make herself a cup of tea in the middle of the night and became obsessed with cleaning kitchen cupboards. She stayed up all night, cleaning every cabinet and drawer in the apartment.

After several days and nights of this, the energy high began to take its toll. Joanna didn't know how to slow down her mind. Thoughts whirled around in her brain. She tried to make sense of them, to link them together in some rational semblance. She felt like she was speeding down the Las Vegas strip at night in a convertible, going a hundred miles an hour, the lights whirring past in a steady line, leaving a psychedelic trail of color behind her. She needed an outlet, a release. She needed to let off steam.

One day on her lunch break, Joanna walked to the marina at Chandler's Cove on the southern tip of Lake Union to browse the specialty shops. She liked looking at all the pretty things, the hand-bags, the dresses hanging on the racks, the jewelry locked in the glass cases. They didn't have the money for these extravagances, but that didn't matter. She bought dresses, jewelry, and shoes and charged them all to her credit card. The total came to over two thousand dollars. When Sam found out, he was furious. "Joanna, for God's sake, we're barely making it!" She told him she'd return everything and get a refund, but instead, she hid them in her closet and wore them when Sam wasn't around.

Only a few months into their marriage, Sam began researching moodiness, depression, and manic episodes and realized Joanna's mood swings weren't typical. He read about bipolar disorder, discovering that the symptoms matched Joanna's behavior almost precisely. He brought it up to her. She admitted to knowing for years that she was bipolar. "Yeah, so now you know I'm crazy, Sam. What do you think? You're married to a crazy woman, whooo!" She was sarcastic, mocking. She waited for his reaction.

Sam remained calm, concerned. "There must be some treatment. What can we do about it?"

"We?" Joanna asked. "*We* don't do anything, Sam. The moods come and go. I know how to deal with them."

"That's news to me, Joanna. If you're doing something to control your mood swings, tell me what it is because I don't think it's working. We have a toddler involved who reacts to everything you do. We need to get a handle on this, see your doctor, or go to therapy. It's not working the way things have been going. Why didn't you tell me about this sooner?"

"It wasn't something we talked about when I lived at home. My parents didn't take an active role. My dad couldn't deal with it. He ignored it and wanted me to do the same." That didn't surprise Sam.

Joanna continued, "There are medications, but I hate 'em. Sometimes I take them for a while, but they have awful side effects. I can't stand to be on them for very long. I can't do my job when I'm on the meds."

Sam got involved and took an active role. He read that family support is essential to successfully manage the condition and encouraged Joanna to keep appointments with her doctor, talk to a therapist, and get on her medications and take them regularly. If untreated, bipolar disorder can worsen, Sam learned, with episodes becoming more extreme and lasting longer. He read that stress can exacerbate the disorder's progression, and drugs and alcohol can trigger the up-and-down mood swings.

He talked openly with her about her condition to normalize it and made it a point to frequently check in with her concerning her moods. Sam read books on ways to communicate with someone when they're manic or depressed and tried not to take Joanna's nasty swipes personally. He listened to her vent when she was on edge and was empathetic when she complained, to avoid making her feel rejected—a big trigger for depression, he learned. He listened for any hint of suicidal thinking when she was depressed.

He learned to recognize when her mood began to swing in the other direction, to identify her manic tendencies. He researched the most effective ways to avoid getting pulled into her arguments and how to de-escalate her behavior during mania. They agreed that Joanna would give Sam her credit cards and cash when she felt herself becoming manic but later she would yell and demand he return them. Occasionally, Sam had to cancel bank accounts and freeze credit cards during these episodes to prevent Joanna from spending everything they had on irrational shopping sprees.

There were times when it took everything Sam had not to blow up. He'd been on the verge many times. He'd tire of tip-toeing around Joanna's current mood to avoid setting her off. But he avoided arguments. The one to suffer the most when an argument broke out was Jamie. It could take Sam an hour or more to calm him, to soothe and quiet his anxiety.

Sam learned to keep his cool and disconnect when Joanna started to escalate. He distanced himself and Jamie from her physically and emotionally, giving her space and letting her quiet down. He learned how to navigate Joanna's moods and get through each one. But Sam lost something in the process. He lost his boyhood dreams, the excitement he used to feel about the future. With each year, he felt his youth fading, his dreams of becoming a writer sliding away out of reach, unfulfilled, unattainable.

He put memories from his past out of his mind, thoughts of what might have been. He didn't dwell on the "what ifs?" He accepted his reality. He stayed focused on raising Jamie and on his law school studies. He put on a determined face. But it felt to him at times like all of them, Joanna, Jamie, and himself, were being whipped around on the tail of a tornado, their lives encased in chaos and turbulence and unhappiness.

22

JOANNA SERENDIPITOUSLY GOT HER CAREER BREAK WHILE WORKING
at the flower shop. After a year of fulfilling paint-by-number flower
arrangements, she was promoted to assistant manager. When the
owner was out, Joanna was in charge. Although slight, it was an im-
provement. She occasionally got the opportunity to problem-solve,
like when an order got mixed up, or a delivery truck was delayed.

On a busy Friday morning, Joanna was sorting through orders
and lining up delivery invoices for the drivers when a local wholesaler
phoned to regretfully say that the shipment of Stephanotis scheduled
to arrive at the flower shop that morning was infested with mealybugs. The Stephanotis were to be used in thirty large cascading
flower arrangements for the wedding of the daughter of a prominent
Seattle banking executive scheduled for six that evening. It was too
late to switch the design.

The flower shop owner was out having a root canal on a tooth
that had been giving her problems for the past week. She couldn't be
reached. Joanna had no choice but to call the event planner in charge
of the wedding to let her know about the Stephanotis. The event
planner, Meryl Himes, owned and operated Big City Events, the
largest and most successful event-planning business in and around

Seattle. She was a steady customer and ordered most of her arrangements from the flower shop. She appreciated the excellent service the flower shop always provided. Today, she blew a fuse. "What do you mean, the Stephanotis are infested with mealybugs? This is unacceptable! I need those thirty arrangements delivered no later than four today, and that's pushing it."

Joanna feared losing her job if she didn't do something right then. The flower shop owner could easily blame her for sitting by and letting this sizable order slip away. Meryl Himes might take her business elsewhere unless something could be done to fix the problem. She was influential, and if something like this got out, that the flower shop couldn't come through on a promise, she could damage the flower shop's reputation.

This was the kind of challenge Joanna thrived on. She was determined to win, knowing something good might happen if she did. She started calling every flower wholesaler in Washington and Oregon. None of them could help her on such short notice. One grower in southern Oregon had the Stephanotis, but to get them to the flower shop in time to complete the arrangements and deliver them to the wedding venue by four o'clock would require having them shipped by private plane. The cost was astronomical.

Finally, when she had exhausted almost every wholesaler on the list, she found one east of the Cascade Mountains, about one hundred and sixty miles from Seattle. They had the Stephanotis and could deliver them by truck by two o'clock that afternoon. Joanna negotiated a price with them, lower than what they originally quoted her. She notified the workers on the assembly line and called in extra help to ensure they could meet the goal. She lined up the delivery truck and arranged to have it at the flower shop by three thirty. Her boss came running in around four o'clock after hearing of the fiasco, her jaw numb from the Novocain. The problem was solved by then, and the wedding event went off without a hitch.

The following Monday, while Joanna was on the phone taking an order for a small wedding event, Meryl Himes walked into the flower shop. She was around fifty years old, slim, and fit. She was dressed in a simple black sheath dress, very expensive, with black heels. Over her shoulder hung a small black Lady Dior handbag that Joanna knew must have cost over two thousand dollars. Her long brown hair, which she regularly colored to hide the gray, was pulled back in a severe ponytail. Her nails, perfectly manicured, were painted a conservative mauve. Meryl Himes reeked of success and wealth. "Excuse me, are you Joanna?" she asked with an air of authority.

"Yes," Joanna braced herself.

"Joanna, I'm Meryl Himes. How can I ever thank you for what you did last Friday? That was a three hundred-thousand-dollar wedding. It could have been disastrous had you not come through. I'm here to let your boss know how pleased I am." As Meryl headed for the owner's office, she turned to Joanna. "You know, I just had an idea. My assistant, who's been with me for over five years, is leaving. Her husband was transferred to Colorado. How would you like to be my new assistant? It's hard work and demanding, but I'll pay you much better than you're making here." She smiled and said the last part in a whisper. "Think about it." She handed Joanna her card. "Call me if you're interested."

Joanna didn't think about it for more than a minute. She accepted the position with Meryl Himes on the spot. Her starting salary was thirty thousand dollars a year, a big step up from eight dollars an hour the flower shop paid her. She breathed a sigh of relief. This was her start. She had no intention of stopping here, but this would be a great way to get her foot in the door.

Joanna's forty hours per week were often stretched to sixty. She worked weekends and evenings, some holidays, and whatever was needed. She never said no.

She loved the demands and the tight deadlines. It energized her and recharged her battery. The strenuous schedule gave her a focus, something to channel her energy into. She had to remind herself to eat and sleep. She got involved in as many aspects of the business as Meryl would allow. She became skilled at knowing how to pull off extravagant events. She oversaw half-a-million-dollar weddings, private retirement parties for top-level executives, and big-stakes fundraisers that required her to book auctioneers, entertainers, musicians, and comedians. Her clients came from multimillion-dollar technology companies, financial institutions, national sports teams, and privately run corporations. Joanna supervised several design teams and oversaw every event from start to finish. She often stayed late into the evenings to check off, for the tenth time, that every detail of an event was addressed.

Meryl gave Joanna a credit card to charge meals, drinks, and whatever was needed to ensure clients were happy and well cared for. Joanna became acquainted with vendors and caterers throughout the area and established partnerships with set-up and clean-up crews to ensure that each event ran smoothly. She met with caterers and learned to work within a company's budget when planning menus while giving the client a gourmet eating experience. Joanna's annual salary jumped to forty-five thousand dollars in less than two years. By now, Sam was in his third year of law school and still struggling as a part-time bartender. Joanna had become the breadwinner.

23

WHILE JOANNA'S CAREER WAS THRIVING, HER PERSONAL LIFE SUF-
fered. She was gone from home more and more. She typically left
for work before Jamie got up in the mornings, and often got home
when he was asleep. Sam and Joanna's biggest quarrels occurred because Joanna would miss major events for Jamie—playdates, birthdays, and Halloween. She'd often plan to go home early, spend the
evening with Jamie, bathe him, and read to him. Still, something
at work would demand her attention, and going home got pushed
aside. She'd have to stay until she got whatever it was worked out.
Sometimes she convinced herself that just saying she wanted to
spend the evening with Jamie exonerated her of guilt and met her
maternal obligations.

When Jamie was almost four, his favorite storybook was *The
Barn on the Farm*. For his fourth birthday, he begged his parents to
take him to a real farm where he could see real live farm animals.
Sam heard about a farm in Skagit Valley, north of Seattle, that gave
tours for kids. Joanna scheduled a party at the farm for Jamie and a
few of his preschool friends and let Jamie help her plan the event. She
arranged for pony rides and a clown to do tricks and ordered Jamie's
favorite cake and ice cream. Jamie was excited for weeks leading up

to the party. It was all he talked about to Sam and Joanna. He told Sam everything he and his mom would do together at the farm.

On the day of the birthday party, there was a wedding event that Joanna was sure would go off without a hitch, but it didn't. It was a relatively small wedding, with one hundred and fifty people on the guest list. The morning of the wedding, the jazz quartet canceled. One of the musicians had come down with a stomach bug. The bride was in tears, and Meryl assured her Joanna would work something out. Joanna sped off to her office late that morning, hoping to find a quick fix and return home to head out for Jamie's party.

Finding a replacement quartet at the last minute was challenging. Finally, after almost three hours of phone calls, Joanna got a group lined up. Jamie's party was already in progress, and she knew she'd miss it if she didn't leave right now. Still, first, she wanted to contact the bride to let her know everything was handled. The bride was grateful and wondered if Joanna could please talk to the chef about the dessert for the sit-down dinner. She decided at the last minute to serve the cherry cobbler with vanilla ice cream instead of whipping cream. Could Joanna please make sure that got handled?

By the time Joanna finished, it was too late to make it to the farm for Jamie's birthday party. "Daddy, where's Mommy?" Jamie asked over and over. Halfway through the party, Jamie grew irritable and cried during the clown's tricks. He refused to eat his cake, claiming he didn't like it and didn't want to pet the farm animals after all. He wanted to go home. When they returned home later that afternoon, Jamie cried, "Mommy will be sad that she missed the animals today, huh, Daddy?"

Joanna arrived home late that afternoon while Jamie was napping. "Sam, I know what you're gonna say, so don't. I had an emergency at work, and I couldn't walk out and leave it. I'll make it up to Jamie."

Sam was in the kitchen when Joanna came in. He walked into the hallway, blocking her way to their bedroom. "You'll have many weddings during your career, Joanna, but Jamie only turns four once. Don't give me any excuses about emergencies. I'm not in the mood to hear them. While you were finding a musical group for some wedding that could have just as easily gone without, I was explaining to your son why you weren't at his party that he'd waited weeks for. Your priorities are backward."

"Move out of my way, Sam. Don't you dare try to make me feel guilty? I'll make this up to Jamie; I don't need to be reprimanded by you for what I do and don't do."

"You have a four-year-old boy that needs his mother. *He's* your priority, Joanna."

"If you recall, Sam, I never signed up for this role," Joanna said on the defensive. "You knew that. I made it very clear to you that I would have a career. I'm not giving that up. Don't try to make me a bad person for doing what you knew all along I'd do. I'll make it up to Jamie. I'll take him someplace special for his birthday. But I don't need you trying to make me feel guilty. So, knock it off, Sam." Joanna pushed past him and then turned to face him. "Not to mention, if it weren't for *my* income, we wouldn't be able to afford *any* party for Jamie. I'm the breadwinner, so, yes, my job *is* my priority." With that, Joanna shut their bedroom door in Sam's face.

Jamie was asleep on their bed. Joanna sat down on the edge of the bed and looked at her son. Tears welled up in her eyes. She reached over and gently brushed his hair off his forehead. "Jamie, I'm sorry," she whispered. Here came those feelings again. The heartache, the guilt. "What kind of a person am I?" Joanna whispered. What kind of mother would stay at work to ensure that some wedding party had a jazz quartet rather than be at her child's birthday party?

Sam was right. Her priority *should* be her son. But she knew her need to be excellent would always win out. She needed to be the best. Failure as a mother was personal, between her and Sam and Jamie, but botching her work was public. All eyes were on her to pull off the perfect event. It took more effort to succeed in public. Every event had to be flawless, or she tortured herself. Plus, she knew Sam would pick up the slack at home. He'd cover for her to Jamie. She'd always known that would be the case. After all, that's why she married him.

Her life became one of juggling success and guilt. She hated seeing the look on Jamie's face when she had to leave him to handle something at work. After the birthday incident, when she knew she'd be home too late to tuck him in, she'd call him to tell him good night. She'd make a big deal about throwing him kisses over the phone, and they'd play a game of him catching each one. Joanna always hung up, feeling guilty. She was being forced to choose between her job and Jamie. The other constantly tugged at her for attention when she focused on one.

In Joanna's mind, she needed her job. Running things for Big City Events helped ward off feelings of depression that could sneak up on her without warning. She had to remain sharp and focused on her job. Her work kept her adrenalin flowing and in a low-level state of mania most of the time, not as extreme as full-blown mania, but with just enough elevation in her energy level to improve her moodiness. She typically had at least three or four large-scale events that she oversaw simultaneously—weddings, business events, and corporate parties. Her responsibilities were stressful, but they kept her in high gear. She seemed to convert stress into octane for her body and brain.

If Joanna gave up her job, her depression might come back. She hated depression. She didn't feel safe when she was depressed. She feared she would hurt herself. She couldn't risk having that happen; she might not survive. She was happiest when she was working. It gave her purpose. She'd be unhappy staying home. She wouldn't be a good mother. She knew her preoccupation with wanting more would take her away from Jamie. She'd physically be there but not mentally. It felt to Joanna like the guilt of pursuing what she wanted was easier to deal with than the fear of the alternative.

24

JOANNA MADE ENOUGH MONEY TO LEAVE AND SUPPORT JAMIE ON HER own within a few years of working for Big City Events. But the thought of going out alone, sharing custody, and having Jamie part of the time without Sam there to help overwhelmed her.

Joanna also knew Jamie wouldn't be happy without Sam around. The truth was that Joanna doubted Jamie would want to stay with her at all if Sam wasn't there. As it was, if Sam were gone for just a few hours, Jamie would ask repeatedly, "When's Daddy coming home, Mommy?" He'd grow irritable and refuse to put away his toys or sit at the table and eat his dinner. With Sam around, Joanna could still look somewhat good in her son's eyes.

Her mood disorder caused her to be self-obsessed, to focus only on herself. Nurturing someone else—even her own son—was foreign to her. When she came home in the evenings, she wanted peace and quiet, time to unwind. She'd want to retreat to the bedroom and lay on the bed in the dark with a drink.

Jamie, however, would want her attention. He'd bombard her with stories about something that happened that day at school, like getting a gold star for sitting quietly through story time or getting mad at a girl in his class for cutting in front of him in the lunch line.

Joanna would try to listen, but she'd find herself shuffling through the mail or digging for something in her purse. She tried to act interested, but her mind would wander, and she'd instead think about the glass of wine waiting to be poured.

Sometimes, though, Joanna's love for Jamie would clutch her heart, and the intensity would bring her to tears. She knew Jamie loved her unconditionally. He forgave her shortcomings, her missing his birthday, or not being available to go on a field trip with his class. Jamie was always ready to let things go, to look ahead to the next hopeful event. Joanna would be overcome with guilt.

When Jamie was young, Joanna would sometimes tiptoe into his room after he'd fallen asleep. She'd brush the hair from his face and take in his features. He mostly resembled Sam, but something in the shape of his nose and mouth was uniquely Joanna's. She'd lay down on the bed next to him and listen to his steady breathing; she'd tuck him into her arms and feel his chest's rhythmic rise and fall. She'd fall asleep lying there beside him.

The more stress Joanna felt in her work life, the easier it was to set her off at home. She picked fights with Sam and looked for things to be critical about. Her voice would raise a couple of octaves when she spoke to him. "Sam, I can't believe you got whole milk. I told you to get two percent. Why is that so hard?" or "Sam, can you go see what Jamie's hollering about. Are you deaf?" She accused him of coming on to other women. If another woman even smiled at Sam, Joanna accused him of inviting the attention.

Joanna knew Sam was friendly with some of the mothers in Jamie's preschool. Once, when they were at a parent event at the school, Joanna observed Sam in a cozy conversation with the mother of a little girl in Jamie's class. The mother and Sam had obviously met before, probably when Sam dropped off Jamie or picked him up after school. Joanna's jealousy ignited as she judged the mother as being too attentive, hanging on Sam's every word, laughing at something funny he said, touching his arm when she said goodbye. It made Joanna furious. When they got home, she accused Sam of coming on to the woman. "If you want to send 'come fuck me looks' to women, Sam, do it when I'm not around."

"Joanna, where's this coming from?"

Once Joanna got going, she couldn't stop herself. She'd continue to provoke Sam, egg him on, trying to get him to react. She'd call him names and refer to women he had a friendly exchange with as "whores" or "bitches." Sam would find himself in the middle of Joanna's verbal onslaughts.

When they were first married, when this happened, Sam would react. He'd become angry and get on the defensive. But he eventually learned that Joanna's hot temper and her attempts to get him into verbal arguments were symptoms of her bipolar disorder. Sometimes the most minor thing could set her off. If Sam responded by arguing back, Joanna could keep up her onslaught for hours, causing Jamie to react. Jamie would shout over both of them to be quiet.

Once when Jamie was three, he greeted Joanna when she came home from work by screaming his words at her. When Sam asked why he was yelling, Jamie replied, "I'm mad, like Mommy!" It was difficult sometimes for Sam to practice what he knew was essential to minimize Joanna's attacks. He'd try to stay calm, refuse to argue with her. He'd disengage, even if it meant taking Jamie and leaving the apartment until Joanna could settle down. Over time, it wore on Sam, the constant effort to stay centered, not to react.

There were times when Sam seriously considered taking Jamie and moving out. But he struggled with what was best for Jamie. Was it better to stay and put Jamie through Joanna's difficulties with mood swings, anger and arguments, and impulsive behavior? Or would it be better to separate and remove Jamie from the situation? Joanna would fight to have custody of Jamie half the time if they split. Her guilt wouldn't allow her to leave Jamie with Sam full-time. He knew Joanna wasn't up to parenting Jamie by herself. She couldn't care for herself when she was caught in one of her episodes. How would she possibly take care of Jamie and ensure his safety?

Sam thought about going to court to fight for full custody of Jamie, but Marty Bigelow talked him out of it. "You won't win, Sam," he warned. "Joanna has a good track record. She runs a million-dollar company, she's never been hospitalized for her condition, and her daddy's loaded. He can afford the best family practice lawyers available. They'll camouflage Joanna's symptoms and make it look like you're just out to get her. Rip can drag you through a financial nightmare. And you'll still lose."

Once, Sam did take Jamie and leave, but only for a couple of days. Jamie was five years old. Sam and Joanna took Jamie to Green Lake one Saturday afternoon, a popular urban hangout for families, joggers, skaters, and anyone who wanted to enjoy the outdoors. They sat on a bench watching a group of twenty-somethings play volleyball while Jamie played close by. The volleyball players needed one more person to even the teams, so Sam volunteered. When Sam and the woman playing on his left dove for the ball, they got tangled up and fell to the ground. They both laughed about it as Sam helped her up. Later, Sam couldn't even remember what she looked like, but Joanna wouldn't let it go. It crescendoed into her yelling, accusing Sam of flirting, calling him names. "You son of a bitch, Sam, don't tell me you weren't coming on to her."

Sam told her he'd take Jamie and leave if she didn't knock it off. When she kept it up, he packed enough clothes for him and Jamie for three or four days. Joanna became hysterical, demanded he not leave, and pleaded with him to stay. She became irrational and threatened to call the police if he took Jamie. Sam ignored her while shoving pajamas, underwear, toothbrushes, Jamie's play clothes, and his stuffed rabbit and blankie into his duffle bag. He'd had enough. Joanna's shouting upset Jamie. He became inconsolable. "You shut up, Mommy!" he yelled over her threats.

Sam picked him up, reassuring him, "It's okay, Bud; you and I are going on an adventure."

He found Jamie's shoes and helped him get them on while Joanna shouted in the background. Sam got Jamie into his coat, carried him and the duffel bag to his car, and took Jamie to his folks. Sam didn't call Joanna while he was there, and he didn't take her calls. Joanna felt panicked. *What if he doesn't come back?* She repeatedly phoned him and left demanding messages for him on his parents' answering machine. "God damn it, Sam, call me back right now!"

Sam and Jamie came home a few days later. Even Sam's parents couldn't get Jamie's mind off his mom. "Where's Mommy? Is she sad, Daddy? I wanna go home."

Joanna ran outside and scooped Jamie up when she saw Sam's car pull into their parking lot. He clung to her neck. She glared at Sam over Jamie's head, "Don't ever take Jamie away like that again, or you'll be sorry."

All Sam could do was offer up empty threats. "Either you get a handle on things, Joanna, or we'll go to court and see about that. I mean it this time. I won't put Jamie through that again." He went about his business, not letting on in front of Jamie that there were problems between him and Joanna, but Joanna knew he wasn't kidding.

She started seeing a therapist about the problems in her marriage. The therapist told Joanna that she was angry at Sam for not being what her parents wanted him to be and that she used anger as a shield to protect herself from feeling rejected. The therapist told her that she hid behind her anger to avoid showing Sam she cared about him. "When you treat Sam with contempt, Joanna, it's *you* you're really angry at," the therapist told her. "You punish Sam for being a good man because you don't believe you're worthy of being cared for." The truth was brutal for Joanna to hear. She stopped going after the fourth session.

25

WHEN SHE WAS ON HER MEDICATIONS, JOANNA'S MOODS WOULD EVEN out. Sometimes her "normal" phase might last for several months. When this occurred, she was more likely to take better care of herself and was easier to get along with. She was more attentive to Jamie during these times, would spend time with him, accompany him on school field trips or take him on special outings, just the two of them. As a family, they'd have dinner together or stay up late on weekends and watch movies on TV. Her marriage ran smoother when she felt this way.

Eventually, however, the side effects of her medications would begin to sneak up on her. She'd gain weight or develop tremors in her hands. She'd feel nauseated, sluggish. She'd have no sexual libido. When convinced that her moods were under control, she'd stop taking all her medications without telling Sam. She'd stop them all at once, cold turkey, without slowly weaning herself off little by little. Within a week or two, she'd feel her mood shift, sometimes up, sometimes down.

She liked it when she was in a state her doctor called "hypomania." It wasn't full-blown mania, just a minor elevation in her energy. Joanna felt at her best when she was in this state. She'd feel it at first as a tingling sensation, an internal excitement. She'd become more alert, energized. Her mood would be light, and her motivation would come back. The feeling she got from hypomania reminded her of summer vacation as a kid, when every day held an adventure, and she had no worries. It was liberating. She was playful with Jamie while in this state and teased with Sam. She'd laugh out loud at funny movies and act out stories with Jamie when she read to him at bedtime.

But that feeling wouldn't last long. Soon, Joanna's mood would escalate. Her thoughts would start to race, making it hard to focus on any one thing. She talked faster than usual and took on extra activities at work. Gradually, her mind and body would reach a crescendo. She wouldn't think things through; her decision-making became reckless and impulsive. Sometimes she'd still be at her office after midnight. She'd forget to eat, to sleep. An undercurrent of sexual arousal would tingle through her body. When alone in her office, or at home, or sometimes in her car, she'd slip her hand inside her panties and masturbate.

Sam became the focus of her sexual fantasies in this state. She'd fixate on his body. Now in his late twenties, he'd physically matured into a man. He was lean and fit. His hair had darkened over the years, the red turning blondish-brown. He habitually ran his fingers through it to keep it off his forehead. He smiled with his eyes, accentuating the laugh lines at the corners. When he went a few days without shaving, he'd sport a stubble beard, a scruffy look Joanna liked. He had reddish-brown hair sprinkled across his mid-chest that trailed down his belly in a fine line that disappeared below the waistband of his pants. He had a natural rugged, outdoorsy look that women of all ages were drawn to.

Sam could gauge when Joanna was becoming manic by her preoccupation with sex, and learned that hypersexuality was a symptom of bipolar disorder. He'd set boundaries to prevent her from sexually exploiting him, often sending her into a rage. He walked a fine line between protecting his personal space and keeping her from feeling rejected.

Joanna's sexual appetite didn't stop with Sam. She'd become promiscuous with other men. She'd stop at a bar on her way home in the evenings for a few drinks. Joanna was striking, with her silvery blonde hair and green eyes. She'd be impeccably dressed. It didn't take long for her to attract an admirer who would sit down on a bar stool next to her. They'd strike up a conversation, and she'd flirt, laugh, lean in, and touch his arm when she talked to him. After a few drinks, she'd let him put his hand on her knee, allowing him to slowly move his hand underneath her dress and up her thigh. She'd rest her hand on his knee, toss her hair, or throw her head back to laugh at something funny he said.

Eventually, he'd suggest they move things along, get a room or go to his place. She'd tell him to wait there; she'd be right back. She had no intention of going home with anyone. Seducing another man was thrilling enough; it somehow made Sam more attractive to her. She'd gotten what she wanted from the stranger in the bar. She'd make a detour when she was out of sight and leave, heading for home.

Joanna would smell like alcohol when she came home. She'd lie to Sam and tell him she got stuck at the office when he questioned her. He'd know she was lying and bring it to her attention. "Joanna, you went off your medications again, didn't you? You need to get back on your meds, Joanna, right now before things get out of hand. I'm calling your doctor."

Her doctor advised Sam to remain neutral around her during these times and to downplay her behavior as much as possible to avoid provoking her. Some nights he slept on the couch. Joanna accused him of avoiding her, cheating on her, and having another woman on the side. She watched for clues, hushed calls from the bedroom, excuses for him to run errands, him traveling out of town to attend a conference. She'd never find any evidence.

After a manic episode ended when Joanna's moods were more stable, she'd think about her behavior, how she'd acted around Sam and picked up strangers in bars. Shame would overcome her. It felt like someone else had taken over her body, and she couldn't stop. It was a drive within her she had no control over. It felt hormonal or chemical; she wasn't sure which, but something would turn on inside her body, and she had no choice but to go with it. It felt good at the time, shameful later.

Intimacy for Joanna had always been a problem, something she wasn't comfortable with. She'd had one long-term sexual relationship when she was an adolescent. During her last two years of high school, she dated Aaron. It wasn't that she liked him so much as that it was the expectation among her group of friends to have a boyfriend—more accurately, a sex partner. Aaron had served the purpose. He played football and was popular. They had sex on occasion, usually in his dad's BMW coupe. It was a tight squeeze, with one or the other constantly trying to reposition themselves to avoid being pinched by the steering wheel or poked by the gear shift. Aaron would practically crush her as he knelt on the car's floorboards, pinning her to the seat with his weight while her legs were splayed across the dashboard.

Occasionally, someone's parents would go out of town, and Joanna and her friends would throw a party. By the night's end, people would couple up and spread out throughout the house, looking for someplace private to halfway undress and have three-minute sex. It was the thing to do. Joanna played along, trying to conform. Still, when she and Aaron went separate ways for college, she never looked back, never gave him a second thought.

Joanna tried unsuccessfully to date a couple of times in college with two different guys she met in nightclubs. She never saw the first guy again after their first date and only dated the second guy twice before giving him the slip. Mostly, her sexual encounters happened with strangers. Sometimes, she'd sneak out of the sorority house in the evenings and go to a bar by herself, someplace removed from campus, to avoid running into someone who might recognize her. She'd have a few drinks, zero in on a guy, flirt, go to his apartment, and have sex with him. She'd give him a fake name and phone number and never see him again after she left. She never felt passion toward these men during sex. She wouldn't even remember their names after a few days. It was just a release for her, a way to let off steam.

Intimacy was an issue in Sam and Joanna's marriage. Typically, Joanna ignored sex or avoided it. When she wasn't in a manic state, she had very little desire for sex and, when depressed, wanted nothing to do with it. It wasn't anything Sam did; he was always attentive and giving, but Joanna was convinced that allowing herself to be intimate with Sam was somehow accepting his mediocrity and settling for less. Had things been different, had she *chosen* to marry, not been backed into a corner, she would have married someone with wealth and success, someone who could give her the lifestyle she was accustomed to. She would never have picked a middle-class guy who didn't have a dime to his name. Sharing intimacy with Sam felt like accepting second best to her, like giving in, losing.

For Sam, their sex life was unfulfilling. He'd become accustomed to Joanna's behaviors, her sexual come-ons when she was manic or had been drinking. He'd learned to expect it. He knew of her inability to enjoy intimacy, to be able to give of herself, and her feelings of disappointment that he wasn't what she believed she deserved. He accepted things the way they were. He'd never been in love with Joanna. He was there to give Jamie a fair shake at a normal childhood. He'd never expected things to be any more than they were.

But sometimes, he thought about the what-ifs: what if he'd found his soulmate somewhere, the one the fortune teller in high school foretold to him? What if things had been different, and he'd ended up with a woman who brought passion to his life, who completed him? He didn't allow himself to dwell on it. The situation was what it was. "Look for the lesson," his mother would say. Sometimes meaning was difficult to find in the empty space that was his marriage.

26

DURING SAM'S SECOND YEAR OF LAW SCHOOL, HE TOOK AN INTERNSHIP
position in a small startup law practice owned and operated by an
attorney named Jeff Billings. Sam wanted to avoid being in a large,
competitive firm where the expectation was to bill out every minute
of his time to put money in the pockets of the firm's partners. Sam
wanted a work environment with heart in it.

What most attracted Sam was that Jeff Billings specialized in
intellectual property law. In his first semester of law school, he'd
taken a course on protecting and enforcing the rights of artists,
writers, designers, inventors, and musicians. Sam immediately felt
a connection with this branch of the law—it was the closest thing
to his love of writing in any of his law classes. If Sam couldn't be a
writer, he could protect those who were.

Jeff was twelve years Sam's senior. He was tall and lean with
short, cropped, sandy-brown hair. The first time Sam met him, he
was wearing a jogging suit, having just returned from a long run.
When Sam arrived, Jeff had a towel around his neck and was dab-
bing at his face.

Jeff's law office was in Ballard, the hip waterfront neighborhood
northwest of Seattle on the Lake Washington Ship Canal. Jeff was

the lone attorney in his office, with two paralegals who assisted with his cases. He'd tried, he told Sam, to meld into a large firm right out of law school but quickly learned something was missing. There was a disconnect; attorneys in the office competed with each other, like they were out to get one another. He opened his firm five years ago and spent most of that time representing small-scale trademark and copyright cases from individual clients and small startup companies. "I'm not looking for attorneys aiming to get rich right out of the chute or who want the prestige of a big firm," he told Sam. Something about Sam's demeanor told Jeff he was the right intern.

The first year, Jeff paid Sam a small wage, not much, but he offered lots of hands-on experience with actual cases. The following year, Sam's final year of law school, Jeff was able to pay Sam enough for him to cut back on his bartending hours.

Sam was a natural in intellectual property law. Jeff acquainted him with every case. He'd shoot questions while Sam was busy completing tasks around the office. How would Sam handle the complaint? What was the most probable liability? What information was missing from the case history? Should the case go to trial or be settled in mediation? How would Sam approach a jury if the case went to trial? It was a steady stream of questions that took strategic thinking. Sam might be busy filing paperwork or searching the law books for some prior ruling and would have to stop and think about what Jeff was asking.

Sam learned everything he could about intellectual property law. He read law books and studied case law and public opinions written by judges on why a case was settled a certain way and what court rules apply to which types of cases. Jeff taught Sam to prepare court documents, file complaints, prepare for evidentiary hearings, and interview witnesses under oath. Sam became skilled in methodically proceeding through the discovery process to confirm whether a client was being truthful, whether they had all the facts, and discovering the sequence of events on which the complaint was founded. The most valuable lesson Jeff taught Sam was to look for surprises, anything that might derail the case. Sam graduated from law school in the spring of 1998, passed his boards, and went to work full-time for Jeff. He was twenty-seven years old.

Billings Law Firm felt right to Sam. He dove in headfirst, hungry to learn. When Sam started working for Jeff, he mostly handled small cases, working with trademark and patent offices to ensure client protection or defending small startup companies being hassled by larger competitors claiming trademark infringement.

Within a few months, Sam handled more complicated cases, like helping a U.S.-based company protect their trademark overseas and defending an artist threatened with a cease-and-desist order from a brand owner trying to censor his work. He worked with artists and writers whose copyrighted words, songs, or images had been used on a company's website or in advertising without authorization and with musicians whose songs were downloaded without permission. One of his first big wins involved a well-known musician whose song was used by an established retailer as their theme song without the artist's permission. He won his client a substantial settlement for the case and earned a reputation as a skilled litigator.

Sam's clientele grew. Those who believed their intellectual property rights had been infringed upon frequently sought his counsel. He collaborated with attorneys from other states on a *pro hac vice* basis when their clients specifically requested him. Within five years, Sam brought in enough work that Billings Law Firm was forced to expand with four additional associate attorneys.

27

SAM AND JOANNA DECIDED TO BUY A HOUSE. SAM HOPED THAT IF THEY
had their own home, Joanna might settle in more, take better care
of herself, and stay on her medications. They may even start to act
more like a family.

Joanna wanted a house for different reasons. She wanted a home
in an up-and-coming area, closer to her work, which supported her
image. Joanna would die if Meryl saw the apartment where they
had lived for six years. She was raised on Mercer Island, in a waterfront mansion with a manicured yard sloped down to the lake, with
housekeepers and gardeners. She wanted to get closer to her roots
and the life she'd grown up with.

They found a house in Newport Shores, a small, upscale community located on the southeast shore of Lake Washington in
Bellevue. The house offered three bedrooms, a playroom for Jamie,
a spacious kitchen, a living room with floor-to-ceiling windows, and
a big backyard. Joanna fell in love with it. She pictured herself plant-
ing flowers in the backyard flowerbeds and lounging on the patio.
While not right on the lake, the house was within walking distance.
The winding streets were great for rollerblading and strolling. They
bought bikes to ride the trails that wove along the shoreline.

Joanna had no interest in associating with her neighbors, didn't chat with other women at the mailbox, and wouldn't carpool with other parents to get Jamie to and from school. Joanna preferred to remain aloof. She had little interest in becoming friendly with anyone who might ring her doorbell unannounced.

Jamie started first grade in the local elementary school, just a short walk from their new home. Joanna typically was gone before Jamie had to leave in the mornings. It was Sam who got Jamie up and ready for school. They walked to Jamie's school before Sam left for work. He arranged for Jamie to stay at an after-hours daycare at the school until Sam or Joanna picked him up in the evening. If Sam picked Jamie up, he'd drive home, put the car in the garage, and walk to the school. Together, they would walk home, hand in hand. Jamie would tell Sam about his day at school and what was fun and scary, like when he didn't know what line to get in when coming in from recess and ended up in the fourth grader's line.

Mornings were frantic for Joanna. If she had to drop Jamie off at school on her way to her office, it would often involve having him in tears before it was over. She'd become impatient when he didn't like what she laid out for him to wear. She'd demand he not dawdle over breakfast, hustle him out the door and into the car, and snap at him if he forgot his backpack, causing her an extra trip back into the house to retrieve it. It would be a bad start to the day for them both. Joanna would drive away feeling guilty, and Jamie's teacher would have to soothe him and wipe away his tears before he would settle into the classroom.

Things other mothers enjoyed about parenting, Joanna didn't. There was no joy in spending her day off at a birthday party for one of Jamie's classmates with mothers she had nothing in common with. They wanted to talk about trivial things that Joanna couldn't be bothered with—how they loved the kids' teacher this year; how she was so much more organized than last year's teacher had been; wasn't Joanna impressed with how well the teacher kept the kids engaged? Didn't the kids seem calmer and less anxious than last year? Joanna hadn't paid any attention; it wasn't something she spent time thinking about.

Occasionally, Joanna pictured herself as the kind of mom who could tolerate kids running through the house, making messes, tracking in mud, and roughhousing. The summer before Jamie started second grade, she agreed to host a slumber party for him at their house. This would be a chance to let Jamie and his friends have a free run of the house. Jamie invited four friends. Joanna had a trampoline delivered to their backyard. She planned to barbeque hot dogs on the grill and brought Jamie's favorite snacks home. She had Sam pitch a tent in the backyard so the boys could pretend they were camping out.

Everything started out well. Jamie was excited. The boys jumped on the trampoline and rough-housed outside. Then the wind kicked up, and the rain came. They had to move the party inside. Joanna watched as they slopped catsup and mustard on the dining room floor, piled into the living room to watch a movie, and discovered that the couches were as good for jumping on as the trampoline. They were loud. They didn't get sleepy. Joanna could hear them from the kitchen, wrestling in the living room.

Sam was easy with it all. "They're kids," he told her. She didn't enjoy it. She started drinking around nine that evening. By eleven, she was drunk. She had to retire to her bedroom, leaving Sam to handle things. She tried to drag herself downstairs in the morning to help with breakfast, but her head felt like it might explode. She could hear Sam making pancakes and laughing with the boys in the kitchen. She stayed in bed until noon, until all the kids were picked up and taken home.

She felt ashamed when she finally came downstairs and had to face Jamie. "Did you have fun last night, Jamie?"

"Uh-huh." He was playing on his PlayStation and didn't look at her when he answered. "It was fun."

She made light of the situation, hoping it would relieve the tension in the air, "I'm sorry I couldn't get up this morning. I woke up with a terrible headache. I may have a touch of the flu."

"It's okay, Mommy," he still didn't look at her.

Joanna turned around to see Sam listening from his den. He was sitting at his desk. He held her gaze, didn't say anything—he didn't have to. His look told her everything she needed to know.

She walked to the door of his den. "Fuck you," she mouthed to him so Jamie couldn't hear.

28

SHORTLY AFTER GOING TO WORK FOR MERYL, JOANNA DISCOVERED that a glass of gin when she got home after work helped to take the edge off. Within a couple of years, one drink was no longer enough. She found it took two, sometimes three drinks to give her the buzz she sought. As one year turned into the next, Joanna began to rely on alcohol to calm her anxiety and numb her guilt. She liked its mellowing effect.

She convinced herself that she could quit any time she wanted. She'd set limits on how much she drank. She'd limit herself to no more than two drinks an evening, but when her day had been particularly stressful, she'd assure herself that one or two more wouldn't hurt. "I'll have a couple more tonight, then I'll lay off for a week," she'd promise herself. She rarely kept her promise.

When Joanna drank, she tended to be harder on Jamie than usual. She'd nag him over little things. It seemed to Jamie that just his presence was upsetting to her. "Jamie, your room is unacceptable. It stinks in there; open the windows. I'm sick of walking past your door and looking at that mess."

Every noise in the house grated on her nerves and created a cacophony of unpleasantness. "Jamie, turn down that TV. I can't hear myself think," or "Must you run the garbage disposal right now?" or "Jamie, if you slam that door one more time, I swear to God ..." She'd leave the threat open-ended.

Jamie learned to avoid her when she drank, to tiptoe around, and try not to upset her. By the time he was ten years old, he'd learned how to avoid a scene. Jamie would jump in if Sam intervened when Joanna's nagging became too much. "It's okay, Dad. I'm going up to my room." He often heard them arguing downstairs. He could hear the exasperation in his dad's voice, "Christ, Joanna, ease up."

His mom came back with remarks that upset Jamie. "Maybe I'll just get an apartment downtown; that way, I won't have to come home at all. What do you think, Sam? Should I get an apartment?"

"Do whatever you need to do, Joanna."

Jamie didn't want his mom to leave. He'd get angry at his dad for not encouraging her to stay. He worried about her. She seemed so unhappy. The next day, he'd tell his dad, "Don't tell her to get an apartment downtown, Dad. She'll think we don't want her to come home."

Sam tried to reason with him, "Jamie, you're not responsible for making your mother happy. She has to do that on her own. It's nothing you or I do that makes her upset."

Joanna felt jealous of the relationship Sam and Jamie shared, and consuming alcohol in the evenings only made her jealousy worse. She felt left out much of the time. From the time Jamie was a toddler, wherever Sam was, Jamie was close at hand. They'd go grocery shopping together, to the bank, the hardware store. When Jamie was in elementary school, he sometimes got to go to work with his dad. He'd hang out in the office with Martha, Sam's assistant, an older woman who had worked for Sam since he'd started at the law firm. Jamie liked her. She'd give him little jobs to do, stacking papers and alphabetizing folders.

By the time he was twelve years old, he could keep up with his dad on a four or five-mile jog. When the weather was nice, they'd often walk to the nearby neighborhood park and toss a football or play frisbee. Sam taught Jamie to play pool. They'd play for hours in their family room. They watched sports on TV and cheered for their favorite teams.

Sam and Jamie occasionally took the ferry to Oak Harbor and spent weekends with Sam's folks. The two people who could trump Sam for Jamie's attention were his grandparents, Jack and Sid. His grandpa Jack taught him to fish. When Jamie knew he and his grandpa were going fishing, he'd wake up around four-thirty or five o'clock in the morning. When he heard his grandpa rattling around in the kitchen, making coffee and sandwiches, he'd jump into his clothes and go downstairs to greet him. "You up already?" Jack would tease.

Jamie loved these early morning fishing trips just like Sam had when he was a kid. They'd fill the thermos with hot coffee, pack the sandwiches and head out. They'd launch Jack's small aluminum fishing boat into the cold, still waters of nearby Cranberry Lake. Jamie would pester Jack to tell stories of his youth or of when his dad was a kid; other times, they'd sit quietly, enjoying the peace and quiet of the early morning.

It was Sid who Jamie was most drawn to. Jamie loved it when she gave him a blank canvas and let him use her paints and brushes. Year after year, he'd sit with her and paint in the early mornings, sipping orange tea while listening to the stories she read him. Together, they devoured all seven volumes of *Harry Potter*. Sid loved the story as much as Jamie. She'd make them root beer floats and pretend it was butterbeer. When they knew the next volume of the *Harry Potter* series was coming out, Sid and Jamie would camp out in front of the bookstore hours before it opened to ensure they'd be first in line for a copy of the sought-after novel. They did crossword puzzles while waiting, ate egg salad sandwiches, and drank apple cider.

When Jamie knew he and Sam were going to Oak Harbor, he invited his mom. Jamie constantly bugged her to come along. He wanted her to be a part of what he knew would be a fun time. Joanna would decline. She'd drink alcohol throughout the weekend, sulking and being angry. It would infuriate her that they were off having fun, forgetting her. Sam should've insisted that she come along. She'd blame him for purposely leaving her out, for excluding her from having a relationship with his parents. Joanna never warmed up to Sid and Jack and was convinced they didn't like her. When Sam and Jamie got home, she pretended to be happy for them, but she didn't feel it. She'd try to fake it, but her resentment came through.

Joanna convinced herself that Sam was trying to turn Jamie against her. She devised notions that assured her it was true and let her anger toward Sam rub off onto Jamie. Joanna was resentful of her son. Somewhere in her brain, where her rational thinking resided, she knew these feelings were unhealthy. She should have encouraged Jamie to have a close relationship with Sam but couldn't do it; she didn't feel it.

She became convinced that Sam was planning to leave with Jamie and worked herself into a frenzy. The separation of rational and irrational thoughts blurred inside her head. Finally, one evening, Joanna confronted Sam when Jamie went with a friend to the school wrestling match. She came into Sam's den when he was reading legal briefs for a case he was working on.

She caught him off guard as she accused him of conspiring with Jamie to leave her. She cried, blamed, and called him names. When Sam told her he wasn't planning to leave, she called him a liar. She used Jamie as a pawn. "Don't think you're leaving with Jamie," she threatened. "I'll take you to court. He's not leaving this house."

Sam attempted to reason with her. "Joanna, I'm not planning on taking Jamie anywhere. He wouldn't leave you. He loves you too much."

"You're lying, Sam."

Sam's attempt to be patient turned to anger. He pushed his chair back from his desk forcefully and stood up. He raised his voice when he addressed her. "Joanna, this is just another one of your crazy notions that happens when you refuse to take care of yourself and take your medications. We are not scheming to leave you. If anything, Jamie wants to spend more time with you, Joanna. He feels responsible for you, for your unhappiness. That's what he's grown up with, trying to figure out how to make you happy. He fears that you'll take too many pills with alcohol, and he'll come home and find you. He keeps hoping he can fix you, fix us, so we can become a normal family. What a joke that is."

This was different from what Joanna had intended. Instead of making Sam feel guilty, he turned on her. She felt tears sting her eyes. She swung around and started walking out of the room.

"Don't walk out that door, Joanna." Sam had a tone to his voice that Joanna hadn't heard before. She stopped. Sam continued, "If I thought Jamie would leave here, would leave you, I'd take him out of here in a minute. No kid should have to endure what he's had to deal with. You don't think about Jamie; you only think about yourself. *Your* troubles, *your* pain, *your* misery. You won't take your meds that keep your moods balanced because they make you feel sluggish or gain a few pounds. So instead, you allow your moods to swing from one extreme to another while making your son's life miserable."

By now, Joanna was sobbing. Her breathing was hitched. "That's ... that's not true, and you know it."

"It *is* true, Joanna." Sam shook his head, rubbed his eyes with his thumb and forefinger, and took a deep breath. "What I've always wanted," he lowered his voice, "is to give Jamie a fair shot at a normal childhood. It's almost too late now. He's nearly a teenager. Joanna, I'm committed to staying until Jamie goes off to college or moves into his own apartment. After that, I can't make any promises. I want peace and quiet. I want time to write. I don't get either here. I want something more."

Tears streamed down Joanna's face. Her nose ran and dripped off her upper lip. She wiped it with the back of her hand. "Sam, I try so hard, but I just ... I can't do it. I keep fucking things up. I'll do better. I promise. Please, don't leave me, Sam. Promise that you won't. I can't ... I can't make it without you. You know that."

"Joanna," Sam's tone softened, "You need help; you need to follow your doctor's advice, stay on your meds, and get your drinking under control."

"I promise ... I'll call my doctor. I'll do better. I promise."

For a couple of months, Joanna kept her word. She participated more with Jamie. She came home early from work, fixed dinner, didn't pick fights with Sam, and curbed her drinking. But slowly, things began to resort back to her old ways; stress began to build up at work, and her insecurities returned.

Joanna made an appointment with a doctor she'd never seen before. She reported struggling with anxiety at work and sometimes losing her temper at home. She explained how nervous she often felt at home and how overly critical she'd become. Her marriage was suffering as a result, she explained. She failed to mention anything about drinking, self-medicating, or being bipolar. The doctor diagnosed her with generalized anxiety and prescribed Xanax. "Take these cautiously, Joanna, and don't mix them with alcohol." Joanna assured him she wouldn't.

Jamie knew his mom sometimes combined prescription pills with alcohol. More than once, Jamie found her passed out. She'd fall into a deep, drunken slumber that scared Jamie because he couldn't wake her. One spring day, Joanna was lying on the chaise lounge on their patio. Jamie was thirteen years old. It was a warm, sunny Saturday, and Joanna had swallowed a couple of Xanax and chased them down with gin. She had the whole day off and wanted to lay on the patio and decompress from a hectic work week. The warm sun felt good on her skin. By early afternoon, she'd refilled her glass numerous times and had consumed well over her limit. Without realizing it, she was smashed. She felt woozy, and when she closed her eyes, she felt like she was on a spinning wheel. She put her head back on the chaise lounge and passed out.

In her semi-conscious state, Joanna's head rolled toward her chest, making it hard for her to breathe. When Jamie found her, she was making loud snoring noises through her gaping mouth. When he couldn't wake her, he yelled for his dad. Sam was able to rouse her and get her into a sitting position. She stared at him through a haze and then vomited down the front of her sundress. "Jesus, Joanna," Sam said. Later, after he cleaned her up and helped her to bed, Sam apologized to Jamie, "Sorry you had to see that, Bud. Drinking alcohol in the hot sun isn't a good combination. She's okay."

Jamie worried about Joanna when she was home alone. He feared she'd fall, cut herself, or forget the stove was on and start a fire. He would back out of plans with friends to stay home to keep an eye on her. He'd spend time in his bedroom or the family room watching TV, where he could listen, observe, and be ready if she needed him.

Sam knew from talking with Joanna's doctor that every time she experienced a bout of depression or a manic episode, it became more and more difficult for her to return to her normal baseline. Without consistent management, the doctor warned, her condition would worsen. Joanna's mood episodes would become even more frequent and extreme if not controlled. They would begin to take a permanent toll on her overall health. Her physical health would suffer, her cognitive ability would wane, her thinking would become more irrational, and she'd be more prone to making hasty decisions and poor choices. The doctor explained to Sam that the goal was to prevent mood episodes from occurring altogether. But Joanna never stayed on her medications long enough to stabilize her moods. As soon as she convinced herself she felt better, she'd quit taking her pills.

Joanna's behavior was typical, the doctor told Sam. "Patients with bipolar disorder often have the illogical belief that they can control their symptoms on their own, by drinking or using drugs, or through obsessive-compulsive behavior."

Joanna learned over the years that she preferred certain prescription medications over others. She didn't want to take mood stabilizers or other medicines for depression. They made her feel worse. The truth was, while she hated feeling depressed, she liked the high she felt when manic. She craved the thrill she felt when her energy began to build.

She learned to doctor-shop for medications she preferred over her doctor's prescriptions. She'd make an appointment with a doctor she'd never seen before and who had no medical history on her. She never mentioned these doctor appointments to Sam. She'd complain to the doctor that she had trouble concentrating, sticking to a task. She'd explain how keeping things running smoothly at work was exhausting when she couldn't focus her attention. She'd describe feeling rattled, trying to accomplish one thing only to have something else grab her attention and pull her away. She'd convince doctors to prescribe medications that would help her stay focused during the day and sleep at night.

When she began to worry that a prescribing doctor might suspect something else was the problem, she'd search for a new doctor. It worked. She had a constant supply of medications in her medicine cabinet that could kick-start her morning, keep her running all day, and help her fall asleep at night. On days when she couldn't get moving and was dragging, she'd start her day with one or two

Dexedrine or sometimes Adderall. She might down another during the day even though the prescription called for just one in the morning. She'd bring herself down when she got home with one or two drinks and maybe a Xanax. When she was unable to sleep, she depended on prescription sleeping pills. When she ran out of those, she switched to Benadryl.

Eventually, she'd burn herself out and crash. One afternoon, when Jamie was in the eighth grade, he arrived home to find Joanna alone. She'd come home from work early, something she hardly ever did. He found her in the living room, sitting alone, crying. He hurried to her, thinking something terrible must have happened. Was his dad alright? "Mom, what's wrong? Are you okay?"

Through glazed eyes, Joanna stared at Jamie standing in front of her. He was fourteen. He was starting to grow into his looks. He looked like his dad, except for his nose and mouth, which resembled hers. "Jamie, m' sorry," her words sounded garbled, slurred. Jamie had trouble understanding her.

"What's wrong, Mom? Why are you crying? Did something happen? What can I do?"

"Nothn'. There's nothn' …. I'm so tired. I wish I were dead. I want to lay down somewhere and sleep and never wake up."

"Mom, what are you saying?" Jamie felt a sense of panic. "Mom, did you take something, pills?"

She mumbled something that he couldn't understand.

Jamie telephoned his dad. "Try to keep her awake, Jamie, until I get there. If you can't wake her up, call 911." Sam rushed home. He got Joanna in a cool shower, warmed a can of soup for her to eat, and helped her to bed. He called her doctor, and Joanna was hospitalized for a week. She insisted her employees at Big City Events be told she had a nasty virus. She rested, slept, and walked with Jamie around the hospital grounds. Her medications were adjusted. A drug and alcohol counselor visited with her about treatment programs available when she was ready.

When Joanna came home a week later, she dismissed the whole affair. She copped an attitude with Sam when he tried to talk to her about what happened, claiming she hadn't been eating right; that was all that was wrong. Ignoring her doctor's recommendations, she returned to work and buried herself in her job.

29

WHEN SAM TURNED THIRTY-SIX, JEFF BILLINGS MADE HIM AN EQUAL partner in the firm. The law practice had grown to include seven associates in their nine years together. They outgrew their Ballard office and relocated to a high-rise office in downtown Bellevue. Sam's reputation as a top-notch litigator preceded him. Each year he accepted more challenging and complex cases. When he believed that beating the odds was possible, he agreed to litigate lawsuits that some said couldn't be won and won them. He'd always been loyal to Jeff, but Jeff knew Sam got offers. A partner from one law firm or another, sometimes one that Sam opposed in court, would make him a generous offer. They promised to double his salary, increase his bonuses. Jeff didn't want to lose him.

Becoming the "Parker" in Billings and Parker Law Firm brought a new level of respect. Attorneys from other law firms sought Sam's glance when they walked past him and gave a nod. Judges stopped him in the hallways of the courthouse to share small talk. Sam handled his new status with grace. He didn't take himself seriously. His demeanor stayed the same.

He often walked around the law firm stopping here or there to visit with an associate, office staff, or an occasional client, to say hello. He'd stroll through the firm, hands in the pockets of his flannel trousers, or holding a mug of coffee in one hand, the sleeves of his herringbone shirt rolled past his wrist to reveal a leather, braided bracelet. Heads would turn when he passed by, and smiles would be waiting to greet him.

He had a casual, effortless way about him that put others at ease. He'd sometimes surprise an associate or paralegal by sauntering into their office and sitting across from them at their desk. He'd sit back, relaxed, one foot resting on his knee. His socks were colorful and playful. They displayed bulldogs, fish, elephants, or geometric designs. He wore suede Amberjack oxfords. He made it a point to know the employees in the firm on a first-name basis, to know whose mother was ill, who'd just had a new baby, whose son or daughter had just graduated from college. "Jill, how's your mother doing? Are her chemo treatments working? Let us know if we can do anything to help."

Sam's title only made him more attractive to others. The handsome young partner, who dressed well and carried himself with ease, who had a winning smile, was hard not to pay attention to. It astonished him how bold women could be. He was sometimes surprised at how easily things could get out of hand. He'd been offered keys to women's hotel rooms when out of town for business. Once, an attractive, well-dressed female attorney Sam met in the hotel bar while at a legal conference asked him, only a few minutes into their conversation, if he'd like to take her to bed. He was taken aback. That scene wasn't for him; it had never been.

In other situations, women were more subtle. He attended a meeting with the opposing council involving a new songwriter's lyrics that sounded very similar to a song already published by a client of Sam's. Sam came to the meeting primarily to support his associate in charge of the case. She was getting her feet wet in intellectual property litigation. Sam was there to jump in if necessary. The litigators for the opposing council knew to avoid pushing one of Sam's associates around if Sam was nearby.

Sam's associate was doing a good job, so he sat back in his chair, relaxed, not paying attention. He looked up to see a woman, a paralegal for the opposing team, sitting across and a few seats down from him at the conference table. She was in her early thirties. Her natural look and the slight color in her cheeks reminded Sam of a snowboarder. She had her elbows on the table and rested her chin on her folded hands as though she were listening intently to what was being discussed. She let her gaze drift down to Sam, where she locked eyes with him. Her eyes spoke volumes. They told him she was available if he wanted to meet her in the bar for a drink afterward. Sam held her gaze briefly, smiled at her, and looked away. He feigned sudden interest in what was being discussed at the table.

Women clients seeking Sam's professional services would often end up paying more attention to him than to what was going on in their legal case. They'd show up at his office for meetings looking their best, full of smiles, issuing vaguely flirtatious remarks, and finding an excuse to linger a bit longer when the meeting was over.

A client known internationally as "Lizzy" hired Sam to defend her in a case against her ex-lover, who she claimed produced a line of knockoffs that closely resembled her multi-thousand-dollar-an-item line of handbags and leather accessories known worldwide, resulting in a loss of hundreds of millions of dollars to her company. Lizzy was a brunette with shoulder-length hair and brown eyes. She was tall, five-nine, and dressed in sheik European-style outfits, trousers, flowing skirts, and tailored dresses.

Lizzy attended meetings with Sam's associates for months, going over specifics of her case with his legal team, always hoping that Sam would be present. Sometimes she wouldn't see him; he'd be out of the office or occupied with another client. When he did occasionally join the meetings, Lizzie perked up. She'd pay more attention to him than to what was being discussed. He'd be dressed in something smart but casual. His shirt sleeves would be rolled up, and he'd have removed his tie. He'd greet her, look her in the eyes, and smile but never give her anything to misconstrue. He never stepped outside of his attorney role. Ultimately, Sam's and his team's strategic planning and attention to detail paid off. The jury returned a guilty verdict and awarded Lizzy eighty-five million in damages.

It wasn't her win that Lizzy thought about when the case ended. It wasn't even that she felt vindicated. A part of Lizzy was sorry the case was over. It was Sam she thought about, his blue-green eyes with their laugh lines at the corners. She'd no longer have an excuse to telephone him or ask to meet him for lunch to discuss her case. Sam had given her no encouragement to stay connected. He'd moved on, already focused on his next case. He'd linger in *her* mind long after she faded from his.

It wasn't that Sam didn't appreciate the attention. It was something to smile about. On the other hand, he didn't want to encourage trouble. He didn't allow himself to get into situations that might be tricky to get out of, that could reflect poorly on him or the firm. He kept his focus on business. He'd smile, engage in conversation, and give a warm handshake to a client or colleague as he showed them to the door. Still, he never gave out vibes that could be misinterpreted as interest.

The real reason Sam didn't get involved with other women was because of the belief he'd carried with him since high school when the old Roma fortune teller at his school fair told him that somewhere out there was his soulmate, the girl he'd traveled through many previous lifetimes with. He liked to imagine how he'd react if his soulmate walked into his office one day and hired him as her attorney.

Would he know it was her? What would she look like? Would she be bold or shy? Would she be exotic or plain? How would he respond if *she* flirted with him?

Sam thought about whether he'd lived previous lives. Maybe it was the storyteller in him, but he couldn't completely rule it out. No one could know for sure. He wondered if he missed his soulmate in this lifetime, would they find each other in the next? Sam liked to think it might strengthen their bond, having lost each other for a lifetime and then finding each other again. They'd be less likely to let go of each other next time. Or, he'd ponder, does it break the spell if two soulmates miss each other during a lifetime? Does it mean they won't travel through any more lives together?

Maybe it was for the best that he didn't find her. What would he do? He was married, had a son, a career, and a life. He liked to pretend, though, that she was looking for him. Sometimes the fantasy would seem so real that he felt sure about it. He could sense her. That Sam didn't cheat with other women wasn't because of his loyalty to Joanna. It seemed foolish to admit, but Sam was committed to a total stranger, a woman he'd never met and probably never would. Even though, thinking about her, thinking about the what-ifs, kept him connected to her. "I'm searching for you," he'd daydream. "Where are you?"

30

OVER THE YEARS, JOANNA'S MOTHER, GLADYS, CAME TO SEE SAM differently. Differently from Rip, but differently from when Sam first entered the scene. It wasn't that Sam had changed, instead, she had. In her early sixties, Gladys was more accepting of herself and others. She was less likely to judge and criticize and had learned that diversity made for a more exciting world. "Like a well-stocked pastry shop," she liked to think.

Rip, on the other hand, had become intolerable to her. While Rip's girth expanded over the years, his viewpoints narrowed. Gladys concluded, years past, that he was a narcissist. He was his own favorite topic of conversation. He bragged about himself repeatedly—his wealth, accomplishments, and material possessions—until it became tiring. Gladys thought money mattered most in her youth, but she was no longer sure. She was wealthy but could hardly bear to sit in the same room with Rip when it was just the two of them. Years earlier, Gladys had learned to block him out. She knew how to nod and interject an "uh-huh" now and then to indicate she was listening.

Gladys had come to think of Sam in contrast to Rip. Sam was strong. Not macho strong but morally strong. He did what was right. He thought about others before himself. She admired that. She wondered, if she'd met someone like Sam in college, would she have had the courage to say to hell with what her parents expected from her and go away with him? Not back then, but now, yes.

She found it embarrassing to face Sam much of the time. It was excruciating to think back and remember how she and Rip had treated him when he and Joanna first got together. They'd schemed to get Joanna to leave him years ago, convinced he wasn't good enough because he hadn't come from money. Now she realized her daughter hadn't done so badly after all. "I must remind Joanna to watch herself," Gladys made a mental note. "A man like Sam might just walk out that door one of these days. If he ever does, there's probably no bringing him back."

As Jamie got older, Gladys became more interested in her grandson, wanting to spend time with him. She'd realized the error of her ways, how she'd failed her daughters when they were growing up. Her fear of how others might see her was replaced with guilt from knowing that she and Rip had fallen short as parents. Gladys hoped to redeem herself through Jamie, giving him what she'd failed to give her daughters. It was hard for her to face, however, that no matter what she did for Jamie now, she could never undo the damage she'd caused Joanna by ignoring her bipolar diagnosis as an adolescent. Through wiser eyes, Gladys watched Joanna's struggles, saw her inability to nurture her son, and the impact it had on Jamie.

Jamie didn't mind hanging out with Gladys. He called her "Gram." She took him to his favorite places. She'd take him for lunch at one of his favorite fast-food restaurants, and they'd eat hamburgers and fries and drink milkshakes. One time she took him to a Mariner's game at Safeco Field in Seattle, just the two of them. "I used to love baseball as a young girl," she told Jamie. Sometimes she'd take him to the mall and let him buy as many new clothes as he wanted—hoodies, cargo pants, sneakers—clothes that were all the big rage.

Years ago, Gladys had established a habit of inviting the three of them, Joanna, Sam, and Jamie, for dinner once a month. It allowed her to catch up with Joanna and spend time with Jamie. But it was Sam who she found the most interesting. She was never sure how things would go when Sam showed up or how Rip would react. Sam could finesse his way around Rip in a way that Gladys enjoyed watching. It was almost like he toyed with Rip and knew how to set him off balance. Rip would typically end up furious by the end of the evening, while Sam would appear to be unmarred.

Sam, on the other hand, found dinners at the Melrose's uncomfortable. There they would all be, seated around the long formal dining room table, while the housekeeper, Camila, made trips back and forth from the kitchen to the dining table to serve them. After dinner, Sam often found himself in the kitchen chatting with Camila. She was living in the United States as an undocumented immigrant with her husband while her children were back home in Mexico, living with her mother. She got teary-eyed talking about them. Sam admired her tenacity, her effort to send money home for her children each month, to better herself and her family, and to go further than her mother had. Sam wondered what she must think of the Melroses, their wealth, their entitlement. Sam much preferred Camila's company over Rip's or Gladys's. Camila had character, substance, and perseverance. She taught Sam and Jamie Spanish. Sam offered to help her out if she ever needed legal counseling.

"Sam, you have to stop hanging out in the kitchen when we visit my folks," Joanna told him on their way home from one of their visits.

"Why is that, Joanna?" Sam had asked her.

"It's just not right. It looks odd, my husband hanging out with the hired help. Can't you just for once sit at the table and have a conversation with my father?"

"You want me to sit at the table while your father puts me down for where I come from, for what my dad did to earn a living? How would you like me to respond?"

"He doesn't mean it to be rude, Sam. He can't help being who he is."

"He's an educated, intelligent, grown man. Of course, he can help being who he is. He *chooses* to be an ass."

"What message are you giving Jamie when you wander out of the room in the middle of my father's conversation?"

"What message? I'm giving him permission to get up and leave any time he finds your father insulting. I'm giving Jamie permission to be his own man."

When Rip heard that Sam had made partner, he looked for ways to downplay it in his mind, to make it trivial. Rip knew he couldn't rely on his same old put-down tactics any longer with Sam. They'd long ago lost their effect. When Rip was willing to be honest with himself, he realized they'd never worked with Sam. It didn't matter, Rip assured himself. Nothing Sam achieved would make the slightest difference to Rip. Sam would never be a Melrose. That Rip was born advantaged automatically elevated his status, putting him on a higher playing field than Sam. That's how he believed the world worked.

Deep in his mind, Rip heard his inner voice caution him about his arrogance. He brushed it aside. He'd ask the priest the following Sunday, when Gladys dragged him to mass, for a special blessing. If the priest thought Rip needed to do penance for his condescension, Rip would contribute to a needy cause, say, starving children in Africa. Rip remembered hearing about a high-rise apartment building somewhere in the South, maybe Oklahoma, that had recently burned down, leaving the occupants homeless. He'd send a check to the relief fund for the victims.

Rip prided himself on being the type of man other men deferred to. He had the loudest voice, the best cigars, and the most money. He flippantly dealt insults to other males to show he was the top dog. They didn't let on to his face if anyone thought Rip was a blowhard. He was accustomed to other men laughing at his jokes, slapping him on the back, and buying him drinks. It had worked for him since he was a boy. His own father taught him by example and demanded Rip follow suit.

The first time Sam, Joanna, and Jamie came out to the house after Sam became a partner in his law firm, Rip offered him a glass of his best whiskey and a cigar. They were on the patio; Sam accepted the whiskey and declined the cigar.

"Come on, Sam, you're a partner in your law firm now; act like one. Have a cigar," Rip slapped him on the back.

"I don't need a cigar to learn how to act, Rip."

"You must feel pretty important now, huh?"

Sam stood. "I don't like where this is headed. I'm going inside."

When Sam turned around to walk inside, Rip said to his back, almost daringly, "You don't like me much, do you, Sam?"

Sam turned around, looked Rip in the eye, "No sir, I do not."

Rip was taken aback. "And why is that? I've done nothing but offer to help you since you married my daughter." There was an edge to Rip's voice. Who the hell did this punk think he was?

"You've done nothing but insult me and your daughter since I've known you. You act like a jackass, Rip."

Rip moved closer to Sam, almost a lunge, his drink sloshing out of the glass. "Who the hell do you think you are, talking to me that way?"

He meant to continue, but Sam stopped him. "Save it, Rip. I know full well who *I* am. You're the one who's confused. You think you're better than everyone else. You're nothing special. You're just a hollow bully. I tolerate you because you're Joanna's father. If it weren't for that, I'd tell you to go straight to hell." Sam turned around and walked into the house, hollering for Joanna. "Joanna, we're leaving; get your coat. Jamie, come on, we're leaving."

Joanna came out of the kitchen where she'd been helping her mother. "Why are we leaving? I just poured myself a cup of tea."

"Because I've had enough. Come on, Jamie." To Joanna, he added, "We'll be in the car."

Joanna started to argue but saw the resolute look on Sam's face and decided against it. She gathered her handbag and jacket and headed for the car. She passed her father coming through the door. "Honestly, Dad, when will you learn? If you can't be nice to my husband, we won't be coming out again." She walked out, letting the screen door slam behind her. She didn't look back to wave. She didn't need him anymore. It felt empowering.

Gladys came out onto the porch. "Joanna, why are you leaving?" She called after Joanna, who had gotten into the car and shut the door by now.

"What'd you do this time, Rip?" Gladys said, turning toward him in anger.

"Shut up, Gladys." Rip turned and walked into the house.

Sam and Joanna's combined incomes gradually allowed them the ability to purchase luxuries. Sam drove a Porsche, Joanna a Mercedes. They had a Land Rover parked in the third garage space for outings. Sam bought a cabin cruiser for fishing that slept four people and had a fully equipped kitchen. The three of them, Sam, Joanna, and Jamie, flew to Hawaii or Mexico once or twice a year. They purchased expensive art. One luxury they didn't have that Joanna wanted was a waterfront home on Lake Washington. It made her smile to think what her father would say if they purchased a house on the lake without his help. She couldn't wait to flaunt it. She'd drop the news casually like it was no big deal. "Oh, did you know, Dad, we bought a house on the lake?"

She found a lake-front home in Bellevue just south of Kirkland with modern-style architecture. It had an open floor plan with wall-to-ceiling windows that opened onto a wrap-around balcony with lake views. The inside was wood, metal, and glass. It had simple, straight lines, recessed lighting, ash floors, and an industrial metal staircase. Its day-light basement opened onto a manicured yard sloping down to the lake, with a swimming pool and entertainment-sized patio. The yard ended at its own private beach and dock. The house spoke luxury, and Joanna wanted it. It was Jamie who convinced Sam to buy it. "Dad, we can moor our boat right in our backyard. We can go fishing whenever we want."

The views from their new home were spectacular. Sam could sit in his den in the evenings and look across the lake to the Seattle skyline. He appreciated the luxury of the house, but it wasn't him. He daydreamed about where he'd like to live if he could. Somewhere up north, a little cabin on the Skagit River, where chinook, coho, and sockeye salmon came to spawn, where his parents used to take him as a child to see bald eagles wintering along the marshlands. A place where he could take long walks, get back to nature, and carve out time for writing.

31

BY THE TIME JAMIE ENTERED HIGH SCHOOL, JOANNA HAD BEGUN TO insist that he learn the art of navigating social-status norms, skills her parents forced onto her when she was a kid that she didn't like then, any more than Jamie did now. She ignored that fact and insisted he learn to play golf and tennis and become adept at sailing. She wanted to shape Jamie's social circle to include friends whose folks belonged to the country club and who appreciated the arts and culture. Jamie preferred fishing or crabbing with his dad and Grandpa Jack, hiking on forest trails, or taking peaceful walks along one of the many walking paths close to their house.

When he was a sophomore in high school, Jamie decided, after taking biology, that he wanted to go to med school. Like Sam, he worked hard throughout high school to get good grades in classes that would make him competitive on college admission applications. That was where the similarities between Sam and Jamie's high school days ended. Jamie's childhood was nothing like Sam's. Jamie didn't have the easy-going time his dad had in school. Jamie didn't play contact sports and wasn't the editor of the high school newspaper. He played on the high school chess team but could have been better and belonged to the chemistry club and, for a while, the physics club until deciding it wasn't his thing. He didn't have a close buddy he palled around with. He wasn't popular.

Jamie was a quiet boy, soft-spoken and gentle. He suffered from anxiety and liked to keep to himself. He tried hard never to disappoint his dad, who he considered his best friend. As for Joanna, Jamie never quit trying to win her attention, her love. Jamie thought she was the most beautiful woman he'd ever seen. She reminded him of a fairy princess with her long silver-blonde hair and green eyes. He was a disappointment to her, he knew. Sometimes just being in the same room agitated her. He knew little things he did made her angry. Jamie tried to stay out of her way much of the time, but he longed to be close to her, feel his hand in hers, rest his head on her chest, smell her, and breathe her in.

He sometimes hung around with a group of teenagers at school considered by other students to be misfits. They were a mismatched group of kids trying to find themselves and instead found each other. Jamie's closest friend was Chelsea, a girl his age. The two had been friends since their last year of junior high school. They bonded over their passion for Coldplay's *Viva la Vida* album. They ate lunch together in the school cafeteria. Unlike Jamie, Chelsea had no interest in chemistry or biology. Her passion was art. She wanted to be a clothing designer. She dreamed of attending fashion design school in Seattle when she graduated, but her mother didn't think they could afford it.

Jamie and Chelsea began sharing secrets soon into their friendship. Shortly after Chelsea was born, her father disappeared, leaving her no recollection of him. Her family consisted of her and her mom, who worked as a loan processor for a mortgage company in downtown Bellevue. She and Chelsea lived near her mother's work in a high-rise apartment building. They lived paycheck to paycheck, and Chelsea didn't have the luxuries that most other kids in her school had. She had a pretty face with long blonde, curly hair. According to her BMI, she was twenty-five pounds overweight for her frame.

Jamie shared everything with Chelsea. He told her about his parents, that his mom was bipolar, and how unpredictable she was.

Jamie told Chelsea how his mom would become so depressed at times that Jamie feared she might hurt herself and other times so high that she'd go days without sleeping and eating. He shared with Chelsea his mom's abuse of alcohol and pills, how frightened he often felt, and how he feared his mom might accidentally take a lethal combination. He told her how his mom ran a big event planning business in Bellevue and was gone most of the time and how things got tense when she was home in the evenings.

He told Chelsea how angry his mother always acted toward his dad, and he didn't know why. It made him feel bad, sometimes angry himself. He wanted to step in and protect his dad but didn't know what to do. He didn't think his parents loved each other. He knew they'd met at a college party and didn't marry until after he was born. Jamie told Chelsea how he worried that his dad would up and leave one day, get sick of it all. He didn't think his mom could make it if that ever happened.

Chelsea was a good listener. She'd empathize with Jamie. He felt understood when he was with her. He could tell her anything, and she'd accept him, no matter what. That's why he sometimes confided to Chelsea about his attraction to other boys. Was it normal? Did other boys feel the same thing? Was Chelsea attracted to other girls?

"Maybe you're gay," Chelsea offered. "It's okay if you are. You should talk to your dad."

"I'm not gay," Jamie was adamant. If he were gay, which he wasn't, he knew his mom wouldn't take it well. If his mom thought he was gay, she might fall into one of her depressions that could last weeks or months. She might refuse to talk to him. Worse yet, he cringed thinking about what his grandparents, Rip and Gladys, would say, particularly Rip. Rip once told him being gay was all in one's head. It was distorted thinking, he called it. He called boys who were gay "fags" and "pretty boys." Jamie pushed his sexual attractions aside and tried to ignore them.

He felt ashamed when the feelings overpowered him. It mostly happened when Zack, a boy on his chess team, was around. Shortly after they became friends, Jamie noticed that when they started teaming up during practice games, Zack talked to him much like he saw girls and guys do when they were flirting. Jamie liked it and looked forward to it. He smiled a lot when Zack was around. Zack would sometimes briefly touch his arm when they were deep in discussion or would let his eyes linger on Jamie's face just a few seconds too long when they said goodbye for the day. It made Jamie feel warm, almost lightheaded.

Jamie graduated from high school when he was eighteen. He got accepted into two biology programs with a pre-med focus, one at OHSU, Oregon Health and Science University in Portland, and the other at the University of Washington in Seattle. Sam and Joanna drove him to Portland to visit the OHSU campus. In the end, he chose the University of Washington. He could live at home and attend classes. It would save his parents a lot of money. Sam assured him that money wasn't an issue. He encouraged Jamie to live on campus, as he and Bobby had done, but Jamie wanted to live at home. He didn't tell his dad that he was afraid to leave home for fear something would happen to his mom, that his sexual urges might get the better of him living in the men's dorms, or that he wanted to live at home forever and never become an adult.

Joanna's present to Jamie for graduating high school was a trip to Paris. Joanna was to represent Meryl at an international trade show in Paris in early June, and she invited Jamie and Sam to come along. The last time she'd been to Europe was long before Jamie was born when she dreamt of moving there and becoming the manager of a European hotel. This was her chance to go back, to get a fresh reminder of the dream she'd left behind.

While Joanna attended the trade show, Sam and Jamie saw the sights of Paris that most tourists see. They went to the top of the Eiffel Tower, walked around the Arc de Triomphe, took a sight-seeing excursion up the Seine River, admired the *Mona Lisa* in the Louvre, drank French coffee and people-watched at a café on the Boulevard Saint-Germaine, and strolled through the charming Montmartre hilltop district where Picasso and Dali came to paint years before and where the domed Basilica of Sacré-Cœur stands sentry over all of Paris.

When Joanna joined them, she took them to places most tourists might miss. They picnicked on the Parc du Champ de Mars. They dined at the historic Le Fouquet's, strolled through Jardin du Luxembourg, one of Paris's best-known parks, snacked on tea and macarons at Ladurée Patisserie, and ambled along the Avenue des Champs-Élysées where they browsed through upscale boutiques.

On their last afternoon before flying home, they discovered a flower shop resembling a French countryside barn while on a final stroll along quaint streets in the antique district. The flower shop had heavy, red wooden doors with brass handles, shiplap walls, and oak floors worn smooth by years of foot traffic. Antique farmhouse tables, distressed armoires, consoles, and benches were strategically positioned throughout the shop and adorned with ivies, hydrangeas, and roses arranged in clear vases.

Topiaries in woven baskets, interlaced and clipped into delicate shapes, were interspersed among worn and weathered flowerpots where lavender, nasturtiums and eucalyptus had taken root. Mirrors hanging from walls with chipped paint reflected tattered milk buckets filled with daffodils, iris, and weeping figs. Flowers and greenery spilled out onto the sidewalk, where shoppers browsed under the protection of large black and white striped awnings. At the checkout counter, customers could purchase fine French chocolates and greeting cards made of parchment paper. The shop was called *La Ferme Bouquet*.

Joanna came alive in the flower shop. She meandered through every inch of the shop, admiring the flowers, running her fingers along the rough surfaces of the tables and benches, fingering the delicate plants, and gazing at the pottery. She and the owner, Raphaël Toussaint, shared a limited conversation between her broken French and his broken English.

Raphaël and his wife, Anna, had owned the flower shop for twenty-five years. They lived in the small apartment above the shop. They considered selling the business in a few years and moving to the country to be closer to their children and grandchildren. Sam, who didn't speak or understand more than a few French words, could pick up just bits and pieces of the conversation. He heard Joanna say, "If you sell, will you contact me first? Who knows," she laughed, "I might be interested."

The following day as they were hurrying to catch the cab to take them to Charles de Gaulle International Airport and back home, Sam made one last sweep around their hotel room to ensure nothing got left behind. On Joanna's nightstand was the business card from the flower shop owner. At first, Sam dismissed the card, but at the last minute, he put it in his jacket pocket. "You never know," he thought. "Never a bad idea to have contacts in other countries."

32

JAMIE'S COLLEGE YEARS PASSED WITHOUT INCIDENT. HE THOUGHT his life should be different than it was. Something was missing. He felt incomplete. He had a constant feeling of dread and anxiety. It wasn't blaring but lay like an animal on the hunt, in the recesses of his mind, crouched and ready to pounce when he let his guard down. He feared, at times, that he was becoming like his mom, depressed and unhappy. He didn't want to lay that burden on his dad.

Jamie missed high school. He missed his group of friends. He still talked to Chelsea occasionally, but she'd gotten accepted into a fashion design school in Seattle on a needs-based stipend. She had to keep her grades up to continue receiving financial assistance, and her fashion design program was demanding. She put in long hours working to perfect her skills. Plus, she'd made friends with a group of fashion design students who, like Chelsea, spent most of their time in the campus design labs. Jamie missed her. He remembered how they used to go to movies and bike on the trails that wove through Bellevue and how they loved to visit coffeehouses where they'd sit for hours sipping coffee, talking, and solving the problems of the world.

It was Zack, though, whom he missed the most. Zack had moved to Los Angeles to study engineering after high school. Zack's friendship had filled a void in Jamie. The two of them shared corny jokes and read passages to each other from their favorite books. They'd sometimes met for dinner at the Beachhouse in Kirkland and afterward would walk on the pier. They'd find a bench where they could sit looking out at Lake Washington and talk until late into the night. They shared their secrets, their future dreams, their fears and anxieties. Jamie sometimes wanted to put his hand on Zack's leg or touch his arm when they sat next to each other, but he never did, and Zack never made a move.

When Zack first moved to Los Angeles, he and Jamie talked on the phone almost daily, but the calls became less frequent as months passed. Finally, Zack told Jamie he'd met a guy in his engineering program with whom he was hanging out. Jamie didn't hear from him again. It broke his heart. Sometimes the pain felt unbearable. He wanted to talk to his dad, to tell him how he felt, but he knew his feelings for Zack weren't normal. He felt ashamed. There was no way he could share his heartbreak with his dad. It would just be one more thing his dad had to deal with.

When Joanna began to see Jamie more as a man instead of a child, her relationship with him shifted. She saw him as someone she could lean on. Jamie would listen, empathize, and show concern when Joanna came home from work stressed out. He started staying home more and more to be available to her.

He tagged along with her to the grocery store, the cleaners, and sometimes Sunday mass. When she occasionally made dinner, she asked Jamie to help her set the table, chop the vegetables, and empty the dishwasher. She began to confide in him about her job, the stress it caused her, client problems, and staff issues.

She'd sometimes encourage Jamie to drink with her. One glass of wine typically led to two; Joanna would soon switch to something more potent. When Joanna started drinking, Jamie's pleasure in hanging out with her would turn to dread. He knew how it would end. She'd need help getting to her bedroom. She'd get sloppy and repeat herself over and over. Sometimes she'd get emotional, cry, and tell him how much she loved him through slurred words. She'd become angry if he found an excuse to go to his room. She'd accuse him of wanting to get away from her. It would be Sam who rescued him. He'd come into the room and tell Jamie, "It's okay, Bud. You've probably got studying to do."

Jamie completed his degree in biology and was accepted into medical school at both OHSU in Portland and the University of Washington in Seattle. When Jamie told his dad he would stay at the University of Washington, where he could continue living at home, Sam told him, "Living at home isn't an option for you any longer, Jamie."

Jamie thought he heard wrong. "What do you mean, it's not an option? Why isn't it an option?"

"It's time for you to go, Jamie. You're nearly twenty-two. You may never leave if you stay here another three or four years while in medical school. You have a life waiting for you. You need to go find it."

"But it would be easier for me here. I have my own room, a place to make meals. I don't want to live in a dorm situation."

"You've had it easy for too long, Jamie. Having a few challenges to figure out along the way is what growing up is all about. It's time, Bud. You worry about your mom, but she'll be okay without you here. It's not your responsibility to keep her company."

"She'll feel sad if I leave. I like keeping her company."

"You can't stay here forever. It's time to make friends and find your own way, Jamie. When was the last time you brought a friend home? When was the last time you went out with Chelsea? What about Zack? What happened to him? You really liked him."

For a second, Sam thought he noticed Jamie's lip quiver ever so slightly. They were standing in Sam's den. At the mention of Zack, Jamie could only focus on a cabin cruiser way out across the lake and stare, daring his eyes not to cloud up. Jamie wanted to tell his dad how much he missed Zack and how lonely he was. "He moved to LA, Dad, don't you remember?" He stared straight ahead.

"Yeah, but you used to talk to him all the time. Did you lose touch?"

Jamie kept his eyes on the boat far out on the lake, afraid to blink. He wanted to turn around and tell his dad everything he was feeling, but he couldn't. Instead, he turned and walked out of the room.

"Jamie, are you alright?" Sam watched as Jamie disappeared through the living room and up the industrial staircase to his room. He continued to stare into the living room after Jamie was gone. His attorney's brain clicked on. He knew when a witness was hiding something or omitting something. He'd seen what holding onto secrets can do to one's psyche. The evidence lined up. His heart ached for his son. "Geez, Bud, come talk to me."

Joanna was furious when Sam informed her that Jamie was moving out and that his living at home was no longer an option. "It isn't your sole decision, Sam," she snapped. "I have a say in what he does."

"Joanna, Jamie would stay forever if he thought you wanted him to. He's going on twenty-two years old. Do you remember how hard it was to give up your dreams when we married? We were his age, Joanna. He shouldn't have to go through that same thing. He needs to find his own way."

In the end, Jamie accepted admission to OHSU. He found a small studio apartment in downtown Portland close to campus. Sam and Joanna paid his expenses. He got a job bartending in a brewery on weekends, two evenings a week. It wasn't much, but it contributed a small amount to his living expenses. He studied hard. One month turned into the next, and he began to make friends with a few classmates.

Now and then, he met up with fellow students for a beer and to lament the drudgery of medical school. His constant worry over his mom slowly began to lessen. He began to enjoy his newfound independence. He buckled down and took his studies seriously. He became interested in neonatology. Caring for tiny babies fighting to stay alive, giving them the life-saving measures needed to survive until they found their footing, resonated with Jamie. He began to shape his studies toward a specialty as a neonatologist.

And then, one day, toward the end of his first year of med school, Jamie walked into his anatomy and physiology lab, and there was Michael Daniels. They paired up and became lab partners. Michael was from Colorado and was planning to specialize in pediatrics. He had red hair and freckles and wore funky glasses. They made each other laugh. They'd sometimes meet in the library on campus and study together, stopping on the way home to grab a beer. Jamie wanted to tell his dad about Michael. Still, when his dad called to catch up, Jamie omitted Michael from his conversation. He rehearsed what to say, but when he heard his dad's voice on the other end of the line, the words wouldn't come.

33

BEFORE JAMIE MOVED TO PORTLAND, WHEN HE WAS STILL LIVING AT home, Joanna purchased Big City Events from Meryl, who was nearing seventy and wanted to retire. Over the years, the company became a multi-million dollar business. It was known throughout the Seattle metropolitan area for its high-profile events. The newest venture Meryl undertook, a couple of years before she retired, was the production and oversight of national conferences for big tech companies and financial institutes. By this time, Joanna was running the company. Her salary had risen to a quarter of a million dollars a year. When Meryl offered to sell the company to Joanna, it was too good to turn down. It was time, Joanna thought, to take the next step.

It turned out that purchasing the business was the tipping point for Joanna, the incident that led to her unraveling. She made the decision after coming out of a rather long depressive episode and as she was beginning to escalate into a manic one. The uplift in her spirits made her feel like she was at peak performance. It was common for her to feel overly emboldened on the upswing. Such was the case with her decision to assume ownership of the company, a decision made without consulting Sam. Meryl agreed to put up the financing and carry the loan for Joanna. The company attorney wrote up the deal, signed, sealed and delivered it without Sam knowing.

Had Joanna discussed the business venture with Sam before she made the purchase, he would have cautioned her against taking on added responsibilities, reminding her that the duties she already oversaw for the business often caused her bipolar mood episodes to escalate. He would have reminded her that when she was depressed, she could hardly function— and when manic, she'd stay up for several nights without sleeping while eating very little. Her decision-making ability was not at its best during these episodes. He would have emphasized how stressed she became when dealing with staff issues, client complaints, and deadlines and how she often relied on alcohol and pills during work hours to get through the day. He would have pointed out how easily she lost her temper over something trivial. "How," he would have asked, "will you handle the added demands of owning the business?"

Joanna naively imagined the transition from manager to owner of Big City Events would be seamless. The employees knew her. Some had worked with her for years. She promoted her assistant, Stephen Forbert, into the role she was vacating, Managing Director. Stephen had been Joanna's assistant for several years. He'd always been competent in his position. But this promotion was a giant step up.

Joanna soon found that owning the business was different from managing it. She no longer had the time to focus on the details of each event as she had before. She had to trust Stephen, as Meryl had done with her. Suddenly, profit and loss statements, balance sheets, assets, liabilities, and rates of return became her everyday worries.

Her first big mistake was failing to listen to her administrative team. In her first year as owner, against the advice of her financial team, she refused to raise event prices. She ignored their warnings that the cost of goods and services would increase. As predicted, the profit margin dropped by the end of the first year. To correct the loss, she again should have considered the advice from her financial team. Instead, she raised prices higher than they recommended, ignoring their warning that doing so might affect client satisfaction. Joanna believed her clientele would support the cost increase. She was wrong. She ended up with unhappy clients, a few who decided to take their business elsewhere.

Joanna needed to get a handle on things. Her anxiety worsened. Quality slipped. Clients complained. Mistakes became frequent; a project manager would order the wrong flowers, miscalculate the number of parking slots needed, or overlook a misspelled word on a flyer. Worse yet, Stephen Forbert sometimes underbid an event. Joanna was left to either absorb the loss or inform the client that getting what they anticipated would cost them substantially more.

Stephen Forbert was in over his head, trying to handle multiple events simultaneously. He performed better in the role of assistant than in the role of director. He continuously came to Joanna for clarification, advice and to get questions answered. Joanna had to update herself with each event to give Stephen the needed information. She'd remind him that this was what she was paying him to do.

Things went from bad to worse. Morale dropped. The enthusiasm staff used to come to work with diminished. Employees began to drag in each morning, and staff were out the door each evening by five p.m. sharp. Negativity crept into the work environment. Turnover increased. Employees, who already felt overworked, might tell a client they couldn't guarantee that this or that would arrive on time for an event. The client would have to call several times to follow up. They complained to Joanna. "What's going on over there?" repeat clients who knew Joanna from years back wanted to know.

Her working relationship with Stephen deteriorated. She began to micromanage him. He began to avoid her. She felt like the enemy. Once she overheard him bad-mouth her to one of the project managers. She confronted him, accusing him of creating a hostile work environment.

Joanna wished she would have remained the Managing Director of Big City Events and let somebody else be the owner, stuck with what she knew. Would managing a European hotel have been everything she hoped for, or would it have been filled with headaches, worry, and stress? Doubt crept into her mind … maybe it was her. Perhaps she wasn't capable of being at the helm. Maybe she was only meant to go so far, and now she'd passed her threshold.

Her alcohol and pill consumption increased to compensate for her failings. By three o'clock in the afternoon, she'd need a boost to calm her nerves. She'd shut her office door and mix herself a martini, straight up, no olive; she couldn't be bothered. She'd taken to keeping a supply of alcohol in her locked cabinet at all times. Sometimes, on a demanding day, she'd swallow one, maybe two Xanax along with the drink. "Take them as prescribed," her doctor warned. "Avoid taking with alcohol." She blew caution to the wind. She needed it, she'd convince herself.

She'd continue her alcohol consumption into the evening. Instead of doing what she hoped it would do, the alcohol brought on feelings of dread and doom. Sam refused to engage with her when she was under the influence. He'd busy himself in his den reviewing a legal case, hit a few balls around the pool table, go running, meet Bobby for a beer, or go to bed before she came in. Other times, he'd stretch out on the couch in his den and not come to bed at all.

To add to Joanna's difficulties, the only woman she considered her friend at the time deceived and deliberately sabotaged her. It was an unhealthy relationship, to begin with, and it catalyzed Joanna's downfall. The friend, Lisa Perry, was Joanna's therapist. Joanna started seeing her a few years into her marriage when things between her and Sam were going poorly. Lisa was close to Joanna's age. She wore French-painted acrylic nails, and her haircut was styled to look messy. Her clothing and accessories spoke money. She wore stiletto heels—she liked to cross one leg over the other and let her stiletto dangle from her foot during therapy sessions with clients.

There was no competition between the two women—in the beginning. They were both successful but in different professions. Lisa claimed to be an advocate for her women clients. If men didn't like her, she saw it as a sign of success. "Husbands fear me," she once told Joanna. "They know I'm on their wife's side. It's threatening to them."

The two women began socializing outside of therapy shortly into their relationship. They often met for lunch or for cocktails after work. Over time, Lisa started sharing stories about her past lovers, recent break-ups, and ex-husbands with Joanna. Sometimes, during a therapy session that Lisa billed Joanna for, Lisa would get sidetracked and tell Joanna details about her newest lover.

Lisa came on to Sam one evening when he agreed to pick Joanna up from the lounge she and Lisa liked to frequent. Joanna's car was in the shop that day, and Sam agreed to pick her up on his way home from his law office. Lisa had met him a few times over the years she and Joanna had known each other and each time had felt an immediate attraction toward him. This evening was no exception. The couple of drinks she'd consumed boosted her confidence and loosened her inhibitions. She'd slept with her friends' husbands before but never a client's, which was more unforgivable. She quickly convinced herself that Joanna was more of a friend than a client.

Sam took a seat at their table and ordered a beer. He didn't plan to stick around more than a few minutes, he didn't want to enable Joanna's drinking but Lisa persuaded him to have just one beer, "for the road." When Joanna excused herself from the table to visit the lady's room, Lisa took no time in making her move. She was used to getting what she wanted and felt sure of herself. She boldly dropped her stiletto heel and rubbed her bare foot up Sam's pant leg. When Sam looked at her quizzically, Lisa stared back at him invitingly. She didn't get the response she was expecting or hoping for.

Sam looked her in the eye. "Doesn't Joanna pay you to be her therapist, Lisa?"

Lisa was taken aback. "She started as my client, but we've become friends. It tends to get confusing. I give her a terrific deal," she laughed, trying to look unaffected.

"Are you gonna tell her you came on to me tonight?"

"I don't know what you're talking about," Lisa tried to sound innocent.

"Joanna will know what I'm talking about if I tell her. I'm curious," he pushed on, like he might cross examine a witness on the stand, "is it possible to have a therapeutic relationship with your clients when you aren't honest with them?"

By then, Joanna was walking back towards the table. Before she sat down, Sam stood. "Joanna, I hate to cut this short, but I have some documents for trial tomorrow that I need to review."

Lisa kept what she'd done from Joanna but worried Sam would say something. He didn't—at first. Thinking about how Sam had shut her down made Lisa furious. She wanted to get back at him, so she concocted a story that Sam came on to *her* that night in the bar when Joanna got up to go to the lady's room. "I told him I wasn't interested," Lisa told Joanna. "I just thought you should know."

Joanna was furious and confronted Sam. He told her the truth. "Actually Joanna, the opposite occurred. You might consider whether Lisa has your best interest in mind and what kind of game she's playin'. Not only should you fire her as your therapist, but you could report her for unethical conduct." But Joanna wasn't open to hearing it. She took Lisa's side, called Sam a liar, and ranted and raged for a week.

During that time, a young female law student interning in his office telephoned Sam one evening at home to ask about a case she was assigned to. When Joanna realized he was talking to a woman on the phone, she stormed into his den and said loud enough that she hoped the intern could hear, "Is that one of your little fucks, Sam?"

Sam found her in the kitchen a few minutes later. "That was the lowest I've yet to see you stoop, Joanna." He was angrier than Joanna could remember ever seeing him. Joanna refused to back down.

"Well is she Sam, is she a good fuck?" Joanna repeated herself defiantly.

Sam turned and walked out of the kitchen. He poured himself a shot of whiskey and walked outside to the deck to avoid a showdown.

Joanna followed him outside, ready to go down fighting. "I'm just wondering. That's all. Don't think I'm stupid, Sam. I see how women bat their eyes at you. Don't try to tell me you don't fuck em. I wasn't born yesterday."

They went days barely speaking to each other after that. One night, Sam went to bed early, and Joanna stayed up late to work on some financial reports she'd brought home from her office. After downing three, maybe four martinis throughout the evening—she'd lost track—she couldn't concentrate on the reports before her; her mind drifted. She thought about Sam. Their marriage was caving in. They were at their lowest point. She knew she was to blame. Regret and insecurity filled her head.

It became glaring that Jamie had been the link that held Sam and her together. With him gone, there was nothing to secure their relationship. Jamie, after all, was the reason she and Sam had married in the first place. She thought about all she had put Sam through over the years of their marriage. Why would he want to stay with her? What did he get out of it? The answer blared in her ears: nothing. Joanna rested her head in her hands, thinking about how badly she'd messed up her marriage.

The numbers on the financial reports blurred. She felt tears fill her eyes. Like the insidious rumble of an earthquake felt far away, her world slipped. Sam had become indifferent. She felt a sudden urgency to fix things, to undo the past twenty-two years. She realized she didn't want to lose him, couldn't lose him; she needed him—loved him.

Joanna was drunker than she realized. She stood up and stumbled down the hall and into the bedroom. While attempting to sit on the edge of the bed, she lost her balance and accidentally bumped Sam. He roused and rolled onto his back. He was unshaven, and his hair was tousled from sleep. Joanna suddenly wanted him more than she ever had; she wanted to tell him she loved him, was sorry, and would make everything up to him. She wanted to create a romantic moment between them but forgot to factor in that she was drunk. She undressed and slipped into bed, pressing against him. She put her hand inside his boxers and groped him. He woke, startled. "Joanna, what the hell!"

"Les fuck, Sam," the words came out in a slur.

"Gawd, Joanna, stop!" Sam pulled himself to a sitting position on the edge of the bed. He sat with his back to her and ran his hand through his hair. He turned to look at her. "Joanna, I'm sick of you coming on to me when you're drunk or drugged up or when you're manic or stressed, or God knows what else. It's cheap, Joanna. I get nothing out of it." He got up and left the room, leaving her in the middle of the bed. She didn't know what to feel—anger, embarrassment, rejection? She couldn't zero in on the correct emotion. They were all mixed up. She laid her head on the bed, tears streaming down her cheeks.

The dam that contained Joanna and Sam's marriage cracked after that, and their relationship collapsed. They barely spoke; they avoided each other. Joanna sometimes stopped off at a bar downtown on her way home and allowed men who were strangers to join her at her table. She'd flirt and let them come on to her. They'd put their hands on her, sometimes kiss her. She'd go home with them and have meaningless sex like she used to do in college. It temporarily filled a void in her.

She'd creep into her and Sam's bedroom in the wee hours of the morning smelling of alcohol, her hair disheveled, her lipstick

smeared. Sam would hear her sneak in, trying to be quiet and unde-
tected. He no longer confronted her about her whereabouts. Sleeping
on the couch in his den had become his norm. He got up early, went
for a three-or-four-mile run, and stopped for coffee, staying away
until Joanna left for work. The distance between them had become
too wide to traverse.

34

WHEN SAM MARRIED JOANNA, HE'D PROMISED HIMSELF THAT HE'D SET aside time every day to write, maybe only an hour, but he'd do it; he'd get up an hour early or stay up an hour late. After Jamie was born, he hadn't been prepared for the barrage of responsibilities that piled on. By the end of every day, he'd fallen into bed exhausted.

As years went by, he never gave up his longing to write. He thought about it and dabbled at it, but he felt out of practice, rusty. He had an idea for a novel that he tinkered with for years but kept rewriting the opening lines and struggled with the plot and character development.

Sam's mom encouraged him to write. Jamie encouraged him to write. Bobby was on him constantly, urging him to write, "Come on man, writing is what you're all about. Don't let it slip away. You're destined to be great, dude." But he'd find excuses to put it off. Now, as he entered his forties, writing wasn't much more than a faded dream.

Bobby had done well for himself during the years since college. He opened his own architectural firm when he turned thirty. He specialized in residential properties and small commercial buildings. His designs felt natural, earthy, and peaceful. He began working with contractors who specialized in high-end homes and, within a couple of years, was creating all of their designs. He worked with city planners and designed blueprints to refurbish old buildings while maintaining their original charm. His clients consistently passed his name on to others, ensuring a steady business flow.

One morning, after being out of college for several years, Bobby was out for a run along the Burke-Gilman Trail. The old Seattle railroad corridor had been converted into a pedestrian trail years ago. He came around a corner while adjusting his MP3 player and ran headlong into another runner. They collided hard enough to knock them both to the ground.

"You son-of-a-bitch!"

To Bobby's dismay, he saw a woman around his age sprawled on the gravel.

"Oh, God, I'm sorry," Bobby said, horrified. "Are you okay?"

"I think so, no thanks to you,"

Bobby had scraped both of his palms and ripped the knee of his running pants. He jumped up to help the woman to her feet. She was examining her scraped arm. Years later, Bobby couldn't remember if it'd been her brown eyes, teasing smile, or French-braided blonde hair that he'd noticed first. Whichever it was, it never grew tiresome to him. He fell for her before she even got to her feet. His charm kicked in. "When we're married and old and gray," he told her as he pulled her up, "we'll remember that the first name you ever called me was a son-of-a-bitch. What's your name, by the way?"

"Kat, short for Katherine. Look at you; you're bleeding." She handed him her bandana from her waist pack. "I live just up ahead in Ballard. Why don't you follow me home and you can bandage your hand?"

"I don't want to bother you. I'm Bobby, by the way."

"You're already bothering me, Bobby."

Bobby didn't need coaxing; he followed her home and allowed her to clean and bandage his scrapes.

They spent the whole day together—in bed. She moved into Bobby's apartment a few months later, and a year after they were married. Kat was a school counselor. She was good-natured, bold, and bossy, and Bobby adored her. They had two children within a few years of getting married, a daughter, Ally, and a son, Luke. By the time they'd been married ten years, they could afford a home in Madrona, an upscale Seattle neighborhood on the west side of Lake Washington. Bobby turned part of the lower level that opened up to their side yard into his office so he could work from home.

Sam and Bobby had been friends for nearly thirty years. They were no longer the carefree school boys they once were. They had families and responsibilities. They were successful, but their success had been reached by following very different paths. Things had gone smoothly for Bobby—he was happily married, had settled into being a family man, and was satisfied with his work, doing what he'd always dreamed of doing. Sam, on the other hand, had made do. He hadn't married for love; now, after years of turmoil, his marriage was in tatters. While a prosperous attorney, his dream of becoming a writer had faded away. "It's okay," he'd convince himself—he'd done it for Jamie.

Sam and Bobby still confided in each other. Sam told Bobby about the problems in his marriage, Joanna's struggles with mood episodes, her erratic, sometimes risky behavior, and the impact Sam worried it had on Jamie. They'd often take a break from work demands and meet for lunch, coffee, or go running together.

It was fishing they mostly bonded over. Sam, Bobby, and sometimes one or two other friends from their Oak Harbor days often took Sam's cabin cruiser out on Puget Sound to fish for salmon. Other times, Sam and Bobby would take a day off and escape to a quiet stream somewhere on one of the San Juan Islands or the Olympic Peninsula to fly fish or troll one of their favorite lakes in

Bobby's small outboard fishing boat; their lines would drag in the water while the two men reclined, beers in hand, sharing the cama- raderie that only comes from being friends since boyhood.

On one such fishing getaway with Bobby in early spring, fate once again intervened in Sam's life and led him further down the path of his destiny. Sam's marriage was barely hanging on. He and Joanna had spoken little since he'd walked out on her in their bedroom. He needed time to think and wanted to get away for the weekend. He and Bobby decided to go fishing for coho salmon in the Strait of Juan de Fuca near Crystal Bay, a tiny fishing town nestled along the western shore of the Olympic Peninsula. They loved fishing for coho this time of year. The fish sometimes grew to over twenty pounds and fought hard when hooked. Neither of them ever tired of the thrill of feeling that tug on their line, that sudden pull that set their reel spinning.

It was early Saturday afternoon when they docked in the Crystal Bay marina. By day's end, after several hours of fishing, once they loaded Sam's cabin cruiser onto the trailer and packed their catch on ice, they didn't feel like rushing to board the Kingston ferry more than one hundred miles away. They wanted to make their day last, sit back and sip a few beers.

They booked motel rooms in Crystal Bay and set out to find something to eat. They were searching for a good meal and were told by the motel desk clerk that The Tavern, located at the marina, offered good burgers and cold beer. The Tavern was an icon on the upper peninsula. Locals, tourists, and sports fishermen who docked their boats in the bay to come ashore for supplies had been enjoying The Tavern's homestyle cooking and cold beers for over fifty years.

It was a dimly lit, somewhat run-down establishment. It was one of those places still sporting tables and chairs from the fifties and had a working jute box in the corner that patrons loved to play.

It was early evening when Sam and Bobby arrived. The idea of a burger and fries with a cold beer sounded good. They were hungry and tired from their day of fishing, and The Tavern promised to provide that homestyle kind of cooking that a day in the wind and rain made appealing.

They sat at the counter and ate juicy and messy burgers and fries with homemade fry sauce. The cold beer tasted good. The proprietor, Skeeter, who also served as chief cook and bottle washer, was working the counter that evening and struck up a friendly conversation with Sam and Bobby. He had a toughness about him, worn and hardened, resulting from alcohol and cigarettes and living hard. Within a short time, the three men fell into a comfortable banter.

"What do you boys fish for?" he asked.

"Just about anything," Sam answered. "Today it was coho. Bobby and I grew up fishing together. We like it all. Probably our favorite is fly fishing. We're always looking for the best river."

"Well, my friends, unless you've fished Gus's Fishing Hole, about six miles inland off Highway 112, I can guarantee you ain't yet found the best river."

"Never heard of it," Bobby said. "It must be a well-kept secret. Sam and I have been fishing in this area for years. I thought we knew every fishing hole up and down the peninsula."

"Gus's is private property located on the North Fork Sekiu River. It belongs to an old boy named Gus Tobler. He has a couple uh cabins on the property that his old man used to rent out to fishermen. Gus occasionally still rents 'em out. Best fly fishin' you'll ever find. The fishin' hole's loaded with smallmouth bass, bluegills, and stripers—a fly fisherman's paradise. Gus is a good ol' boy. His wife, Mary, died a year ago. He likes company now and then. He'll never turn down a game of poker. He'll supply the booze, too. There's nothin' better 'n sittin' on his porch playin' Texas Hold'em or just enjoyin' the peacefulness of the surroundings. It can't be beat. Take my word."

That night, Sam lay awake in the dark, alone in his motel room. He couldn't get the image of Gus's Fishing Hole out of his mind. It sounded like the place he'd been dreaming of for years, a little cabin on the river where he could write, finish his novel, and figure things out. Knowing there was a place like Gus's Fishing Hole, not so far away, gave him a sense of comfort. Somewhere for him to escape to in his mind when reality got rough.

35

JOANNA'S LIFE WAS FALLING APART. HER BRAIN HAD BEEN IDLING IN overdrive for a few days, a hypomanic state. But she could sense a full-blown manic state coming. Obsessive thoughts ran through her head that made it hard to concentrate. She felt others were laughing at her, sneering, mocking her. She wanted to open the door and start running—she didn't care where. *The Catcher in the Rye,* one of her favorite stories when she was young, came to her mind. "I'm about to fly over the edge, Holden," she said to herself. "Are you there to catch me?"

Her marriage was in crisis. Plus, her therapist, Lisa, was trying to pick a fight with her. Since the night when she and Sam and Lisa met for drinks, Lisa couldn't stop talking about Sam whenever she and Joanna were together. She'd bring Sam up every chance she got and say things to deliberately put doubt in Joanna's mind. "You should have seen how he kept looking at me that night—I'm just telling you, Joanna, so you're aware."

Joanna became suspicious of Lisa's motives. Lisa reminded Joanna of girls from her high school days who would compete for some other girl's boyfriend by telling lies and spreading rumors. It dawned on Joanna that maybe Sam was telling the truth, maybe

Lisa was the one who came on to Sam that night, not the other way around. She'd listened for years to Lisa's stories of coming on to men—work associates, husbands, or other women's boyfriends; it didn't matter to Lisa. She let nothing get in her way if she wanted a man, even friendship. But Joanna was her client. Even in her mixed-up mind, something about that felt like Lisa had overstepped some sacred ethical standard—do no harm.

Joanna sensed a catfight brewing. She was ready for it. She began rubbing Sam in Lisa's face. "Sam and I did this last weekend ... Sam and I did that." Tension between the two women mounted. Joanna didn't show for her next scheduled therapy appointment with Lisa and didn't call to cancel. When she saw a message on her phone from Lisa, she responded with her own message: "Fuck off, bitch!"

On top of her troubles with Lisa, the tension at work between Joanna and Stephen Forbert reached a boiling point. It was apparent they no longer saw eye-to-eye. Stephen got friendly with some project managers, and Joanna knew he occasionally went out with them after hours. That was against business policy. Management does not socialize with staff. It had been Meryl's policy. When they started working together many years ago, Meryl told Joanna, "It's hard enough to manage others when you hardly know them, but when they're your drinking buddy ... That's when things get messy!"

Stephen had put himself in charge of overseeing an information technology conference hosted by a local IT company in one of Bellevue's most prestigious hotels. He feared it might be too much for a less experienced project manager. The conference was due to open in two days. Over three thousand attendees were registered. The cost to produce the event was more than four hundred thousand dollars, which the IT company hosting the event expected to recover with hefty registration fees. It was to be an elaborate event with prominent IT experts from around the world scheduled to speak.

Joanna received a telephone call from John Presto, the IT company's chief technology manager, two days before the event. John had been put in charge of ensuring the conference went off without a hitch. He told Joanna he didn't want to cause problems, but he was worried that Stephen wasn't up to handling such a big event. Some important things had been missed or forgotten. John told Joanna that when he brought it up, Stephen got defensive. "We would appreciate it if you could review things and ensure everything's on track."

Stephen copped an attitude when Joanna confronted him about John Presto's complaints. He blamed her for the problems. "I can't come to you with questions, Joanna. You're not available. Everyone knows you're drinking on the job. We can smell it on you. You're half-looped most of the time, scattered. I can't count on your help. The employees are unhappy, and our customers are becoming dissatisfied. It's a shame when you think of what this business used to be."

Joanna, under different circumstances and with a different mindset, might have heard Stephen's feedback as constructive. Still, all she heard at the time was Stephen's accusations. How dare he accuse her of drinking and being scattered! Who did he think he was, talking to her that way? She couldn't let it slide. It would get around the office that he'd accused her of drinking on the job. She couldn't let that happen. She made a hasty, impulsive decision. She fired him.

The one positive thing about her decision was that the angst that propelled her to fire Stephen threw her into high gear. She felt a surge of energy kick in. How dare Stephen confront and accuse her—this was *her* company, after all. If her employees were as unhappy as Stephen suggested, they could quit, or better yet, she'd fire them too, get rid of them all.

As for the IT conference, she'd handle it on her own. She relished the opportunity. She felt like getting her hands dirty, getting back to doing what she loved. She had a new focus. Her issues at home diminished in scope—she had more urgent matters to deal with.

Joanna called John Presto and told him not to worry; she was taking charge of the conference. She promised it would go off without a hitch. They arranged to meet at the hotel where the conference would take place. John was in his mid-sixties and in okay shape, nothing to brag about. He had a full head of gray hair and was casually dressed in running pants and a pullover shirt. He was pleasant looking.

John knew nothing about event planning. Being put in the position of overseeing the conference placed him outside his comfort zone. He was thrilled to learn that Joanna, herself, would be taking over supervision of the event. He offered to help Joanna in any way he could be of service.

They worked from early morning until late into the evening for the next two days, ensuring every detail—room setups, menus, table decorations, lighting and sound, reservations, parking, check-in procedures, posters, and flowers—was attended to. Joanna issued orders to the hotel staff assigned to set up the conference. She insisted things be redone if they didn't meet her expectations. Her engine revved, propelling her along, allowing her to juggle several balls in the air without floundering. She was unstoppable.

Joanna didn't sleep the two days she and John Presto worked to prepare for the conference. She barely ate. Her diet consisted mainly of alcohol, a swallow here, a swallow there, to keep her moving—the hard stuff, the stuff with some push behind it. She hadn't combed her hair or changed her clothes. At one point, she snuck into a hotel room when she saw the housekeeper step out for a minute and brushed her teeth with one of the new toothbrushes lying on the bathroom counter.

At the end of the second day, she sat in the hotel bar trying to recoup, her mind and body exhausted. The energy that had driven her the past two days had drained away. She felt like a rag doll, floppy and empty. She had a sudden sense of clarity, much like one feels during grief when all barriers are down.

She felt like she was standing naked in the middle of her life and seeing it for what it was. She was in it alone. There was no one she could turn to. She wanted to give up everything she'd worked for and disappear to someplace where life was simple and easy. She didn't crave the power she once thought she did. It was her father that wanted it, not her.

She knew she was losing the business. She felt guilty. Meryl had put her faith in Joanna and believed she could take over and run the company. She had let everyone she cared about down, Sam, Jamie, Meryl, Stephen, and her employees. She'd followed in her dad's footsteps only to find no prize at the end. He'd lied to her.

She sat at the bar, sipping a drink with these thoughts running through her mind, when John Presto came in. "I think we pulled it off, Joanna. The conference is ready to open tomorrow morning. How can I thank you?" He noticed Joanna's disheveled look, the circles under her eyes, the wrinkled dress she'd been wearing for the past two days. He thanked her for her dedication. "You're a trooper, Joanna," he told her. "You're the best. Can I buy you a drink?" he offered. He took the stool next to her. There was something about his attentiveness that filled a void inside Joanna. She focused in on him. They decided to have dinner together. John suggested they dine in the hotel dining room. It was elegant, and the food was known to be superb. It had dim lighting and live piano music.

They started off with a couple more drinks. When they finally got around to ordering their meal, their heads felt dizzy, and their bodies relaxed, the stress from the previous couple of days dissipating like late-morning fog. They opened up to each other about why the conference was such a big deal to both of them. Joanna found herself telling John about her struggles to maintain her business. She told him how Stephen had turned against her and turned staff against her, that she might have to fire everyone and start over. "But that kind of thing gets around. I might have trouble finding good designers. They'll blackball me," she confided to John. The thought frightened her.

John had his own grievances to bear. He missed a lot of work over the past year. His wife had been ill and finally passed away four months ago. He missed her terribly, he told Joanna. But the company, he explained, had yet to cut him any slack. They were watching his performance. He had to pull off this conference. His job was on the line. How could he effectively grieve for his late wife with that kind of stress hanging over his head, he wondered aloud to Joanna? He was convinced upper management was looking for a reason to fire him because of his age.

They ate very little of their meal and ordered more drinks. Their conversation moved closer to the line they knew not to cross. Joanna asked about his late wife. "The grief must be awful," her words sounded garbled. She leaned in across the table to let him know that she understood. She put her hand over his.

It was unbearable, he told her. Some nights he thought he'd die of loneliness.

Joanna told John about her marriage. The circumstances she and Sam had married under. How righteous Sam always came across to her, how he always had to show her up. "He never makes a mistake," she told John. "No matter what I do, it's never good enough," she allowed her tone to become vulnerable. "He practically turned my son against me." To show he understood, John ordered a bottle of wine.

Joanna had a blackout sometime during dinner. Her head was "totally fucked up," as she described it to John, and she told him things that sounded like they were coming out of someone else's mouth. She told him about her sex life with Sam and how she fantasized about quarreling with him and then using sex to make up.

John listened attentively, nodding his head. The alcohol gave him a glazed look. His words sounded smeared, like wet ink across the written page. "Joanna, we're too drunk to drive home. We're gonna have to get a room here tonight. We'd get a DUI, we could kill someone." For some reason, the thought struck them both as hilariously funny. They laughed uncontrollably.

"I'll put the room on my personal credit card. My supervisors won't authorize a hotel room when I live in Bellevue."

"Don't worry about it," Joanna's tongue felt too big to fit in her mouth. "I'll bill it to my expense account. Don't tell anyone," Joanna warned, "it's against policy." They both found what she said to be hilarious. They hooted with laughter. Joanna was so drunk that she could no longer speak coherently.

Thankfully, the hotel had a room available. It had two king-size beds and a sitting area. "We'll just rest for a couple of hours," John said. "We have our own beds."

At the door to their hotel room, John couldn't get the key card to work in the lock. Joanna was leaning against the wall attempting to remain vertical. While John fumbled with the key card, Joanna shifted her weight and swayed from the wall to John, pressing against him, primarily for balance. "Wassa problem?" She threw her arm around his neck and leaned back, trying to focus on his face. The further back she bent, the more forward John came until they both lost their balance and tumbled to the floor. They tried to right themselves, first by getting on their hands and knees and then clinging to each other for support. They laughed so hard that they had to lower themselves back to the floor. They were able to finally resume a vertical position by using the wall to help pull themselves up. Their hooting and laughter could be heard up and down the corridor.

At some point, before heading up to her room, Joanna had left Sam a message on his cell phone to tell him she was too drunk to drive home. She didn't remember doing it. She omitted to tell him she was getting a room with the host company's chief technology manager. Sam interpreted her message as her needing a ride home. He found it concerning that she'd gotten so drunk while on the job that she couldn't drive. He was fed up. He was ready to make some serious decisions. He just needed one more thing to push him over the edge.

When Joanna and John got inside the hotel room, Joanna sat down on the end of one of the beds. She flung herself backward. It felt good to be horizontal. She had the spins. It felt like the room was swirling out of control. She thought she might be sick. John sat on the edge of the bed beside her. "Should we finish the bottle?" He held the wine bottle in the air so they could both see how much wine was left.

"Why not!" Joanna tried to push herself up into a sitting position. She found she couldn't. "John, I can't get up." They were laughing again.

John took her arm and tried to pull her up. Instead of Joanna coming up, John went down. He landed on top of her. Somehow, they ended up naked. Joanna had no recollection of them both getting undressed. They were too drunk to have sex. John couldn't perform, and Joanna tried to open her legs but found it too complicated. She'd get one to open, but when trying to open both, she became knocked kneed. The two were rubbing against each other, half laughing, half panting. They didn't hear the click of the door unlock when a second key card was inserted. They didn't hear the door open. All Joanna remembered was turning her head to see Sam standing in the doorway.

When Sam got to the hotel, he couldn't find Joanna in the bar or the lobby. He asked a young woman at the front desk who wore a "Trainee" badge on her lapel if she'd seen Joanna. He explained that Joanna was in charge of the IT conference opening in the morning.

"Well," the trainee said, half teasingly, "can you prove you're her husband? She has a room, but I'm not supposed to give you a key unless I have proof that you're who you say you are."

Sam showed her his driver's license. She looked at it, handed him the key card, and told him what room Joanna was in. He hurried to catch the elevator, knowing full well the trainee at the front desk was supposed to call the room first to get Joanna's permission to send Sam to her room. He didn't want the trainee's supervisor chasing him down and demanding he follow the correct procedures. Joanna might be passed out, too drunk to even hear the room phone.

He'd make it quick, he thought, as the elevator doors opened on Joanna's floor.

As he started down the corridor toward her room, it dawned on him that he could turn around and leave, return to his car, and drive home. She could sleep it off in the hotel room. He thought about how Jamie would feel if he knew Sam left her at the hotel, too drunk to drive home. Sam would get her and take her home. Tomorrow they'd come to some conclusions.

When he knocked on the hotel door and got no answer, he unlocked it with the key card. When he entered the hotel room, it took him a moment to grasp what he saw. His wife and some guy, both naked, were writhing around on the bed together. He was seeing it in slow motion. It took Joanna a moment to see Sam standing in the doorway.

"Oh my god, Sam," Joanna gasped, pulling herself to a seated position. Her hair splayed across her face, and her intoxicated condition made it hard to bring Sam into focus. She could barely make him out. She tried to cover her nakedness with the bedspread, but there wasn't enough loose fabric to pull around her body because they were lying on it. Her feet and the bottom of her legs were the most she could cover up.

John jumped up. "Fuck!" he yelled while pulling on one sock and trying to locate his clothes in the dimness of the room through drunken eyes.

Sam was quicker. He scooped up John's pants, shirt, boxers, and shoes and tossed them into the corridor. He held the door open, "Get out of here."

"Can I dress first?" John's voice was whimpering. He was naked except for one sock.

"You can dress out there," Sam pointed to the hotel corridor. Sam shut the door as John stepped into the hall, stumbling to pick up his clothes. He could hear John on the other side of the door trying to explain in an almost childlike voice to someone, probably a housekeeper walking by, why he was in the corridor naked.

Joanna stood at the side of the bed, leaning into it for balance. She had a dreaded sense of what she'd done. She was crying. Her voice sounded weary and pleading. "Sam, it's not what you think. We were so drunk. Nothing happened."

Sam opened the door. He stood in the doorway, deciding his next move. John was nowhere to be seen. Sam looked at Joanna for a moment. There was a time when he would have felt empathy for her. She was so unhappy, so tormented, so lost. But his compassion was used up. Instead, he got clarity. It was time to go. Without saying a word, he left the room, shutting the door quietly behind him.

PART III

SAM

36

THE EDMONDS FERRY LEAVING FOR KINGSTON ON THE KITSAP
Peninsula was delayed by thirty minutes. There was a line of cars
waiting to board. Sam turned off the engine of his Land Rover and
stepped out. Leaning against his door, he scanned Puget Sound and
the Olympic Mountains stretching along the southern edge of the
Olympic Peninsula. He tried to remember all he had packed: fishing
gear, boots, waders, rain gear, his laptop, and a few clothes, mostly
outdoor items. At the last minute, Sam tossed in a pair of flannel
trousers, a casual dress shirt, his suede oxfords, and a tie, just in case.

It was Bobby's idea for Sam to go. "Man, remember a few weeks
ago when we stopped at The Tavern in Crystal Bay, out on the
peninsula? Skeeter, the owner, told us about that fishing hole, Gus's
Fishing Hole, I think he called it. He said it was a fisherman's paradise. You gotta go find out, man. For both of us."

It was Sid who convinced him to go. "Sam, you need time to
yourself for a while—time to figure things out. Everything here will
be fine. Jamie will be fine. Your dad and I are here if he needs us. Go
lose yourself somewhere for a few months."

When Skeeter called Sam earlier that morning to say that Gus
agreed to rent him one of the cabins, Sam said yes, that he'd be there

by that evening. If he didn't do it spontaneously, he might not do it. Gus's Fishing Hole was remote, rustic, bare bones, according to Skeeter. "You don't need much there, son. It ain't fancy."

The night that Sam found Joanna in bed with John Presto, the night Sam walked out on her and left her there in the hotel room alone, Joanna took a lethal combination of Xanax, Klonopin, and Ambien, on top of the alcohol she'd consumed. She swallowed everything she had in her bag. The hotel housekeeping staff found her. Somehow— Sam wasn't clear how she managed to do it—Joanna had called the front desk and mumbled something that alarmed the desk clerk enough to send housekeeping up to check on her. When Joanna was unable to be aroused, the hotel staff called 911. The paramedics transported her to the emergency room where she was administered Flumazenil to try to bring her around.

When he got the call from the hospital, Sam was sitting in the dark on their patio, sipping brandy from a snifter, watching the lights from the Seattle skyline across the lake. The chill in the air was typical of spring in the Pacific Northwest. The brandy was fortifying. He needed something reinforcing. When his cell phone rang, he wasn't going to answer, thinking it was Joanna, calling in her drunken stupor, furious that Sam had left her at the hotel. When he saw it wasn't her number, he answered. "Is this Sam Parker?" the male voice on the other end of the line asked.

"Yeah, who's this?"

"This is Dr. Li from Overlake Medical Center in Bellevue. Mr. Parker, I hate to inform you that the paramedics brought in your wife for a serious overdose of benzodiazepines, sleeping pills, and alcohol. Her condition is critical. We gave her a medication that reversed the effects of some of the drugs she took, but she was out for a long time before being brought in by the paramedics. She's not coming around the way we'd like to see." There was silence on the other end of the line.

"Mr. Parker, are you there?"

"Yeah. I'm on my way."

When Sam arrived at the ER, the nurse barred him from entering her room. "They're putting a breathing tube in right now," the charge nurse explained. "Her oxygen levels were deficient. The respirator will breathe for her; make sure she's oxygenated."

"What if she isn't able to breathe on her own?" Sam asked.

"We're hopeful," the nurse responded. She was used to this type of life-or-death drama. She had rehearsed her response well.

The next few hours were a blur. The waiting room outside of the ER became the family gathering sight. Jamie flew in from Portland in the wee hours of the morning. Sam spared the details of John Presto with Jamie. He wanted to protect Jamie from knowing he found his mother in bed naked with another man. Jamie called his grandmother, Gladys, as soon as he arrived. She and Rip came right away. Rip barged into the waiting room, bellowing, "What the hell happened?" He found a place near the window where he sat staring out into the darkness. Sam's parents, Jack and Sid, took the early morning ferry. Sam telephoned Bobby while he was waiting for Jamie to arrive. He and Kat came right away and stayed through most of the next day.

Joanna regained consciousness around eight a.m. the following day, and the medical team weaned her off the respirator and transferred her to the intensive care unit for observation. She was admitted to the mental health unit two days later on an involuntary commitment. The medical team refused to release her. She was considered a threat to herself.

When Sam visited Joanna in the mental health unit, he braced for her hostility. He expected her to demand that he get her discharged. Instead, Joanna was quiet and subdued. When he walked into her room, she rose from her chair slowly. Her exhaustion showed through. She looked older—the whole ordeal had aged her, weakened her. She reminded Sam of a flickering candle about to go out. "Sam," her voice quivered. "I'm so sorry that I did this to you and Jamie. Everything seemed so hopeless at the time. I promise I'll make it up to you and Jamie, Sam."

Sam listened; he'd heard it before. "Joanna ..."

Joanna interrupted him. "Sam, let me finish. I mean it this time. I want to get better. I want to get well. I'll do whatever I have to do. I know I'm an alcoholic and addict. I need to go to a treatment program. I'll go. I'll sell the business. I'll take my meds consistently. I need to know, Sam, that you forgive me for what I've done. I'm so ashamed. Please, Sam, tell me you forgive me."

"It's too late, Joanna. I wish I felt differently, but I don't. I'm not interested in sticking around any longer. I care about what happens to you, but I'm taking time for myself." Sam spoke to her like he might a client he had to present with unwelcome information. He kept his tone careful but honest.

"I plan to take a leave of absence from my law practice. I probably won't go back. You need to figure out what you want. We both do. Please don't wait around for me, Joanna, don't spend your time thinking I'm coming back. I filed for divorce. I've talked to Marty Bigelow; he's drawing up the papers. We'll always have Jamie together," he added. "That won't end, but as for us, it's over."

Despair swept over Joanna. Old behaviors from the past during moments like this were futile now. The anger, the demanding, ridiculing tone in her voice, the tears, the threats, he was beyond it all. Nothing could reach him; it was like trying to talk someone back from the dead. She pleaded with him, this time with no manipulation, no drama. It was her last chance, a plea for mercy. She knew it was too little, too late. "Sam, please. Don't say your decision is final.

Give it some time. Let me show you, Sam. We have twenty-two years of marriage. We have a history. We have a son."

The line had been crossed. Joanna was on one side, Sam on the other. She watched him drift away, beyond her reach, with no way to pull him back. His mind was made up. She reached out from where she sat and took his hand in hers. "Sam, please, give me one more chance. I know you've given me so many, but my head is clear now. I mean it this time. I'll change. I love you; I need you. I can't make it without you."

"You don't need me, Joanna. You rely on me. That's different. Our marriage was based on so many wrong reasons. We knew it when we got married. We stayed for Jamie; we both did, but what a mess we made of it. He's spent his whole life trying to protect you, fix us, and make us happy. Our marriage traumatized him. He may never get over it. Sometimes I wonder if I did him a disservice by keeping that couple who wanted to adopt him from raising him. He wouldn't have known us, wouldn't have known any of the pain. My biggest regret, Joanna, is what we did to him. He loves both of us, and we let him down."

Sam wondered many times over the years what the final incident would be that resulted in his filing for divorce. In the past, something had always happened to change his mind. Something inside him warned that if he stayed this time, he'd never leave. It had to be now. This time, Joanna would need to figure things out for herself. It would be her demise if she continued the same bad habits. He couldn't save her. If she decided to make some much-needed changes to her lifestyle—quit drinking, get off the pills, take her medication as prescribed, reduce her stress—then she could live a reasonably stable life, the doctor had told Sam. Sam was handing her the reins. It would be up to her from here on out.

He had no intention of leaving her high and dry. He'd ensure she was taken care of and had what she needed to get her life going again. They could sell the lake house. It cost them a fortune to maintain and was more than they needed. Joanna could use the profits they'd make on the house to buy a smaller place, still on the lake, if she wanted. Maybe a townhouse. They'd made good money over the years and had saved well. Joanna's finances were secure. Regardless, he'd help her get settled. They didn't have to be enemies; Sam didn't want that. They had Jamie to think of.

Jamie finally came out to Sam about being gay. It happened quite by accident. Jamie was trying to figure out how to arrange time away from his summer classes to return and help his mom when she got discharged from the hospital. "I want to be here for her, Dad." Without thinking, he mentioned that Michael could send him his coursework so he could keep up.

"Who's Michael?" Sam had asked. They were in the ICU waiting room, just the two of them drinking a cup of coffee from the vending machine. The medical team had taken Joanna off the critical list, and she was waiting to transfer to the mental health unit.

Jamie faltered for a moment. Finally, he said, "Michael's my boyfriend, Dad. I'm gay. I've known it for a long time. I didn't know how to tell you."

Sam embraced him and held him tightly. "Thanks for telling me. I don't care who you love, Jamie, as long as that person makes you happy, respects you, and treats you well."

Sam listened while Jamie told him all about Michael, how they made each other laugh, how they both loved the outdoors and liked to do the same things, that Michael was planning to specialize in pediatrics, and their plans to move to San Francisco when they finished their residencies.

Sam told Jamie, "I filed for divorce from your mother, Jamie. I need to do something different. I know I'm picking a terrible time to spring it on her, but she's known it was coming for a long time."

"Wow, Dad," Jamie was surprised. "I didn't think you'd ever really do it. I think Mom's gonna have a hard time with it. I'm not sure she'll be able to handle things without you."

"Jamie, I know it's hard, but you can't let your mom dictate your life. You have your own life to live. Our marriage wasn't good for either her or me, and it especially wasn't good for you, Bud. We have to try something new, all of us. I hope to find something that makes me happy. I hope your mom does the same. Nothing will change between you and me, Jamie."

Sam didn't return to visit Joanna on the mental health ward. There was no reason to go back. There was nothing left to be said. Seeing him only upset her. Jamie returned to Portland to start his summer classes. He hadn't wanted to leave, but Sam talked him into going. According to Jamie, Joanna telephoned him at least once a day from the hospital, sometimes more. "Every time we talk, she starts to cry. I don't know how to help her."

"You can't help her, Jamie," Sam told him. "None of us can unless she's willing to help herself."

"I'm worried about her, Dad. She just tried to kill herself. Who's to say she won't try again."

Sam called Meryl Himes. She agreed to come out of retirement and take over the management of Big City Events until a new owner could be found. Sam met with his law partner, Jeff, to let him know that he would be taking what would most likely be a permanent leave of absence.

"What are you gonna do, Sam?" Jeff asked.

"I'm gonna do what I've wanted to do for a long time, rent a cabin on a river, somewhere remote. I plan to write the novel I've put off for the past twenty-two years."

Joanna entered a two-month rehabilitation program for patients with difficult-to-manage mental health issues. The goal was to detox her off drugs and alcohol and find the proper medications and treatment approach to stabilize her moods. The hospital psychiatrist had secured a bed for her in the program. "Without this intervention, Joanna, your prognosis is not good. This disorder," the doctor spared her no room for misunderstanding, "can take twenty years off your life if untreated."

While Joanna entered the rehab program in Woodinville, a small bedroom community north of Seattle, Sam said goodbye to his law firm. He walked away quietly, without a big fuss. Jeff threw a small going-away party for him. His associates told him how much they'd miss him. His long-term clients told him how sorry they were to see him go.

Sam's colleagues called to wish him the best. "If you come back and you're looking to join a law firm, come see us," law partners from other firms told him. Martha, his longtime assistant, decided to retire when Sam left. Sam took her to lunch and gifted her with tickets for a two-week European cruise for her and her husband. Her eyes spilled over when she opened the card and saw the tickets. She wished him well and made him promise to stay in touch. He said he would.

Now he was waiting for the ferry to take him across Puget Sound to a place he'd never been, that he knew nothing about. He was trading his multi-million-dollar home on the lake for a rustic cabin on the river at Gus's Fishing Hole. His thoughts were interrupted by the announcement that the ferry would begin boarding. He got back into his SUV and started the engine. He drove his Land Rover onto the ferry, facing south. He barely felt the tug as the ferry pulled away from the dock. He watched as the Edmonds shoreline became smaller and smaller. Ahead, he could faintly make out the Kingston ferry terminal—a symbol, he thought, a passage, a new beginning.

The ferry glided smoothly into the Kingston slip and docked. Sam followed the departing cars and turned right onto Highway 104, heading west. He crossed Hood Canal and eventually merged onto Highway 101, heading south and then again onto Highway 112, just south of Port Angeles on the western edge of the Olympic Peninsula. The two-lane highway became a tangle of corkscrew turns, with thick forest growth on the inland side and the coastline on the right, which offered panoramic views of the Strait of Juan de Fuca through the thinning trees. Sam could see two huge barges heading out to sea in the distance. A cruise ship coming into the Port of Seattle from Alaska was slipping by in the opposite direction.

He drove through the tiny towns of Clallam Bay and then Sekiu, more of a marina and RV park than an actual town. He saw a highway sign indicating the Makah Indian Reservation and Neah Bay forty miles ahead. "Visitors welcome," another sign read. On the coastal side of the highway, farms began to emerge, old farmhouses and weathered barns, vegetable gardens, and hay fields, most with views of the Strait of Juan de Fuca. He wound his way to the tiny town of Crystal Bay, a bustling last stop for tourists, boaters, and fishermen on their way to other places. It was where he and Bobby had met Skeeter in The Tavern weeks earlier.

Sam stopped at the local grocery store and picked up a few items—eggs, milk, coffee, bread, butter—staples he'd need for simple meals. He intended to catch most of his dinners at the fishing hole on Gus's property. He steered his SUV south, back onto Highway 112, groceries in tow. Glancing once in his rearview mirror, Sam set his sights on what lay ahead.

37

IT TOOK A BIT OF HUNTING TO FIND THE DIRT ROAD OFF THE HIGHWAY that led to Gus's Fishing Hole. Skeeter told Sam it was about three miles south of Crystal Bay on Highway 112 and about five miles east down a dirt road that wove through the forest and over a ridge. The turnoff was easy to miss, just a nondescript dirt road carved from tire traffic over the years. It was bumpy and rough. Sam missed it the first time and had to turn around. The road cut through the forest where Eastern hemlock, Sitka spruce, and Pacific yew flourished and led inland away from the coastline. Years ago, someone had cleared the trees, leaving just enough room for the road to wind through. Dappled light from the late afternoon sun filtered through the tall branches. Creeping Jenny and other low-growing plants carpeted the forest floor. Lilly of the valley, ferns, hydrangeas, hostas, and Japanese Spurge speckled the scenery like a painter had smudged them into the background with a delicate finger. Occasionally, the forest receded away from the roadside, creating space for small meadows of grass and wildflowers.

About two miles inland, the road wound upward to the crest of a small ridge and then down the back side to where the forest began to thin out until it opened into a valley of fields and meadows. The trees had receded to allow a basin of fertile farmland to thrive. A sign on which someone had carved the words, "No Trespassing-Private Property," hung from a wooden arch constructed over the dirt road. A metal gate hung between the posts of the arch to deter trespassers from coming any further. At the site where the arch stood was a wide turnaround area formed by curious motorists over the years, drivers wandering too far inland and needing to turn back toward the highway.

Sam pulled over. He turned off the engine and stepped out of the Land Rover. He wanted to get a better view of the valley. It was picturesque, like a postcard. Nestled deep in the forest, miles from the nearest neighbor, the setting had a magical quality, a peacefulness, a feeling of solitude. The North Fork Sekiu River was visible off in the distance meandering west toward its destination, Puget Sound. Far off at the valley's edges, the forest stood guard like a row of sentries, forming a barrier to shelter the farmland, keeping it hidden from the rest of the world. Across the valley, situated at the forest's edge, Sam could make out what he assumed was Gus's Fishing Hole. From where he stood, it looked more like a farm. He remembered Skeeter telling him and Bobby, "If there's a heaven for fishermen, Gus's is it." A sense of anticipation came over him. He could write here. Gus's Fishing Hole was the place he'd been dreaming of.

While he stood there, taking in the view and feeling the peacefulness of the surroundings, something caught Sam's attention out of the corner of his eye—movement. Someone or something was in the woods to his right. He instinctively swung around to face, whomever or whatever was there. He felt a surge of adrenalin. He hadn't been expecting to run into anyone so far out.

As he stood posed to move, a horse stepped out of the trees and into the clearing. The horse was almost the size of a Clydesdale, black with white spots. Long, white, feathery hair that started at his knees hung to the ground. His mane and tail, both black, were equally spectacular; his mane, lifted by the breeze, flowed out behind him as he walked into the clearing. Almost to the ground, his tail remained sturdy, nearly erect with confidence. His grooming was meticulous like he was about to enter a show arena. He was the most magnificent horse Sam had ever seen except in pictures. There was no lead rope or harness on him. He was completely free.

When he spotted Sam, the horse stopped and whinnied slightly, giving a toss of his head, causing his mane to flow away from his neck. He strode a few steps into the clearing to grab a tasty mouthful of leaves from a low-hanging tree. He chewed, unconcerned with Sam.

Somewhere back in the woods, Sam heard a dog barking. "Ahh," he thought, "someone must be coming. The horse must have gotten loose somehow." The barking was getting closer. It wasn't a threatening bark; it sounded playful and excited. Sam watched the clearing, waiting, unsure. Dogs in a backcountry like this might be vicious, trained to scare off trespassers. Sam turned to head back to his Land Rover. As he was about to climb in, the dog trotted out into the clearing from the same forest path the horse had come from.

He was one of those dogs that looked like he should belong to a kid. He was medium-sized, shaggy, and wiry, with ash-brown fur and golden eyes. Sam recognized him as a Berger Piccard Shepard. He was the same breed as the dog in the *Winn-Dixie* movie. Sam and Jamie had watched that movie many times when Jamie was young. The dog stopped next to the horse upon seeing Sam. He barked a couple more times, curiously, sizing up Sam.

"Hey pal," Sam tried to sound non-threatening. "Are you friendly?"

Sam worried the horse might run off through the woods, back toward the highway. He didn't know much about horses, and this wasn't just any horse; this horse was one and a half times the size of an average horse. If he could find a rope in his trunk, he might be able to slip it over the horse's neck, but then what? And what about the dog? It didn't appear to be a threat, but if Sam tried to approach the horse, he wasn't sure how the dog would respond.

While standing there trying to decide what to do, a woman in her early thirties stepped through the trees and into the clearing to join her animals. Sam did a double-take. To say she was beautiful would be an understatement; mesmerizing came to Sam's mind. She had a mystique, an aura, unlike any woman Sam had ever seen.

She had thick, dark, chestnut curls that tumbled loosely below her shoulders to the middle of her back, with short fly-away wisps that framed her face. There was a wildness about her, windswept, alluring. She looked out from dark brown eyes that took Sam in before he could get his bearings. Her olive complexion was flawless and smooth, without makeup. Her looks were effortless, natural. She was about five-foot-five, slim, and fit like an athlete. She reminded Sam of Dryads from Greek mythology, nymphs of trees and forests, soft and delicate but with great strength and power.

She wore a loose-fitting white dress made of soft fabric, and necklaces of different lengths made of silver and turquoise adorned her neck. Bracelets of braided leather and beads decorated her wrists and forearms. She wore buckskin boots, worn and tattered and trimmed with fringe strung with delicate turquoise beads.

She came to stand beside the horse. The breeze played with her hair. She brushed it away from her face. The dog watched her for cues. She gazed curiously at Sam. He felt that she knew everything there was to know about him without knowing anything about him. She held his gaze momentarily, then turned away, back to the forest. She made a soft clucking noise, and the horse turned and followed her. The dog trotted behind. None of them looked back.

"Wait, don't go," the words came out before Sam could stop them. Whether she heard him or not, Sam didn't know; the threesome disappeared around a bend in the path and was gone. Sam walked toward the spot where they'd been, the horse, the dog, and the woman. He peered down the trail, but they were nowhere to be seen.

PART IV

ESME

38

HER NAME WAS ESMERELDA HORVAT. SHE WAS THE DAUGHTER OF
Elena and Bo Horvat and the granddaughter of Django and Analetta
Horvat. She was Roma, a true black blood, considered by her people
to be gifted. She came from a long line of circus entertainers, starting
with her great grandfather, Vano Horvat, a tightrope walker for the
Ringling Brothers and Barnum and Bailey Circus.

In 1918, when he was ten, Vano immigrated from Bulgaria
to America with his family. They came by boat, past the Statue of
Liberty, and landed at Ellis Island. His family found New York City
as unwelcoming of Romani people as Bulgaria had been. Treated as
outcasts, undesirables, shooed out of restaurants, refused work and
lodging, and left to scour for food in the garbage bins behind small
eateries and bakeries, Vano's family struggled to survive. Vano's father was arrested shortly upon landing in New York for shoplifting,
having grabbed a slab of meat hanging near the entrance of a local
butcher shop so he could feed his family.

After traveling by horse-drawn caravan across the country with
other Romani immigrants from Bulgaria and Serbia, camping in
the forests during the winter, and journeying in small groups when
the weather allowed, Vano's family migrated to Washington State.

After two years of back-breaking work on the docks while living in cramped quarters in run-down tenement housing in Seattle's Central District, Vano's father was able to purchase a small plot of land that lay tucked away in a remote valley east of the tiny town of Crystal Bay on the Olympic Peninsula. There they set up farming.

When Vano was sixteen, he ran away to escape the doldrums of farming and headed to Seattle, where he hopped a circus train heading east. The circus proved to be his haven. It was the tightrope that captured his interest. By the time he was twenty-two, he was the main draw of the circus, able to perform death-defying feats on a thin wire high above the ground. He married his tightrope partner, Tina, also Roma, and together they had three children. Only their youngest son, Django, stuck around to become a part of the circus. Their two older children became disillusioned with circus life. They wanted to live in a bustling city and make their way, far removed from the migratory life of their parents.

Django was soft-spoken with a gentle nature. He had no desire to make his name as a stuntman, performing death-defying acts on a high wire or trapeze. It was the dog and horse act that Django fell in love with. The head trainer was an old equestrian instructor with a special knack for relating to animals. His method was to develop trust with his animals to make them feel safe. He was patient and kind and worked in a slow, methodical manner. He carried on conversations with his animals and rewarded them when they progressed. He didn't allow whips when training his animals; he used small flags on the end of long poles that he would gently brush over the horse's body to introduce a touch or redirect a movement.

The trainer began letting Django assist him during his training practices when Django was just ten years old. He taught Django everything he knew. In 1954, when the trainer suddenly died of a heart attack, Django, at seventeen, found himself head circus trainer for the dog and pony show, a favorite among the audience.

It was around this time that the circus changed. The eighteen-ton big top tent with its pennants that flew from its peaks, with its heat, dust, and tanbark, came down for the last time after its final performance in Baltimore. It had become too expensive and labor-intensive to maintain. Venues such as sports or concert arenas replaced the big top. While the circus still traveled from city to city by train, gone was the excitement that Django and the other circus performers anticipated, the side shows and parades that drew the crowds during the assembly of the colossal canvas tent.

Django fell in love during that time, so what happened to the circus didn't much affect him. It was Analetta that stole his attention. She was sixteen, from a long line of Serbian Romas. She was fair-skinned with jet-black hair and piercing black eyes. She immigrated to America as a toddler with her parents and grandparents to escape persecution by Tito and guerilla fighters who instituted a reign of terror throughout her homeland, Serbia, that resulted in the murder of over 20,000 Romani people, including Roma children who were marched out of their schoolhouses and executed.

Analetta's family settled in Pittsburg. Being unable to afford to purchase farmland, Analetta's grandfather and father took inner city factory jobs. They were discriminated against and shunned. Analetta was made fun of, ridiculed, and called names when she entered school. She had difficulty learning English. Her teachers reprimanded her if she accidentally spoke in her native tongue.

She left school without graduating and, at sixteen, talked her way into a job with the circus repairing sewing machines when it stopped in Pittsburg for a two-day performance. As a bonus, Analetta was a superior seamstress. To a circus operation, her skills were valuable. She spent her days repairing sewing machines that broke down and mending and sewing costumes.

Without trying she won Django's heart. Even growing up in America, Analetta found it challenging to assimilate into American culture. She often slipped into her native Serbian language that her grandparents and parents spoke at home, making it difficult for others to understand her. Django found her charming. He felt protective of her and wanted to cushion her from the cruelty

Romani immigrants often experienced at the hands of the Gadjo, non-Roma people.

Django and Analetta married in 1959 when Django was twenty-two, and Analetta was nineteen. They dreamed of having three or four children and settling on Django's grandparents' farm, far away on Washington's Olympic Peninsula. But as life sometimes happens, Analetta lost two pregnancies within the next two years. It broke her heart, and she didn't want to try for more babies. But when they least expected it, Analetta became pregnant again. She feared that her body would reject her baby, that her heart would break once more. But the heartbreak never came. Nine months later, Analetta delivered a healthy eight-pound boy who they named Bo.

Bo grew up loving the circus. By the time he was fifteen, he had become a trapeze artist, the aerialist, the flyer who swings and jumps high above the ground, from one bar to another or to a catcher, another aerialist who catches him in mid-air while hanging from a second trapeze. Bo was on target to become the best aerialist in the circus. He was young, fearless, and fit. While muscular, he was lightweight and easy for the catcher to catch. Bo never allowed himself to become distracted. He kept his eye on the prize—until Elena arrived at the circus wanting a job.

Elena swept Bo away like a fallen leaf in an autumn breeze. She was the most beautiful girl Bo had ever seen, fifteen, a black blood Roma. Five-foot-five with a body trim and fit, she was natural and exotic for her age. Her long chestnut hair cascaded down her back in untamed curls that gave her a bohemian, wild look. She donned traditional Roma attire, colorful sashes, head scarves, skirts and peasant blouses called *ie* and *camasa,* and necklaces of gold coins. Bangles and bracelets of silver and gold adorned her forearms. She was unencumbered, free, both spiritually and physically. She said what she thought and wasn't afraid to stick up for her ideas, even if they went against the grain of others. Bo compared her to an untamed Mustang running wild. She attracted admirers wherever she went.

Elena was a psychic, a seer. She read palms and tarot cards, a skill her aunt taught her. Those who knew her, however, wondered if she'd inherited more than just knowledge—perhaps an extraordinary power. She had an uncanny ability to look past a person's persona deep into their psyche. By the time Elena was fourteen, she could focus on a stranger, someone she'd never met before, look deep into their eyes, and channel information she couldn't have known. She could tell the most intimate things about people whose palms or tarot cards she read, their fears, desires, and secrets. They'd gasp and question how! No one knew for sure if she was just very good at guessing one's psychic journey or if she had a unique sense, a psychic ability. Elena claimed the latter, that she was gifted.

From the moment they saw each other, Bo and Elena were captivated. They shared a love for adventure and freedom of soul and spirit. They threw caution to the wind, allowing their youthful desires to rule their emotions. They'd sneak out at night and find somewhere removed, an old barn on a nearby farm, a secluded shack on the pier, or a place by a river. They'd spend the night wrapped in each other's arms, making love, talking, laughing, and dreaming of their future together.

They never thought about the consequences of their love, to be careful, and take protective measures. When Elena was just sixteen, and Bo was eighteen, she became pregnant. Bo went to his parents, Django and Analetta, for advice. "Do you love her?" Django asked.

"Yes." There was no doubt in Bo's mind. Elena was his forever girl.

"Then marry her," Django concluded.

They married with their family of circus entertainers in attendance. Elena wore the beautiful costume designed for the performer who rode atop the lead elephant, and Bo wore the ringmaster's top hat. In 1981, three months before Elena turned seventeen, she delivered a seven-pound girl with a combination of looks from both Bo and Elena, Bo's dark olive skin and Elena's dark piercing brown eyes. Bo and Elena were mesmerized by their tiny baby. "She came from us, from our love," Elena proclaimed. Elena wrapped a scarf around her chest and carried the baby, who they named Esmerelda, close to her during the day. If the baby became fussy or squirmy in the carrier, there was never a shortage of circus performers to hold and rock her.

The baby became known as Esme by her circus family. As she grew, she had the run of the circus and was loved by all. Even at an early age, Esme would slip away from the watchful eye of Elena and Bo. She might be found in the clown arena, sitting atop a clown's shoulders as they prepared to launch a comrade from a cannon or holding a hoop for dogs to jump through in Django's training tent, or sitting atop a massive elephant in the arms of a performer.

As time passed, Bo made his name as the circus star, thrilling the audience and making them gasp and cover their eyes as he flew from the trapeze gracefully and effortlessly. Once when Esme was six years old, to her joy, Bo lowered the trapeze and strapped Esme into a harness attached to the high wire and allowed her to swing out over the arena. After that, she begged Bo to let her do it again and again.

Elena busied her days doing odd jobs around the circus, always with Esme close by, ready to help. It was Elena's fortune telling that Esme most looked forward to. Before each show, Esme helped her mother set up her booth. As patrons filed in, Elena read the fortunes of the excited circusgoers who came anxious to see the performers and to marvel at the daring acts, the costumes, the animals, and the clowns. Often, though, it was Elena's readings they would remember. Word of mouth spread. Elena's psychic abilities became a significant draw for the circus. Folks sought her out, paid to have her read their fortune, and raved about her uncanny ability to get it right.

Esme sat next to her mother during readings and carefully observed as Elena took the hand of a curious patron, turned it over, and interpreted the lines on the person's palm to reveal their past, present, and future. Esme watched and learned. By the time she was just nine years old, Esme had developed a knack for palmistry that, with enough practice, threatened to outshine even her mother's uncanny abilities.

Esme learned the art of reading tarot cards from her mother. Elena taught Esme to shuffle the cards seven times when prepping the deck and how to spread elaborate variations of the cards depending on the type of reading. From Elena, Esme learned to carefully interpret the cosmic energy that drives each person's psyche journey, the emotional self, the physical self, and the mind. Esme listened as Elena explained the prophecy of each card and the cosmic forces at play in a person's life. Even before she could read, Esme played with tarot cards, turning each one over and learning its meaning and prophesy.

"You're gifted," Elena told her. "You're a very old soul, Esme. You've lived many lives. You have powers you are yet to discover. Remember," Elena had lifted Esme's chin with her fingertips so that Esme was looking into her mother's eyes, "always use your powers wisely, but don't be afraid of your own strength."

39

ESME'S CHILDHOOD WAS EVERYTHING A CHILDHOOD SHOULD BE. SHE
had loving parents, grandparents, and a circus as her playground.
But when she was nine years old, tragedy struck. It was an evening
in early summer; the circus had completed its final performance in
Omaha. The packing and loading of equipment, animals, tents, and
costumes onto the circus train was complete. It was a time when the
performers could take a break, catch up on much-needed sleep, get
drunk, or write letters home to loved ones. Some performers chose
to stay in their living quarters while others gathered in the dining
cars at the back of the train to congratulate each other on a job well
done, to strum musical instruments, sing, dance, and celebrate. The
circus train pulled out, heading south for Kansas City. Bo and Elena
arranged for Django and Analetta to put Esme to bed in their car
while they joined the celebration at the back of the train.

It was never determined if the switch that controls the direction
of the rails malfunctioned or if it was human error, but as the circus
train gained momentum and was clamoring down the track at top
speed, another train traveling in the same direction, but from a
different route, collided with the back of the circus train, derailing
seven of its eighty cars. The seven derailed carriages spun off the

track in different directions, tossing down the embankment, rolling front-over-end until finally coming to a fiery stop. Thirty-three circus performers died in the crash, Bo and Elena among the deceased.

The news that carried the story claimed it was a miracle that more people didn't die in the crash. It was a godsend that none of the animals, all housed toward the front and middle of the train, were injured. To Esme, none of this mattered. Her mother and father were gone without even so much as a goodbye. Her life as she knew it ended that night. She fell into despair and became inconsolable, even to her grandparents.

Staying with the circus was too painful for Django, Analetta, and Esme. They were too grief-stricken to pick up where things left off. The beautiful fortune teller Elena was gone, never to interpret one's past and future again. The trapeze swung empty without Bo. Esme was despondent—she wouldn't eat or sleep and refused to let others comfort her. Django and Analetta decided to do what they had always wanted to do, but now under different circumstances. The three of them, Django, Analetta, and Esme, left the circus and settled in Washington, on the Olympic Peninsula, on the tiny farm first established by Django's grandfather. They took up farming while their hearts, heavy from grief and loss, slowly healed.

When Esme's parents were part of the circus, Esme learned how to play the fiddle. One of the cirky's, a laborer who helped construct the circus props and de-assemble them when the carnival was ready to move on, was a young Irishman who immigrated to America as a kid. His fiddle was the only thing he had left from his home country. The Irishman coveted it. In the evenings, he'd fiddle while performers and circus workers finished last-minute details for the next day's performance. The soft, sweet, merry sounds made by his bow would fill the air.

Esme loved how he would tuck the instrument under his chin and run the bow across the strings to make beautiful sounds. She'd sit beside him and listen. It delighted her. Over time, the Irishman taught her to play. He taught her how to position the fiddle under her shoulder instead of her chin so she could sing while playing. He showed her how to rosin the bow and read notes and bars of music. He taught her which notes belong to which strings and how to strum the bow in a down-and-up motion. By the time she was nine, Esme had mastered the basics of the fiddle. Within a short time, she played beginner songs, *Drunken Sailor* and *Little Liza Jane*.

The Irishman was among those killed in the deadly train crash that took the lives of Esme's parents. Before Django and Analetta took Esme and left the circus, a few performers brought the Irishman's fiddle to Esme. "Take this," they told her. "When you play it, let it remind you of the circus you loved, which brought you joy. Let it remind you of the good times."

The first few months after she arrived on the farm with her grandparents, Esme's grief and sadness felt at times like it might crush her. One day Django handed her the fiddle as she sat on the porch looking out at their farm. At first, she sat with it in her lap. Finally, she placed the fiddle in position and began to strum a few notes. She found it lifted her spirits ever so slightly. Each day, she played a little more. She remembered the lessons the Irishman had taught her. Analetta bought her a book of fiddling music, and Esme taught herself to play more complicated songs. Before long, she played more advanced pieces, *Old Joe Clark, Old Molly Hare,* and *Arkansas Traveler.* She'd walk around the farm with the instrument positioned at her shoulder and fiddle. The farm animals became accustomed to her instrument's sweet, lively sound. It created a soothing atmosphere for everyone on the farm.

Django brought Esme a Border Collie that someone from the nearby Makah Indian Reservation had to rehome. Esme and the dog became inseparable. She and Django trained the dog to do tricks when she played the fiddle, to stand on his back legs and turn in a circle as though he was dancing.

Django bought a couple of Gypsy Vanner draft horses known for their feathery hair hanging from their knees and hocks and beautiful free-flowing manes and tails. Initially bred in Ireland, the horses were the same breed used by Django's grandfather to pull their wagon and vardos when they caravanned from New York to Washington state years ago. Django used the draft horses on the farm to pull heavy wagons and other farm equipment. After a few years, he bred them and traded their foals to the Makah Indians for farm supplies.

Django and Esme trained their two Gypsy Vanners to do tricks; they became family pets. When she played her fiddle, the horses would shake their beautiful manes back and forth and lift one forelimb and then the other as though they were dancing. At the same time, the Border Collie would stand on his hind legs and dance in a circle. It reminded Esme of the circus when she used to help Django train the dogs and horses. Gus and Mary Toblar, the nearest neighbors to their west, whose farm was known as Gus's Fishing Hole, would come for the show and, along with Django and Analetta, would sit on the porch and watch and listen as Esme fiddled and the animals performed. They'd applaud and cheer. Over time, the smile returned to Esme's beautiful face.

Her Border Collie lived to be seventeen and died of old age when Esme was twenty-two. Django helped her bury him in a field under a tall bigleaf maple. Esme insisted Analetta leave the dog's blanket on the front porch after he died so his spirit would have a place to rest when he occasionally slipped back to visit the farm.

The Gypsy Vanners lived to be in their late twenties. Django held on to their last foal and kept it on the farm as a pet. Esme named the colt Homer—Homie for short. She let him follow her around from the time he was born. He imprinted onto Esme and formed an attachment to her, much like her border collie. Homie followed Esme wherever she went, unbridled and untethered. He'd nuzzle her neck and dance when she played her fiddle. He'd shake his head back and forth, causing his beautiful long mane to whip around, and like his parents before him, lift his front legs one by one and hold out his hoofs in front of him.

40

DJANGO AND ANALETTA ENROLLED ESME IN SCHOOL PER THE STATE
requirement and saw to it that she attended class. The elementary
school was in the small town of Crystal Bay. The tiny seaport village
was named after the bay on whose shores it sat, which was more of
an indent along the coastline than an actual bay. Crystal Bay was a
bustling marina, the last place to gas up one's boat or to buy supplies
before making it to the very most western tip of the United States,
Neah Bay on the Makah Indian Reservation, and then on out to the
waters of the Pacific Ocean.

Slightly south of the town lay Shipwreck Point, a three-mile
stretch of open beach that attracted tourists and visitors from near
and far. Visitors to the beach could expect to catch sight of marine
life, including porpoises, seals, sea lions, and otters. Mostly it was
a haven for whale watching. Whether it was because of visitors on
their way to Shipwreck Point who'd stop off in Crystal Bay for a
beer or a meal or to spend the night in one of the beachfront motels
or because of boaters who came ashore for last-minute supplies and
groceries, Crystal Bay was a bustling town.

Its less than three thousand residents made their living either
from the commercial fishing industry, whose businesses dotted the

shore along Highway 112 or from the tourists who found Crystal Bay a charming place to visit. To the outside eye, it looked like the perfect seaside town. Visitors loved to meander up and down Main Street and visit the quaint shops, including a coffeehouse, bakery, ice-cream store, and eateries. An old-fashioned general store stood in the center of Main Street next to the courthouse. It sold everything from groceries—primarily canned goods and packaged meals—to fishing supplies, farming tools, and hiking gear. It was partly a museum, displaying old farming equipment and fishing paraphernalia from years back and old photos dating back to 1893, when the town was established. The Tavern, situated on the beach next to the marina, took in the most business of any facility in the community. Its iconic burgers and beers made Crystal Bay noteworthy.

Anyone sticking around long enough soon discovered that the town of Crystal Bay was different from what it appeared to visitors. Its true nature was another story altogether. It was a close-knit community, a place where everyone knew everyone. Like most small towns, it was hard to keep a secret in Crystal Bay; nobody's business was private, and what wasn't known was filled in with gossip.

There was very little diversity among the residents of Crystal Bay. The townsfolk were Caucasian, lower-middle-class individuals who considered themselves hard-working, honest Americans— church-going people who were always ready to lend a hand or help a neighbor down on their luck unless the neighbor was undesirable. They held on to conservative values and fought hard to maintain the status quo. There was little room for anyone who didn't fit in or who had ideas that challenged those of the majority. The Crystal Bay residents were only welcoming to people who matched their image. As a town, they banded together to deter outsiders from settling there. The nearby Makah Indian Reservation was often a bone of contention for the Crystal Bay city council members.

Esme had never attended public school and had always done her school lessons with the teacher who traveled with the circus. When Django and Analetta enrolled Esme in fifth grade at the Crystal Bay elementary school, they hoped it might help her adjust and get her mind off her sorrow and the grief of losing her parents. Still, their experience warned them that probably wouldn't be the case. They'd grown accustomed to being treated like outcasts since leaving the circus. It was a known fact among Roma immigrants that they weren't always welcome in America. Roma people were used to racist slurs, racially motivated attacks, police abuse, segregation, hate speech, and hate crimes committed against them.

The attitudes that prevailed toward Romani people were no different in Crystal Bay than in mainstream America. When asked what the residents of the town thought of Romas, words like "thieves," "pickpockets," and "liars" were heard. When the Crystal Bay locals heard that a family of "Gypsies" had moved in close by, they braced for the worst. Shop owners kept a close eye on their cash registers when Django or Analetta came in to shop, and restaurant owners were careful to ensure that the Horvats didn't try to sneak out without paying their bill. When Analetta and Django walked down the streets of Crystal Bay, sometimes with Esme, the townfolk barely acknowledged them, talked about them behind their backs, avoided them, and did little to welcome them. Only Skeeter at The Tavern welcomed them to the town.

Django and Analetta knew there was little they could do to prevent the prejudice that prevailed in Crystal Bay. They knew the townspeople tossed around rumors that Romas could cast spells and put curses or jinxes on people. For the most part, Django and Analetta stayed to themselves on their farm and went into town only for necessities. They didn't cause trouble for anyone and weren't disrespectful, but they worried that the Gadjo in Crystal Bay wouldn't return the courtesy. They worried about the problems Esme might encounter while at school when they weren't there to protect her.

The elementary school in Crystal Bay was small, with just over sixty students. The stern, middle-aged principal, Jeff Thompson, had been a teacher for ten years before moving into the principal position for both the Crystal Bay elementary and middle schools. He was a man who liked to do things his way. He wasn't a big fan of change, and he feared diversity. He made it a point to be on a first-name basis with city council members. He felt his responsibility was to pull back on "radical" progression in his community. He didn't believe that Crystal Bay was where "those people" should be moving to. "It's just not fair to 'those' folks," he would explain with feigned empathy to the sheriff or anyone who would listen. "They need a place with their own people, where they feel like they belong."

The sheriff, a somewhat reasonable man, would question, "Who are you referring to, Jeff?"

"Oh, you know," Jeff Thompson would reply. "Kids from the reservation, immigrants, illegals, families that just don't belong, who have different values. We can't stand by and have our kids influenced by these outsiders."

Jeff Thompson immediately disliked Esme when Django and Analetta showed up to enroll her in school. He didn't trust her. "For God's sake," he lamented to a school board member whom he telephoned that evening to complain to. "Everyone knows you can't trust a Gypsy. What's to become of the community if this is allowed?"

He tended to hire educators who believed as he did. He thought his teachers were an excellent team, "hard-working, honest folks," he liked to brag, "who are shaping good-hearted American kids who will be valuable to society." Based on their prevailing attitudes, it wasn't surprising that the school could have done a better job introducing Esme to other students and helping her integrate into the school environment. As a result, students ignored her, excluded her, and refused to invite her to join them in the lunchroom or play-ground. Esme was disregarded and soon lost in the shuffle.

One girl, Shelby, was the ringleader in Esme's combined fourth and fifth-grade class. The locals perceived her family as wealthy, con-sidering the average income in the area. Her father was a rancher and had a lot of influence with city council members and the police chief. Because of her parents' social standing in the community and Shelby's sense of entitlement that came with it, the other kids automatically deferred to her as their leader.

Esme threatened Shelby, mainly because the other girls in the classroom were fascinated by her. They wanted to touch the pretty dress Analetta made special for Esme's first school day. They wanted to play with her long unruly hair and get as close to her as possible. Shelby refused to participate. She wasted no time planning her strat-egy for getting Esme out of the way.

It wasn't problematic for Shelby to turn the other girls against Esme, who was, after all, ethnic, a Roma. Everyone knew Romas were thieves and con artists, as her parents had warned her when Shelby told them Esme had enrolled in her classroom.

"Where do you think the word 'gypped' came from?" Shelby's dad asked her. "Those folks will rip you off. Mark my word. Keep your distance from that little knacker. She'll be nothin' but trouble."

"Not to mention," Shelby's mother warned, "Gypsies cast spells and put bad luck hoaxes on people. Stay away from her, Shelby, don't have nothin' to do with her." Within a few days, all the girls in her class ignored Esme. They went out of their way to avoid her, refusing to let her join in on the playground or sit at their table in the cafeteria at lunchtime.

The boys in Esme's classroom were at first smitten with Esme, mesmerized by her looks. She looked exotic, like a foreign princess. The way they expressed it was to taunt and tease her, vying for her attention. Eventually, though, it got out of hand, and the taunts became more extreme and cruel while they tried to one-up each other. It became a game for the boys to make fun of her looks, olive skin, and hair. They called her "Gypsy" and "pikey."

Esme learned to keep to herself. She became shy and quiet to avoid bringing attention to herself. But things didn't improve for her. By the time she progressed to the sixth grade, all the students in her grade ignored her and went out of their way to avoid her. She spent her time at school alone.

One teacher, an older woman who had taught for over thirty years, took Esme under her wing. Often, she would invite Esme to her classroom to help with small chores—erasing the chalkboard, wiping down tables, filling water cups—while the other kids played on the playground during recess or lunch break. The teacher frequently told the other teachers and Jeff Thompson that Esme was struggling and spoke of how the other kids often bullied her.

"Well, maybe that's what you see," Jeff Thompson responded, "but I've had that girl in my office on many occasions for interfering with another student, stealing school supplies, hiding books, you name it. Just the other day, a boy in her class discovered that she'd stolen his pencils from his backpack. That little knacker wouldn't admit to it. I made her sit in my office for a week during recess while the other students played outside, but she still wouldn't fess up. She's sullen and difficult. It's because she's a Gypsy. They aren't to be trusted. They'd steal from their own mother."

Esme didn't understand why the students hated her. She remembered her circus family and how loved she felt around the circus performers. Her heart ached with missing her parents and circus family. She longed to feel her mother's touch. Thinking about Elena, how she could read someone's palm or tarot cards or know their whole past and future by looking deep into their eyes, was comforting to Esme. She wished her mother would have passed her secrets on to her before she died, that she'd inherited Elena's power.

Esme hated school. She thought it was a waste of her time and figured anything that needed learning could occur outside of school just as easily. She'd much rather be on the farm with her grandparents, her dog, and horses, wandering the forest or fishing in the river with Django. She took to leaving school during school hours, against the rules. She'd cross Highway 112 and head for the beach.

One day, she found an injured seagull and watched while other seagulls dragged the poor bird through the sand, trying to get it to fly. When the seagulls realized the wounded bird wouldn't recover they flew away. Esme picked up the injured bird and gently carried it back to the beach, away from the lapping waves. She sat beside the bird, singing songs her grandmother taught her of home so far away. When the seagull finally died, Esme carried it to the shoreline and gently placed it in the sand so the waves could take it out to sea. "Goodbye, friend," she whispered, "I'll see you in the next life."

41

DJANGO AND ANALETTA WERE AWARE OF THE BULLYING ESME ENDURED
daily at school. Several times during Esme's first couple of years at
Crystal Bay Elementary School, Django visited Jeff Thompson to
insist that the taunts and name-calling levelled at Esme stop. Each
time, Jeff Thompson copped an attitude and turned the blame back
onto Esme. "She's incorrigible," he claimed. "Esme leaves the school
grounds when she's not supposed to, comes back to class late, and
takes things from other students that don't belong to her. We've tried
to get her to stop, but she won't. It would seem to me," he concluded
during one of his meetings with Django, "that you and your wife
might want to enforce a bit more discipline at home. That's a good
place to start."

When Django heard that one of Esme's classmates accused
her of stealing pencils from his backpack, he'd had enough. He
demanded that Jeff Thompson arrange a meeting with the boy who
accused Esme of the theft and his parents. Django threatened to
go to the school board and then the State Board of Education if it
didn't happen.

When the meeting finally occurred a couple of days later in
Jeff Thompson's office, Django asked the boy, in the presence of his

parents, what reason he had for accusing Esme of stealing from him. Django was gentle with the boy, soft-spoken, and non-demanding. The boy hemmed and hawed around and finally admitted that he didn't have a reason other than that his parents—he looked to both of them for support when he said it—told him that Gypsies were thieves. He finally admitted that he later found his pencils in his coat pocket. He'd forgotten he'd put them there earlier.

An uncomfortable silence settled over Jeff Thompson's office then. The boy's parents and Jeff Thompson didn't have much to say. They all fidgeted and didn't want to look at Django when he stood to leave. Before he left, Django reminded the boy, his parents, and Jeff Thompson that falsely accusing someone of a crime is considered libel and punishable by law. "If I hear of anyone bullying my granddaughter and falsely accusing her of a crime, I'll take it to the highest level to ensure justice is done."

Back at their farm that evening, Django and Analetta talked to Esme over dinner. They offered to move Esme to another school, maybe the school on the reservation or the one in Clallam Bay. They told Esme to sleep on it and let them know in the morning what she wanted to do.

That night Esme had a dream. She dreamed that her mother, Elena, entered her room and sat on the edge of her bed, as she had done every night before she died. Esme felt her mother's presence in her room, her closeness and warmth. "I have a gift for you," she told Esme.

"What is it, Mama?" Esme asked excitedly.

"It was my special gift; now I'm giving it to you. It's the ability to *see*, Esme, beyond the surface. When you look into a person's eyes, you can see their soul. You'll see their thoughts, dreams, fears, and desires. It will give you great power. Don't be afraid of it, but use it wisely." It was the same advice Elena had given Esme shortly before she died. Elena smiled at Esme then. "When you awake in the morning, you'll feel strong, warrior strong." Then she was gone.

Esme awoke the following day. She remembered the dream, remembered her mother's smile, her words. She dressed and went downstairs, and found her grandparents in the kitchen. "I don't need to go to a different school; I'll stay where I am."

"But Esme …" Analetta started to argue.

"Mama said that I'm strong like a warrior." Esme proclaimed. "I'll be okay."

After the dream, Esme felt powerful, more capable of withstanding her classmates' meanness toward her. Following the meeting with Django, where it became clear that Esme did not steal from another student, Jeff Thompson warned the teachers not to allow other students to bully Esme in their presence. "We want to avoid problems from the higher-ups," he'd told them. What Jeff Thompson didn't do was make it a policy that bullying was not to be tolerated at all. As a result, students continued to pick on Esme out of earshot of adults.

When Shelby, who led the pack of Esme's bullies, was turning twelve, she came to school with birthday invitations for every girl in the sixth-grade classroom except for Esme. Shelby promised it would be a grand party to be held in the public park on the beach. The weather report predicted it would be sunny and mild on Saturday, the day of the party. There would be balloons, games, an inflatable trampoline shaped like a castle, ice cream and cake.

It was all the girls in Esme's class talked about all week. Shelby made a point to bring it up whenever Esme was within earshot. When the other girls in the classroom saw Esme coming, they lowered their talk to a whisper, looking her way now and then to see if she could hear. Some girls felt ashamed for how they treated Esme, but no one was willing to challenge Shelby. Everyone kept still or looked the other way.

On Friday afternoon, the day before the party, Shelby cornered Esme in the hallway outside their classroom. "Too bad I couldn't invite you to my party, Esme. My mom doesn't want a pikey spoiling things. She said you know how to cast spells and can't be trusted, not to mention you steal. My mom told me you'd jinx my party if you came."

Esme was weary of Shelby's taunts; she wanted to end them. She remembered her mother's words in her dream: "I'm giving you my special gift, Esme. The ability to *see*. Don't be afraid to use it." Esme looked directly into Shelby's eyes as she had seen her mother do to others. She discovered she could see into Shelby's mind, deep into her psyche, and read Shelby like a book. She saw Shelby's frail ego, insecurities, jealousy, and fear.

Esme saw the writing on the wall. "Shelby," Esme said as she continued to look directly into Shelby's eyes, "nobody but you is going to spoil your party. You're the one putting a jinx on it, nobody else."

"You're just jealous you aren't invited. My party will be amazing."

Esme walked past Shelby back into the classroom. Shelby would need to learn her lessons the hard way.

That Saturday, the day of Shelby's party, started gloriously. The sun was out and felt warm enough to allow the girls to swim in the bay. Shelby's parents decorated the pavilion with crepe paper and balloons. A big "Happy Birthday" banner hung from the rafters—fancy birthday tablecloths and matching paper plates and cups decorated the picnic tables. A large sheet cake decorated with balloons and flowers in pink and yellow icing and Shelby's name scrolled in blue icing was sitting in the middle of one of the picnic tables. Shelby's parents set aside a picnic bench for birthday presents wrapped with pretty tissue and ribbons. The party guests were noisy, laughing and calling out to each other, excited for the fun ahead.

At first, the party was everything Shelby had promised until the wind began to blow. The clouds moved in from the west rather quickly. No one noticed until the sun disappeared. "Mom," Shelby whined, "do something! The wind is blowing all the decorations."

"It's okay, Shelby, it'll pass," her mother assured her. Her mother was wrong. Within minutes the wind picked up, clocking in with gusts of over fifty miles per hour. With the wind came the rain, a torrential downpour. Girls screamed and ran for the safety of the pavilion. The wind and the rain found them. The wind whipped through the pavilion, blowing presents off the bench, across the lawn, and out to sea. Howling gusts ripped crepe paper, banners, and table decorations from the pavilion and blew them away out of sight. The cake was set in motion and slid off the table, landing upside down on the pavilion's cement floor. The balloons that didn't pop from the force of the wind blew away out above the sea.

Lightening flashed across the sky, followed by loud crashes of thunder. The partygoers huddled together, screaming that they wanted to go home. Parents showed up out of nowhere to retrieve their children. Within twenty minutes, the storm blew the party to smithereens and then, as quickly as it came, subsided. The only thing left of the party was Shelby, who stood in the middle of the pavilion, soaking wet, the fancy hairdo that her mother had curled and set for her now limp and hanging in her eyes. There was no cake, no presents, no decorations, no guests to sing happy birthday, nothing. Shelby stood, staring out toward the bay. "This is Esme's doing," she wailed. "She put a jinx on my party. She's a witch, a Gypsy witch!"

Stories about Shelby's party spread around Crystal Bay, about how the storm forced the children to be rescued by their parents. It was such a shame—poor Shelby. But the main focus of gossip was Esme. "That Gypsy girl put a curse on the party, caused the whole mess," they hissed to each other at church on Sunday, in the diner, at the grocery store, at the gas pump. "She cornered poor Shelby in the hall at school last week and did some hocus pocus that put a jinx on Shelby's party. I tell ya, it was a sad day that Gypsy enrolled at school."

People who lived in the area were familiar with sudden storms that roll in from the sea. They weren't uncommon. At least on some level, people knew that Esme didn't cause the storm that blew in. But the people of Crystal Bay loved a good story, something to gossip about, something to divert attention away from the humdrum of everyday life, so the story spread, was embellished, and grew in size.

When Esme heard about Shelby's party, she wasn't surprised. When she'd looked deep into Shelby's eyes, she saw what was coming and tried to warn Shelby. Looking into Shelby's eyes, Esme knew what she had learned from her mother, Elena, before she died: a bad attitude can't result in a happy ending, that hate and mistrust festers and grows and eventually turns on the person who harbors it. Esme didn't even try to say this to Shelby, and Shelby would never have been able to hear it.

Following Shelby's party, the locals started calling Esme a witch behind her back. "That Gypsy witch ...," they'd say to each other under their breath. While the locals' hatred of Esme and her grandparents deepened, their name-calling grew quieter and more secretive. Shelby quit bullying Esme to her face and stopped making it a point to turn the other girls against her. They left Esme to herself without bothering her. The truth was Shelby, and the other girls feared Esme and what she might do to them if they tried to cause her more trouble.

By the time Esme got into middle school, things had quieted down for her. Her classmates didn't bully her to her face anymore. They'd gotten accustomed to having her around. They avoided and ignored her and left her to herself. Esme preferred it that way. She turned her attention to her studies and found she liked learning, loved reading, and solving problems. Esme was a good student. She got her assignments in on time, got good grades, and was quiet and attentive in class. Some of her teachers started to notice and appreciate that she wasn't disruptive, turned in her homework on time, and paid attention in class. A few teachers, on occasion, would even ask her to stay after class and help out with a particular project.

Toward the end of her middle school years, a few girls—a couple older than Esme and a few younger—started sitting at Esme's table during lunch. These girls, like Esme, were shunned by their classmates, made fun of, and bullied. They weren't beautiful, didn't have smooth and silky skin, didn't have "perfect" hair or bodies, or didn't wear the latest trend in clothes. These girls didn't get asked to the school dances or receive valentines and invitations to birthday parties. But when Esme looked into their eyes, she saw something real. These were girls learning early on how to be resilient, who would, Esme could see, become strong, empathetic women. She'd smile when she saw one of them approaching her in the school halls. They'd smile back. It was a fellowship that would continue through high school, a buffer for each of them in an otherwise hostile environment.

Esme and her grandparents continued to be a topic of conversation among the townsfolk. They'd share myths and mistruths about "Gypsies" with each other and insert the Horvats' names into their storytelling as if they were talking about them directly. Over time, Esme and her grandparents became notorious among the residents of Crystal Bay for things they'd never done, for accusations that weren't true. The townsfolk especially loved to talk about Esme. She was an object of fascination. With each passing year, Esme grew more beautiful and mysterious. She was a combination of her parent's traits: her father's strength and his dark-olive skin and intent, brown eyes, and her mother's compassion and her wild, dark hair and sultry, bewitching looks.

By the time Esme entered high school, no other girl in the school could arguably compete with her physical beauty, and most of the boys, and some grown men, secretly pined for her. While boys outwardly rejected her, reminding themselves that she was Roma and not anyone you'd ever be caught dead with, secretly they yearned for her, dreamed of possessing her, some even of running away with her, professing their love away from the scrutiny of Crystal Bay. A few thought about being her hero and standing up for her in front of their peers, but there was only one of her secret admirers who was brave enough to do so.

42

HIS NAME WAS TOM JOHNSON, AND HE WAS A MEMBER OF THE MAKAH Indian Nation. Tom met Esme when they were both freshmen in high school when they were fourteen. Tom's family had been living in Crystal Bay for the past year, where his father drove a delivery truck for a grocery store distribution center that delivered produce and other groceries from Port Angeles to grocery stores in Crystal Bay and other seaport towns along Highway 112.

Tom's father got the job after being laid off from the small fishery on the reservation where he'd worked for twelve years. The fishery went under when the owner suddenly died. Tom's family planned to return to the reservation when his father found work there among their people.

Like Esme, Tom was an outcast at Crystal Bay High School. At that time, he was the only American Indian who attended high school in Crystal Bay, and despite his agility and athleticism—he'd played left receiver on his high school football team when he lived on the reservation, and they typically made it into the division playoffs each year—the team excluded him from playing football for Crystal Bay High School. The senior players fought hard to keep him off the team. They didn't want some "res" kid taking a position that could go to one of them.

Their parents felt the same way. They went to the school board as a group, claiming that all positions on the football team were assigned before Tom signed up. They convinced the school board members that Crystal Bay High School couldn't afford the cost of supporting an extra player with uniforms and helmets. It was a flimsy excuse, but it sufficed. The school board voted four to three to exclude Tom from playing on the team, using budgetary constraints as the reason.

Like Esme, Tom often got bullied by kids at school. He was, after all, a "res" kid, an outsider. Tom kept to himself. He wasn't afraid of bullies; he wasn't afraid to defend himself if necessary, but he went out of his way to avoid problems. His father and grandfather taught him to use reason over force, walk away from trouble when possible, and respectfully treat others, even his enemies.

Like other boys at school, Tom was captivated by Esme's beauty but even more so by her mystique. It impressed him how she shielded herself against the gossip and remarks that followed her wherever she went. He met her by chance. One day, when Tom was fourteen, he rode out to Esme's grandparents' farm with his uncle, Dakota Hastings. The tribal council, of which Dakota was an elected official, had been granted custody by the Bureau of Land Management of several wild mustangs captured illegally and abused by their captors when the horses proved too difficult to break for ranch work.

Under *The Wild Free-Roaming Horses and Burros Act*, the Bureau of Land Management hoped to return the mustangs to the wild. However, the horses' conditions were grave. They were malnourished. Whips had been used to saddle-break them, and some were hobbled from tiny stress fractures on the front of their shins called bucked shins, and all of them were frenzied when approached by humans.

Dakota heard of Django's skill as a horse trainer in the circus and wanted to persuade him to board the horses and work with them to restore them to a healthy condition so that they could survive if released back to their natural environment. Dakota came prepared to bargain with Django. The Makah tribe, he offered, would provide hay and supplies needed to care for the horses, and pay for any other expenses caring for the horses might incur.

Django agreed to board the horses on his farm and care for them. Django and Esme, who worked alongside him in caring for the animals, took careful precautions not to domesticate the horses, to avoid touching them except when necessary, and to prevent bonding with them. The horses would survive better in the wild if they didn't lose their feral nature. When tamed, they lost their edge. Rather than using their hands, Django and Esme used the same small flags on the ends of long poles that Django had used with his circus animals to communicate with the mustangs and direct them in and out of the barn. After months, the horses were healthy, well-fed, and free of injury. They were ready to return to the wild.

Thus began a friendship between Django and the Makah tribal members. Django became known as an animal whisperer among members of the tribe who would often turn up at the farm with animals and fowl in need of rehabilitation or just a place to live out the remaining years of their life—cows too old to provide milk, horses too old to be of any use, injured fowl with broken wings or sprained necks, or chunks of their feet or talons maimed, horses that needed to be saddle broken or dogs that needed training.

The first time Tom drove with his uncle to Django's farm, he didn't know it was where Esme lived. When Esme came out of the farmhouse that morning, Tom stared in disbelief, not realizing that she was Django's granddaughter. He felt shy and didn't know what to say. It was Esme who approached him. She came down the steps, smiling, her border collie close in tow. She walked up to Tom, who was loitering around Dakota's pickup, and, without an introduction, asked, "Do you want to pet our Gypsy Vanners?"

After his first visit, Tom found excuses to ride along with members of the Makah Tribe whenever they drove to Django's farm. Even at his young age, Esme swept Tom away. He looked up to her and was awed by her. They began palling around together at school. After he got his driver's permit, Tom would drive his dad's old pickup truck the five miles through the forest to Esme's grandparents' farm. On weekends, he and Esme explored the nearby woods, played in the river and fields, fished, and climbed trees. Over time, Tom's presence at Esme's grandparents' farm became a natural occurrence. In the summers, Tom would often spend two or three days at a stretch with the Horvats. Analetta got in the habit of making Tom a bed on the couch at night and setting an extra place for him at the table.

As time passed, an enduring friendship developed between Tom and Esme, a lasting bond. As their relationship deepened, Tom hesitated to return to the reservation. He wanted to finish out high school in Crystal Bay. While recognizing Esme's strength, he felt protective of her. He knew she got bullied, they both did, for that matter, and he didn't feel it was right to abandon her to face her bullies alone.

Like his parents and grandparents, Tom adhered to a philosophy of peace and gratitude. Even at his young age, Tom was spiritual and introspective. He loved nature and had great respect for the earth and her bounties. Like his father and uncle, Tom dreamed of earning a place as a paddler in his people's yearly canoe journey through ocean waters to visit other Indian tribes along the Washington and British Columbia coast. He took pride in his people's traditions and his American Indian heritage.

As was customary among his people, Tom believed in powerful spiritual forces capable of creating unity and equilibrium in the world. He grew up believing in *Hohoeapbess*, two mythical characters said to be the brothers of the sun and moon. According to Makah legend, these fabled characters transform ancient spiritual forces into people, animals, and landscapes on earth that have strong healing capabilities and that create balance and harmony wherever they are. Even when they were kids, Tom sensed a spirit emanating from Esme, a strength behind her that he interpreted as coming from a special *Hohoeapbess* blessing. Tom recognized a powerful healing source in Esme and saw her as one who brought tranquility and joy to her surroundings.

Tom believed Esme was more spiritual than even his grandmother, whom the Makah people revered as a shaman, a prophet, and a healer gifted with special powers. Tom's grandmother was honored by her people as the guardian of their cultural traditions.

Esme read Tom's palm once, and he listened as she told his life story to him precisely as things had happened. Even his grandmother couldn't do that. How did Esme do it, he wondered? She read his tarot cards and revealed personal information about him, his fears, his dreams, that were right on, things he'd never talked about to anyone before.

More than anything, Esme could see past the obvious, look deep into one's soul, and relate to all living things, animals, birds, plants, and trees, which made Tom know she was a seer. She connected to the earth itself. Esme could communicate with the soil in her garden. She could tell what it needed, lacked, or was getting too much of by digging deep into the ground with her bare, ungloved hands to feel the earth, listen to what it was telling her, what it was asking of her. In return, her garden produced succulent, healthy vegetables and herbs, and the fruit trees flourished with pears, cherries, and apples that fed them year-round.

When Esme was sixteen, an elderly Makah tribesman from the reservation showed up at the farm with a young female bald eaglet who'd been abandoned in her nest atop a telephone pole after some reckless and insensitive hunter took aim at the mother and killed her in mid-air. Esme took the young eaglet into her care. She fed the eaglet raw meat eight times a day, day and night, that she would tear into small bits and offer with an ungloved hand. She and Django constructed a nest for the eaglet on top of a tall post near the barn. Esme worked with the young bird daily, feeding and caring for it until the young eaglet mastered the art of flying. Esme never tried to tame the eaglet; instead, she hoped the bird would grow strong enough to take to the countryside and make her own way.

As the eagle matured, she began to fly farther away from the farm, sometimes disappearing for days. Then she would come soaring back toward the farm, where she'd perch in a nearby tree for a day or two before rising again into the sky. When she reached full maturity, the eagle nested in a tall Sitka Spruce in the field in the back of Esme's farm, out where the forest stood guard over the valley. She became a permanent fixture to the farm, frequently seen soaring high in the sky, diving for food in the river or the open fields behind the farm, gliding and dipping low over the barn before vanishing behind the tall trees lining the river.

Tom remembered stories his grandfather told him when he was very young of spirit guides and animal totems, the eagle being the most powerful among them. "The eagle," Tom's grandfather taught him, "is connected to the earth by her strong talons but can soar to great heights, keeping her resilient and in complete harmony with the universe." Esme reminded Tom of the eagles from his grandfather's stories. She was grounded to the earth but could soar higher than most people only dreamed of.

43

TROUBLE STARTED AGAIN FOR ESME WHEN SHE ENTERED HIGH SCHOOL.
This time, Mark Kipling, quarterback of the Crystal Bay High
School football team, was the ringleader of her torment. Whenever
Mark saw Esme coming down the halls at school, he'd call her
"Gypsy," "Little Witch Girl," or some other derogatory term or ra-
cial slang, loud enough for everyone around him to hear. When he
bullied Esme, it pumped him up and made others notice him. He
was the most popular kid in high school, and he could do no wrong
in the eyes of his fellow students.

Crystal Bay loved their high school football squad. For the past
few years, the locals had watched as the team became one to be reck-
oned with. Folks throughout Clallam County came out in droves
for every game to cheer the players on. By Esme's senior year, the
Crystal Bay High School football team had won all their division
playoffs. They were on target to win the state championship. It was
down to Crystal Bay and the opposing team to see who would take
home the coveted championship trophy.

The football team players were treated like superstars in the community. They got special privileges—free soft drinks at their favorite
fast-food hang-out and free movie tickets; even the local cops cut

them slack when they were caught speeding down Main Street or missed curfew. The players were admired for their cockiness, for the way they'd strut their stuff in the halls at school and on the streets in town.

Mark was the team's star player. He was a skilled leader on the field, known for carefully orchestrating plays that could tip the opposing team off balance and for his downfield throwing that kept his team advancing toward victory each game. Mark enjoyed holding the title of top dog at school and being glorified by the locals. Being the quarterback gave Mark his identity, a sense of self and allowed him to *be* someone. By all accounts, the locals agreed that Mark was the best thing to happen to Crystal Bay in years. It seemed there was nothing he could do that would turn public opinion against him—his status was secure.

Mark had a rough upbringing. He'd been raised by his dad ever since his mother ran away when Mark was five and his brother was just two. His mother had left one morning with no warning or even a goodbye to the boys, just climbed into the passenger side of a logging truck next to the driver and rolled away down the highway, never to be heard from again.

Mark lived with his dad and brother in a run-down house on Highway 112, just south of Crystal Bay. The house was nothing more than a musty and dank shack. The property was littered with trash and old cars. Used tires were piled in the yard. Long ago abandoned, the shell of an empty camper lay next to the house. A filthy, battered couch, moldy and tattered from years in the weather, stood center in the front yard. The grass had died long ago and was worn away to mostly dirt and a few tall weeds.

Mark's dad had always been a drinker. After his wife walked out on him, his drinking worsened. Over the years, he'd become known by the locals as a drunk. Some talked behind his back that it was no wonder his wife ran away; rumor had it that he beat her when he got drunk. Others said he drank because she left him. Either way, after she left, his rage turned to the boys. He raised Mark and his brother with an iron fist. Their dad didn't believe in talking. He communicated by connecting his fist to the side of his boys' heads when they fell out of line.

Mark hated Tom Johnson. If Tom was nearby and overheard Mark taunt Esme, he'd intervene and confront Mark in front of other students. It infuriated Mark that some good-for-nothing Indian, some punk from the "res," wasn't afraid to outwardly challenge him or show he cared about Esme. The truth was Mark also cared about Esme. In fact, he was secretly infatuated with her. Esme was Mark's own private fantasy. He couldn't let anyone know how badly he had it for her. He'd be the laughingstock among his friends and fellow team players. "That Gypsy?" they'd ask. "Are you crazy, man?" They'd spread it around that Mark, the big man on campus, had the hots for the "Gypsy witch." But deep down, Mark believed that Esme was the girl who would make him a better man.

Mark would sit in class when he was supposed to be paying attention to a math lesson or memorizing lines from *The Road Not Taken* by Robert Frost and daydream about Esme. He thought she was beautiful. He liked her calm attitude, the way she'd walk down the halls, ignoring the taunts and names she got called. She was different from the other girls at school. She didn't worry about her looks. She didn't flirt with boys or try to fit in. She wasn't silly like the other girls; she didn't scream, giggle, or mess with her hair. She didn't have to hang out in a group at all times to avoid being seen by herself. She was good with herself the way she was. Mark thought Esme was the finest thing he'd ever seen.

Mark didn't know what to do with his feelings for her. He'd never felt that way for anybody. His feelings embarrassed him. He was afraid others would see through him, recognize the love-struck look in his eye when Esme walked by. The only way he knew to camouflage his feelings for her was to bully her. When she walked down the hall at school, Mark would make hooting noises and call her a "knacker" and a "pikey" so his friends would hear. "Hey, little Gypsy witch," he'd shout as he put his hands over his pockets in an exaggerated motion. "Don't get any ideas about trying to pickpocket me …" He and his buddies' laughter could be heard up and down the school halls.

When Mark was alone, Esme consumed his thoughts. He fantasized about situations where they'd be together, holding hands, strolling along the beach. He would imagine walking down the hall at school, her coming toward him, their eyes locking. They'd both feel the electricity in the air as they passed.

He'd lay awake at night and imagine her slipping into his room, sitting on the edge of his bed, leaning over him. She'd kiss him gently on the lips. He dreamed of undressing her, running his hands over every inch of her naked body, causing her to moan and beg him to take her. He'd become aroused, roll around on his sheets, squirming, stifling moans, whispering her name to see how it sounded on his lips. In the morning, all that was left of his fantasy was the mess on his sheets.

When Django heard that Mark and his football buddies were harassing Esme at school and that the teachers and administrators were doing nothing to stop it, he bypassed the high school principal and went to the school board president. The president of the school board, an avid fan of the high school football team, downplayed the problem. "You know how boys are, Mr. Horvat," he said patronizingly. "These boys don't mean any harm; they're just strutting their stuff. After all, they're on track to put Crystal Bay on the map—the state championship!"

Django went to the police chief to complain that Esme was being bullied at school and that the school board chose to turn a blind eye. While the police chief agreed to speak to the high school principal to remind him that bullying and name-calling shouldn't be tolerated, he told Django that because no crime had been committed, the police couldn't intervene.

Django wanted more. The football players weren't like the young girls who had caused Esme problems in elementary school. The football players were rough and tough, filled with male hormones, and egged on by the community who believed aggression made for a more exciting football team.

Esme was just months from graduating. She wanted to finish high school and be done with it. Analetta talked to her about ways to protect herself, to avoid the football players, especially Mark Kipling, and to report him to the principal when he taunted her to force the principal's hand. Esme promised her grandmother that she'd be cautious, go out of her way to avoid problems, and report any bullying to the office. But the truth was, Esme had no fear of Mark Kipling. When Esme looked at Mark, she felt her own inner protection that came from her mother. She could look deep inside his mind and see him for what he was, a scared, hurt, weak coward. He was driven by anger, rage, and resentment, and Esme was wise enough to know where it came from. She could see that Mark would soon bring about his own downfall and that he'd do it in front of his entire community.

His downfall started when Mark began to bully a fifth-grade boy named Patrick Donovan. When a teacher from the elementary school found out and reported it to the high school principal, the school administrators downplayed the situation just as they'd done with Esme. They convinced themselves that their star football player was having a little fun, that he didn't mean anything by it. Mark's coach and the principal told him to stop it and not let it happen again, but no one did anything more to intervene.

The situation got worse. One afternoon, Patrick was ahead of Mark as they walked home from school. Patrick was a shy, awkward, effeminate boy. He was everything Mark detested, everything, according to Mark, that made a person worthless. Mark wanted to know what it would feel like to terrorize Patrick. There was no one around but the two of them. The thought of having so much power over Patrick induced a rush of testosterone through Mark, an exciting electrical charge he could barely contain. He picked up a switch from a nearby willow tree and caught up to Patrick. As he walked behind him, just a few feet, he tickled Patrick's legs with the switch and threatened to beat him up if he turned around. When Patrick was finally within sight of his house, he started to run with Mark in close pursuit. As Patrick got closer to home, he began to scream, which brought his mother out onto the porch. When she saw what was happening, she recognized Mark and yelled at him, "Hey you, shame on you, scaring someone so much younger than you are! Get out of here right now! I'm gonna report you to your coach!"

"Ahh, I didn't mean to scare him," Mark jested. "I was just walking him home from school."

Patrick's mother was true to her word. She contacted the football coach and demanded that Mark sit out the next football game. Bullying should not be acceptable she insisted and threatened to make a big stink if Mark didn't get a consequence. The coach knew there was no way he would let his star football player sit out one of the playoff games. After all, the championship was at stake. The town wouldn't allow it. Instead, the coach set up a meeting with Mark, Patrick, his mother, the school principal, and the school board president and made Mark promise out loud that he would leave Patrick alone. But there was nothing sincere about Mark's promise. As soon as the meeting ended, Mark and his football buddies doubled down on Patrick as their target.

From then on, whenever Mark and his pals saw Patrick, they'd gang up on him. It might be when Patrick was skateboarding, playing on the beach, or walking home alone from school. They would close in on Patrick, follow a few steps behind him, and harass him. They'd call him "gay boy," "sissy," "faggot." They'd mimic him running and screaming for his mother and scare him into keeping quiet. "I'll beat the crap out of you," Mark would threaten, "if you tell anyone."

44

THE TOWN WENT WILD WHEN THE CRYSTAL BAY FOOTBALL TEAM MADE
it into the state championship playoff game. Community picnics
were held at the beach, and a make-do parade, comprised of locals,
wound its way down Main Street. The bars were packed the weekend before the game with rowdy folks who got drunk. Still, unlike
other weekends when fights would break out and eventually someone would get hauled off to jail, there was a sense of camaraderie
this weekend. The townspeople stood together, behind their team,
against the opponent.

Thursday afternoon, the day before the game, the high school
held a pep rally in the gymnasium that brought together students,
parents, teachers, and administrators from the elementary, middle,
and high schools. The football players were center stage along with
their coach. Some players made short speeches, thanking the community for their support, praising their coach, and giving a shout-out
to their parents, who sat proudly in the audience. The cheerleaders
were there leading the crowd in rah-rah-sis-boom-bah chants.

Mark was at the center of the pep rally. He proudly wore his
letterman's jacket and football jersey. Halfway through the players'
speeches, the audience began to chant, "Mark! Mark! Mark!" Mark

sidled up to the microphone in the center of the stage. His speech was all about himself; he bragged about how he would lead his team to victory, call the plays and throw the passes that would guarantee the trophy. He should have thanked his coach, the townspeople who supported him throughout his high school football career, and his fellow team players. He should have acknowledged his little brother, but he didn't. The crowd didn't notice or care. They cheered for him, and when he finished his speech, they stood and applauded for a full minute.

Patrick, the fifth grader who'd become the target of Mark's bullying, was in attendance that afternoon. He hadn't wanted to attend the rally, but the entire elementary school was required to participate. Patrick went out of his way to avoid being in Mark's eyesight. When no one was watching, Patrick managed to sneak out the side door of the gymnasium. He wandered out to the football field and stayed out of sight by hiding beneath the bleachers. He got caught up looking for loose change and trinkets that had fallen out of spectators' pockets during the last game.

Patrick got so enthralled in his search that he failed to notice when the students from the elementary school filed out of the gym, boarded the school bus, and drove away. He panicked and wasn't sure what to do when he realized he'd been left behind. He ran back to the gym, hoping to find someone from the elementary school who might still be there. Unfortunately, who he found instead was Mark.

After everyone else had exited the gym, Mark wanted a few minutes to himself. He stayed behind to bask in his pending glory and visualize his victory in the upcoming game. He stood on the stage, reliving what it had felt like to have everyone in the audience stand and cheer for him. He was on a high and could almost feel the adrenalin pumping through his bloodstream. He felt aggressive, ready for tomorrow's game, and was prepared to lead his team to victory against all odds, a win that would put his name in the high school annals for years to come. Mark visualized a dedicated glass showcase in the halls of Crystal Bay High School in honor of him, his retired jersey, helmet, the championship trophy, newspaper articles, and pictures that would be taken at tomorrow's game, highlighting his passes and downfield throws.

Mark was enjoying his private moment of glory when he heard the gym door open. He looked over to see Patrick standing frozen on the gym floor. Patrick looked like a snared rabbit to Mark, and Mark was the coyote. Without skipping a beat, Mark hooted, "Oh, look who's here; it's the little gay boy." He walked to the edge of the stage and jumped down.

Patrick couldn't move. He looked around. There was no one else there to help him. When he could get his feet working again, he started running back toward the door. They say never to run from a vicious dog; it sets the dog in motion. Thus was the case with Mark. As soon as Patrick set off, Mark sprinted across the gym floor and grabbed Patrick by the collar before he could escape out the door. He half pulled, half shoved Patrick to the middle of the gym floor. All his built-up adrenalin for tomorrow's game somehow converted into the pent-up rage Mark had carried with him for many years. Patrick's weakness and fear infuriated Mark. "Quit sniveling, bitch," he hissed at Patrick. He grabbed Patrick under his arms and swung him in a circle, chanting, "Faggot!" and "Mama's little sissy!" He twirled Patrick so hard that Patrick flew out of his grasp and crashed onto the floor several feet away, his head banging into the hard surface of the gym floor.

"Please," Patrick wailed, "let me go!" He tried crawling away from Mark, but Mark grabbed him, flipped him over, and put his foot on his chest, making it hard for Patrick to breathe.

Patrick sobbed and pleaded for help. He lay pressed against the gymnasium floor, gagging and gasping for air, while Mark stood over him, his foot still on Patrick's chest, daring him to move.

"Let him go!" someone from the back of the gymnasium yelled. Mark turned to see where the voice was coming from. "I said, let him go," the voice repeated. It was Tom Johnson, who was walking by the gym and heard the commotion. Tom ran over to where Mark was still holding Patrick down.

"Let him go, Mark. What kind of jerk are you? He's just a kid!"

By now, Mark was seeing nothing but red. Still with one foot on Patrick's chest, he turned his anger and rage onto Tom. "Oh, look, it's the Injun to the rescue."

In his blind fury, Mark didn't see Tom's right fist coming at his jaw. When it connected, Mark fell to the ground. He was back up instantly; Patrick forgotten for the time being. Mark doubled his fist and landed a hard blow to Tom's temple, knocking him to the ground. Tom rolled to his side, pain shooting through his head. Mark's foot connected with Tom's back with a hard kick to his kidney. Tom groaned in pain. He found it hard to take in a breath.

Patrick was too scared to run, so he curled into a fetal position in the center of the commotion. Tom got to his feet, only to be taken down again by the upper thrust of Mark's left fist to his jaw. Tom and Mark were focused on each other, Mark out to destroy Tom and Tom trying to regroup so he could defend himself. Tom wasn't a fighter and knew he would lose this fight, but he'd try his best to ward off severe damage. In their concentration, neither saw Esme enter the gym and make her way to the spot where Patrick lay huddled on the floor.

Esme didn't speak. Instead, she raised her right hand out in front of her in a stopping gesture. She held her hand out and looked directly at Mark, who stopped in his tracks, then turned to look at Tom, who had managed to get himself into a standing position. Blood dripped from his nose and a gash above his right eye from hitting the floor. Dirt from the gym floor was smeared across his face and t-shirt. Mark would always remember the look Esme gave Tom at that moment. It was a look of deference and admiration. It was the look that Mark had fantasized about for so long that Esme would give him. Instead, when she turned back to Mark, her expression made him feel cold. She looked at him with contempt and shook her head in disgust as though she pitied him.

Esme stepped over to Patrick, still on the ground, his sobs turning to gags. Snot ran from his nose and was smeared across his cheeks and mouth. She offered Patrick her hand and helped him to his feet. He clung to her, still heaving with sobs.

Esme nodded to Tom and turned to leave, with her arm around Patrick and Tom following close behind. She paused and turned back to face Mark. She could feel the presence of her mother beside her and hear Elina's words echoing in her mind, "Don't be afraid to use your power, Esme." Esme looked directly into Mark's eyes and saw the deep insecurities he tried to conceal. She could view his weaknesses, self-doubt, and pain. She brought them all to the surface, shone a light on them, and stripped him down to his most profound vulnerability.

When Esme looked into Mark's eyes, into his psyche, she saw it: his pending demise, his downfall, the shame and disgrace he'd bring upon himself and his community. She saw the mistake he would make and the consequences that were looming in front of him. When Esme spoke, she did so clearly and distinctly. "Tomorrow, at the game, Mark, you'll go down. Your team will lose, and it will be your own doing." She turned then, and walked across the gym and out the door, Patrick clinging to her hand, Tom walking behind.

True to Esme's prediction, Crystal Bay High School lost the championship to their opponents. It was Mark's error that cost them the game. It was the fourth quarter, and the score was tied, twenty-one to twenty-one; Crystal Bay had the ball, and they were at the forty-yard line. It was the second down. There was one minute left in the game.

When Esme had warned Mark that he'd lose the championship game, he tried to ignore it, to put it out of his mind. He tried to tell himself that her purpose was to up-end and unsettle him. He wanted to convince himself that it meant nothing. She didn't have any power to put a spell on him. But he couldn't shake the look she'd given him. She'd seen the shame and disgrace that defined him. Tom and even Patrick had seen it. Esme had made Mark look weak. Worse, she'd looked at him with disgust. The girl Mark secretly lusted after, wanted to win over, dreamed of running away with, saw him for what he really was, and was disgusted by him.

As Mark stood in the huddle with his team players, ready to call the game's final play, his mind wasn't focused on the move; it was on Esme and her warning. It was at that moment that Mark knew. He knew he'd lose the game during those last remaining seconds. He knew that Esme's curse would bring him down in front of the entire crowd of fans, his teammates, teachers, school administrators, and townsfolk. Esme would bring Mark to his knees in front of the whole town.

Mark called the play: he'd pass the ball to the left receiver, who'd run the ball down the field to the goal line. The team took their positions. The receiver was ready to accept the pass. But at the last second, just as the center snapped the ball to Mark, he saw an opening downfield. Instead of passing the ball to the receiver, he threw the ball to a running back at the ten-yard line. Mark knew that it was his fatal blow when the ball left his hand. He miscalculated. The running back wasn't prepared, expecting the ball to be passed off to the receiver. He missed the throw. A player from the opposing team intercepted and ran the ball downfield to the opponent's twenty-yard line before being tackled. In the last ten seconds of the game, the opposing team made a field goal for three points to become the new state champions.

Crystal Bay High School lost. Mark, the renowned quarterback, the school's pride, and the town's hero, lost the championship. He wouldn't get a chance to return and try again, showing the good folks of Crystal Bay that he was the winner they thought he was. Mark Kipling would finish out his high school football career as a loser, as the one who deprived his town of being champions.

The residents of Crystal Bay were distraught, having lost the state championship when it was so close at hand. Many had anticipated telling stories for years to come about winning the championship trophy. They'd hoped it would become a story that would put Crystal Bay on the map, make it stand out, and make it a legend. Instead, they were left with the story of how their prized quarterback made a foolish error that cost them the game.

It was important for the Crystal Bay locals to have a rationale, a reason that helped explain why things turned out the way they did. It didn't sit well that their hero, Mark, could have made a poor judgment call. The Mark they knew would never have done that. Something must have happened. There had to be a reason. Mark was the town hero folks talked about while mingling after church, in the diner over burgers and milkshakes, in line at the cleaners, and in the check-out line at the grocery store. He was the one neighbors bragged about over the fence when mowing their lawns or walking out to get their mail. Not only did the residents of Crystal Bay lose the championship, but they also lost their bragging rights and sense of significance, the common thread that held them together as a community.

Talking about Mark's fatal error grew tiresome. They needed something new to weave their community together and soothe their unrest. It was Esme who gave them what they were looking for. "You know," one bored housewife said to another one morning shortly after the football game while standing in line at the grocery store, "my son happened to be sitting on a bench outside near the gym on the day of the pep rally, the day before the game. He was waiting for his girlfriend to come out of the library, and he saw that Gypsy girl and that Indian kid coming out of the gym together after everyone else had left. That little witch girl was dragging some younger kid by the hand. The kid looked like he'd been crying. A short time later, my son told me he saw Mark come out of the gym looking dazed. He was obviously distressed, according to my son."

"We all know that Gypsy is nothin' but trouble," the second housewife added. "And that Indian kid! He's not much better. I heard those Indians on the reservation pray to spirits and practice sorcery. Who's to say she and that Indian didn't put some curse on Mark?"

"That Gypsy's done it before," the first housewife added. "Remember how she ruined that little girl's birthday party years ago? I think her name was Shelby or something like that. I knew there'd be trouble if we let people like those two into our schools."

Folks in line at the grocery store that morning couldn't help but overhear. One older gentleman repeated the story to the pharmacist at the local drugstore. At the same time, a twenty-something woman told her nursing-home coworkers, who told their spouses that evening over dinner, who went to work the next day and told their own coworkers. Like adding oxygen to fire, the story spread.

As often happened in Crystal Bay, no one ever stopped to question the story's validity. It was simply a story the locals loved to believe, to talk about when they mingled for cookies and coffee after church or in the cafeteria at work. Esme's notoriety spread, with stories of her witchery and unnatural ability to know one's past and predict one's future, her power to put curses on people. She'll steal from you if you turn your back, they insisted. She'll entice men away from their women and convince women to turn against their men they gossiped. Esme became the common thread that wove the people of Crystal Bay back together, that reunited them after the disappointing loss. She became their sacrificial lamb, someone to unleash their prejudices, hatred, and biases upon.

The town's children learned the story, too, and Esme became the focus of their make-believe play. Esme, the powerful witch who lived in the forest, could cast spells and turn children into toads or rats if they trespassed on her property; she could turn herself into a raven and pluck small children off the ground and fly them away to her secret dungeon if they misbehaved.

Over the years, on the rare occasions that Django, Analetta, or Esme went into town, folks shunned them. If folks saw the Horvats coming, they'd look the other way and appear preoccupied with something or someone else. No one in Crystal Bay offered to help if Django had a problem on the farm, nor would anyone greet Analetta when she entered the market to shop. There was an unspoken agreement among the people of Crystal Bay, and no one would be caught dead being nice to Esme or her grandparents; not one person was willing to break the pact they all agreed to adhere to.

Despite it all, Esme's beauty—her untamed, fiery looks and mystique—continued to fascinate the residents of Crystal Bay. That the town's men collectively avoided her kept them safe from outwardly longing for her. That the women all agreed to hate her kept their envy at bay. They convinced each other, and themselves, that she would bring them bad luck, jinx them, that she wasn't one of them, that she was an undesirable, someone to be shunned. The townsfolk of Crystal Bay officially made Esme an outcast.

45

AFTER HIGH SCHOOL, ESME RARELY LEFT HER FARM. SHE HAD NO desire to venture farther away than to visit their closest neighbors, Gus and Mary. Her life happened on the farm. At first, Analetta and Django encouraged her to go out into the world and make her way, to meet new people, fall in love, get married, raise a family. But Esme was content to stay. The farm was what she wanted. It was a part of her. There were times when Esme couldn't tell where she ended, and the farm began. Its essence was alive and breathing through her. She felt like she'd always been a part of the farm. It was her place in the world, where she belonged.

By the time she was out of high school, she could do anything Django could do on the farm. She learned to care for the wild mustangs brought to the farm for rehabilitation before being released back into the wild. Django taught Esme how to relate to wild horses and communicate with them. He taught her never to approach a wild horse but rather to let the horse approach her. He coached her to stand in the fenced pasture with an apple in her outstretched hand, waiting for a horse to come close enough to retrieve it. One time she stood for over three hours holding out an apple, waiting for a horse to feel safe enough to snatch it from her outstretched hand.

Once the mustangs became accustomed to her mingling among them, Esme could tend to their injuries and wounds without them shying away. She learned how to calm the horses and keep them from spooking with the tone of her voice, the assuredness of her touch, and the reward of an apple when she had to massage and wrap an injured ligament or tendon or clean a wound or remove a burr from a horse's hide.

She worked alongside Django and cared for wounded fowl. She learned how to set a broken wing and clean the wound of an injured talon or claw. She learned how to birth farm animals, clean stalls, construct a hen house out of old lumber, and keep the irrigation flowing through the front pasture from a tiny tributary that branched off the main river and flowed south of the farm.

Esme and Django created a sanctuary for wildfowl on their farm. Often, as many as a hundred wild birds would fly onto the property—geese, ducks, cormorants, herons, wild turkeys, and pheasants. Esme would entice them with insects that Django taught her to collect using molasses. When they heard the spoon clang against the metal bucket containing the insects, wild birds and fowl would fly onto the farm. They'd crowd each other, snapping and scolding, trying to push each other aside to get a sample of the tasty treats. Esme taught her border collie to "belly down" when the birds were on the farm. "Look with your eyes," she'd tell the dog. "They're our friends."

The fields behind their farm, on the north side of the river, were often dotted with deer and elk that would wander out from the forest to graze, knowing they were safe there. They sometimes wandered onto the farm, hoping to grab a nibble from Analetta's vegetable garden. It took only minutes for a whole row of lettuce or beet greens to disappear when a few hungry deer found their way in. Esme helped Django build a wire fence with wooden posts around the garden and bury it deep into the ground to keep out deer and other intruders, moles, and badgers.

Esme refused to eat wild game or fowl, claiming they would lose the trust of the deer, elk, and wild birds that frequented their farm. Over time, Django and Gus from the farm next door put their guns away and kept them just for protection. Once, Django agreed to board an aging Black Angus steer that a farmer from the reservation couldn't sell at auction. Esme grew fond of the steer, claiming she could see its soul when she looked into its eyes. After that, she refused to eat red meat or pork.

Esme became known by the Makah people as someone who could communicate with animals, birds, the earth, and the universe. People from the reservation thought her to be a spiritual healer, an animal whisperer, a seer who could read one's past and predict one's future; someone blessed by *Hohoeapbess,* someone they held in the highest regard. Over time, the Makah people blessed her with special protections: protection of her land, animals, and safety.

While it was the farm and its bounties, the Makah people defined Esme by—her animals, the wild mustangs and fowl, the deer and elk, the open fields, the eagle that nested in the Sitka Spruce at the edge of the forest, the river that wound its way through Esme's farm to its final destination, stocked with fish that fed her year around, her garden—it was her grandmother, Analetta, who instilled in Esme a strong sense of Roma tradition. Analetta told stories to Esme of Serbia and Bulgaria, as told to her by her parents and grandparents when she was growing up. She taught Esme to dance the kolo and the horo, the traditional dances of their homeland. She'd intwine her arm through Esme's, and together, they'd laugh and sing and sway their hips as they danced in a circle around the kitchen while preparing meals.

Analetta taught Esme to cook traditional ethnic dishes and to bake the flatbreads and pastries loved by their people. They worked side-by-side in the kitchen, making goulash with fresh seafood and vegetables from their garden, set off with garlic and green peppers. They made sarma, cabbage leaves stuffed with rice and salmon, accented with kale and chard and always served with mashed potatoes. They prepared Placinte cu cartofi, patties made from dough stuffed with mashed potatoes, cheese, and sauteed onions and then fried to a golden brown on both sides. Esme learned from Analetta the art of seasoning and using fresh herbs and fruits from the garden to bring out just the right flavors.

In the early mornings, they'd tie on aprons and roll out dough to make traditional Roma bread and pastries, savory breadsticks called prestige, pufe from fried flour, and xaritsa from fried cornmeal. They made grits called mamaliga and gogosi, donuts flavored with vanilla and grated orange peel and papaya, and cheese donuts served with fruit jam and powdered sugar. Sometimes for lunch, they'd snack on placinta, flatbread stuffed with soft urda cheese, jam, and boiled cherries picked from their garden and fried to a crispy golden brown.

Analetta passed on her skill as a seamstress to Esme. On cold winter days, when the weather turned damp and drizzly, when rain pelted the ground, making it soggy and difficult to walk without sinking into mud, when the garden lay dormant and the hens huddled in their hen house to keep warm, Analetta gave Esme lessons on how to repair and service the two sewing machines they set up in the tiny attic of their farmhouse. Together, they cut patterns out of fabrics traded to them by the Makah people in return for favors or services.

Under Analetta's vigilant tutorage, Esme learned to cut and sew bohemian-style dresses and skirts traditional of her people, loose-fitting, soft, and flowy. She learned to make shirts and peasant blouses from voile or silk. In honor of her Roma heritage, she created colorful sashes and head scarves with long tails that hung to her shoulder.

Esme blended her self-made dresses and skirts with clothing and jewelry from the Makah people. Members of the tribe brought her handcrafted offerings as a sign of their friendship and a way to recognize her special skills. They gifted her with boots and moccasins, jackets, and long coats for winter made from buckskin that they handmade just for her, adorned with fringe, furs, and beads. They endowed her with necklaces of silver and turquoise and bracelets woven from soft leather and silver, fired into delicate shapes. Esme honored the Makah people by wearing their handcrafted gifts. It was a sign of respect she showed them, an acknowledgment of friendship between Esme and the Makah Indians. Esme's look became distinct, a combination of Roma and American Indian, accentuating and defining her uniqueness.

When Esme was twenty-six, she lost both her grandparents within a short time of each other. Analetta passed away quietly in her sleep following a bout of pneumonia. Esme and Mary from the farm next door tended to Analetta during her illness, Esme never leaving her side. Less than a year later, Django suddenly died of a heart attack while working in the barn. Esme had been helping him repair a section of siding on the barn when he keeled over and dropped to the ground, dead. The farm was passed down to Esme.

After her grandparents died, Esme's world became reclusive. Her farm was her lifeblood. It suited her, but at times loneliness seeped in, and she found herself yearning for the company of another. It was Tom Johnson she turned to. Her bond with him had deepened with each passing year. He picked up the slack when she was too grief-stricken to move off her porch. He saw to her animals, barn, and garden, brought her meals that people from the reservation made for her, and encouraged her to eat. He sat with her on her porch, sometimes not saying anything, until the sharp pain of loss eventually began to subside, and she could once again go about her life tending to the farm.

A few months after losing her grandparents, a member of the Makah tribe brought her a Berger Piccard Shepard, a few months old, that had been abandoned. The dog had been tied to a stake in the backyard by its previous owner, who had moved away and left him just one bowl of water and a bone to chew on. The dog had suffered in that spot for five days before someone walking by heard him whimper and came into the yard to see if the dog was hurt. He was emaciated and dehydrated and waiting at death's door. The tribal vet cared for, hydrated, and fed him with IVs for a few days until he slowly regained his strength.

When Esme saw the dog, she fell in love with him. They had something in common, the two of them, both abandoned as they'd been. She nurtured the dog back to health. She taught him to follow hand signals and short verbal commands. She named him Jake. Like her border collie, Jake learned to dance to the music of her fiddle. He was more agile than the border collie had been; he could balance on his hind legs for a full minute, twirling slowly in a circle.

46

AFTER TOM GRADUATED FROM HIGH SCHOOL, HE ATTENDED THE University of Washington on an *American Indian Educational Fund* scholarship. He got a degree in law with a focus on American Indian heritage. He took up causes that impacted his people and the reservation and fought for and helped win the rights of the Makah people to participate in whaling, a passionate and spiritual custom central to their culture. Upon turning twenty-eight, Tom was elected to the Makah Tribal Council.

Tom married a woman from his tribe. In his heart, he believed it was essential that he marry someone who shared his Indian heritage. He'd grown up with the woman he married, they'd lived on the reservation together, had played together as kids, and their two families had attended traditional Makah events together. She was a school teacher and taught in the high school on the reservation. She was soft-spoken and proud of her Indian culture. She and Tom had three children.

It was Esme, though, who held Tom's heart. His soul aligned with hers. He visited her often on her farm. Sometimes he'd walk with her out through the fields, and other times they'd sit together on her porch and enjoy the sunset or watch the stars in the night sky. Sometimes Esme would play her fiddle for him or cook him a traditional Roma meal. He was always there to lend a hand if she needed help with something around the farm.

Tom was strong and proud and never made excuses about his relationship with Esme to his elders or wife. Esme and Django, before he died, provided services to the Makah people, and tribal members maintained a close relationship with both of them. Besides, Tom had known Esme since they were kids—she'd been his best friend. Tom left it at that.

Tom knew that Esme's heart was searching for her one true love. She'd confided in him when they were kids what her mother told her before she died, that somewhere in the world was Esme's soulmate, the person she traveled through eternity with. During one of Tom's visits to her farm, Esme told him how she often dreamed of being an eagle and soaring high above the land where she could see infinity from her perspective. "What does it mean, Tom?" she asked.

Tom asked his grandmother. "Esme's gifted," Tom's grandmother told him. "In her dreams, she can shapeshift. She can transform her body into the shape of an animal or bird. As an eagle, she can soar to great heights and observe the world from a grander vantage point. When she soars high above the earth, she can more easily find her soulmate, the one destined to travel with her and complete her journey."

Tom knew he wasn't Esme's soulmate, not the one her heart searched for. He knew their destinies were not to be lovers. They came from different worlds, different cultures. But somehow, their souls were intertwined. He was drawn to her, pulled in her direction. Like the powerful force that binds together an atom, she was the nucleus that his orbit circled. He would never be able to leave her, to distance himself from her. That he would journey through life in her company was enough for Tom. Though he wouldn't possess her, he would walk alongside her, always.

Esme learned about destiny from her mother, about the karmic journey each person must follow. Her mother taught her that each lifetime offers opportunities to break old patterns, overcome challenges, and gain the wisdom to fuel one's soul.

"Our journey," Elena taught Esme, "isn't always easy. Often it's painful, but it's necessary for one's soul to master life's lessons, to break karmic cycles. Our soulmate," Elena explained, "is the person who helps to guide our destiny, who walks beside us when our journey becomes difficult, when the challenges seem insurmountable. Our soulmate is the person who keeps us from straying too far from our karmic path, who helps steer our journey toward its ultimate goal."

Before the train wreck claimed her life, Elena had spread tarot cards and studied Esme's karmic prophecy. It had been a special occasion for Esme when she was barely nine. On a beautiful, warm spring day, when the circus was between shows, the train camped outside a small town in upstate New York. Elena had prepared a picnic, and she and Esme had walked out through the open fields of the countryside until they'd found a spot under a giant oak tree to have lunch. Elena had carefully shuffled the tarot cards that would reveal Esme's karmic journey and laid them on a blanket where they sat. Elena shared with Esme just enough to prepare her for what lie ahead for her future. "You are strong, Esme like a warrior is strong. You will be able to handle what life brings your way. You are passionate, fierce."

"Where will my journey take me?" Esme had pleaded to know. "Will I meet someone special like Papa?" she had asked.

"There is one person in your journey, Esme, who stands out, who will match your strength. You travel together during each lifetime. He is your one true love, your soulmate. He is searching for you even now. He completes your cycle in this lifetime. He is coming for you, Esme. Be patient."

After her parents were killed and taken from her, Esme often remembered that day in late spring with her mother, their walk through the field, their picnic under the old oak tree, and her mother's reading of her tarot cards. She wondered if her mother had seen what was coming in Esme's life, that she would shortly be left alone, and of her struggles ahead.

After her grandparents' death, Esme yearned for the soulmate her mother promised would find her. She was aware of his absence and the space in her heart waiting for him to fill. As the years slipped by, her impatience turned to anticipation, a knowing that his journey was bringing him closer to her. The time was getting nearer. She'd wait. She'd be ready when the time came.

Esme sometimes wondered if Tom was her soulmate, her true love. She somehow knew they would travel side-by-side throughout their lives and felt sure she'd known him in other lifetimes, that she'd know him again in lifetimes to come. He'd always be a part of her; she'd love and hold him dearly in her heart forever.

She sometimes allowed herself to think about being with Tom intimately. He was fierce but gentle, handsome, and proud. When he occasionally held her hand to help her over a fence or to wade across the river in the shallow spot behind her house, a feeling of warmth came over her. They were good together. He made her laugh, and she could tell him anything, confide in him.

He occasionally brought his children to her farm when he came to check on the wild mustangs she was tending or to help her with a repair or a fence that needed mending. Tom's children were fascinated by Esme's wild, unruly hair, so different from their straight and sleek hair. They loved the pastries Esme baked, the breads, and the donuts. They'd beg her to walk them through the fields, hoping to glimpse the female eagle. They'd help her collect the insects she fed to the wildfowl who came from all directions when Esme clanked the metal spoon against the side of the bucket. The children would pile atop Homie and ride around on his back, no reins, as he followed Esme around the farm. They'd delight in watching Jake and Homie dance to the music of her fiddle.

In time, Esme learned that Tom was not the soulmate she was searching for. He was pulled by his destiny to marry within his tribe. If it were possible to have more than one soulmate, two people in a lifetime that could fulfill one's heart, she knew Tom would be that second person. But somewhere, she was sure, was one other who offered even a stronger bond, someone she hadn't yet met, someone destined to be her lover.

Over time Esme settled into her solitary life on the farm with her animals. She learned to adjust without Django and Analetta like she'd learned to adapt to losing her parents and Border Collie years ago. She became content in her solitude, her world consisting of a tiny farm nestled within a small, remote valley, hidden deep in the forest, away from the rest of the world.

But in her dreams she'd fly, sometimes far away. She'd turn herself into a powerful bird, an eagle, and soar thousands of feet above land. She'd use her wing feathers to control her flight, turn the front edges inward to gain speed, and slow herself down by turning the broad surface of her wings into the breeze. She'd spread her tail feathers to increase her lift and tilt her wings to turn. Her eyes were like a telescope. She could make out every detail far below on the ground. She'd soar effortlessly, out over land, across the water, and above the city, using her instincts to guide her. If she wanted a closer view, she'd adjust her tail feathers to give her balance and dive and dip low. When she'd seen enough and felt content in her journey, she'd rise again, bend the front edges of her wings inward and gain speed. She'd head back to her farm. She'd wake up.

PART V

SAM

47

SAM RETURNED TO HIS LAND ROVER, CLIMBED IN, AND STARTED THE
engine. He looked again at the spot where the woman and her
animals had been. "Of all the strange coincidences," Sam thought.
"Out here in the middle of nowhere, I stop my car just as a woman
walks out of the woods."

"There are no coincidences," his mother would say.

Sam opened the gate that led onto Gus's property and drove
forward. He came to a fork in the road in less than a mile. There
was a sign pointing left that read, "Welcome to Gus's Fishing Hole."
The road to the right was unmarked, narrower, and less traveled,
just two worn tire tracks barely visible through the grass and weeds.
Sam went left. A few hundred yards ahead, the road opened onto a
small gravel clearing. He parked the Land Rover and got out. He'd
arrived. Gus's Fishing Hole was a small, weathered, and rustic farm.

No longer maintained, the surrounding fields had been over-
taken by tall grasses, some green and some golden. A run-down
split-rail fence, decaying from years of dampness, meandered around
the property, adding a touch of charm. Across from the gravel clearing sat two distressed barns, their siding rough and weather-beaten.
Two cabins, rustic and craggy, each with a front porch, were nestled

into the bend of the river as it curved southward on the property's northwest corner, and on the farm's northeast corner, along the river's edge, sat a faded farmhouse, its years of exposure to the elements noticeable. Its front porch was scattered with a mismatch of lawn chairs in different colors and sizes, an old picnic table, and a hammock.

The North Fork Sekiu River flowed west along the property's northern edge and gently wound south. It burbled and tumbled as the clear, clean water hit the rocks. A bridge made of logs, just east of the farmhouse and constructed years ago to allow farm equipment back and forth to the outer fields, provided passage across the river. Along both sides of the riverbank, dirt paths, perfect for walking, had been carved out over the years by small farm equipment and foot traffic, mostly fishermen. The trails called to Sam, "Come get lost."

Bigleaf maple and cottonwood trees grew along the river's edge, offering protection from the rain, and shade on hot summer days. Vast, open fields surrounded the farm in all directions. Hemlocks and Sitka spruce, tall and majestic, grew sporadically in the open fields, and gradually merged with Douglas firs and western red cedars to form thick forest growth, where moss hung from tree branches like finely crocheted cloaks, and bog, lichen, and mushrooms blanked the ground. Here and there, a withered tree's rotting and decaying trunk lay in the open fields, feeding the ecosystem and providing shelter to small woodland creatures.

Sam took a deep breath. He breathed it in. The air smelled of moss, wet tree trunks, and needle-covered pathways. It was a smell Sam loved. It brought back images of camping and fishing with his dad when he was a kid, both of them standing on the bank of a river in their waders, casting their lines back and forth, his dad telling him stories, Sam listening, laughing. They'd share a cup of black coffee, a bonding ritual they grew to love.

A screen door slammed and brought Sam to attention. An older man emerged from the farmhouse with an old black Lab with a silvery white muzzle hobbling close behind. "You Sam Parker?"

"I am," Sam replied. Sam estimated the man was in his late seventies, and the Lab was close to the same age in dog years. He reminded Sam of a Mark Twain character, short and stout with gray, unkempt hair that poked out from beneath an old fisherman's hat, like a trapped animal trying to escape its crate. His shaggy, over-hanging eyebrows reached almost to his eyelids, and he peered out from beneath them through gray-green eyes that looked to Sam as though they held the mystery of life. The older man's face, wizened and saggy from age and years at sea, reminded Sam of an unmade, comfortable bed. When he smiled, his expression captured a twinkle from his younger day. Sam liked him immediately.

"I'm Gus."

As he came off the porch, Sam noted a slight limp, the remnant of an accident obtained at sea that he would later tell Sam about over a glass of whiskey. His hands were gnarled, his voice gravely. He was dressed in khaki workman's pants cinched up with a belt and a long-sleeved undershirt, moccasins on his feet. He held a pipe between his teeth that appeared to be a permanent fixture. Such an outdated smoking habit somehow looked natural on Gus.

"I've been waitin' for yeh. Hope you didn't have any trouble finding the place."

"Not too much trouble," Sam replied. Any apprehension he might have felt faded.

"Welcome to the fishing hole. I'm sure you'll find it very accom-modating. Let me show you to your cabin."

Both cabins looked alike. Gus led Sam to the one farthest from the farmhouse. "Here you are, Sam. Pull your rig in. Unload your stuff. Get comfortable. Everything you need should be there. I set it up just like Mary used to before she died. If you need any-thing, holler."

"Can I hook up to the Internet?" Sam asked.

"Yep, the codes and passwords and any other instructions you need are taped to the refrigerator door."

"How do you get reception so far back here?"

"They put up a tower not too far away to service Crystal Bay, the Makah Reservation, and the farms in between. We get pretty good internet reception out here, but the phone service ain't worth a damn. You'll have to rely on texting, which could be better. Or email. I'll let ya' get settled. If you feel like it after you get unpacked, come on over, and we'll toast your arrival with a shot of my best whiskey."

"Deal," Sam said.

The cabin was as rustic on the inside as on the outside but clean and fresh. It had a kitchen, small but stocked with everything Sam would need. The bathroom had fresh towels, and the bed was crisp and clean, with an extra blanket folded neatly at the foot. The combined kitchen and sitting room held an old worn couch that faced a stone fireplace and a small rickety table with three wooden chairs. The plank floors were worn smooth. The first thing Sam noticed was the absence of a TV.

Sam unloaded the Land Rover, put away his groceries, set up his laptop, and threw cold water on his face. He decided to take Gus up on his offer of a glass of whiskey. Gus was sitting on his front porch smoking his pipe, his ole black lab at his side, when Sam arrived.

"Come on up, Sam. Take any chair you want." Sam choose an old rocker. Gus poured them each a glass of whiskey. Sam took a sip and could feel the fiery warmth of the liquor deep in his belly. It felt rejuvenating.

"What brings you out here to the fishing hole, Sam?" Gus sat back in his chair and puffed on his pipe.

"Skeeter told my buddy and me about your place when we stopped at The Tavern after fishing for coho off Crystal Bay," Sam said. "I'm a writer," he added. " I've been looking for someplace like this where I can work on a novel that I've shelved for most of my life. It may be too late if I don't get back into it now." Sam paused and decided to say more. "I've been dealing with some heavy stuff back home. It feels like meeting Skeeter and learning about your place was fate. I haven't been able to get it out of my mind. I've been dreaming about a place like this for a long time."

Gus sat back, relaxed, puffing his pipe. He nodded in understanding and smiled at Sam. "Well, you've come to the right place. Life moves pretty slowly around these parts. It's a good place for figuring things out."

The whiskey, the rocking chair, and Gus's storytelling were hypnotic to Sam. He sat back and let Gus's stories carry him away. Gus grew up at the fishing hole as a young boy. Back then, it was a working farm. His parents mainly grew wheat and fruit—apples, berries, and melons. When he turned eighteen, just out of high school, Gus joined the merchant marines. "I wanted adventure, something more than this place had to offer at the time." Eventually, he became the captain of a large cargo transport ship that moved freight throughout domestic and international waters.

Sam would come to know Gus as a tough and crusty old sea captain, able in his youth to take care of himself in any situation but who preferred to harness friends over enemies. He met his late wife, Mary, while docked at a port-of-call to transfer cargo in Juneau, Alaska, when he was still a deckhand in his twenties. They married.

"She was the one who kept me sane while I was out on those waters for months at a time," he told Sam. Their life happened in increments, in between Gus's sea voyages. "We were happy," Gus told Sam. "Sometimes I think that's the best way to live. Absence makes the heart grow fonder. She was everything I ever wanted. She waited for me loyally when I was out at sea."

When he was in his late fifties, Gus and Mary returned to the farm after his parents passed. "Mary loved this place. We never wanted to go anywhere else. We were content, filled up, back here, away from everyone else. It's funny how my ideas changed from when I was young and couldn't get out of here fast enough."

"Mary breathed life into the place. She died a little over a year ago. Life ain't the same without her." Gus stopped, lost in thought. Finally, he added, "I sense her close by. It's uncanny, sometimes, how close she feels. It's as if she's hanging around, waiting for me. I look forward to the day I see her again."

The men sat in silence. Sam could almost feel time slow down. Finally, he spoke. "Today, when I was driving in, I stopped and got out to stretch my legs. As I stood there, a horse, a dog, and a beautiful woman stepped out of the forest. All three of them were so unique that it was almost disorienting. They weren't what I expected to see way out here. For a minute, I thought maybe I'd imagined it."

Gus chuckled. "That was Esme and her dog Jake and her horse Homer. Homie, she calls him. She owns the little farm next door. My dad sold that parcel of land to her great-great grandfather years ago. Her family's owned it ever since. Her grandparents passed it on to her when they died. She keeps to herself and lives there alone with her animals. Rarely goes into town."

That was all Gus offered. Sam didn't push for more. Instead, he leaned back in the rocker. They sat together, watching the night sky filled with stars and listening to the harmonious chirp of the crickets. They didn't talk much, just shared the peacefulness. Sam loved the damp smell of the air and the subtle noises coming from the darkness surrounding them. Off in the distance, a great horned owl hooted. He felt the stress leave his body, and the whiskey kick in and do its thing.

Somewhere around midnight, Sam bid Gus goodnight and headed for his cabin. Instead of going straight to bed, he sat on his porch, letting the cool air clear his head. He checked his laptop and saw he had an email from Jamie:

"Hey, Dad, hope you're getting settled. Mom's doctor called me yesterday to tell me that someone has to be the contact person for Mom, someone he can call with regular updates on Mom's status. I told him I'd do it."

Sam made a mental note to email him the next day about having Gladys do it instead. After all, she was right there in town, close by.

He'd deal with it tomorrow. He sat back and let his mind wander. His thoughts drifted to the woman in the woods. He couldn't get her eyes out of his mind; her gaze had been direct and penetrating. It was haunting.

Sam got up, went into the bathroom, splashed water on his face, and brushed his teeth. He lay on the bed, closed his eyes, and let his thoughts drift. It felt like Gus's Fishing Hole had been waiting for him his whole life. He couldn't remember ever feeling more like he belonged. He'd found his cabin by the river. He couldn't explain it, but he felt sure this was where he was supposed to be.

Sam fell asleep and woke a few hours later to the river's babble outside his bedroom window. The sounds of birds filled the air. It was still dark; dawn was barely peeking over the eastern horizon. He couldn't go back to sleep. He got up, made a pot of coffee in the percolator, and stepped out to the front porch. The coffee tasted good. He sat on one of the plastic lawn chairs and looked across the clearing to the barns. There was a peacefulness about the place that reminded Sam of early morning fishing excursions when he was a kid.

He remembered those carefree days of his youth when he didn't have a worry in the world, before his life took a U-turn. Childhood memories of his dreams and aspirations stirred inside him as he sat on the porch, listening to the river, and watching the night sky slip away. The hopes and dreams he'd let go of years ago suddenly seemed within reach. He remembered it wasn't that long ago when he was excited about his future. He felt those old feelings stir as he sipped his coffee and reminisced.

Sam went back into the cabin and sat down at the small table. He turned on his laptop, opened a blank document, and typed a sentence—read it, then deleted it. He tried again and deleted it again. He constructed one sentence, then another. Within twenty minutes, he'd typed three pages. He got up, poured another cup of coffee, and sat back down. He started typing again, slowly and methodically at first, but then faster. Words and sentences began to pour out of his head. He focused on the page and blocked everything else out. The next time he looked up, it was ten o'clock. He'd typed the book's first chapter he'd carried around in his head for over twenty years.

Sam scrambled a couple of eggs and made toast. He ate the eggs from the skillet and washed them down with the last of his coffee. He showered, dressed in trekking pants and lightweight hiking shoes, and decided to explore. There was a slight drizzle coming down. He donned his rain jacket and walked around to the back of his cabin to get a closer look at the river, scoping out places that looked good for fishing. A section of the river that lay between the cabins and Gus's farmhouse deepened, and the flow of the water was slower than the shallow water flowing into it. "This must be the hole," Sam figured.

"The fish love the seam, just at the edge of the hole," Sam turned around to see Gus standing on his porch. He pointed to the place where the water slowed. "Where the fast water merges with the slower, deeper water, that's where the fish are," Gus told Sam. "They don't have to fight the current so hard where it's slow, while the faster water brings their food right to 'em. Fish the seam; that's where you'll catch 'em."

"Thanks, Gus. I'll give it a shot."

Sam decided to meander around the farm and check out the barns and the outfields. He followed a dirt path through the clearing toward the smaller barn. The sliding doors were open. Years ago, the barn was converted into a place to do laundry, obviously a necessity for laundering bedding and towels back when there was a fast turn-over of fishermen who rented the cabins on Gus's property. There were a couple of washers, dryers, and a table for folding clothes. There was a big wash basin and a mop closet in the corner. "This will be convenient," Sam thought. It would allow him to limit his trips to and from Crystal Bay.

The larger of the two barns had a lean-to off to the side that housed yard tools, old bicycles, and fishing gear. It was apparent it was once a working barn, a place to store farm equipment, tractors, and flatbed trailers. Several rustic stalls once used to stable and shelter farm animals needed repair, their wooden gates rotting and covered with moss from years of dampness. The attic had an empty hay loft, its door open to the weather.

On the east edge of the farm, where the road came to an end in front of Gus's property, grew a thick cluster of Douglas firs blocking the view beyond and giving the farm a sense of privacy. Sam stood and took it all in, the rustic buildings, the open fields, the river, shimmering and bubbly, flowing through the property, and the thick, dense forest surrounding the valley like a protective shield. Skeeter had been correct; Gus's Fishing Hole was like a little piece of heaven. A little bit of perfection tucked away from the rest of the world.

July 8. "Dad got your message. I don't mind being the go-to person for Mom's doctor. Gram didn't take care of her bipolar disorder when Mom was young. Why would I think she'd do it now? Talk soon. Hope you are lovin your new pad!"

48

SAM FELL INTO AN EASY ROUTINE. HE GOT UP BEFORE DAWN EVERY morning, wrote for several hours, and then fished. Gus had been correct; the seam where the fast water merged with the slower, deeper water was the spot. Sam was in no short supply of fish for his meals. At night, he wandered to Gus's porch, where he'd sit and enjoy a glass of whiskey while listening to Gus tell stories about his adventures at sea. Occasionally, they'd play a few hands of poker.

Every afternoon, Sam took off walking through the fields and meadows until he came to the forest's edge. Sometimes he'd find a trail leading into the dense trees and follow it. He loved the damp coolness, how the air grew musty the further into the forest he ventured. Mother Nature resided there—Sam could smell her, feel her cool touch.

But it was the river he was most drawn to. Each day the river, and the paths that meandered in both directions along the riverbanks, called to him. He'd avoided those paths up to now. The woman he'd first seen the day he arrived, Esme, Gus told him, lived on a farm to the east. He felt pulled in her direction and wanted to glimpse where she lived. He remembered Gus's warning, "She likes her solitude. She avoids people." Sam didn't know if he could casually walk past her farm without gawking, without making it look obvious that he was looking for her farm, for her.

One afternoon, he decided to do it. He'd walk east along the riverbank. If he came to Esme's farm and she noticed, he'd casually wave and keep walking like he had a destination in mind. He crossed the bridge to the north side so the river would be between him and her farm. He started walking. Esme's farm was closer than he expected. It was located around the crook in the path and nestled where the river bent slightly south. Sam approached it cautiously. He felt like a voyeur, a trespasser.

The setting reminded him of a painting, a farm taken from the pages of storybooks his mother read to him as a child. It was a small farm, no more than a couple of acres. As Sam approached from the west, he could see where the narrow dirt road ended in front of the farm. A rustic fence made of old cedar posts with interlocking rails wove like a serpentine across the front of the property. Left to rot long ago, it was still performing its function. A climbing rose enshrined an old arbor that stood at the entrance to the farm, rickety from years of rain and sun. Free to meander, the climbing rose spread out and crept along the fence rails smothering them with delicate pink blossoms.

Mountain wildflowers, daisies, lupine, and sedum, left to themselves, grew with reckless abandon around the property. A small farmhouse, aged and stripped bare of paint, stood on the river's edge. Its wrap-around porch allowed views of the river in the back and the farm in front. Soft, cushioned rattan chairs and ottomans sat empty.

There was a chicken coop and hen house and a well-tended vegetable garden with a worn and battered gardening shed close by. The vegetable patch, situated only feet from the river, was enclosed with tall cedar posts, aged and rotting like the fence, with heavy wire panels in between to keep the deer out. A run-down weather-beaten barn, held together by years of patching and mending, provided shelter for animals. Two mustangs grazed on tall grass in a pasture to the side of the barn. When they caught Sam's whiff, they raised their heads, nostrils flaring, their breath coming in snorts. When they determined no real threat, they returned to grazing, flicking flies from their hides with their tails.

The Gypsy Vanner, Homie, was unhaltered, grazing on tall grass at the side of the farmhouse. A Guernsey milk cow, reddish brown with white spots, lazily grazed on tufts of grass she found in the clearing in front of the barn. Like the horse, the cow was unhaltered except for a gold bell that hung from a heavy leather collar around her neck. The bell clanged with every step she took.

Sam stopped walking. He stood, taking in the details. Having picked up Sam's scent, Jake, the dog, trotted out of the barn and gave a couple of warning barks. It brought Sam back to attention. He turned around and took a few steps back toward Gus's farm to give the appearance he was walking past. As he was about to pick up stride, Esme stepped out of the barn. She was bohemian, unconventional, and fiery. Wisps of curls from her hair, knotted in the back, escaped and blew around her face in the breeze. She had on a loose-fitting, flowy dress. The dampness from the drizzle made the fabric cling to her body. She wore a pair of red rubber galoshes. Under her left arm, she held a black-and-white striped hen with a red comb and wattle. The hen appeared to be perched in the crook of her arm, comfortable, like she'd hitched a ride there many times.

Sam stopped—he couldn't move. The attraction was like a magnetic pull, powerful. He was aware that he was staring. Her beauty was like a trap; she snared him. "Thanks, Jake," Sam heard Esme say to the dog. She reached into the pocket of her dress, retrieved a treat, and tossed it to Jake, which he caught in mid-air.

Sam stood rooted to the path watching her.

Esme stared back at Sam across the river. A flock of geese flew onto the property, landing close to her. Jake, who had wandered off to check out something near the barn, came trotting back, intent on harassing the wildfowl. "Belly down, Jake." Esme's command to the dog was soft, non-demanding. The dog immediately dropped to his belly and let out a slight, impatient whine. "Look with your eyes, Jake; they're our friends." She tossed him another treat to show her approval.

Sam forced himself to take a step toward Gus's farm, then another. He slowly started walking away, looking over his shoulder several times to find her standing at the barn door, still watching him. Before turning the bend and disappearing out of sight, he stopped and turned around. He couldn't help himself. She was still standing there, observing him. Even from that distance, her eyes found his. Time stood still. For a fleeting moment, Sam experienced déjà vu, like he'd been there before, with her, like he knew her, like she was a part of him.

After that, Esme was in Sam's head all the time. She consumed his thoughts. He tried not to think about her, but then he'd find his mind wandering back to the image of her standing at the barn door with the hen under her arm, her hair blowing around her face. He started walking past her farm every day, hoping to glimpse her.

Sometimes there'd be signs of activity. The animals, Jake, Homie, the Guernsey milk cow, would be out, free to wander the farm. Unlike the other animals, the mustangs were always in the pasture. Now and then, they'd absentmindedly flick a fly from their hide with their tails, but mainly they were preoccupied with feasting on the tall grass. Once, Sam noticed that one of them had his front leg wrapped in a compression bandage.

Sometimes Sam would see the black-and-white hen strutting around the grounds, plucking at insects. Two other hens, one white, the other brown, would be scavenging with her. Once in a while, the farm lay deserted. Esme and the animals were nowhere to be seen, the barn door closed, and the hens secured in their coop. "She's somewhere out in the woods," Sam figured.

On one of Sam's walks, a few days later, rather than crossing the log bridge to the north side of the river, he decided to walk down the path along the south side nearest Esme's property. As he approached her farm, he saw her in her garden, tilling the space between each row of vegetables, bending now and then to break up a clod of soil. She wore a pink floral dress with short sleeves that barely floated over her shoulders and a V-shaped neckline. Sam's eyes traveled to the neckline. Her logging boots, old and worn, were caked with mud from the garden.

It was Jake who warned Esme that Sam was approaching. The dog, sensing Sam was on the side of the river closest to Esme, barked several times, threatening him to keep his distance. Sam stopped, not sure if it was safe to proceed. Esme looked up, saw it was Sam, and turned to the dog, "It's okay, Jake." She reached into her pocket, retrieved a treat, tossed it to Jake, and then turned to face Sam. "I wanted you to come," she said softly, almost to herself.

As her eyes sought his, Sam had the sensation of being lifted off his feet and tossed into the air. She was who he'd been searching for, he knew it, the woman who the fortune teller told him about years ago. He found her on this tiny farm in the middle of nowhere. He'd felt lost for years, now he was found. "I've been searching for you." Sam couldn't tell if he said it aloud or just thought it.

He walked from the path, through the tall grasses and wildflowers, and onto her property. They watched each other, neither saying a word. She didn't try to stop him, and Jake didn't interfere. Sam saw a hoe leaning against the garden shed. Retrieving it, he entered her garden and began to scratch between a row of plants, watching the ground, careful not to dig up a plant or disrupt a vine. He glanced her way now and then. She went back to tilling. Sometimes when he looked up, she'd be watching him. She was leaning on her hoe when he looked up again, the breeze gently lifting her hair, fluttering the skirt of her dress. "What's your name?" she asked.

"Sam. Sam Parker."

"Sam." She said the word tentatively. She went back to tilling and a few minutes later said, "Go deep enough with the hoe to turn over the soil, Sam. Break up any dirt clods, keep the ground loose and the soil fine, allow it to breathe."

Sam looked at her face, her brown eyes and lips, her hair tied back in a loose ribbon, stray strands curling around her face, the V-shape of her neckline. He nodded.

They worked for an hour or more. When they had tilled every row in the garden, Esme took the hoe from him and put the tools in the garden shed. They stood facing each other. Sam smiled at her, studying her face, taking in every detail. "I'll come tomorrow."

Esme nodded. She turned and walked toward her house, Jake in tow. When she got to her porch, she looked to see if he'd gone. He was still there, standing in the same spot, not moving, watching her. He didn't return to the river path until she disappeared into her house.

The next day, Sam cautiously walked onto her farm. He looked around for Jake, waiting for him to warn Esme of his arrival. Instead, Jake came trotting up to Sam from around the side of the barn, wagging his tail. He'd decided Sam wasn't a threat, perhaps even a friend. "Hey pal," Sam squatted to be at eye-level with the dog. He scratched behind Jake's ears. Jake licked his face. Homie was grazing near the gravel driveway on the opposite side of the yard. When he saw Jake with Sam, he turned and trotted closer, stopping in front of Sam. "Hey, Homie," Sam said as he reached out his hand. Homie sniffed it, tossed his head, and dipped his neck to retrieve a tuft of long grass near Sam's feet.

Sam found Esme in the barn cleaning stalls, wearing faded bib overalls rolled up to her calves and a striped long-sleeve t-shirt, the sleeves pushed past her elbows, her red galoshes on her feet. She wore leather gloves and, with a pitchfork, was depositing dung and wet sawdust from one of the stalls into a wheelbarrow. A second wheelbarrow stood by, piled with fresh sawdust.

She looked up and saw him. Her hair was loosely knotted at the back of her head, stray wisps escaped and lay against her neck and down her shoulders. They looked at each other, neither speaking. She smiled slightly.

"Can I help?" Sam asked.

She nodded and pointed toward a tack room at the back of the barn. "You'll need a rake, pitchfork, and shovel. You'll want some gloves, too."

Sam gathered his tools and returned. "What do I do?"

Esme nodded toward the next stall. "Use the pitchfork and shovel to remove the wet sawdust and dung. Put the waste in the wheelbarrow. Then muck again. Use the broom to sweep up any remaining wet sawdust." She pointed to a broom and dustpan standing against the wall. "Then spread fresh sawdust around the stall from this wheelbarrow," she nodded toward the second wheelbarrow. Be sure to clean out the water bucket; there's a spigot outside on the side of the barn." With that, she went back to cleaning her stall.

Sam began. They worked in silence. Now and then, Sam glanced over at her. Once, she looked up and met his eyes. They gazed at each other, neither wanting to turn away. Sam smiled at her. He was captivated by her mouth, her nose and deep brown eyes, her eyebrows perfectly arched, and the wisps of curls framing her face like a piece of art.

His eyes lingered on her. She didn't look away. He wanted to go to her, to put his hands in her hair, bury his face in her neck, breathe her in, feel her against him. He felt his breath catch in his throat. He looked away. She stood for a few seconds longer and watched him. He was aware of her eyes on him. He had to concentrate on his task at hand. If he turned around to meet her gaze, he wouldn't be able to stop himself; he'd go to her and pull her into his arms.

49

SAM WENT EVERY DAY TO HER FARM. ESME WOULD ANTICIPATE HIS arrival. She dreamed of him at night. He occupied her thoughts during the day while busying herself around her farm. She wanted to be near him, smell his scent, feel his energy when he was close. Once when they were in the barn laying down fresh sawdust for the animals, his hand brushed against hers as he'd reached out to take a rake from her and hang it on the rack. She felt her body react, come alive. When she looked into his face, she felt as though she were falling backward through space. "Catch me, Sam," did she say it or think it?.

Esme watched for his arrival each day. When she'd finally see Sam coming down the riverbank, she'd memorize him, his steps, the way he kept his hands in his pockets when he walked, relaxed, and the way he pushed his hair off his forehead with his fingers when the breeze caught it. She anticipated his smile when he saw her. They'd find each other's eyes. They didn't need words. Their eyes spoke of a thousand lifetimes past, a thousand lifetimes to come.

He worked beside her, gardening, cleaning the barn, mending a broken fence or a section of the chicken coop. He gathered eggs. He learned how to clean out the hen house. Esme taught him the mustangs on the farm were wild, only there to get stronger and return to the wilderness. Together, they herded the mustangs back into the barn each evening. Esme showed Sam how to talk to the horses, tell them what he wanted them to do, praise them when they made the correct move, and assure them they were safe. Sam learned to be calm and determined when herding the mustangs, avoiding sudden movements, and walking slowly but deliberately when corralling them toward the barn. Esme instructed him to use flags to communicate with the horses and gently tickle them on the flank, shoulder, or rump to keep them moving in the desired direction.

Sam learned the Guernsey milk cow's name was Bessy. For most of her life, she belonged to a commercial dairy farmer who bred her each year so she'd produce a calf to keep her milk coming in. She wasn't allowed to care for her any of her calves; they would be taken away from her at birth and either killed to be sold as veal or if a female, raised to become a milk cow. Bessy would be frantic for days after each birth, bleating a high-pitched moo repeatedly, searching with her eyes and nose for her calf. She never got to fulfill her instinctual motherly role. Her milk became sporadic. Finally, when she got too old to be a productive source of milk, the dairy farmer sent her to auction to be sold and sent to the slaughterhouse so her meat could be used as low-grade ground beef. Animal activists saved her, and Esme took her in and gave her a home, a little peace to an otherwise tortured life.

Sam learned the names of Esme's hens: Beulah, Betty, and Bertie. Inevitably one of the hens would fly onto Esme's lap without warning when she sat with Sam on her porch. She hardly noticed. The intruding hen would nestle down, get comfortable and doze while Esme paid little attention. Bertie, the black and white striped hen with the red comb and wattle, had a special affection for humans. Sam learned how to coax Bertie to fly up just high enough so he could catch her. She'd settle in the crux of his arm, content to ride along wherever Sam went.

"Why does Bertie like to be so close to people?" Sam asked one afternoon while they were sitting on Esme's porch, Bertie on her lap.

"It makes her feel secure. When my hens feel safe, they're less stressed and they lay better eggs. They depend on me for security. It's like Saint-Exupéry's *Little Prince*," Esme said softly. "Did you ever read that book, Sam? My hens are my rose. They need me."

It had been one's of Sam's favorite books as a child, and even as an adult, he still loved it. Sam remembered the *Little Prince's* rose, how demanding she was, how prickly, but in the end, the Little Prince sacrificed his life to return to her on his far-away planet because she needed him. Sam sat there on Esme's porch, contemplating her words. He felt a chill for a moment, like when the sun goes behind a cloud. He looked over to find Esme watching him.

"Esme," he couldn't stop the words from coming out, "*I* need you." Saying it made him feel vulnerable, like one of her hens. He wanted to cling to her at that moment, never let go.

She stood, disrupting Bertie, walked over to where Sam was sitting, and reached out her hand. Sam took it. "Come here, Sam," she said, gently tugging his hand. He stood. Esme stepped into his arms and nestled her body into his. They melded into one. Their scents, their breathing, and the sound of their hearts were all in perfect sync. Now that he'd found her, Sam knew he'd never let her go. He couldn't.

One day, Sam walked with Esme through the backfield east of the barn. Jake ran ahead as though he knew what they were there to do. Homie trailed behind, stopping now and then to nibble tasty morsels of tall grass. There, Sam and Esme buried several quart jars containing water and molasses into the earth, leaving only the necks of the jars sticking out. They returned with a strainer, a metal bucket, and clean jars the next day. The liquid molasses had collected June bugs and a plethora of other insects. Esme caught the bugs in the strainer and poured the liquid from the used jars into the clean ones. She dumped the insects into the bucket and reburied the new jars containing water and molasses.

They carried the bucket of insects back to the farm to feed the hens. She tapped the side of the bucket with the metal scoop she used to toss the insects. When the hens heard her coming, they ran to greet her. Wood ducks, geese, cormorants, and pheasants joined the feast. "Belly down," Esme said to Jake when he saw the birds fly in. "They're our friends," she reminded him, tossing him a treat.

One afternoon, when the sun was out, and there were no clouds in the sky, Esme and Sam loaded up Homie and set out on a walk with him and Jake through the woods. She put a halter on Homie and cinched two soft leather saddle bags over his back. She packed bottles of water for her and Sam and the animals, homemade bread and cheese and smoked salmon, vegetables from her garden, and apples from her trees. She poured enough whiskey for two shots into a glass jar and packed it in the saddle bags. She took her rifle, ammunition, and a blanket for them to sit on. She tied a wet scarf around Jake's neck. They set out through the fields in the back of Esme's farm and into the woods.

It was a beautiful, warm day. They walked along the forest trail, taking in the wonders of nature, the giant trees towering above them: western red cedar, Sitka spruce, Douglas fir, bigleaf maple. They followed a brook on its way to meet up with the North Fork Sekiu River. The only sounds they could hear were those belonging to the forest itself, that of birds, an occasional insect, the burble of the brook, and the rustle of tree branches when the breeze swooshed through.

They stopped at a clearing to have a picnic. Esme untacked Homie and tethered him to a nearby tree. It was unfamiliar territory to him, and she didn't want him to get spooked and run off. There were lots of tasty grasses and leaves to nibble on that would occupy his time. Jake was left to wander and explore. They sat on the blanket and ate the picnic lunch Esme brought. They each finished a shot of whiskey. Sam laid back, using Homie's saddlebags as a headrest. Esme sat beside him on the blanket. She lifted his palm and looked at the lines and creases. He was aware of her fingers on his skin. "What's your story, Sam? You've left behind some sort of turmoil." She studied his palm. She reached up and brushed the hair off his forehead. He could see his reflection in her eyes. He gently put his finger over her lips as if to quiet her.

She brushed his fingers away. "Sam, you have a wife back home, don't you? A family? Why are you running away?"

Sam was quiet for a moment. His family felt a million miles away. He didn't want them to be a part of this setting, being in the woods, alone with Esme, just the two of them with Homie and Jake. Today was just for him and Esme. "I'd prefer to think that I ran to you." He reached up and touched her hair, rubbed his thumb slowly across her bottom lip, and let his fingers caress her neck.

"I've been looking for you my whole life, Esme. When I was seventeen, an old Roma fortune teller read my palm and told me I had a soulmate, someone I'm destined to be with. She said I'd know her the minute I saw her. I knew it was you that day you stepped out of the woods when I was driving in. You feel it too, I can tell."

"I feel it, Sam. I feel like I've known you forever. All the pain from my past melts away when I'm with you. I wish we could stay in this spot forever. Just like this." She lay down alongside him. She ran her hand up his shirt and felt his chest. "Take off your shirt, Sam; I want to feel you next to me."

They undressed each other, item by item. They weren't in a hurry. They took their time. They explored each other's bodies. Their passion took them away. To Sam, it felt like he was falling off a cliff in slow motion, tumbling through space, falling into her, becoming one with her. To Esme, it felt like she was melding into him, his energy, his heat consuming her—the more he gave, the more she took.

Later, they lay on the blanket in the sun and dozed, wrapped in each other's arms. Homie stood, head down, resting under the nearby tree. Jake napped at the end of the blanket. It was peaceful, perfect.

Esme dreamed she was an eagle flying high in the sky. Below, she could see a deck of tarot cards lying on the blanket next to where Sam slept. Somewhere in the deck, Esme knew, lay Sam's journey, the lessons he came to learn, his karmic and spiritual path. She could see his past, present, and future from her vantage point. As she dipped lower to get a closer look, she woke up.

July 22. *"Hi, Dad. I'm in between classes right now. I only have a few minutes, but Dr. Stewart from the treatment facility phoned me today. He told me mom is detoxed from alcohol and pills, and they're trying her on a medication called Lithium. I know a little about it from my pharmacology class. It can have some nasty side effects. But so far, it's stabilizing her moods, so Dr. Stewart feels optimistic that it might be a good one to keep her on.*

"The bad news he shared with me is that he thinks mom has brain damage, cognitive, from going for so many years without consistently treating her bipolar disorder. He says the damage can occur from losing amino acids that build proteins that insulate the brain. I didn't understand it. But he's finding that her memory is impaired, and she has trouble concentrating and paying attention for more than a few minutes. Her impulse control is poor, according to Dr. Stewart. The tests they have put her through show that she tends to make hasty decisions and has difficulty planning. Go figure.

"He told me this will likely never improve. I'm just worried that she'll do something stupid when she goes home, that she'll make a careless decision. I mentioned to her that she might consider a live-in, someone who can do the housework, cook for her and do the shopping. Mom has never been good at those things. She refuses to talk about it. I hate having to depend on email. I wish you had phone service."

50

SAM LIKED TO TEASINGLY CAJOLE ESME INTO TELLING HIM WHAT
their future together looked like. He never wanted to know significant details, like how old they'd be when they died or whether
he'd become a successful writer. Instead, he asked her about small,
insignificant details they most looked forward to sharing, like where
they'd go to chop down their Christmas tree that year or how many
pumpkins they'd carve for Halloween. It was simplicity they both
sought. Their days together, they dreamed, would roll by with no
fanfare. He'd write, and she'd tend the farm. He'd help with chores.
They'd go on walks, cook together, he'd read his manuscripts to her,
they'd make love in the afternoon. They dreamed of growing old
together, caring for each other.

Sometimes when Sam fished or sat on Esme's porch or at the
rickety table in his cabin where he wrote, he'd think about whether
or not he and Esme had shared previous lives. The writer in him, the
dreamer, made him ponder the possibility. What little he knew of
quantum physics told him everything was a possibility. He wanted
to believe it. He'd wonder how they'd met in their previous lives. He
wished he could remember. He tried to imagine how they'd meet
in their next life. Would they recognize each other? No, he knew

they wouldn't, but they'd remember the feeling when their hands would first touch. It would be like a lock opening up, like walking into the sun, like completing a circle. They'd have a moment of déjà vu when they'd know that somewhere far away and long ago, they'd experienced the same feeling, and it would feel right.

They surrendered to it completely, loving each other. It was as though they were sailing down a river on a raft with no oars; their only choice was to cling to each other and let the current take them where it would. They gave into their passion and allowed it to carry them along like a feather in the breeze. The rest of the world ceased to exist.

It was a sweltering afternoon. Sam had stretched out on a lawn chair on Esme's porch, reading, and had dozed off, the book open on his chest. He woke up, went inside, and poured himself a small glass of whiskey with ice. He returned and walked around the porch to the back of the house, his drink in hand. A clearing in the back of the farmhouse served as a backyard. A sandy beach had formed along the river in that spot over the years. The water there at the beach was shallow and slow. It was a great place to cool off, pull up a lawn chair and dip one's feet in the water, or sit around a campfire on cool nights and listen to the sound of the river as it flowed by on its way to the ocean.

Esme was hanging laundry, wet sheets and pillowcases on two makeshift clotheslines that Django had built years ago for Analetta. It was a beautiful day. The sky was cobalt blue. Soft, puffy, cotton-top clouds drifted across the horizon. Esme was barefoot, her hair blowing around her face in the breeze. She wore a simple white dress made of sheer fabric that Sam could see the outline of her legs through. He could see a trickle of sweat roll down her neck and disappear in the space between her breasts.

Sam stood on the porch where he knew she could see him and studied her like an artist examines his model, intent on her every move. He sipped his whiskey, occasionally holding the glass to his face, letting the chill from the ice cubes cool him in the hot sun. He watched as Esme bent to retrieve a wet sheet and then stretched to pin it to the line. The breeze caused her dress to cling to her legs.

She disappeared behind a row of sheets, so only her bare feet and calves were visible. Sam watched her reappear to retrieve a wet pillowcase from her basket. The laundry on the line fluttered, and Esme's dress blew softly in the breeze. Sam stood at the railing, holding his glass of whiskey. Esme could feel his eyes on her. She turned to meet his gaze. She didn't look away, instead drawing him in, inviting him.

Sam stepped off the porch, the glass of whiskey in his hand, and walked to where Esme stood between the two rows of billowing sheets. No one was around except for Jake, who dozed in the shade of a nearby tree. Sam put his free arm around Esme's waist and gently pulled her to him. She let her head fall back. He trickled a droplet of whiskey from his glass onto her neck and let it puddle in the indent at the base of her throat. His lips were on her neck; his tongue found the whiskey.

She touched the rim of his glass with her lips. He fed her a swallow of whiskey and then softly kissed her mouth to catch the flavor. Their gaze told each other what they wanted. Her body pressed and moved against him. She could feel him respond. She was receptive, willing. He laid her down on a wet sheet in the sand next to the river. The sun drifted overhead, the breeze blew the clouds out to sea, and the river rolled by. But Esme and Sam failed to notice; the world was forgotten. They drank each other in, fed on each other, and when at last they were satiated, they slept, cooled by the breeze.

They cooked meals together. Esme prepared authentic Romani dishes, goulash and sarma. Often the aroma of Ciorba de fasole, white bean and vegetable soup thickened with roux and seasoned with sweet and hot paprika drifted from her kitchen and wafted onto her porch. She taught Sam the art of chopping vegetables just so for each dish, how much of a fresh herb to sprinkle over a stew or to mix with rice pilaf to set off the flavor, and when to toss in fresh tomatoes or a dribble of fresh lime to add a final zest. She'd stand at the stove and sample a taste of sauce or the broth of a soup. She'd offer Sam a taste. He'd gently push the spoon aside and sample the broth from her lips, his tongue, ever so lightly, finding the flavor. Later they'd eat the meal in mismatched bowls with thick slices of homemade bread with butter. They'd sit on the porch savoring the meal, watching the day end, listening to the sounds of the forest, nourishing their souls.

They baked together. Esme taught Sam how to make pufe and xaritsa as Analetta had taught her. They made baklava and prestige that she and Sam would eat with hot coffee before they began their day. Together they'd knead the dough. The trick, she taught him, was not to over-knead. She'd put her hands over his, and together, they'd work the dough lightly until it was of the right consistency. Sam would lose his concentration, forget about the kneading, and become distracted by her closeness, her hands on his, the feel of the dough oozing up through their fingers. He'd turn his head and breathe her in, feel her hair on his cheek, her neck close to his lips. She'd laugh and redirect him. Some loaves got tossed out, the kneading overworked until it was too late to salvage.

51

ONE MORNING WHEN SAM FINISHED WRITING AND WAS ON HIS WAY TO the fishing hole, a pickup truck drove onto Gus's property and parked in front of the farmhouse. Tom Johnson stepped out of the driver's seat, his long black hair parted in the middle and braided behind each ear. The braids hung to his chest and were intertwined with red suede. He wore jeans over black western boots, a black sports jacket over a black jersey. Around his neck he wore three silver chains of different lengths, ornamented with turquoise and silver pendants. Small turquoise studs decorated both ears. A hand-carved eagle adorned his belt buckle. He was lean and fit, striking. Sam couldn't help but notice.

Gus came out of his house, "Hey, Tom. What brings you out this morning?"

"I've been to the courthouse. I saw on the docket that Mark Kipling has scheduled a formal hearing with Judge John Milton in a couple of weeks for this cougar issue concerning Esme."

With the mention of Esme, Sam perked up.

"Why?" Gus sounded concerned.

"He's accusing her of bypassing legal channels to relocate that cougar that came onto her property last year. Twice she's missed the deadline to pay the two thousand dollar fine he issued her. Now he's ordered her to appear in court. If she misses the court date, he plans to issue a warrant for her arrest."

"That's outrageous," Gus said. "She didn't even transport the cougar. Does Mark know that?"

"I'm pretty sure she told him. But he hates her, remember?" Tom said. "Either he hasn't done his homework, or he intends to lie about her to the judge. People in Crystal Bay hear her name and they'll come out in droves. Mark's had it out for Esme for years. He'd like nothing more than to arrest her and send her to jail in front of the whole town. I've had it with Kipling. I've had it with the whole damn town to be honest. I mean to do something about it. I intend to represent her."

Sam forgot about fishing. He stepped onto Gus's porch, where the two men stood talking. "Morning, Gus." He turned to Tom. "My name's Sam, Sam Parker," he said, extending his hand. Tom shook Sam's hand. "I couldn't help but overhear what you said. What kind of trouble is someone trying to cause Esme?"

Tom and Sam faced off, each one taking in the other. It was Gus who responded. "Sam, this is Tom Johnson, he's from the reservation, lives in Neah Bay, he's on the Tribal Council. Tom, this is Sam Parker. Sam's been staying here for a while. You men have something in common, you're both attorneys."

For a second, Sam expected Gus to say what they both had in common was Esme.

Tom finally spoke, "I take it you know Esme?"

"Yeah, I know her. What kind of trouble is this guy trying to cause her, what's he accusing her of?"

The two men sized each other up. Neither knew what role the other played in Esme's life.

It was Gus again who answered Sam's question. "Mark Kipling is the fish and game warden who was assigned to work the area around Crystal Bay a couple of years ago. He's fairly new at his job. He's been trying to get on with the Fish and Game Department for years. He grew up in Crystal Bay. He's a hard-nosed, hard-drinking guy with a nasty disposition. He was big man on campus back in high school. He was the star quarterback. Folks around here still put him on a pedestal. Truth is, he's a bully, always has been and now that he wears a badge, he likes to use his law enforcement authority to throw his weight around. The person he most likes to bully is Esme. His beef with her goes all the way back to high school. It's a long story."

"What's his beef with her?" Sam asked.

Gus and Tom exchanged looks. Tom wasn't willing to share stories about Esme with someone he'd never met. Finally, Gus spoke. "Let's fill our coffee cups and have a seat, boys. Sam here needs to know what Esme's dealing with. She won't tell you, Sam, I know her. She's used to figuring stuff out on her own."

For the next couple of hours, Gus and Tom filled Sam in on Esme's connection to Mark Kipling, how he bullied her in high school, along with his football buddies, and how she caught him beating up on a ten-year-old boy the day before the big championship football game back when they were seniors in high school. They told Sam how the whole town of Crystal Bay shunned Esme from the time she arrived in Crystal Bay when she was nine years old, how they spun stories about her being a witch and made her an outcast.

Tom concluded the story. "Last year, a cougar started prowling around Esme's farm. Gus texted Mark five times at Esme's request to ask the Fish and Game to relocate the cougar. She didn't want to shoot it, she wanted it relocated. Mark never responded. Later, when Mark learned the cougar had been relocated, he assumed she did it without permission."

"Thing is," Tom laughed sarcastically, "folks from the reservation relocated the cougar. It was all done according to Fish and Game policy. Mark thinks he has her cornered, but really, he's the fool. He's counting on her showing up alone, thinking it'll be her word against his. The whole town will turn out; you can count on it. They'll squeeze into the courtroom to watch what they think will be a showdown, the 'witch' against the town hero. I intend to put a stop to it once and for all."

The three men sat silently, each thinking about the spectacle the hearing could entail. Sam looked up to find Tom watching him. The two men looked at each other, and an understanding passed between them. "Do you want to help me out with this, Sam?" Tom asked him. A look of agreement passed between them, a knowing.

"I do," Sam replied.

Esme was out picking blackberries that morning. Sam sat on her porch, waiting for her, Jake, and Homie to walk home through the field east of her barn. When he saw her coming, he got up and walked to the barn to meet her. "Es, we have to talk."

"What about?" Esme saw the concerned look on Sam's face. "What's wrong, Sam?"

"I met Tom Johnson this morning. Tell me about Mark Kipling, Es. What happened back when you were in school?"

Sam emailed Marty Bigelow. "I need your help Marty. I need you to find someone for me."

52

The temperature dropped, and the rain set in. It wasn't the type of day to typically draw folks out of their houses. But on this day, residents of Crystal Bay dropped everything to crowd into the courthouse. The gallery, including the balcony, was packed, and the areas in the back of the courtroom and along the outer isles were crowded with spectators standing, pressed together. It was a rare chance to see the "gypsy" up close and watch how she would respond to the complaint filed against her by Mark Kipling.

Nothing exciting had happened in their town for a long time, and folks were looking for something to distract them from their boredom. Anticipation of the hearing reignited stories of Esme, her witchcraft, her power to cast spells, and her ability to read one's future and tell one's past. "Watch your men," the women of the town warned while their husbands joked, "Watch your wallets."

Mark and a Fish and Game Commissioner were seated at the council table to the right facing the judge's bench. The commissioner was there to support Mark, to show that the Fish and Game Department was backing him. Mark's complaint against Esme was outlined in the Washington Code, which stipulates the unlawful transfer of wildlife as a class C felony punishable by up to five years in jail and/or a fine of up to $10,000. Mark was confident he had an open-and-shut case against Esme. He had, after all, fined her only two thousand dollars and didn't expect the judge to hesitate to enforce his penalty. Esme either needed to pay the fine or go to jail, which Mark secretly hoped would happen. The thought of Esme sitting in the slammer for a few days would feel like a victory to him, a long overdue win.

The wall clock indicated it was twelve fifty-nine, one minute before the hearing was due to begin. Mark was impatient, shifting in his seat as he looked over his shoulder at the crowded courtroom gallery. He knew most of the faces who'd come to watch the hearing. Mark saw a few of his old football buddies from high school sitting together toward the back of the gallery, some with their wives. Jeff Thompson, the long-retired principal from the Crystal Bay Elementary and Middle School, was there, as were many of the parents of the kids Mark grew up with. Sitting about halfway back in the gallery was Shelby and her mother, the girl who'd bullied Esme in elementary school. Mark remembered Shelby had her own beef with Esme years ago. When Mark caught Shelby's eye, she smiled at him.

The spectators were fidgeting, waiting for the show to begin. They hyped themselves up as they always did when Esme was involved. They whispered and jeered, stood in small groups, and talked amongst themselves. It felt like the same camaraderie they remembered when they went out to cheer for their football team. Now, here they were again, out to support Mark, their former football hero, the man of the hour. The talk, however, focused on Esme, the anticipation of getting to see her up close and personal. Though they didn't admit it to each other, this would be their chance to watch her, study her, and stare at her beauty without pretending they weren't interested.

Mark turned around to make contact with the spectators. He was anxious to show the commissioner how much support the community gave him. This was his chance to shine in front of his superior. Someone in the front row from Mark's football days caught his eye when he turned around and assured him, "Hey Mark, we've got your back."

The feeling in the gallery made Mark think of what it used to feel like when he'd look up into the bleachers from the football field and see the faces of his fans, good people who came out to cheer him on during a football game. They were here today. It gave Mark a feeling of warmth, of recognition, and significance. This was his chance to show the people of Crystal Bay that he was still a winner.

Mark had prepared notes to keep him on track. He'd carefully outlined every infraction that Esme had violated. She wouldn't have a leg to stand on. Mark wouldn't be aggressive. He'd smile at her and be friendly toward the judge. He'd come at her nice and slow, methodically, clarifying every point, leaving no room for argument, leaving her tongue-tied. He'd point out that she was getting off easy; a two thousand dollars fine was all. Of course, she'd be looking at jail time if she couldn't come up with the money.

It wasn't because Esme refused to pay the fine he issued her regarding the cougar; it wasn't even that he'd lost the game because of her years ago; he wanted to shame her in front of the townsfolk for how she'd made him feel that day she walked into the high school gym and found him with Patrick Donovan. Her look that day had been revealing. He disgusted her; he was a brute in her mind, someone who picks on weaker prey to feel powerful, just like his dad had done to him and his brother. Her look made him feel like he was no different than his father.

The girl Mark had secretly idolized, glorified, and lusted after, was disgusted by him. Esme had reached into his soul that day and pulled open the curtain on who he really was. She'd revealed his true nature, left him feeling naked and exposed, and then walked away, spurned him. Now was his chance to bring that little bitch down in front of God and all of Crystal Bay.

Mark glanced toward the back of the courtroom, waiting to see Esme push open the door and enter the gallery. "Maybe she won't show," he thought. That might be even better. "Everyone would think she was too afraid to face me."

53

AT PRECISELY ONE O'CLOCK, THE DOOR AT THE BACK OF THE GALLERY
opened, and Tom Johnson walked into the courtroom. All eyes
watched him walk down the aisle and sit at the defendant's council
table. He didn't acknowledge anyone in the gallery as he strode
toward the front of the courtroom. He wore his hair in a man bun
secured with a hand-carved wooden comb and was dressed casually
but professionally. Jewelry, hand-made by the Makah people, adorned
his neck and wrists. He carried a worn leather satchel in one hand.

No one in the gallery expected Esme to come to court with
representation. Moreover, they didn't expect an attorney from the
reservation to show up on Esme's side. The Makah Tribe typically
kept to themselves and didn't get involved in business outside the
reservation unless it concerned community issues that impacted the
Indian Nation. But here was Tom Johnson, the quiet kid from high
school who went to law school and now sat on the tribal council.

"Why's that Indian here?" somebody asked. "And what's he got
to do with the Gypsy?"

"This isn't a reservation issue," said another.

And where was Esme? They all wanted to know, although none
of them asked it aloud. The courtroom door opened before they could

speculate, and Esme walked in. The townsfolk expected her to come into court feeling timid. After all, they figured she'd be on her own while Mark had the support of the whole town. Instead, she seemed poised, dressed in traditional Roma attire. Rather than trying to blend in to avoid making a scene, it was as though she wanted to show off her differences.

Wearing a blue velvet mid-length skirt, a peasant blouse with short, puffed sleeves, and a low-cut neckline, suggestive but not revealing, she walked down the aisle. Around her waist, she wore a colorful sash and soft deerskin boots on her feet. A necklace of gold coins encircled her neck, and gold hoops adorned her ears. Both her wrists were embellished with silver and gold bangles. Her hair, tied back in a vibrant headscarf with long tails that hung to her shoulder on one side, cascaded down her back with loose strands escaping around her face. Esme was unconventional, unique, and untamed. She dimmed the lights on every woman and man in the gallery. She was like a fine piece of art. The spectators were taken off guard, spellbound. They craned their necks to get a better look.

Equally captivating was the man at her side. He was handsome, with windblown hair and blue-green eyes, and dressed in khakis, a tattersall shirt, and expensive oxfords. "Who's he?" was on the tips of everyone's tongue. The locals didn't know him; none in the courtroom had seen him. But his manner gave the impression of someone not to be ignored. He looked like a prominent city attorney, professional, and competent. All eyes in the courtroom were riveted on him, women and men alike. But, like Esme, he ignored the spectators in the gallery. The two of them walked up the aisle and sat at the defendant's table next to Tom, Esme in the middle, and the men on either side.

"You didn't tell me, Mark, that Esme would be represented by legal counsel," the commissioner whispered. "We should have had our attorney here."

"I didn't know," Mark whispered back in a type of hiss. It was the first flicker in Mark's mind that things might not be as cut and dried as he'd counted on.

The bailiff called the court to order. "The court is now in session, the Honorable Judge John Milton presiding."

The judge entered the courtroom and took his seat on the bench. "Please be seated," Judge Milton announced. He pounded his gavel and nearly shouted to be heard over the commotion. Folks hurried to their seats. Judge Milton looked at Sam and then Tom before addressing him. "Tom, I'm aware of your status as an attorney from the Makah Tribe. Does the complaint from the Fish and Game Department against Ms. Horvat involve the Makah Indian Tribe?"

Tom stood and faced the judge. "It does, your Honor. It was members of the Makah Tribe who relocated the cougar, not Esme."

There was a rumble from the gallery. Judge Milton pounded his gavel. "Quiet," he practically shouted to the spectators. "Why am I just now hearing about this?" He turned to Mark and repeated himself. "Why am I just now hearing this?"

Mark sat at the counsel table looking perplexed, like someone who had slept through all the stops on the transit, and woke up to find he was at the end of the line and miles from his destination. "That's not true, he's lying."

"Mark, watch yourself. I'll not have you blurting out accusations in my courtroom. You'll be given time to make your points and we'll determine if someone is lying."

Judge Milton glanced at the notes provided to him by the judicial clerk and turned to Sam. "I presume you are Sam Parker. Please rise and state your name and purpose for being here today."

Sam stood, as instructed by the judge, and stated his full name and credentials for the record. "I'm also representing Esme, your Honor. Like Tom, I have additional evidence to bring forward today that impacts the complaint against our client."

Once again, there was a loud reaction from the spectators, a reverberation that rolled through the gallery. And once again, the judge pounded his gavel to quiet the courtroom.

Judge Milton turned to Esme. "May I call you Esme?" he asked. Esme nodded. "Do these two gentleman, Esme, have your permission to speak on your behalf in this courtroom today regarding the complaint filed against you by the Fish and Game Department?"

Esme stood, "Yes, your honor."

"Are you aware, Esme, of the charges being filed against you today?"

Esme briefly glanced at Sam. He smiled at her and nodded his head. "I am, your Honor," Esme spoke softly but clearly.

The judge looked at Mark and then at Tom and Sam, addressing them all. "Gentlemen, please approach the bench." He'd hoped to finish court early to get in nine holes of golf before dinner. Suddenly, what he'd thought would be a simple open-and-shut complaint had become convoluted. He regretted allowing spectators to be present.

"I want to know what the hell's going on," he said out of earshot of the spectators.

It was Tom who responded. "Your Honor, I will present evidence that was omitted in the official complaint filed against Esme."

"What additional evidence?" The judge looked at all three men, wondering which ones would be to blame for making a circus out of his courtroom.

"Your Honor," Tom kept his voice low, "I will present evidence that counters the points Mark Kipling will bring against Esme. Everything I will present is documented and we have witnesses in the gallery who are willing to testify in support of the evidence I am submitting."

Judge Milton looked at Mark, who looked like the last one to get the joke. The judge considered and then said to Tom, "I'll allow this evidence to be presented." He turned to Sam, "Mr. Parker, Sam, is there anything else I need to know before we start?"

"Your Honor, I intend to show proof of a long history of bullying from Mark Kipling against our client and have witnesses ready to testify who will validate my testimony. I can show that Mark Kipling deliberately refused to respond to Esme when her neighbor, Gus Toblar, texted him on five separate occasions to ask for assistance from the Fish and Game Department."

"Your Honor, that's a lie," Mark practically shouted, his voice audible throughout the courtroom.

"Mark." The judge's tone had taken on an attitude of authority. "Let me remind you where you are. I'll not tolerate outbursts in *my* courtroom." When he said, "My courtroom," Judge Milton pounded his index finger on his desk to show ownership. He turned back to Sam. "Continue."

"My testimony, your Honor, will put into question whether or not Mark Kipling is qualified to wear a badge and serve in the capacity of law enforcement." Sam looked at Mark when he spoke.

The spectators strained to hear what was being discussed at the judge's bench. Mark slammed his fist against the judge's bench. "John, this is crazy. They're just trying to evade the situation that we're here for. What this guy," Mark waved his hand in Sam's direction, "is proposing is complete nonsense and has nothing to do with why we're here today."

"Mark, you are inching closer and closer to trouble." The judge leaned forward over his bench to get closer to Mark. "When you're in my courtroom, you'll address me as 'Your Honor.' Don't make me explain the rules of this courtroom one more time."

"Sorry, Your Honor, but this is all bullshit."

The judge stared at Mark. "One more fuck up from you, Mark," he said low, under his breath, to keep the spectators from hearing, "and I'll cite you for contempt. Make one more stupid remark and see if I'm kidding." Judge Milton's tone had become impatient, disgusted. The worst possible situation in a hearing was being caught unprepared. Someone would pay for this debacle; the judge needed to find out who.

Judge Milton continued, "Sam, these are serious allegations you're proposing."

Mark was red-faced with anger. He butted in before Sam could respond, willing to ignore the judge's previous threat. "Your Honor, these allegations are outrageous and have nothing to do with the complaint we're here to present. We're here to discuss a Fish and

Game violation. No bullying occurred. Wildlife was endangered by the defendant's actions and needs to be addressed." Mark spoke indignantly, louder than he meant to, so those in the front rows of the gallery could hear. He could feel the eyes of the spectators on him and somehow he had to get things back into focus. This wasn't a football game where he could call a play and make things happen his way.

The judge pondered the situation. Finally, he spoke, "Gentlemen, it appears we have a mess to sort out. I'll allow this additional testimony to be presented. If the defendant has been bullied I want to know about it. But let me be very clear, Sam, this better be valid. If you are falsely accusing Mark of something this serious without proper evidence, your ass will be on the line. Have I made myself clear?"

"My testimony will be valid, your Honor."

Next, Judge Milton turned to Mark. "If I find that you failed to provide accurate facts about this case, your head will roll. Are you clear on that?"

Mark nodded. He had no idea what was coming his way. He felt caught off guard.

"Let's get this ball rolling then," the judge ordered Mark. "Present your complaint. You'll be given the opportunity to defend any evidence levied against you today."

"But, your honor," Mark began.

The judge didn't say anything; he just looked at Mark. His look said everything. The Fish and Game commissioner hissed at Mark from the counsel table to be quiet.

Mark turned and walked to his counsel table, looking out at the spectators while they were looking back at him in anticipation. The self-confidence he brought into the courtroom disappeared, leaving him feeling shaky and uncertain. He blamed Esme. She was doing it to him again, toying with him. "That bitch," he thought. He glanced over at her. She sat quietly, looking right at him.

Mark tried to muster up his courage. He had no idea what Sam Parker had in mind, but one thing Mark knew for sure was that he had not bullied Esme. He might hate Esme, but there was no crime in that. Sure, he came onto her farm occasionally, checking for Fish and Game violations, and sometimes gave her a bit of a hard time, but that wasn't the same as bullying her. He'd never laid a hand on her. Mark didn't know what Parker had up his sleeve, but he was dealing with the wrong guy. Sam Parker didn't know anything about him. Mark had friends in this courtroom. Folks present today would stand up for him. He felt some of his swagger return.

Still standing, Mark glanced down at the commissioner, who looked up at him with a questioning expression. Mark cleared his throat, faced the judge, and began in his most convincing voice. "Esme Horvat is guilty of violating the Washington code, RCW 77.15, that states it's an offense punishable by law to unlawfully traffic, take, or remove big game or protected wildlife without proper authority."

Mark finished and stood staring at Judge Milton, who impatiently replied, "Go on, Mark, explain to the court what specifically the defendant did."

"Well, it's obvious," Mark had a defensive tone. He picked up his notes for moral support. There on the page were his complaints, outlined and numbered. His points were all valid. He would carry on as he'd rehearsed.

Esme sat calmly at the defendant's table. She turned to look at Mark, waiting for him to speak. Her eyes on him made him feel exposed. Tom had a pad of paper before him, ready to take notes. Sam, however, had pulled his chair out from the table and leaned back, relaxed, with one foot crossed over his knee. He was watching Mark. When Mark glanced at him, Sam smiled. Mark didn't like anything about him.

Mark steadied himself, glanced down at his notes, and then addressed the judge. "First of all, your honor," he began, "the cougar was injected with an unauthorized sedative. The sedative could have seriously injured or killed the cougar. The amount needs to be determined by a qualified vet." He planned to go into more detail but lost his train of thought, so he moved on.

"Secondly, she put everyone who helped her in danger."

The judge interrupted. "Mark, hold on a second. According to Tom here, Esme wasn't the person who relocated the cougar. If that's true, your testimony is worthless. I want to hear how you happen to know that Esme was the one who carried out the relocation of the cougar. That's what you've charged her with. I need proof of that before we move on."

It was hard to hear Mark over the rumble from the spectators. The judge banged his gavel. Mark didn't know how to respond. He sounded defensive. "Your Honor, Gus Toblar informed me in his texts that Esme wanted the cougar relocated and then he notified me later that Esme had resolved the cougar issue herself."

"So, what?" Judge Milton thundered. "That doesn't prove anything. Sit down, Mark, I want to hear from Tom, here."

Mark felt like a fool in front of everyone in the gallery. This felt like a redo from the championship football game years before. He remembered the feeling, knowing everyone in the bleachers had just witnessed him lose. Today felt the same. But worst of all, it was happening in front of Esme. He was being made a fool of in front of her. He glanced her way. There she sat, looking right at him, right into him.

54

TOM STOOD AND FACED JUDGE MILTON. HE CAREFULLY LAID OUT THE facts of the case, that a young cougar that probably wandered down the mountains and into the valley near Esme's farm began stalking her animals. "Typically," Tom explained, "these animals will turn around and head back up to higher ground. But this was a very young cougar who most likely became disoriented when he wandered outside of his hunting territory." The cougar, he explained, had become bolder each day, finally coming onto Esme's property in broad daylight. Tom presented the judge with a photo taken by someone from the reservation of the cougar on Esme's property near her barn.

Tom then showed evidence from the phone company of the multiple texts from Gus's phone to Mark during this time. "Your Honor, Mark was notified five times from Gus's phone asking for assistance from the Fish and Game Department. Mark did not respond to one of those messages."

Tom continued, "Finally, Esme contacted the Tribal Council and asked for our help. There are members of the Makah Tribe who are familiar with relocating wild animals and who use the same protocol that the Fish and Game Department uses. The animal was sedated with a dart gun prepared by one of the Tribal vets and moved by members of the tribe who've done it many times before. The cougar was collared for tracking and moved to a location about ninety miles southeast that's had no cougar sightings in over five years. The goal was to avoid putting the young cougar in another cougar's hunting territory."

"The bottom line, your Honor," Tom turned and faced Mark, "is that Mark Kipling failed to respond to a resident within his jurisdiction when he'd been informed that a cougar was prowling on the resident's farm and stalking her domestic animals. The cougar was becoming aggressive as a result of hunger and fear. Protecting farmers and domestic animals is a top priority of the Fish and Game Department, as is protecting wildlife. Mark Kipling failed to do his job and left a resident within his jurisdiction unassisted, putting Esme's life and that of her farm animals in jeopardy, as well as compromising the safety of the cougar. If Mr. Kipling wants to file a complaint, he needs to direct it to the Makah Tribal Council, who will argue that the Makah Tribe got involved due to Mark's negligence."

Judge Milton, who'd been taking notes during Tom's testimony, finally looked up. He turned his attention to Mark. "Mark, do you have anything to say about Tom's testimony?"

Mark's mouth was dry. He felt like his throat might have closed, preventing him from speaking. "Your Honor," he heard the weakness in his own voice, "are you aware of how many requests for assistance I receive as part of my job? It's not feasible that I can respond at the drop of a hat to every request I receive."

Tom stood again to address the judge, "Your Honor, I would like to point out that the Fish and Game warden, on average, in this jurisdiction, receives maybe one or two requests each month asking for help. I repeat, your Honor, one or two requests each month. It would not be difficult to have responded to Esme's texts within a twenty-four-hour period."

The judge turned his attention once again back to Mark. "Mark, either you deliberately presented incorrect evidence or yours is an example of the sloppiest testimony I've ever heard in my courtroom. Do you have facts to present that might dispute Tom's testimony? A record of all those requests that kept you too busy to respond to this one?"

Mark felt the color rise in his neck and creep into his face. He hadn't considered that the Makah Tribe would step in and take care of the cougar for Esme. He should have known better. Tom Johnson had been protecting Esme for as long as Mark could remember. This all felt like déjà vu.

"Your Honor …," Mark began but couldn't find the words to continue.

"Mark," Judge Milton's tone was that of a frustrated adult trying to reason with an illogical child, "since you failed to respond to Esme's need for assistance, her only options were to shoot and kill the cougar or ask the Makah Tribe for help. Which would you have preferred she do? Would you have preferred she shoot and kill the cougar?"

"Of course not, your Honor, but …"

Judge Milton didn't give Mark the chance to finish. "Sit down, Mark. We need to move on."

The courtroom gallery was abuzz. Spectators ignored the signs posted around the room to maintain silence and reacted boisterously, shaking their heads in bewilderment. Mark Kipling, their man, just went down. Again! Esme had him by the crosshairs. The Gypsy had done it once more. Through all this, Esme sat quietly in her chair at the defendant's counsel table, not saying a word.

The judge banged his gavel. "I'll have order in my court," he demanded. "If there's one more outburst from the spectators, they'll be removed from the courtroom. This is your final warning." When order was re-established, Judge Milton turned to Sam. "Sam, please stand and present your testimony."

Esme looked at Sam. He looked at her and smiled. "It's okay," he said to her quietly. "Trust me." He stood and moved to the center of the courtroom in front of the judge. "Your Honor, I request permission to ask Mark Kipling a few questions."

Judge Milton thought about it for a moment. He was known for running his courtroom like a tight ship. Today would go down as the exception. He braced himself for what would come next. Again, he regretted not having banned spectators from the hearing. Finally, he spoke, "This is highly unusual, Sam, in this type of a hearing, but I will allow it this one time. You may proceed with your questioning, and Mr. Kipling will be given the opportunity to redirect."

"Fair enough, your Honor." Sam walked close to Mark's counsel table, forcing Mark to make eye contact with him. Mark had the look on his face of a cornered animal. When Sam addressed him, his tone was almost gentle. "Mark, can you tell the court how you know Esme Horvat?"

"I don't know her." Mark replied defensively.

"Oh, I think you do, Mark," Sam corrected him. "You've known her since you were both in high school. Tell us what you remember about Esme from school."

"I didn't know her in school."

"Yes, you did, Mark," Sam corrected. "Tell the court how you used to address her in the halls at school."

There was an uncomfortable shuffling in the gallery as folks shifted in their seats, waiting for what was coming next.

"I don't know what you're talking about." Mark's face by now was flushed. He needed to get his thoughts straight, but he couldn't focus. He was finding it hard to catch his breath. He could feel the eyes of the spectators drilling holes through the back of his head. His buddies from high school were present in the gallery. They'd stick up for him if need be. But this was a courtroom. He couldn't just call out his friends to back him. He was in this alone.

"Let me help you remember." Sam's tone was like an adult coaxing a small child. "You and your friends used to call Esme a 'Gypsy,' a 'witch,' a 'knacker,' a 'pikey,' when you saw her coming down the halls at school." Sam said each derogatory term carefully and slowly to make his impact. "You'd make comments when she walk past you in school accusing her of being a thief, a pickpocket, a tramp." Sam gave Mark a moment to respond. When he didn't, Sam continued. "You'd laugh and hoot with your friends, bullying Esme when you saw her."

"We might have made a few jokes. It didn't mean anything," Mark tried to sound nonchalant, unconcerned. Still, he was finding it hard to talk and breathe simultaneously. He was on the verge of hyperventilating. There was an uncomfortable silence in the gallery. People began staring at their laps to avoid making eye contact with Sam. The judge had quit taking notes. He waited to hear what was coming,

Sam continued, "I'm sure that you, as well as everyone in the courtroom," Sam looked up and swept his arm across the gallery to indicate he was addressing the spectators, "know that the names you called the defendant are derogatory terms used against Roma people. Isn't that right, Mark?" Sam was looking at the spectators in the gallery, waiting for Mark to answer. Mark looked at Sam defiantly, refusing to respond.

Sam went on, "What's more, I'm sure that you, Mark, as well as everyone in the courtroom, know that when you attach a negative label to another person, like witch or thief, for example ..." Sam looked around the gallery, taking in each individual as he did so. "When you misrepresent a person over and over like that, the person becomes known by that label, it ostracizes that person, isolates them, turns them into a target."

Sam positioned himself in front of Mark to look down directly into Mark's face and over Mark's head at the spectators in the gallery. "I'm sure, Mark, that you, as well as everyone here in the courtroom, know that making up stories to embarrass or ridicule another person, stories you know aren't true, is considered defamatory by law and makes any propagator of those stories, by definition, a bully." With that, Sam paused and swept his gaze over the spectators, who had now lowered their eyes and were fidgeting uncomfortably in their seats. "Do you agree with that definition of a bully, Mark?"

Mark refused to look at Sam. Instead, he turned his head to try to catch the eye of his supporters in the gallery. No one was looking at him. The spectators were avoiding eye contact altogether. Some were eyeing the exit door, trying to figure out a way to leave without looking obvious.

"Are you remembering any better what your relationship with Esme was like, Mark, when you and your football buddies used to bully her in high school?" Sam looked toward the back of the courtroom and let his eyes rest on the now-grown men who played high school football with Mark.

Mark's reply could barely be heard, "We might have made a few jokes. We weren't bullying her. It didn't mean anything."

"To you and your friends, it didn't mean anything. It got you laughs and attention. How do you think it made Esme, your target feel? What do you envision it feeling like to be labeled with the kind of words you called the defendant?" Again, Sam shifted his gaze from Mark to the spectators in the courtroom, and again the spectators averted their eyes.

Sam was silent momentarily, letting the unease settle over the courtroom. "It seems a bit uncomfortable in the courtroom right now, doesn't it, Mark? Let's change the subject." Sam's voice sounded almost soothing. "Let's go back fourteen years to the championship football game that your team lost when you were a senior in high school. Let's talk about the pep rally that took place the day before the big game."

"Your Honor," Mark jumped to his feet. He refused to be put on the witness stand. He was not on trial here; this hearing was about Esme, not him. "I'm not on trial. None of this has anything to do with the reason we're here today!"

The judge banged his gavel. "Sit down, Mark. I'm finding Sam's testimony to be quite revealing. Please continue, Sam."

"Mark, please tell the court what happened at the pep rally when you stayed behind in the gym, after everyone else left."

"How am I supposed to remember what happened fourteen years ago?" Mark snapped at Sam.

"Let me help you remember," Sam offered. "Do you remember a young boy by the name of Patrick Donovan? He was ten years old at the time and you were eighteen. I'm sure you remember, because your coach, the school principal and the president of the school board met with you and Patrick and his mother earlier that school year. You remember, don't you, Mark? Patrick's mother made an official complaint about an incident in which you followed Patrick home from school, threatening to beat him with a switch if he didn't do exactly what you told him to do. Now do you remember Patrick, Mark?"

"No, I don't. I'm sure it was no big deal."

"Come on, Mark." Sam's tone became more forceful. He wasn't easing up. "You remember Patrick very well. You remember what happened after the pep rally ended and everyone but you had left the gym. Patrick came into the gym looking for his classmates and ended up alone with you."

"I don't know what you're getting at, but it's hearsay. You weren't there, you're grabbing at straws," Mark's tone was defiant.

"You're right, Mark, I wasn't there. No one was there except you and Patrick. That's why you got by with what you did. That's why when the whole town turned against Esme and made up stories that the reason you made a bad play that lost the championship football game was because she jinxed you, you were relieved. You wanted the town to spread their stories about Esme. It kept the focus off you, kept the truth from coming out."

Sam paused, and the courtroom was silent. People squirmed uncomfortably in their seats. Hearing Sam talk about the stories they all helped to spread about Esme suddenly sounded indefensible. Sam refused to ease up, "You didn't lose the game, Mark, because Esme cursed you. You lost the game because you got caught abusing a child. Esme walked in on you and saw you for who you really are, a bully, a coward. She caught you in the act. And because you got caught, you felt vulnerable and were unable to perform at the game. You lost the game because you felt guilty, you knew what you had done was wrong. The incident with the cougar is just your latest attempt to harass Esme, to keep her in line, and to prevent the rest of the town from knowing who you really are, what you did."

Mark jumped up. "Is that what that stupid little bitch has been telling you?" he practically screamed at Sam while he pointed at Esme. "She's evil, everyone who knows of her knows that to be true. You can ask people. People here today know what I'm talking about. She's doing it right now. Look at her, sitting there not saying a word, spewing her voodoo throughout the courtroom!"

The gallery erupted into chaos. "Silence!" Judge Milton hollered over the uproar. To the bailiff, he ordered, "Remove anyone who makes even the slightest peep in my courtroom." Turning to Mark, he said, "Mark, I'm holding you in contempt of court."

During the chaos, Esme turned to look directly at Mark, right into his eyes. In an instant, Mark realized his folly, that he had no power over Esme. He never had. She held the power. She would always be a reminder to him of his weakness, his incompetence, and his inadequacy. His bravado drained under her gaze. Her stare disarmed him, leaving him vulnerable, aware that his self-imposed disgrace could have been avoided.

Sam turned to the judge when things settled down, "Your Honor, I would like to call a special witness to the stand."

The judge looked at Sam and considered his request. "Go ahead and proceed, Sam."

With that, the bailiff opened the courtroom door and motioned a young person into the courtroom. He was very slight in build and dressed effeminately. His short, shaggy hair was dyed blue, and he wore blue fingernail polish on his nails. Earrings dangled from both ears. He wore eyeliner and lipstick. His clothing was snug to show off his body, tight black jeans and black ankle boots with a white t-shirt. He was obviously nervous and avoided looking at the spectators as he walked down the aisle. Sam greeted him with a smile and assisted him to the witness stand, where he was officially sworn in by the bailiff.

"Will you please state your name for the record?" the bailiff asked.

"Well," the witness's voice cracked when he tried to speak. When the words came out, they were barely more than a whisper. "I go by Dessa, but my birth name is Patrick Donovan."

Mark sat frozen in his seat, like someone who ran into an intruder in the dark. The color drained from his face. The Fish and Game commissioner had a look of puzzlement on his face. The sound of people shifting in their seats could be heard.

Once again, Mark tried to protest. "Your Honor, this is a violation of my rights. This line of questioning has no business in today's hearing. You need to put a stop to this."

"Sit down, Mark," the judge said. Then, to Sam, "Please continue."

Sam turned to face his witness. "Dessa," Sam was gentle in his approach. "Thank you for agreeing to testify today. I'm going to ask you a few questions. You can direct your answers to me. To begin, what is your relationship with Mark Kipling?"

It took Dessa a moment to gather himself. Finally, he took a deep breath and began, "When I was in the fifth grade, he and some of his football friends bullied me."

"What do you mean by 'bullied'?"

"Well, he would follow me home from school or he and his friends would find me when I was alone. They called me a 'faggot,' 'gay boy,' horrible names. Mark taunted me because my mother caught him threatening to beat me with a switch and reported him. It made him angry, so after that, every time he saw me he'd torment me, make fun of me, call me names. He threatened to beat me up if I told anyone he was bullying me."

"Were you afraid of Mark?"

"I was terrified of him. He was mean. I thought he might really hurt me, maybe even kill me." With this, a loud murmur went up through the gallery causing the judge to pound his gavel again. The bailiff removed three people from their seats for being loud and showed them to the door. He stood in the middle of the aisle, threatening anyone else who made a sound.

Sam continued. "What happened at the pep rally, Dessa, the one that occurred the day before the big championship football game when you were in the fifth grade?"

"I didn't want to go to the pep rally because Mark and his football friends were there, so I snuck out and hung around outside until it ended, but I accidentally got left behind when my class took off without me. I ran back to the gym, hoping someone from my class would still be there, and ended up in the gym alone with Mark. He was the only person in the gym when I got there."

"And what happened when he saw you?" Sam presented the question carefully.

"He saw me and said something like, 'Oh, look who's here. It's little Patrick. Don't you want to call your mama so she can come and save you?' I was terrified, so I turned and started to run out of the gym, but he came running after me and grabbed me by my collar and drug me back into the middle of the gym. He pulled me so hard that I fell down and he continued to pull me by my arms."

There was silence in the courtroom. The spectators sat motionless. The judge fought the urge to shake his head in disgust as he listened to Dessa testify.

"What happened next, Dessa?" Sam's voice was gentle, encouraging.

"He got me under both arms and made me stand up. Then he started swinging me around in a circle until my feet were off the ground. The whole time he was taunting me, calling me a bawl baby. I was screaming in fear. Suddenly, he let me go, and I flew out of his grasp and landed on my back. My head banged into the floor." Dessa's voice waivered as he fought back sobs, making it hard to finish his story. "Then he put his foot on my chest, hard, so I couldn't breathe. I thought I was going to die." Tears rolled down Dessa's cheeks.

"I know this is hard to relive, Dessa. Can you tell us what made Mark finally stop terrorizing you?" Sam kept his voice low, supportive.

"Tom Johnson." Dessa leaned forward and pointed at Tom, sitting at the defendant's counsel table. "He came into the gym and yelled for Mark to stop. He slugged Mark in the face, trying to get him off me. They got into a fistfight. Mark kept hitting Tom and knocking him down, but Tom kept getting back up and then Mark would knock him down again. At one point Mark kicked Tom in the kidneys really hard."

"Then what happened?" Sam again coaxed Dessa to continue.

"It was Esme, sitting right there," Dessa leaned forward and pointed at Esme, "who came into the gym and stopped the whole thing. She walked up to Mark and put her hand out indicating for him to stop." Dessa held his hand out to demonstrate. "She didn't say anything, she just stood with her hand out in front of her, looking straight at Mark. Finally, she helped me get up off the floor. Then she led us out, Tom and me. On her way out, she turned back to Mark and told him that the Crystal Bay football team would lose the championship game the next day and that it would be entirely Mark's own doing."

"Is that everything that happened, Dessa?"

"Yes. Tom walked me to the office so I could call my mom. I never said anything to anyone for fear Mark would come after me and kill me. I refused to go back to school. Shortly after that my dad took a job up north and we moved away."

"How has your life been since that day, Dessa?"

"I live in Portland. I suffer from anxiety. I've gone to counseling for years. I'm glad I got to tell my story in front of Mark." Dessa turned to address Mark directly. "You're a terrible person. You don't scare me anymore. You're a small-minded bully."

"Thank you, Dessa. That's all the questions I have for you," Sam said before returning to the defendant's counsel table.

Judge Milton sat silently throughout Dessa's testimony and turned to Mark. "Mark, would you like to cross-examine the witness?"

"No." Mark's voice had sunk to barely a whisper.

Spectators in the gallery silently watched as Dessa walked down the aisle and out the courtroom door. The judge watched as he left. When the courtroom door closed behind Dessa, the judge spoke.

"Sam, Tom, wrap up, please."

Sam took his seat next to Esme. Tom pushed his chair back and stood; he would offer the closing remarks. He felt confident knowing that his and Sam's testimonies were enough to keep Mark from ever bothering Esme again.

"Your Honor," Tom began, "the residents of Crystal Bay know what happened after the championship football game was lost. They didn't want to accept that their esteemed quarterback, Mark Kipling, made a poor decision that cost them the game. They had to make it somebody else's fault, so they blamed Esme—again. They made up a story about how she jinxed Mark with witchcraft that caused him to make a bad pass. They knew it wasn't true, but they all covertly agreed to believe it. They taught it to their children and to newcomers who moved into town. It became the gossip that held the town together. It's still the gossip that gets told over and over by the people of Crystal Bay. They were talking about it in the courtroom today before this hearing began."

Tom waited a few seconds, letting his words sink in. He began to weave his comments into a story, the way he and Sam had prepared during the days leading up to the hearing.

"The Crystal Bay locals began to bully Esme when her grandparents settled here when Esme was nine years old. They bullied her because she's Roma. The principal of the elementary school tried to keep her out of his school by going to the school board." Tom looked directly at Jeff Thompson in the gallery, who quickly looked away. "There were parents who told their children not to play with Esme back then, claiming she was a thief or would bring bad luck to their family.

"Long before the incident with Dessa and Mark, when Esme was just twelve years old, the whole town made up a story about her being a witch. I'm sure many spectators in the gallery today remember the incident. After being excluded from attending a birthday party for one of her classmates, back when Esme was in the sixth grade, parents and classmates accused her of causing a windstorm that swept through the town and ruined the party. I find it baffling that grown adults could actually convince themselves that a twelve-year-old child could control the weather. Even worse, they taught their children to believe it."

Tom paused and looked around the gallery. He had the whole town's attention. He continued. "At a time when Esme needed the support of adults, of teachers, of friends, the townspeople labeled her a witch, a thief, and called her disparaging names ... 'gypsy' ... 'pikey' ... 'knacker'. They made her an outcast and left her to face a barrage of bullying every day on her own. I know, I was there."

There was silence in the courtroom. Tom went on, "I can't believe the folks of Crystal Bay are bad people. But anyone who has ever participated in spreading bigotry, hate, and lies has behaved poorly. I ask you," Tom gazed around the gallery, looking spectators in the eye, "what can be said about a parent who turns their child against another child based on bigotry? What can be said about a parent who teaches their child that anyone different is dangerous and should be shunned?"

Tom paced himself. He was methodical and deliberate. "What can be said about a parent who refuses a child an invitation to a birthday party based on the false belief that because of that child's race, she's a thief, someone who can't be trusted?" Tom's eyes rested on Shelby and her mother. "What can be said about people who stand in line at the grocery store, or in the local coffeehouse, or

God forbid, at church, and make up false stories that ostracize an innocent child or an adolescent?"

He refused to ease up, "What can be said about teachers or school administrators who allow bigotry, prejudice, and fear to preside in their classrooms and not intervene? What can be said about townsfolk who sacrifice one of their own to allow a bully like Mark Kipling to be worshipped as a hero?" Tom stopped for a few seconds to let his remarks sink in.

"Ask yourselves, people of Crystal Bay, what did Esme ever do to you? Did she rob you, steal from you, take your men, turn your women against you, insult you, hurt you in any way? Does she deserve to be the target of your malicious bullying and gossip?" Tom hesitated and looked at the uncomfortable faces in the gallery. Some people were looking at him, some were nodding, and a few had tears in their eyes. Others looked at their laps, unwilling to face Tom.

"Let me tell you about Esme," Tom continued. "Does she have special powers? I don't know; I'm not here to argue that. People from my tribe claim she's a spiritual leader, an animal whisperer. She has a gentle spirit that animals and birds relate to. Eagles nest on her property. Deer graze in her fields. She provides a sanctuary for waterfowl. She rehabilitates wild mustangs so they can be set free, returned to the wild. She's kind, giving, generous." Tom looked at Esme and let his eyes rest on her momentarily.

"She doesn't judge. She's strong, and stands up for what's good. She doesn't let bullying and lies stop her from doing what's right. If one of *your* children were being bullied," Tom swept his arm across the gallery, "if one of *your* children were being made fun of, Esme would step in and stop it, she'd protect *your* child, even if it meant being bullied herself." Tom stopped talking and looked down at the floor before continuing. When he spoke again, his voice was low, softer. "In short, people, Esme's the best of Crystal Bay. She's everything that's good about it."

When Tom finished talking, no sound could be heard in the courtroom. Mark was relieved the focus had gone from him to the

ESME

people in the gallery. Let them take some of the blame, he thought. The Fish and Game commissioner stared straight ahead, silent. Finally, Judge Milton spoke. "This has been a very revealing hearing. Mark, do you have any final words?" Mark gave a slight shake of his head. The judge continued, directing his words to Mark and the commissioner. "Rather than fine the defendant two thousand dollars, it seems like Fish and Game should pay the Makah Tribe that amount for doing your job, Mark. I'm ordering all charges against Esme Horvat dropped."

Mark stood to leave. He wanted to slip out quickly before having to face anyone—before the commissioner had time to corner him—but the judge stopped him. "Sit down, Mark. I haven't dismissed court, and you're in contempt, if you'll remember." He looked directly at the commissioner while his words were directed to Mark, "I strongly recommend that Fish and Game strip you of your right to carry a firearm. Any person who beats on young children and covers it up by bullying another, in my mind, belongs behind bars. It's my opinion that that person certainly shouldn't be carrying a weapon and pretending to protect the citizens. I also strongly encourage Fish and Game to conduct a thorough investigation of your eligibility for continued employment. As for your contempt charge, I'm sentencing you to three days in jail. You can sit there while Fish and Game decides what to do about you."

To the spectators in the gallery, the judge said, "Today is not our proudest day. It saddens me to think people can be so cruel. I thought we were all better than that."

He turned to Esme, who continued to sit at the table with her hands folded. "Esme, you have my most sincere apology for what has transpired. Go in peace."

Tom and Sam walked with Esme toward the exit door of the courtroom. A young couple sitting on the aisle near the middle of the gallery stood as she approached. They were new to Crystal Bay and hoped to set up an irrigation business for the farmers in the area. Like others that day, they came to observe. They'd heard it would be a show, so they came to see what all the fuss was about. Now they were wondering if Crystal Bay was a place they wanted to remain in.

When Esme got close, the young woman smiled, and her husband removed his hat, and gave her a slight nod as she walked by. No one else looked her way as she exited the courtroom. The spectators sat quietly in their seats. No one spoke. Finally, the spectators got up and departed the courtroom one by one. They didn't linger in the parking lot, they didn't stand around talking with each other, they didn't feel like facing each other. They got in their cars and drove off as discreetly as they could.

55

SAM AND TOM AGREED A GLASS OF WHISKEY WAS IN ORDER WHEN THEY returned to Esme's farm. They'd succeeded in doing what they went to court to do. A camaraderie had developed between the two men, a bond. Like soldiers on the battlefield, they had stood together to fight for a single purpose: for the woman they both loved.

Esme sat on the steps of her porch, watching the two men who had fought for her in front of the whole town toast each other. She had known them both, she was sure, forever, but in different ways. One was her ally, her warrior, her friend; the other was her heart's desire, her lifeblood, her soulmate.

She stood, leaving them to celebrate, and walked down the steps and across the yard to the barn, Jake in tow. She could hear Homie whinny for her. He'd been in his stall all day and wanted to be set free into the yard. Esme felt something stirring inside her and needed time to think about what had happened at today's hearing. Mark Kipling wouldn't bully her again. For that, she was grateful. As for the townsfolk, she expected things to change very little. Folks don't typically adjust their attitudes just because somebody holds a mirror to their face. But they probably wouldn't make up stories about her any longer. Sam and Tom had squelched that for them. They'd given the townspeople a strong dose of the truth that couldn't be denied.

Esme was thankful, but it didn't matter; she had no intention of going into town any more often now than in the past. She liked her solitude, away from the townspeople, alone on her farm with her animals. There was Gus and Tom—and Sam. At the thought of Sam, she felt her eyes cloud up and a tear slip down her cheek. She brushed it away with the back of her hand.

"What's wrong, Es? Are you okay?"

She turned to see Sam standing in the doorway of the barn. He must have walked in while her mind was elsewhere. Esme opened the gate to Homie's stall and shooed him out. "Go on," she told him, gently patting his rump to nudge him. He gratefully trotted past Sam and into the yard. Esme shut the stall gate and stood looking at Sam. He reached for her. Esme walked into his arms and rested her head on his chest. He held her close.

It would be a moment Esme would never forget, the feel of Sam's arms around her, his strength. She closed her eyes and drank it in. At that moment, they were the only two people in the world. They were all they needed; they belonged to no one but each other.

The day following the court hearing, Esme was tilling her garden when an older-model pickup truck stopped in front of the farm. Sam and Gus were fishing at the hole. A young couple got out of the pickup and came through the arbor. Esme recognized them as the couple who'd stood as she, Sam, and Tom exited the courtroom the day before.

The man looked to be in his mid-thirties, the woman a bit younger. They were both casually dressed: he in an old pair of jeans, workman's boots, and a worn work shirt, the sleeves rolled up past his elbows, and she in jeans and a t-shirt. The woman was carrying a pie in a covered container.

"Greetings!" the man hollered. Esme stopped tilling. Jake gave a bark, sure there was no apparent danger, but he wanted to alert the strangers that he was nearby. "We're the Douglases. I'm Leo, this here's my wife, Jen."

"I hope we're not intruding," Jen broke in, sounding uneasy. "We wanted to stop by and introduce ourselves. We're new in town and don't know many people." She hesitated, then nervously burst out, "I made you a fresh peach pie, thought you might enjoy it."

Esme wiped her hands on her pink summer dress. The slight breeze caused it to flutter around her legs. Her logging boots were muddied from her garden. Wisps of hair had managed to escape from her head scarf. Shutting the gate behind her so the deer wouldn't sneak in, she walked to where the couple stood, reached out, and accepted the pie.

There was a moment of awkward silence before Leo continued. "My wife and I were having dinner at The Tavern last night and Skeeter, who we've gotten to know, mentioned that you've had some trouble with the irrigation gate in your pasture. We thought we'd take the opportunity to drive out. I can take a look at it and repair it for you if you'd like. I brought my tools."

Esme looked from Leo to Jen and back to Leo. They stood looking at her, smiling warmly. "Thanks," Esme replied, smiling slightly.

"Glad to be of help. I'll grab my tools and get to work."

As Leo returned to their pickup, Bertie, the hen, flew onto Jen's outstretched arm, flapping her wings to get her balance while clucking loudly. "Leo, look!" Jen called out as she situated Bertie into the crux of her arm, more enthusiastic than alarmed. "She flew right onto my arm!" Jen lost her nervousness, her face all smiles now. "Hon," she called after Leo, "we need to get a few chickens!"

The vegetable garden next caught Jen's eye. "Wow, your garden, Esme! How do you get it to grow so well? Mine just limps along."

Esme stood holding the peach pie, not knowing for sure how to respond. But there was something playful in Jen's demeanor that appealed to her. "Would you like to see it?" she offered.

The two women walked toward Esme's garden, Jake in tow, Bertie still settled in the crux of Jen's arm. Esme glanced back over her shoulder to see Leo bent over the irrigation gate on his knees out in the pasture. "Hmmm," Esme wasn't sure what to think. But these folks were friends with Skeeter, and Esme trusted him. Not to mention when she turned and looked into Jen's eyes, she saw a genuine smile looking back.

The result of Esme's court hearing impacted the little town of Crystal Bay. Judge Milton scheduled a meeting with the City Council president the following Monday. The City Council members, in turn, ordered a meeting with members of the school board, who then met with school administrators, who mandated training for all of the teachers in the schools. Bullying was addressed in the classrooms and on school campuses, and a zero-tolerance policy was enacted.

The president of the City Council met with the police chief. An ordinance that outlawed bullying in any public setting in Crystal Bay was passed, and mandatory meetings were conducted with all local police officers on anti-bullying tactics. The Department of Fish and Game ordered a thorough investigation into how procedures with local residents were carried out.

On Sunday morning following the court hearing, the minister of the Congregational Church offered a sermon on the sins of gossip. The local chapter of the Elks Lodge brought in a speaker from Port Angeles to address cultural competence at the high school auditorium for anyone who wanted to attend. While Mark Kipling served his three days in jail, a hearing was conducted by the Department of Fish and Game to evaluate his ongoing employment. It was unanimously decided to immediately discharge Mark from the department due to dereliction of duty and harassment. He left town shortly after that. He didn't leave a forwarding address, and no one knew where he might have gone.

In the week following the hearing, Tom received three calls from residents of Crystal Bay requesting to meet with him for legal advice. Word-of-mouth spread. Within a short time, Tom's law practice grew to include not only folks from the reservation but residents of Crystal Bay and the nearby farms and seaport towns.

56

THINGS SETTLED DOWN, AND DAYS DRIFTED BY, BUT FOR SAM AND Esme, time stood still. A fragility surrounded them, an avoidance of looking beyond their world. They were content, hidden away deep in the forest on Esme's tiny farm. They wanted nothing more; the simplicity of their routine was everything they needed. Their passion nourished and sustained them and made them forget there was a world outside their orbit.

Late one afternoon, Sam and Esme went blackberry picking. They set off with Homie and Jake through the open grasslands behind Esme's barn. The temperature registered eighty-eight degrees Fahrenheit. They followed the river. The blackberry bushes grew wild along the banks. Esme hoped there would be fruit left on the branches—once the deer and other wildlife found them, the berries disappeared quickly. But on this day, they were in luck. The bushes were heavy with their bounty. The berries were plump and dark black, a good sign they were sweet. Sam and Esme filled several canvas bags, sampling the juicy, ripe berries as they picked. Esme climbed onto Homie's back when they were done and packed the berries into the saddle bags cinched around Homie's belly.

The sun had begun to set in the western sky. Sam climbed onto Homie's back behind Esme and wrapped his arms around her. She could feel his chest pressed against her back through her dress, and the beating of his heart. She felt his breath on her cheek and his lips on her neck. She could sense the power of Homie beneath them, and the rise and fall of his belly with each breath he took.

"Take us home, Homie," Esme gently nudged the horse. Homie obediently started back through the fields. It was a unforgetable moment, a snapshot captured in Esme's mind: the two of them atop Homie, his magnificent mane billowing out with each step, his tail erect, Jake trotting alongside, Sam's arms around her. It was the perfect end to a perfect day.

Esme leaned into Sam, resting her head against his shoulder, her hands resting on his arms that encircled her. Suddenly, a feeling of lightheadedness overcame her, making her feel disoriented. A faint memory surfaced in her mind that she couldn't put her finger on. It might have been a dream, yet, a sense of distant familiarity washed over her. She knew she'd been in this same place before, long ago, with Sam, just like now. But like a dream, the memory quickly faded.

August 1. "Hi, Dad; I tried to call you, but the reception wouldn't let me complete the call. Sorry to have to write all this in an email. Long story short, Mom's being discharged from the treatment facility on Thursday. The lithium is keeping her bipolar symptoms stabilized. They tried to add another drug, an antipsychotic medication that helps with depression. She couldn't handle it; she slept all the time and complained of dry mouth and eyes.

"I'm flying home this weekend with Michael. We're going to help her get settled at the house. I plan to tell her about Michael. I hope it doesn't cause her to relapse. I'll keep you informed."

August 6. "*Mom's back home. Michael and I got her situated. When I told her about Michael and me, that I'm gay, she hardly reacted. She looked at both of us, first at me and then Michael, and said, 'So you're gay, huh?' She sounded flat, with no emotion. But at least she knows. She was okay with Michael; he spoiled and catered to her.*

"I met with Dr. Stewart before we left the treatment program. He emphasized that keeping Mom stable will require close attention to her moods. He told me that even with medications, there's the risk, as Mom gets older, that while the manic phases may diminish or remain stable, the depressive episodes could increase or become worse. He considers her high risk for another suicide attempt.

"It worries me sick. It's like balancing her on a tight rope with no net. Thank God she's not boozing and taking pills anymore. For now, anyway. She's at the house alone. She wouldn't go to Rip and Gram's. You can hardly blame her. I tried to get her to come to Portland for a while. Maybe get a little place close to Michael and me. She refused. Gram's going to check in with her every day. I plan to call her every day. I don't know what else to do, Dad."

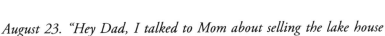

August 23. "*Hey Dad, I talked to Mom about selling the lake house and getting something more manageable. She's got this idea that she's gonna move to Paris. Remember when we were there for my high school graduation and Mom met the owner of that little flower shop, La Ferme Bouquet? I think the owner's name was Raphael. Remember that she told him if he ever wanted to sell, to contact her first? Well, he did! His wife died and he wants to move out to the country to be closer to his kids and grandkids. He called Mom to see if she might be interested in buying his shop. She says she's gonna sell her business and the house and move to France. This spells disaster! She sounds manic to me. She hasn't given any details about her plan, but she's determined to go. I think she's trying to find something to hang on to. I can hear it in her voice.*"

That night, Sam tossed and turned. He couldn't sleep. He got up quietly to avoid disturbing Esme and grabbed his faded jeans and sweatshirt. Jake woke up and followed him out of the bedroom. He dressed in the kitchen and stepped out onto the porch. The night air was chilly. He sat on the porch steps, Jake beside him. "Hey pal," Sam looked into Jake's golden eyes and scratched him behind the ears. Jake licked his face.

It was overcast. The stars were hidden behind clouds. The night sky was black, with no light coming from anywhere. Sam had Jamie and Joanna on his mind. He pictured his son in a rowboat on a lake with just one oar. He put his head in his hands.

Esme woke up. She reached for Sam and then realized he was gone. So was Jake. She sat up on the edge of the bed. She lit a candle on her nightstand, then sat with her hands in her lap, staring at the floor, lost in thought. A deck of Tarot cards lay next to the candle. She picked them up and began to shuffle. She shuffled the cards seven times and laid the deck on the bed before her. Slowly she turned over the top card. She stared at it. It was the Five of Cups, the card of sorrow and loss.

57

EARLY ONE MORNING, A FEW DAYS LATER, AFTER SAM HAD FINISHED writing for the day, while the dew was still clinging to the tall grass, Esme and Sam, with Jake and Homie, walked out through the back fields to look for the eagle who lived near Esme's farm. "She lives in that tall Sitka spruce, straight ahead," Esme said, pointing to a clump of tall evergreens at the far corner of the field. Sam could see her nest toward the top of the tallest trees. "She's sixteen years old, in the middle of her life span. She's lived on the property her whole life. I nourished her when she was a fledgling until she was ready to go out alone. Eaglets stay with their parents from birth until their wings become strong enough to support their flight while hunting. That's when they know they're ready to make their own way. Usually, a fledging flies far away from where they grew up. But this one stuck around."

"They mate for life," Esme continued. "Her mate returns every year, and they breed. When he returns each year, they add new branches and twigs to their nest to make it bigger and stronger. It's a sign of their fidelity, their commitment to each other. She typically hatches two eggs a season but a couple of seasons she's hatched three. Usually, she hatches in February or March. All summer the eaglets grow and learn to hunt on their own. Then in the fall they're ready to fly away. It's always a bit sad. I always hope they'll make it. A short time later, the male flies away and doesn't return until the next mating season. All winter, the female is here alone."

"Doesn't she get lonely?" Sam asked.

"I used to think so, but the longer I observed her the more I came to realize she's okay with it. She knows she'll see her mate next season, so she settles into her solitude."

They both saw her at the same time, the female eagle. She stood on the edge of her nest, spread her mighty wings, and soared into the air. Her mate followed close behind. Together they glided over the field, high above the treetops. They circled the meadow twice, dipping low, then flexed their powerful wings to rise hundreds of feet, only to drop again and glide across the field.

The scene reminded Sam of riding with his parents each winter, so many years ago, through the back country roads of Skagit Valley, where they would spot eagles roosting along the soggy marshlands. Watching the two eagles soar low over the grassy field reawakened the wonder Sam remembered feeling as a boy. Standing in the tall grass with Esme, watching the eagles in flight, tied his boyhood memories to the present, making him forget that in between then and now, he had lost his way and had let his dreams slip into forgetfulness.

"They're amazing," Sam exclaimed.

"I often dream I'm an eagle," Esme told Sam, craning to watch the birds perform their acrobats.

"What does it mean?" Sam asked.

"I'm not sure. Tom's Grandma is a shaman, a sage. She says I become an eagle in my dreams. She calls it shape-shifting. The dreams are so real, Sam. I can fly and soar and glide. I can feel myself leave the ground. I can feel the wind currents carry me along, and the power of my wings as I rise into the air. I can see every detail on the ground below. I can see where a person's been and where they're going. It's like a map, where everything behind the person is their past and everything in front of them is their future, except when I look at it from so high up, there is no past or future, it's all one space."

Esme took Sam's hand and looked into his eyes, "Sam, if we ever have to part, I'll find you in my dreams. If ever you must leave me, know that when you see an eagle soaring high above, it's me. It'll be me, Sam, letting you know that I'm waiting, until next season when you come back to me again."

Sam pulled her to him and held her. A melancholy feeling swept over him. Standing out in the middle of the field, close to the forest's edge, watching the magnificent eagles soar overhead, knowing that soon the male would fly away and leave his mate, made Sam want to hang onto Esme tight, never let go.

September 9. "Sam, Marty here. I heard from Joanna that she wants to put the lake house on the market and sell her business. She wants to buy a flower shop in Paris. You both will need to sign some paperwork before I can get the house ready to sell. Plus I've been prodding her to sign the divorce papers. I've been trying to reach her for the past couple of days but she hasn't called me back. As soon as she does, I'll let you know. I'll be in touch."

September 12. "Dad, I'm losing it. Mom's back in the hospital. I tried reaching her for two days, but she wouldn't pick up. Gram drove over there to check on her this afternoon and found her in bed with all the blinds pulled. There was food left out on the counter, she hasn't been eating, she hasn't been taking her meds. The place was a mess. The hospital is gonna keep her for a couple of days, adjust her meds. When I phoned her in the hospital, all she did was cry. God, Dad, I don't know what to do. I wish she'd come to Portland where I could keep an eye on her."

Sam stood at the edge of the river in the back of Esme's farmhouse, both hands in his pockets, pensive, lost in thought. He had his back to the house and didn't hear Esme when she came around the corner of the porch. She stood quietly for a moment, observing him. She didn't disturb him. Instead, she walked back to the front of the porch, down the steps, and across the clearing to the barn.

September 16. "Mom's back home. She sounds a bit better. The doctor at the hospital added a new antidepressant and upped her dose of lithium. Gram has arranged for their housekeeper, Camilla, to spend a couple of days a week at Mom's to help her out. Mom spoke to Marty Bigelow about selling her business. Marty's talking to another event planning business that might be interested in buying Mom out.

"School is really kicking my butt. Summer classes sucked. Just a short break and fall semester begins. Miss you."

September 22. "Oh my God, Gram had to rush Mom to the hospital this morning. She should've called 911. Mom called her earlier to say she was sick and throwing up; her vision was blurry, and her hands were shaking. Gram said her words slurred, and she sounded confused—didn't know what time it was, morning or night. Gram thought she'd gone off the wagon and was on a bender.

"Turns out she had lithium toxicity. They raised her dose when she was in the hospital a few days ago and her body couldn't handle the increase. They put her in ICU for observation. They were afraid she might start to have seizures. They started her on IVs. She's stable now. I spoke to her. She cried, told me she was really tired of it all."

Back in Bellevue, Joanna stared out the living room window at the Seattle skyline across the lake. It was that period just before dawn, not dark, not light, but she could see that the approaching day warned of rain. The skyline glittered, as, one by one, the lights dimmed in the coming dawn. She watched the twinkling lights, void of feelings, numb.

She thought about what her doctor had told her just before being discharged from the hospital two days ago. To block her depression and the strong urge of wanting to hurt herself, to take her own life, she'd need to be on several powerful medications. The combination of meds in her system was as challenging to Joanna as the ups and downs in her moods. She felt relieved that her feelings of sadness and impending doom were less, not gone totally, but blunted. But also gone were her energy surges, the high that she had come to think of as an old friend, her savior, her rescuer. All that was left was a void.

She felt like she was living in a maze of brain fog. She couldn't get a clear thought to surface. She didn't know if it was from the meds or if this is what being bipolar without the reliance on pills and alcohol feels like. She feared that a big downer was waiting in the shadows, waiting to jump her the minute she let her guard down, forgot to take her pills, or became the least bit stressed.

As she stood staring across the lake, her stomach tossed, the noxious sensation she had learned to expect. Physical symptoms were the only feelings she could readily identify, nausea, a lack of appetite, and the inability to sleep through the night, even though she felt sedated most of the time. Her mouth felt so dry at times that she found it hard to swallow, and her eyes were so dry they burned. Sometimes she was unable to pee when she felt like she had to. Tremors made it laborious to use her hands. Apathy made it hard to focus and concentrate.

She figured she'd probably need another med adjustment in a few weeks. She sighed and thought about the game of chase her

ESME

doctor played with her medications. He'd lowered her lithium after the dose she'd been taking poisoned her and made her deathly ill. To compensate for the reduced amount, he'd added an antipsychotic drug and a second antidepressant that he told her would work synergistically with the antidepressant she was already taking. A cocktail, the medical folks called it. Joanna called it a lobotomy.

Her thoughts drifted to Jamie, to Michael. Jamie had confessed when he and Michael came home to help her get settled that they were more than friends. Joanna tried to wrap her head around her son being gay. She remembered Rip's reaction when he and Gladys stopped by to check on her a few evenings after Jamie and Michael returned to Portland. She told them what Jamie had shared with her, that Jamie and Michael were a couple.

"You don't need to worry about any of that right now, Joanna," Gladys had tried to sound comforting.

Rip had plenty to say. "Hell, I'm not surprised. I knew that kid was too wimpy to be a real man. We should have figured it out long ago."

When Rip spoke the words, Joanna heard a loud snap inside her head, like a tree limb breaking. "Get the fuck out of my house, Dad." There was no fear behind her words; she didn't care what he thought, but something deep inside her stirred for a moment—she felt it, and it felt good. "Leave," she repeated. "Don't ever talk about my son like that again."

Rip had turned and walked out. Gladys, who stood rooted to the living room floor, finally spoke. "Good for you, Joanna. He had that coming. I may tell him to get the fuck out of my house, as well. It sounded pretty good when you said it." She'd grinned at Joanna then. Joanna couldn't remember if she'd smiled back. She just remembered feeling grateful to her mom at that moment, cared for somehow.

"I'll call you tomorrow," Gladys told her, following Rip to the car.

Joanna's thoughts drifted back to the present moment. Outside, dawn had pushed aside the darkness. Joanna wandered into Sam's

— 359 —

den. Thoughts of him awakened something in her, deep down, feelings even the medications couldn't block. She foolishly hoped that when she walked past his den, he'd be sitting at his desk, the way he'd done so often, reading a legal brief or researching something on the Internet. Things worked better when he was around. If he'd come home, she rationalized, she'd feel better, less anxious, more settled. She pretended that he hadn't gone away and that they would move to France, buy a country home outside of Paris. She'd buy the flower shop *La Ferme Bouquet*. It would be enough to keep her focused, her brain firing—but manageable. Sam could write during the day, take walks in the country. He could get a dog. She clung to the fantasy.

His sweater still lay over the back of his chair where he'd last left it. Joanna picked it up, brought it to her face, and breathed it in. His scent was still there; she could sense him all around her. She felt something wet on her cheeks and realized she was crying. Without warning, like a thunderbolt, grief swept over her, awakened the sadness inside her, and caught her unprepared. She leaned against the wall, still holding the sweater.

October 12. "Dad, things here are not good. I dropped out of school for this semester. I have to figure some stuff out about Mom. She didn't answer her phone again for a couple of days. Gram says she's depressed, not bathing, dressing, or eating. Gram doesn't think she's been taking her meds. I can't juggle school and worry about her at the same time. The school's being understanding. Michael's upset, but we're working through it. I've decided to move in with Mom for the next few months. She needs someone with her. She can't live alone. It's so obvious now how much she depended on you, how you kept things steady when you were there. She can't do it on her own.

"From talking to her doctor, she'll never be free from the daily struggle of handling her mood swings. Left alone, she'll likely go off her

meds and become manic or depressed. God only knows what she'll do in a manic phase, but if she becomes depressed, we both know what she might do. I can't live with that worry hanging over my head.

"I wish mom weren't sick. I wish she were strong and able to handle life, but she can't. She's handicapped, and it isn't her fault. That's not the best way to describe her, but she is. She has fewer resources to draw from than you and me. I can't turn my back on her. It's the straw I drew. I think if I'm there consistently, she'll settle in better. I talked to Grandma Sid. She and Grandpa Jack plan to visit me when I get settled there.

"Michael and I are going out to get drunk this evening. I need a release. I wish the phone reception was better where you are so you and I could talk person-to-person. It feels like you've disappeared off the radar."

It was the wee hours of the morning. Sam couldn't sleep. He got up quietly to avoid disturbing Esme and pulled on his jeans and a sweater. He made coffee and left Esme the note he wrote her every morning, "Gone off to write, my love." Outside, it was still dark, just a hint of daybreak peeking over the horizon.

He didn't walk directly to his cabin at Gus's to write. Instead, he walked across the clearing to the pasture. He stood at the fence, his hands in his pockets, his foot resting on the lower rail, and stared across the field. He was pensive.

His emails to Jamie up to now had been bandages, armchair advice, and encouragement that he knew wasn't helpful. He'd hoped things would improve, stabilize. But Jamie was drowning. He couldn't stand by and watch his son struggle and do nothing. He remembered the old fortune teller's warning years ago, "Your destiny," she had cautioned, "involves sacrifice. You'll have to choose." The ache in his heart was deep, debilitating. He saw the writing on the wall. The choice the old Roma had warned he would have to make was looming in front of him.

58

FALL HAD ARRIVED. THERE WAS A CHILL IN THE AIR. THE LEAVES FROM the bigleaf maples were beginning to turn a dramatic orange-red. Sam walked alone through the back fields toward the forest edge. He wanted to check on the eagles to see if the male was still hanging around or if he'd flown away, leaving the female alone. Their two eaglets had matured and learned to hunt on their own. Sam and Esme had watched each day as they grew into adults and became adept at finding their prey. And then, just last week, they were both gone. They'd flown away to find their own hunting grounds, look for a mate, and begin their lives as adults. Next would be the male. He typically hung around a few days after the eaglets departed, but then he, too, would take to the skies. "What a fool," Sam thought.

There was no sign of the male or the female eagle. Sam strolled along the outskirts of the field, near the forest edge, hoping to catch a glimpse of one, hopefully both, but they were nowhere to be seen. A fallen tree trunk lying on the ground beckoned him to sit. He sat down, looking toward the forest, watching the eagle's nest high up in the Sitka spruce.

It was one of those beautiful autumn days when the sun was out, warm but not hot, the leaves were a brilliant array of yellow, orange, and reds, and the tall meadow grass was transitioning from green to a golden wheat color. There was something nostalgic about autumn that Sam loved.

He saw Esme's approach when she was halfway across the field. He smiled at her when he saw her coming. He watched her, photographed her in his memory. Her hair was free and wild, blowing out behind her. She wore a soft flowy dress that danced around her legs in the breeze. The fringe from her buckskin boots swayed with each step. A soft knit shawl draped her shoulders.

"I've been looking for you," she smiled as she approached.

"Sorry, my love," Sam patted the spot next to him. "Come sit."

Esme sat down. Sam tugged her body closer to his and wrapped his arm around her. She rested her head on his shoulder. For a while, they sat like that, neither of them speaking. Finally, Sam broke the silence, "I came out to check on the eagles, hoping that maybe the male is still here, that he'll decide to stay with his mate and not leave her."

"He's gone, Sam. I'm pretty sure I saw him fly north, just this morning, when you were writing. There was no fanfare, he just took his leave."

"Does the female follow after him, accompany him for part of his journey?"

"No, he leaves her when she's least expecting it. He takes off and glides away when the time feels right. I imagine it's easier that way for both of them."

Esme sat up. She took his hand in hers and looked into his eyes. "Sam, that's what I want you to do, when you know the time's right. Don't say goodbye, just slip away."

"What are you talking about, Es? I'm not going anywhere."

Esme reached up and gently pushed the hair off Sam's forehead. "Sam, your son needs you. Joanna needs you. They're your family. It's killing you; I know it is. You're torn between your love for me and your commitment to them."

The two looked deep into each other's eyes, into each other's souls. Sam leaned forward and kissed her gently. She touched his cheek. His eyes filled; tears he'd held back for several days spilled over.

"I don't want to go back, Esme. I care about what happens to Joanna, but I'm not in love with her. I love my son with all my heart, but he's starting his own life. Soon he won't need me."

"If you don't go back, Jamie can't start his own life, Sam. They both depend on you. They're your rose, Sam. They're waiting for you."

Sam's voice caught in his throat, "Esme, I can't do it. Don't expect me to. I can't say goodbye. Even if it means letting them down, I can't do it, Es." Tears rolled down his cheeks. Esme wiped them with her hand.

"What I love most about you, Sam, is that you always choose what's right. It'll haunt you if you don't choose them. You won't be able to live with it."

"What about us, Esme? What happens to us?"

"We'll always be 'us.' We've been 'us' forever. We'll find each other again, another time."

"I wouldn't know how to leave you, Es. I wouldn't know when or how."

"Don't tell me, Sam. When the time feels right, just slip away. Don't say goodbye. It's never goodbye for us."

He pulled her to him, wrapped his arms around her. She sank into him. Their tears flowed and mingled together on their cheeks. They clung to each other. There were no words, only the mingling of their tears and the synchronous beating of their hearts.

59

SAM HEADED FOR THE FISHING HOLE. HE WORE HIS RAINCOAT—
a slight drizzle was falling from the sky. The air was chilly, damp.
The day had barely dawned. "You're gonna get an early start on it,
huh?" Sam looked up to see Gus and his ole black lab standing on
his porch.

"Yeah, I'll see if they're biting this morning. Care to join me?"

"Be right there."

The two men fell into the rhythm of fishing as they'd done so
many mornings before. They concentrated on their lines, casting
back and forth, coaxing their lures to their target. The soggy, damp
air added a layer of tranquility to the setting. Sam watched the river,
the way it flowed toward its final destination, determined, with a
purpose. It knew where it was going. It didn't stop along the way,
it was anxious to complete its journey. The river, Sam thought, had
been flowing through the fishing hole for many years and would
continue to flow through it for many more. It was consistent, de-
pendable. It could be counted on not to change. He could come back
to this spot for many years in his mind and know that it would be
the same. Knowing that was comforting in a way.

"You're quiet this morning. Everything okay, Sam?"

Sam looked at Gus standing at the river's edge, his hair trying to escape from under the rim of his fishing hat, his pipe clenched in his teeth, and his waders held up with suspenders. Sam studied the older man's face for a moment, the eyebrows bushing out over his eyes that contained infinite wisdom.

"Gus, I have to go home," the words tumbled out of Sam's mouth. "Joanna's not doing well, and my son needs me. I have to go back."

Gus was quiet momentarily, letting what Sam told him sink in. "I'll hate to see you go, Sam. I'll miss these mornings, fishing together." Then, on a more tentative note, he added, "What about your situation here? That's going to be hard for both of you."

"I couldn't make the decision; I wouldn't have been able to. Esme's much stronger than me." The two men looked at each other. There was sorrow on Sam's face.

"When I was just a kid," Sam told Gus, "a fortune teller told me that somewhere in the world was my soulmate. The woman I'm destined to be with. I've been searching for her ever since, Gus. I didn't think I'd ever find her, but I did, right here, in the most unlikely place. Now I have to let her go."

"Isn't it lucky that you found each other, that you know who she is? Where she is? You don't have to search anymore."

Sam forgot about his line and let it drift downriver. "I don't know, Gus. The goodbye might kill me."

"It's not goodbye, Sam. Love has no ending. You'll find each other again, count on it." He paused and studied Sam's face.

"Do you think we meet our loved ones after we die, Gus, maybe even meet up again in another life?"

Gus thought about it for a minute. "I can't say for sure, Sam, but when I used to be out at sea, no land in sight in any direction for hundreds of miles, at night I'd look up at the sky filled with stars and get the feeling that the universe holds mysteries we aren't privy to. Mary and I made a pact that every evening we'd both step outside and look for the Big Dipper. That we could both see it no matter how vast the distance between us, was comforting. It connected us, thousands of miles apart. It taught me there is no distance, that being apart is just a perception."

The wild mustangs were ready for release. They'd be taken to a wild horse sanctuary over the Snoqualmie Mountains to Yakama Valley. Esme had cared for them for over a year, mostly just letting them graze in her pasture and drink from her stream, occasionally giving them ointment rubs for sore tendons or muscles. Every night she rounded them up and stabled them in her barn to keep them safe from possible predators. In the mornings, she let them back out to graze.

She never tried to tame them, domesticate them. She did the opposite. She didn't put her hands on them any more than necessary. She wanted them to maintain their sense of freedom, of being feral. If they lost that instinct, they'd have trouble surviving when released. After a year on her farm, they were healthy and ready to go. Ready to make it on their own, to mate, run free, eat on the plains, and drink from the natural waters on the land. It was a celebration of sorts.

The Bureau of Land Management had secured the placement for the horses. The Tribal Council had seen to the details. Two ranch hands from the reservation agreed to drive them to their destination. Tom made the arrangements. It was early morning when the truck and horse trailer pulled up in front of Esme's farm. The plan was to get an early start before the traffic got heavy. Two men from the Makah tribe got out. Esme met them in the yard. "They're ready," she told the men.

"Will they be hard to load?" one of the men asked.

"No, I can load 'em. I'm around 'em every day. They're used to me." Esme had on bib-overalls rolled up mid-calf to reveal western boots, worn and scuffed, and a long-sleeved t-shirt. She pulled her hair back in a knot and pulled on a pair of leather gloves. "Whenever you're ready."

"Let's get to it," the older man said.

Sam stood on the front porch, coffee mug in hand, observing. Esme had no fear of the wild horses. She knew how to handle them, to settle them down, calm them. Sam loved watching her interact with them, talk to them, and direct them using poles and flags. She'd gently touch the flag to their flank, shoulder, and underbelly, guiding them to move in her desired direction. They'd let her get close, close enough to look her in the eye. There'd be an exchange between them, a form of communication and trust.

Sam asked her once if she got attached to the Mustangs she boarded. "No," had been her answer. The plan was always to set them free. "Getting attached would only hurt me. They have to be ready to go when the time comes, no regrets, no doubts. They were born to be free."

"Will they remember you?" Sam asked.

"My scent," Esme had replied. "They'll remember my scent."

Now Sam watched as their days in captivity came to an end. They'd leave and never think of Esme again unless one picked up her scent from the other; then, a distant memory might cross their minds. Sam envied the horses. They'd forget all about this place within a short time. They wouldn't know that Esme had withheld her touch to keep them from forming an attachment to her. Sam knew her touch all too well. Oh, to be a wild Mustang, to put her out of his mind.

A second pickup pulled up; it was Tom from the reservation. His long black hair hung in braids below his shoulders. Sam went to greet him. The two men embraced. Sam felt a special bond with Tom, a brotherhood of sorts. They both loved the same woman. It wasn't a love that set them at odds with each other. It was a shared love, one that enhanced the other.

"Good to see you, man," Tom said. "Thought I'd take the opportunity to drive out and say hello."

"Want some coffee?"

"Would love a cup."

Sam disappeared into the farmhouse. It had come to feel like home to Sam. He kept his belongings at his cabin at Gus's and went there every morning to lose himself in his writing. Still, he slept with Esme every night in her bed, prepared meals in her kitchen, ate at her table, and sat on her porch. She had initially encouraged it. Before long, it had become the only natural place to be.

Sam returned with a mug of steaming hot coffee for Tom. "Glad you came. I've been meaning to talk to you."

"Sure, what's up?"

They were standing on Esme's porch, leaning on the railing. Sam tried to speak, but the words caught in his throat. His mouth felt dry. He stared straight ahead. He ran his fingers over his lips. He feared if he said anything, his eyes would cloud up.

"You okay, Sam?"

Sam forced his words, "Tom, I have a favor to ask of you, man."

"Anything, Sam."

Both men turned at the sound of the horse trailer door clanging open. The younger ranch hand had backed the trailer up to the pasture gate, where they would load the horses. Esme and the older ranch hand were directing the horses toward the trailer.

Tom turned back to Sam, "What is it, Sam?"

"Tom, I need to know that you'll always look out for Esme, that you'll always be here for her."

Tom looked at Sam for a long moment. "Always, man. You can count on it."

Sam handed Tom a business card that he had taken from his pocket. "Keep this card, Tom. It's for my attorney, Marty Bigelow. There will be a financial account set up for Esme that Marty will manage. Anything she ever needs, money, medical care, help with her property taxes, repairs to her farm, whatever, call Marty. He'll see that it gets taken care of."

Tom placed the card in his pocket. "What's going on, Sam?"

Sam shook his head. There was a tightness at the back of this throat, a burning. He felt tears at the back of his eyes. Words didn't come easy. "I have to go away, Tom, I have to go back. I'm needed there. I can't leave without knowing that Esme will be taken care of."

The two men stood looking at each other. Neither spoke. They didn't have to. Tom understood. He reached up and undid the clasp of a thin leather strap from which a turquoise pendant hung that he wore around his neck. He took Sam's hand and placed the necklace in Sam's palm. "To our brotherhood, Sam. Take this and wear it with honor. My grandfather gave it to me when he died. His grandfather gave it to him. I'm passing it on to you. Let it be a token of our kinship, always."

The Mustangs were trailered. The lift gate was shut and secured. The truck pulling the trailer idled. The older ranch hand called to Tom, "Can you follow us over the ridge and make sure the taillights are working properly?" Tom turned and walked to his pickup. As he opened the door to climb in, he looked across the clearing to where Sam and Esme were standing, Sam with his arm around Esme's shoulders. The two men exchanged a final look. Without saying goodbye, Tom stepped into the cab of his pickup and drove away. He didn't look back.

60

SAM AND ESME SAT ON HER PORCH THE NEXT AFTERNOON, SIPPING A glass of whiskey. They'd spent the day working in her garden. It was mid-autumn, time to harvest the remaining vegetables and ready the soil for approaching winter. Sam climbed the tall ladder and picked the last apples from the trees. Esme harvested the vegetables still thriving in the cool weather, tuberous plants, broccoli, cauliflower, pumpkins, and other vine plants. They tilled each row in the garden, pulling up old roots and withered plants. They used their hoes to reach deep into the soil, aerating it so it could breathe. They piled fallen leaves on top of the earth to blanket the ground as protection from the onslaught of impending winter.

Sam was sitting across from her, one foot resting on his knee, his hand holding his whiskey glass resting on the arm of the lawn chair. He was thinking about how he and Esme had planned to compete to see who could carve the most unique pumpkin for Halloween. He forced the thought out of his mind. "Will you miss the garden in the winter?" he asked her. Esme had tied her hair back with a ribbon to keep it out of her eyes. She'd replaced her summer dress with a floppy button-up sweater and a worn, soft-suede skirt. Mud from her logging boots scattered around her feet.

"Yes," she replied, "but it's always exciting to see it wake up in spring, ready to start again. It needs the winter to rest, to prepare for another season."

"Thanks for teaching me how to garden. Thanks for everything, Es. I'll never, ever forget." He tried to force a smile but couldn't pull it off.

He thought she might start to cry, but then she smiled. "Neither will I."

Sam and Esme stared deeply into each other's eyes. There was no timidness in their gaze. They spoke to each other from their hearts at that moment, from a deep understanding. They both knew that there would be no coming and going, that Sam would never give Esme only part of himself, and that he couldn't live two lives, one that he'd have to keep from the other. They both knew that they could never share each other with anyone else and never allow their love to become a juggling act. What they shared belonged just to them. It was theirs and theirs alone. Anything short of what they had would cheapen it, make it ordinary. Theirs was extraordinary. That's how it would end.

It was evening. Sam sat at Esme's kitchen table and typed. He'd taken to writing when she was nearby. She was his muse, the one that inspired his words, his story. He glanced over at her. She was watching him. She sat curled up in an overstuffed chair in a pair of worn flannel pajamas. Her hair was down, wild, and tangly. She held a page of his manuscript in her hand.

"You're gonna be a great writer, Sam. I know it. You're gonna sell a lot of books. You found your passion. Don't ever let it slip away. Write about us, write our love story, tell it a thousand different ways." There was a soft blush to her cheeks from the nearby fire. She wore a pair of readers. Sam had never seen her look so beautiful.

He studied her. He tried to memorize every feature on her face, every freckle, the shape of her eyebrows, the exact color of her eyes. He knew he'd forget the details in time. He wondered how long he could hold on to them. He wished he were a painter so he could capture her for eternity.

He removed his glasses and got up. He walked across the room to where Esme sat. He held out his hand. She lifted her eyes, looked into his face, and put her hand in his. He gently pulled her to her feet, removed her readers, and tossed them onto the chair. He touched her face, slowly tracing his finger over her nose and mouth, down her neck. He kissed her gently on the lips, on the tip of her nose. She watched his face, felt his hands on her, the hands she loved. He led her to the bedroom, where they undressed each other slowly, deliberately. They weren't in a hurry; they wanted to make the moment last, to feel every touch, taste every kiss, and hear every sigh.

Their emotions were laid bare, their passion raw and exposed. Their bodies knew each other, what to do, how to move. Their kisses, mingled with tears, tasted salty and warm.

They let time carry them to a place where the past and future merged, where yesterday became tomorrow and today became eternity. It was a place they would return to for years to come, where they would always find each other. A place that only they would know, their secret, hidden from the rest of the world.

The full moon, a vast round lantern in the night sky, brightened the valley like a nightlight. It shone down on the tiny farm and illuminated the fields, river, and forest off in the distance. Sam and Esme sat on the porch steps. Esme tuned her fiddle and rosined her bow. She strummed the bow back and forth across the strings, playing chords and parts of simple tunes. When she was satisfied that the hairs of her bow were coated with the right amount of rosin dust, when she had adjusted the tension of each string on the fiddle with her tuning peg so that the notes were crystal clear, she stood and walked out to the clearing, the makeshift yard in front of the farmhouse.

She wore a white, flowy dress with long crinkly sleeves that puddled at her wrists. She wore her buckskin boots. Her hair tumbled down her back and around her face. She placed the fiddle at her shoulder, checked her wrist position, and pulled the bow back and forth over the strings in a down-and-up motion that produced a sweet, clear, woody sound as she played. She started slowly, working into it tentatively, and then, without warning, let the bow fly across the strings, playing tunes that only the fiddle can produce, hand-clapping, uplifting sounds.

Jake, napping on the porch, raised his head and listened. He pushed himself up, trotted down the porch steps, and into the yard where Esme played. He stood in front of her and barked. "Come on, boy," she coaxed him. "Dance." With that, Jake stood on his hind feet, his two front paws dangling in front of him. He spun in a circle, balancing on his hind legs, his movements choppy and jumpy. Esme laughed. She twirled with him, whirling in circles as she played, her hair flowing out behind her.

Homie came trotting over from the side of the barn where he'd been having a late-night snack of tall grass. He stopped in front of Esme and began to shake his head from side to side, his tail swishing back and forth, his mane flowing out from his neck. "Dance, Homie," Esme coaxed the horse. Homie danced, lifting one leg and extending one hoof out in front of him and then the other while Jake stood on his hind legs and twirled. Esme fiddled, her bow rocked back and forth over the strings, making a sweet, musical sound that filled the night sky and echoed throughout the valley.

Sam stood and walked to the porch rail. He couldn't help but smile. He watched Esme make her music, watched Jake and Homie perform their tricks, the three of them lost in the moment. Maybe it was the way the moon caught her reflection, the way her dress swirled around her like liquid, or the way her hair whipped around her face almost in slow motion. Sam wasn't sure, but a radiance illuminated Esme for a moment, like an ethereal glow that seemed to come from somewhere other than this world. She was laughing; her face lit up with pure delight. She twirled and danced with the horse and the dog, reminding Sam of a moonbeam or a firefly that flutters in the night darkness like a tiny star that has fallen to earth.

61

THE DAY BEGAN LIKE ANY OTHER. SAM AROSE LIKE IT WAS JUST AN-other morning to write before Esme awoke and before dawn broke. He stepped into his jeans and canvas Dockers and pulled a sweater over his head. His fingers lightly grazed the turquoise stone worn around his neck. He sat down softly on the edge of the bed. Esme slept on her side, facing him, her hair spilling out over the pillow, her face soft and beautiful, her hands, that he loved the touch of, were tucked under her chin.

He wondered as he studied her face, whether, in their previous lives, they had to say goodbye early or leave each other before their time was up. The pain in his chest told him no. He'd never felt this pain before, he was sure. "She helps guide your destiny," the old fortune teller told him many years ago. Is that what was happening? Did he find Esme only so she could put him back on the path home? He hoped someday he'd get the answer.

He reached out and gently touched her cheek, careful not to wake her. "Goodbye, my love," he whispered. "Like the eagle, I have to leave you now." A tear slid down his cheek. He brushed it away with a finger. He got up and quietly walked to the bedroom door. When he got to the doorway, he looked back one last time.

He made a pot of coffee and wrote a message to Esme like he did every morning, folding the paper in half. He set out a clean coffee mug, carefully laying the note beside it where she would easily see it. He quietly slipped out of the farmhouse, careful not to let the screen door slam. He stood momentarily on the porch, looking out at the tiny farm. The hens were already awake and making soft clucking noises from the hen house, anxious for breakfast. Inside the barn, Homie and Bessy would still be dozing.

He felt something wet graze the palm of his hand and looked down to see Jake standing next to him, looking up into his face, his golden eyes kind and insightful. Sam squatted down so he was at eye level with the dog. He ran his hands through the wiry fur on Jake's neck. "Look after her, Jake. I'm leaving her in your hands." Jake whined and licked Sam's face. Sam kissed the top of his head. He opened the screen door. "Go on in, boy," he coaxed. Jake hesitated a moment and then stepped inside. "Belly down, Jake," Sam instructed the dog. "Wait there for her." He stepped off the porch, turning back just once to see Jake lying inside the door, his head on his paws, his eyes intent on Sam.

Sam made the short walk along the riverbank to his cabin at Gus's place. The farm was quiet. Gus was probably awake, drinking strong coffee at his kitchen counter in the dark. Sam wanted to slip by without being noticed. He went into his cabin for the last time. He packed his laptop, manuscript, and notes into his tote bag, then gathered his fishing gear and stuffed his raincoat and clothes in his duffel bag. Before closing the door behind him, he looked around one last time and then walked around the corner of his cabin to where his Land Rover was parked. He hesitated, his hand resting on the door handle, and observed the river to his right. He'd wanted to live in a little cabin beside a river his whole life. Gus had granted him that wish. But he'd gotten so much more. Had he known how things would turn out, would he have still come? Yes, his heart didn't hesitate. A thousand heartbreaks wouldn't have kept him away.

Sam climbed into the driver's seat and started the engine. Ever so slowly, he backed out and turned the SUV toward the gravel road leading away from Gus's farm. From inside his house, Gus heard the sound of tires on the gravel as Sam swung the Land Rover onto the dirt road leading toward the ridge and Highway 112. He'd been expecting it.

In her farmhouse, Esme stirred and rolled over. She stretched her arm across the bed where Sam had recently lain. He was already up. She swung her feet over the side of the bed, pulled on her flannel pajamas and baggy sweater, and stepped into her moccasins. She heard Jake whining from the front room. Esme walked into the kitchen to pour herself a cup of coffee.

"What is it, Jake?" Esme went to the front door and stepped onto her porch, Jake following her. The air was brisk. She stood at the porch rail and looked out at her farm. Jake came over and stood beside her, whimpering softly. She stood quietly, listening to the stillness, and stared out toward her pasture, void now of the mustangs. A knowing settled over her. Jake whimpered once more. "I know, Jake." She reached down and ran her fingers through his fur. "I know."

She found the note. She fingered it lightly, then unfolded and read it. "I've gone away to write our story, my love. I'll watch for you, and wait, until we find each other again." She brought the note close to her face and smelled its scent. She felt her heart skip a beat. Tears formed in the back of her eyes.

"Sam ..."

Esme grabbed a blanket off the back of the couch, walked out to the porch, and lay back on the chaise lounge, resting her head on the cushion. Jake lay down on the porch floor next to her. She reached down and put her hand on his head, steadying her breathing, and closed her outward eyes, opening the ones inside her mind, the eyes that could look into one's soul, into one's psyche, that could see beyond perceptions. Esme concentrated and focused her attention. At first, there was nothing, but then she felt the rise, the wind beneath her, being swept along, the sight, the clarity.

Sam drove the short distance to the base of the ridge that led away from the valley, away from Gus's Fishing Hole and Esme. He stopped, got out to open the gate, and then drove under the arch whose sign warned of private property. There was the pull-out along the road, just beyond the arch, where he'd stopped the day he arrived and saw Esme for the first time. He pulled over, turned off his engine, and rested his forehead on the steering wheel. Feelings he hadn't felt since boyhood rose up inside him. Tears filled his eyes, and the back of his throat felt thick. A sob shook his body. He wept. For how long he sat like that, leaning on the steering wheel, he didn't know.

Eventually, he raised his head, staring out the window before him. He couldn't do it, couldn't drive away. He belonged here. But his son, what about Jamie? His mind took him through one rationale after another. It was like deciding between his breath or his circulation—without either one, he couldn't live. He pushed open the driver's side door; he had to get outside and feel the cool air.

Sam stepped out of the Land Rover and walked to the spot in the middle of the clearing where he'd first seen Esme, tears blurring his vision. He wiped them away with his hand and searched the valley with his eyes. Far off to his left was the outline of Gus's farm. He knew Esme's farm was just beyond his view, to his right. He couldn't see it through the trees. Like a war victim searching the ruins for signs of life, Sam was desperate to glimpse her barn, the roofline of her farmhouse. A sense of bleakness gripped him, like a man drowning in the river while watching his life raft drift away, out of reach, lost forever.

He let his gaze drift skyward to try to steady himself, to get a grip. Far out at the edge of his vision, he glimpsed the speck of something on the horizon, hardly visible, a plane, maybe. He ignored it. He focused on breathing. He stared straight ahead. Whatever the speck was far off in the distance was approaching him, becoming more distinct. He watched as it gradually took form. It was a bird, he realized, flying in his direction, gliding high above the ground. He watched it come into focus. It was flying straight toward him, getting closer and closer. He felt his heart lurch and his knees weaken. His breath caught in his throat. It was the female eagle. She was several hundred feet above the ground. She let the strong wind current carry her along, wings outstretched, gliding effortlessly toward him.

As she got closer, he saw the white tips of her wings and her talons tucked into her underbelly. He stood frozen. She was right above him, circling the trees. He craned his neck backward so he could watch her. When she neared the clearing, she tipped her wings and dove until she was no more than six feet above the ground, all the while her eyes locked onto his, targeting him. She flew within a few feet of where he stood in the middle of the clearing. He could see every detail of her body. She glided past him as though in slow motion, her wings outstretched—so close that Sam could hear the whoosh of the energy propelling her forward, so near he could have reached out and touched her. She was pure grace and majesty, her strength unmatched. She steadied him, grounded him.

His lips formed a smile. He could feel Esme's closeness and hear her voice. "I'll be waiting," the breeze whispered her words. He watched as she caught an air current and soared upward, circling the trees two more times, drifting like a kite on a string. Finally, she lifted her powerful wings to push herself forward and flew off toward home. Sam watched as she became smaller and smaller until she eventually disappeared over the horizon. He spread his arms as if to embrace her. "Esme," he whispered. "Esme."

He stood rooted to the ground after she disappeared, searching with his eyes where she was last visible. He felt calmer. Finally, he turned and walked back to his Land Rover. He climbed in and started the engine. He sat for a moment, tears filling his eyes again, and wiped them away with his hand. He looked back one last time in the direction of Esme's farm, of Gus's Fishing Hole, and then pulled forward, slowly, hesitantly at first, and headed for the ridge. He drove the windy road over the hill and down the other side. He continued until he came to Highway 112. There, he turned right toward Crystal Bay and the ferry terminal—and home.

The End

ACKNOWLEDGEMENTS

I WOULD LIKE TO EXPRESS MY GRATITUDE TO J REUBEN APPELMAN, author of *The Kill Jar* and *While Idaho Slept,* for your editing expertise and support of *Esme.* You were the first person to read *Esme,* and your encouragement and advice gave me the confidence to keep going. Thank you, thank you.

I also want to thank Cortni Merritt at SRD Editing Services. Your tutelage and expertise helped me overcome that final hurdle, and I can't thank you enough.

Thanks to MK Williams, author of *Self-Publishing for the First Time Author,* for guiding me through some tricky steps. Your advice was incredibly helpful.

A special thanks to my daughter, Hollis Welsh, Heart-Led Advocate at www.mamahollis.com. You read every word of every line of *Esme* at least three times, searching for errors and ways to improve. Thanks to you, Hollis, we have a polished final product. I take full responsibility for any remaining errors that may have slipped through, and I apologize wholeheartedly to my readers.

How can I thank you enough, Judie Cosgriff, my lifelong "Spitzie?" You hung in with me from page one and knew Sam, Joanna, Esme, and all the characters in the book as well as I did, and sometimes better. Thank you for helping me shape my story and keeping me focused and on track.

To my friends, Viv and Steve Schrader, thank you for touring me along Highway 112 of the Olympic Peninsula to visit Sekiu, Clallam Bay, the Makah Indian Reservation, and the Makah Cultural and Research

Center Museum. We explored dirt roads leading inland from Highway 112 and found the North Fork Sekiu River—quite by accident!

I am grateful to my beta readers whose advice and feedback were immeasurably appreciated: Joyce Holte, Susan Donnelly, Vanessa Laurella, Darbi McKean, and Jeff Gabeka. Mostly, thanks for your support and encouragement. You gave me the confidence to push forward when I sometimes felt discouraged.

Thank you to The Overbooked Ladies Literary Society of Gig Harbor, Washington: Lori Williams, Lori Hammond, Sharon Smith, Traci Landrith, Karina Hammond, Mary Beth Hines, Lisa Nicholson, and Lauren Hammond. Your critique and comments on *Esme* were constructive and much appreciated. It was great meeting you all. I can't thank you enough.

My heartfelt thanks go to my dear friends who supported and encouraged me through this journey: Mary Kontgis, who listened and loved it, Wanda Cane for your armchair advice, Kathy Baker and Alana Hughes, who listened to my struggles and progress in creating *Esme* during long walks. We drank a lot of coffee in the process!

Thank you to Kryssha, Karen, Klefford and the staff at Formatted Books for your professional input and talent. Only with your hand-holding and expertise could I have gotten the book published. It was a pleasure working with you.

I want to give a special tribute to the many healthcare professionals who provide endless and tireless help, support, and healing to those individuals enduring mental health disorders and addiction. It is not an easy job, and we sometimes go unnoticed, but what you do is appreciated beyond words.

And to individuals and family members living with mental illness and addiction, don't be afraid to reach out; help is available.

Finally, I want to express my gratitude to all my readers. I hope you enjoy *Esme*. If you want to contact me, please send an email to the address on the copyright page. I would love to hear from you.

And most importantly, thanks to all the folks who, like me, believe that everything is possible!

ABOUT THE AUTHOR

A RETIRED PH.D. NURSE, SPECIALIZING IN MENTAL HEALTH, SHONI Davis lives in Boise, Idaho. She devoted much of her forty-year nursing career to working with women experiencing mental health and addiction issues. She learned as much from them about life as she hoped they learned from her.

Shoni is the mother of two grown daughters and five awesome grandkids. Quantum physics intrigues her. Don't ask her to repeat back what she just read—but the part about everything being possible she finds fascinating.

Esme is Shoni's debut novel.

Printed in Great Britain
by Amazon

babc2dfa-7c1b-426f-805b-b701e94ab83eR01